D1826090

Defender of the Faith

by

Marjorie Bowen

BOOK TWO IN THE WILLIAM OF ORANGE TRILOGY

First published by Methuen & Co., London, 1911

TABLE OF CONTENTS

- Appendix

Genealogy of William III of Orange
Nassau and Mary Stewart II

LIST OF ILLUSTRATIONS

Amalia of Solms (1602-1675). Wife of Frederick Henry of Orange and Grandmother of William III. Engraving by W. J. Delff, after Van Mierevelt.
William Bentinck (1649-1709). Engraving by J. Houbraken.
William II of Orange (1626-1650). Painting by Gerard van Hondthorst.

Map of Holland

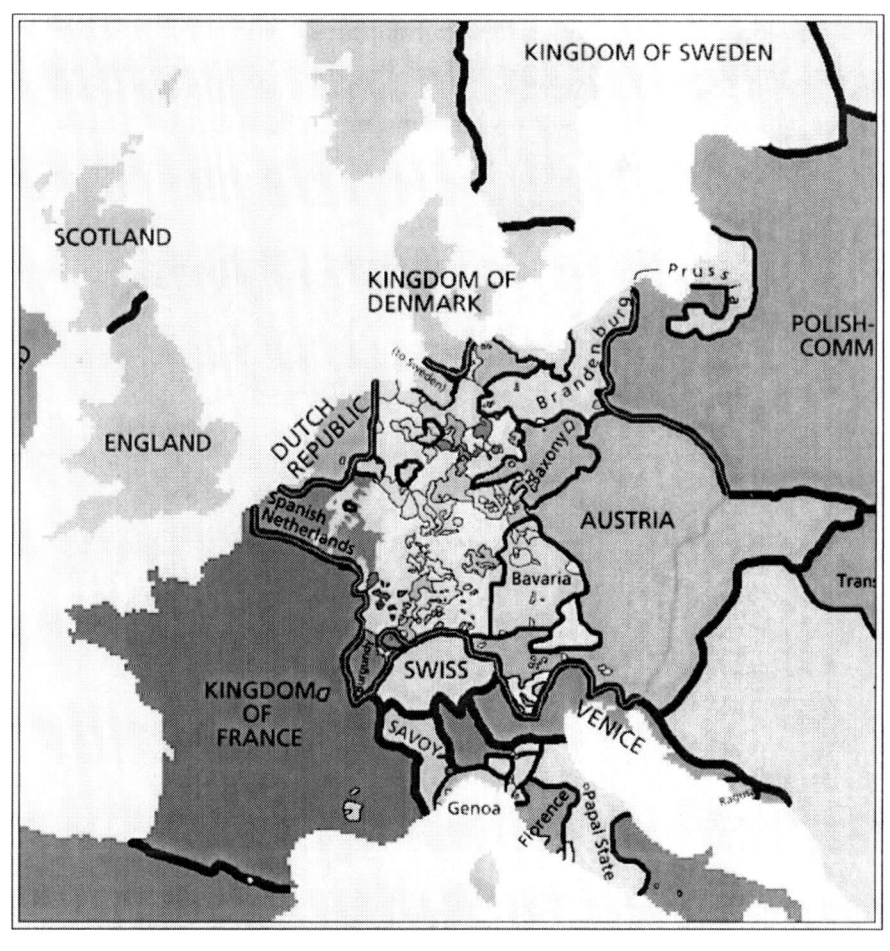

Map of Europe, ca. 1650

PART I. THE DIPLOMATS

"For, Sir, you that see all the great motions of the world and can so well judge of them, know there is no reliance on anything that is not steady to principles and prefers not the common good before private interest." —The Bishop of London to the Prince of Orange.

Prince of Orange, (1650-1702). Engraving by G. Valck.

CHAPTER I. THE MIND OF THE KING

"Mr. Mompesson," said the King serenely, "do you believe in God?"

The young man answered evenly: "Most assuredly, Sir."

The King looked at him steadily out of dark clear eyes and smiled a little like one considering. "Any particular form or manner of God?" he asked, holding his olive-hued hands to the fire blaze.

Bab Mompesson glanced up at his questioner. "I do not take your Majesty's meaning," he answered in a tone of hesitation.

The King kept his soft yet powerful gaze fixed on the man before him as he replied in the smoothest accents of his pleasing voice: "If you believe in God and go no further, Mr. Mompesson, you are scarce the man I want. My Lord Buckingham, my Lord Arlington would say as much—at times. If you would serve me you must have a creed as well as a God."

"I am of the Church of England, Sir," said Mr. Mompesson, "and zealous for the Reformed faith."

"You mean that—honestly?" asked Charles Stewart slowly.

Mr. Mompesson smiled now and returned the King's strong look strongly. "My father was of the Lord Cromwell's party as your Majesty knows—a dissenter—we have never favoured Popery."

The King placed his dark hand on the crimson sleeve of the young man. "I have no wish to convert you to the Church of Rome," he smiled. "You are here because I heard from my brother that you were the most obstinate Puritan at the Admiralty, a man of old-fashioned virtues, Mr. Mompesson."

"Sir, I hope his Highness cannot call me lacking in my duties," answered Bab Mompesson stiffly; but he slightly flushed under the continued scrutiny of the powerful dark eyes.

The King rose from the tapestry chair with a graceful abruptness and looked down on the hearth where logs burnt to a clear gold flame; he leant against the mantle that bore the arms of England and France, and stared, not now at Bab Mompesson, but at the two tall, uncurtained windows.

The sky was a foreboding grey, a few flakes of snow fluttered against its leaden depth; the trees and walks sloping down to Whitehall steps and the river swollen between its banks were bitten with frost and smitten with a keen wind.

Mr. Mompesson, following the King's gaze, glanced at this prospect without interest, then took advantage of the silence to observe the King, whom he had never spoken with before this afternoon.

The face of Charles Stewart was dark and lowering now, his mouth set with a drag of scorn, his brilliant eyes frowning under the heavy brows; the thick curls of his black peruke half concealed his worn cheeks and lined brow; he rested his strongly shaped chin in the palm of his swarthy, elegant hand and his elbow against the mantleboard as he gazed sombrely out at that dull chill view of Whitehall Gardens. He carried himself very stately when he moved to again look at Bab Mompesson, who waited silently to know the King's will.

"Mr. Mompesson," he said, "I have resolved to trust you."

The harsh lines of his face vanished as he smiled gaily; the firelight cast a glow of colour up his tall figure and struck glitter from the paste buttons of his black satins.

Mr. Mompesson bowed.

"Are you surprised?" asked the King. His rich voice had fallen again to a flattering softness; he laughed with his eyes.

"Your Majesty knows that I must be."

"Pleased—you do not add," said Charles lightly. "Well, that is no matter at all—you will serve me, I take it?"

"With all my powers, Sir."

The King laughed, not unkindly. "Look you, Mr. Mompesson, I'll put a few questions. How old are you?"

"Thirty-three, Sir."

"You have travelled somewhat?"

"In Italy, France, and Germany, Sir."

"In the train of our ambassadors?"

"Yes, Sir."

"You have learned, Mr. Mompesson, to keep a secret, to control your feelings, to watch wisely, to report concisely?"

"I have, I think, learnt those things, your Majesty."

The King fondled the ribbon that fastened his glass. "What is your wage at the Admiralty?"

"Three hundred a year, Sir."

"Paid regularly?" smiled Charles in a friendly manner.

"Not always, Sir."

"Well, I am not paid regularly myself, Mr. Mompesson."

The King glowered into the fire, showing his commanding profile toward Bab Mompesson. "You are a gentleman'?" he asked sharply.

"We have written esquire after our name for three hundred years, Sir; our lands are in Berkshire; I am a third son."

"I think you have all the qualifications, Mr. Mompesson, for the service I desire of you."

The King turned to face him full. "You and I must talk politics awhile," he added; "you know something of them?"

"Something—yes."

The King's gaze searched him intently. "Do you remember my Lord Arlington's journey to Holland two years ago?"

"Perfectly, Sir."

"And the object of it?"

"That was kept something secret. I believe he went to arrange a marriage between the Princess Mary and the Stadtholder, your Majesty's nephew."

The King seated himself again in the great chair by the hearth and leant back indolently. "He went to offer my niece's hand to my nephew and it was refused," he said, paused a moment, then added in an authoritative tone: "This is the mission I will send you on— and this time the hand of Mary Stewart must not be refused."

Bab Mompesson flushed. "I, your Majesty?"

"You," said the King. "You are the man for this. My nephew will not speak to Arlington, who bungled sadly—Temple is no better than a tool of the Dutch—and I have no man here in Whitehall whom the Prince would trust."

He smiled wickedly. "The Prince believes in God, Mr. Mompesson, a Calvinistic God; he is a fanatic in his way and honest—such another as himself alone can deal with him, do you understand? I sent Buckingham, I sent Arlington—each time a mistake. No courtier of mine can influence my nephew—he has suspicions of us all—and I will send no great men, for I do not want this news noised through Europe—you follow me?"

The King spoke rapidly, earnestly, yet with a smile. Mr. Mompesson was in every way overcome and bewildered by his Majesty's amazing frankness.

"I follow you, Sir," he made answer; "you would put a great responsibility on me. Sir William Temple is your Minister at the Hague..."

"Temple is a good soul," interrupted the King, "and the Prince liked him, but he does not, I take it, have much influence with his Highness since he has once tried to arrange this match and failed."

Mr. Mompesson endeavoured to grasp the situation. "I am to go to the Hague on a mission unknown to Sir William, a secret messenger from your Majesty to his Highness?"

The King nodded. "Do you undertake the commission?"

Bab Mompesson laughed. "Of course, your Majesty."

The King's smile was unchanging. "You are ambitious, then? My faith, I am glad of it—succeed and I'll make something of you yet. Don't cost me too much in Holland, though, Sir; we are not rich at present."

Mr. Mompesson was flushed and breathing rather thickly; this was the finest chance he had ever had in his well-filled life. The King's trust, the King's graciousness roused a warm response of loyalty in the King's subject; he stood silent, but Charles seemed pleased with his look of flattered gratitude.

"Now I'll tell you something of my policy," said his Majesty very pleasantly. "To begin with—I have done with France."

Charles II (1631-1685). Painting by John Smith, after G. Kneller.

Mr. Mompesson raised his eyes quickly; the King continued with his unalterable air of ease and authority, talking of great things in a casual, commanding fashion.

"The Parliament will not endure that French alliance. My brother's faith and his Popish marriage have cost me a great deal of popularity. You English are stiff as mulets in these matters, Mr. Mompesson—the moment has come when you must be conciliated."

He paused a moment to take note of the gratification expressed in Mr. Mompesson's frank face.

"I must have this Protestant match—England wishes it. I must have peace in Europe; for two years a useless congress has sat at Nymegen—I must have peace!"

Bab Mompesson made a simple answer: "Is this brilliant marriage a bribe to the Prince to conclude that peace he has hitherto refused, Sir? It is as well I should understand your Majesty's mind."

The King's heavy lids flickered. "No bribe," he said with distinct emphasis. "I would not bribe my nephew, but I would give him the hand of the girl who is heiress of England as guarantee of my faith in this new alliance I will make with him—you may tell him so much."

With that he looked into the steady heart of the fire with calm eyes and Mr. Mompesson replied warmly:

"Sir, what your Majesty proposes will delight England—Parliament, and people, Sir, will rejoice at your Majesty's goodness."

"But my brother and my court will have no words hard enough," said the King frankly. "Therefore go carefully, Sir. I would not have the opposition roused. Be secret, avoid the Jesuits and the French their first news of this must be that it is accomplished."

He glanced round and his lip curled freakishly. "I'll go warrant James would miss his ears to prevent this journey of yours. He suspects me, I'll warn you that—but this is my Lord Danby's policy I follow."

From the pocket of his black coat he drew out a long packet. "Here are your instructions, Sir—I and Danby drew them up. I have advised the Prince of your coming; you will live quietly at the Hague and avoid Sir William, who will be put about at not being admitted to this secret, I doubt not—so do your best, Sir."

He rose and held out the letter. "Danby will send you money and write to you; the key of the cipher is in this."

Mr. Mompesson took his instructions, kissed the hand that offered them and was leaving in elated spirits when the smiling quiet of the King, the expression of his humorous eyes struck him suddenly with a sense of danger; he knew something of the intrigues of the Stewart and Bourbon courts.

"Sir," he said on the impulse of his reflection, "your Majesty means what you have said to me? You said you would not send a great man—forgive me, Sir, was it because you would sacrifice a little one?"

"In what way, Mr. Mompesson?" asked Charles calmly.

"Your Majesty is sincere?"

"From my soul, Sir."

"Your Majesty has done with the French alliance?"

The King smiled charmingly. "Come, Mr. Mompesson, you suspect me of being a double fellow! Here is my word on it. I mean what I have said—rupture with France, peace with Holland...The Protestant match. Am I not the Defender of the Faith?" He lifted his head slowly and, still smiling but with a subtle change to slightly disdainful dignity, repeated, "My word on it, Sir."

Bab Mompesson bowed very low. "Am I to sail at once, Sir?"

Charles glanced at the bitter prospect of snow. "As soon as you may for the weather."

"And what am I to pass for, Sir?"

"A gentleman traveling for curiosity. Your wits must teach you what complexion to put upon your mission. Remember I trust you." The King's sparkling eyes contradicted the King's grave words. Bab Mompesson was not wholly satisfied, though overborne and silenced.

Charles dismissed him with the quiet, "I trust you," and turned away half restlessly, but before Mr. Mompesson had opened the door the King had swung round again on his gold heels.

"Sir," he said in a different and haughtier tone, "if my nephew prove obstinate you shall not fail to remind him of his duty to me and of the many grievous defeats he has suffered in this campaign—if he reject my alliance he is no better than lost." Then he laughed and after a few quick steps had his envoy by the arm.

"God bless you, Mr. Mompesson. I trust the damp will not give you an ague—and so farewell."

Mr. Mompesson withdrew very lowly, leaving Charles of England smiling after him. As he descended the great stairs he met three people. The first, Monsieur Barillon, representative of France powdered and gorgeous, carrying his hat with great purple feathers before his lips. Bab Mompesson, bowing himself aside on the wide landing, watched the Frenchman's light figure turn into the room at the end of the long gallery where the Duchess of Portsmouth kept court for the French faction. His uneasy reflection found voice in the quick words with which he greeted the man he found himself face to face with on the next turn of the stairs, Lord Danby, the King's first Minister, Sir Thomas Osborne once a friend of Bab Mompesson; his patron now.

"My lord—one whispered word—is the King sincere?"

Lord Danby paused; his fair face, shaded by the soft cavalier ringlets, showed anxious; he took Mr. Mompesson affectionately by the arm. "Do you think I would be party to sending you on a fool's errand, Bab?" he asked. "You were surprised at what the King had to say to you?"

"Amazed, my lord—I never looked for such distinction..."

Danby interrupted. "Do not think the King knows nothing of you. I have been begging a post for you these six months—

"And the King is sincere?" repeated Bab. "In the matter of the French? I cannot credit it."

"I dare assure you of it—Parliament would force us even if we were not willing. Hush, no more—I will come round to your lodging tonight."

With a little nod my lord passed up the great stairway, his blue and white satins disappearing round the passage that led to the King's cabinet.

Mr. Mompesson, striving to repress a flutter of excitement and to leave the palace as carelessly as he had entered it, though the secret he was entrusted with seemed to him to be written on his forehead, was a third time arrested. A girl in a mutch and cloak of grey satin was waiting by the newel-post, and when the King's messenger set foot in the hall she imperiously caught hold of his sleeve.

"Mr. Baptist Mompesson," she said sternly, "I wish to speak to you."

He stopped abashed; she was a stranger to him. "Madam," he began with a stammer, but she gave him no time for more.

"Oh!" she cried angrily, "there is a silly moppet!"

A childish laugh from behind the stair rails showed Bab that his enemies were two; a taller lady was in ambush in the shadows of the waning afternoon.

He hesitated, half annoyed, half flattered, and while he was framing some manner of speech, the girl in the grey hood gave his arm an impatient shake.

"Come with me," she commanded. "I am Mary Stewart."

Thomas Osborne, Lord of Danby.

CHAPTER II. THE MIND OF THE PRINCESS

Bab Mompesson flushed as he bowed. "Your Highness must excuse my ignorance..."

She laughed shortly, interrupting him, "Follow me, Sir." With a proud little wave of her hand she beckoned him after her and turned rapidly down the corridor.

The other lady, plain-featured, dark, young, graceful and sprightly, flashed a sharp glance at Bab. "You had best obey the Princess."

Mr. Mompesson came stiffly. He wished he was outside Whitehall, outside, London; he had no liking for this instant interruption to his business; he was vexed that the Princess knew something of a matter he had thought secret.

The two ladies stopped before the unlatched door of the banqueting hall and the Princess struck it open with an impatient hand, entering; followed closely by her companion—and reluctantly by Baptist Mompesson. The vast chill chamber was filled with a dreary grey light of winter; the snow-flakes thickened starkly against the woodwork of the tall windows and blotted out the prospect of trees and sky.

Mr. Mompesson had been in the place once or twice before when the King dined in public, but always beyond the rope that divided the spectators from the court; now he stood near the head of the table close to the King's great chair and under the gilt gallery hung with arras of Italy and Flanders.

The tall lady closed the door cautiously, a smothered laugh from her breaking the quiet; the Princess cast her riding-mask on to the kings's chair and clasped her hands angrily, facing Bab, who looked from one to another, half amused, half perturbed.

"On what errand does my uncle send you to Holland, Sir?" demanded Mary.

Bab considered her. She was slender, stately, on the verge of beauty, the Stewart chestnut in her thick curls, and the soft short-sighted weak eyes she narrowed in an effort to see more distinctly; her mouth held an expression of gentle sweetness, even now, in her anger. Her extreme youth disarmed Bab's resentment; she had, too, an air of simplicity that put him completely at his ease; he stood meekly before her.

"His Majesty has given me no leave to speak of my errand, Madam," he answered humbly.

She swept aside his excuse. "I know, Sir—it is to find me a husband." Her lips quivered and in search of help she glanced at her friend, who leant indolently against the King's chair.

That lady smiled up at Mr. Mompesson. "Come," she said lightly, "you see we know your intrigues—confess and be absolved. What said the King?"

"Who are you, Madam?" asked Bab bluntly.

"Lady Monmouth," she answered and looked at him hardly.

"Then I cannot see your interest in the matter, Madam," he said, disliking her half-insolent air.

"You must speak for yourself, Moll," remarked my lady indifferently. "I am not like to get a good hearing, it seems, from this gallant."

The Princess darted an indignant glance over Bab's tall person and good-tempered face. "You are a proper envoy," she said scornfully, "to carry the hand of a Princess to be huckstered abroad. Oh, what a pass are we come to?"

Bab was silent.

Lady Monmouth kept her eyes fixed on him intently. "The King's brother," she said quietly, "knows as much as the King. Danby thinks he is vastly secret but his scheme entertains the court. The Duke knows Monsieur Barillon knows, I dare swear."

Bab, though disconcerted, held his ground. "Neither will prevent me from fulfilling the King's commands," he said. He fixed his eyes on the lengths of tapestry before him, resolved to foil them both by silence.

The Princess stamped her foot. "My father is as much against this as I am," she declared, and the carnation of passion stained her cheeks. "Between us we have some authority. Do you hear me, Sir? I will never marry in Holland."

Bab bowed.

In an increasing agitation the Princess continued: "I have been offered once to my cousin and refused—that was against my father's wish. I will not be cried in that market again..."

Mr. Mompesson was bound to make some protest. "Your Highness does not understand—this is a question of politics..."

"Nay, I do not understand your politics," she made quick retort. "But I see that I am to marry to please my uncle. Holland is the dullest place in the world. I cannot leave England, can I, Anne?"

The short-sighted eyes turned an appealing glance toward the Duchess. "Why, if you must," that lady made reply, "you can give some trouble first..."

The Princess's anger gave place to a wilful laugh, she tossed her head. "You know my mind, Mr. Mompesson, and you know my father's mind. You are like to have a fool's errand if you offer me to my cousin. Mr. Barillon can help me to a fine match in France."

"Do you favour the Papists, Madam'?" asked Bab sternly.

"Maybe," she returned haughtily. "At least I have no love for the Puritans, and do not mean to sit strait-laced at the Hague for the rest of time."

Bab smiled. "Shall I tell his Highness that'?" he asked. He looked upon her only as a child, the almost unconscious instrument of the French policy of the Romish Duke, her father.

"You may tell him worse if you will," she answered. "Say what he refused once is not offered again with any wish of mine. Say I was a child then but am more now and have some power, and if he likes not my message, say I have sharper for the asking."

Bab smiled and shook his head. "I fear Your Highness must find another messenger; my business is with affairs of State."

Mary came a step nearer, melting into a sudden tempting softness of anxious supplication. "Surely now, Sir, you will not go after all I have said." The lovely brown eyes opened wide on him as she approached. "Stay at Whitehall and in a day or so the King will change his mind, I'll be warrant he will."

Bab's smile deepened at her childish suggestion. "It wounds me that I must refuse Your Highness..."

She interrupted him. "Is the King's favour so much to you, Sir?"

There was a certain depth in her tone and expression as she spoke that belied her flippant pose and speech and moved Bab to answer seriously.

"Not the favour of the King only, Madam, but security in England, peace in Europe, and safety to the Reformed faith depend on success of my mission."

He spoke so gravely that the Princess was quelled, but Lady Monmouth turned his speech with her childish laugh. "Moll, my dear," she said, slipping her arm round Mary's waist, "they never lack specious excuses when they are going to sacrifice us, these men!"

Bab knew enough of her history to forbear a retort, and the Duchess, as if wishful to cover the bitterness in her tone, added with a indolent accent, "Madam, we have gossiped here long enough to unleash a pack of surmises. If some babble discovered us we are like to be rated for interfering with the King's messenger."

Reluctant, half pouting, with wilful tears and trembling lips Mary moved toward the door. It was cold in the empty hall and she shuddered under her cloak. "Mr. Mompesson," she said, pausing to face and dismiss him, with a sudden air of the great lady, "I wish you adverse winds, a rough sea, an ill welcome in port and no success at all in your mission, and now you know my mind." She paused breathless.

"I hope Your Highness may come to change it," answered Bab bowing. "In wishes sit heavy on the sails of any man, and if I drown betwixt here and Holland it will be an evil thought for my last that Your Highness rejoices in my disaster."

Mary looked at him doubtfully. "I meant no ill to you," she conceded with a sigh. "Now, you will put me down a vixen. God, He knows my heart is heavy in my bosom as lead in the hand—but if I cannot wish you fair sailing, I'll wish you a better errand." With that manner of high-spirited gaiety that was hers even in her trouble she gave him a little curtsy and quitted the hall on Lady Monmouth's arm.

They left the door ajar behind them, and Bab could hear the sound of high-heeled shoes and the little stir of petticoats for a moment before silence fell unbroken. Thoughtfully he stood by the King's chair on which still lay the Princess Mary's mask and reflected on what he had that afternoon seen and heard in Whitehall. Large issue and small detail—the gentle speech of the black-eyed King; the instant's impression of Monsieur Barillon, discrete, splendid, with downcast lids and a light step directed to the room at the end of the gallery; Danby's anxiety and gesture of caution; the unexpected appearance of Mary Stewart with her impetuous words and troubled loveliness; Lady Monmouth's restless spirit showing in her half-bitter sentences—were woven together across the background of the palace, as figures, trees, and flowers were woven into interchanging lines of red and blue, gold and silver in these tapestries of Ypres and Mortlock that hung from the gallery of the empty banqueting hall. And as behind all the fantasy of the arras was one colour of blue and stars never to be quite obscured, so behind Bab's racing thoughts was the purpose of his mission, the leagues with Holland, the Protestant marriage, the break with the French alliance the country loathed, the policy of the King forced at length by Parliament to the national will. Bab was proud of his task; he felt grateful to the ancient friendship of Danby that had put him in the way of such honours and to the graciousness of Charles, but he was not yet hardened diplomat enough to consider without discomfort the reluctant tears of the Princess, whose appealing youth had endeavoured foolishly to arrest his journey.

The grey clouds thickened, darkened, seemed to close down and overwhelm the land. Bab could not see the river nor the trees nor anything but a steady swirl of snow that beat noiselessly against the tall windows. The fierce weather excited him, he longed to be aboard the boat making for Holland, regardless of the most sullen seas or powerful storms. In the lowering moment of the sudden fall of snow the banqueting hall became so dark that the glowing and flamboyant painting on the ceiling disappeared in the great shadows that obscured the splendours of the place, as breath dims brightness on a glass.

Bab, roused by the gathering darkness from elated reflections, turned to leave. As he moved toward the door he thought that he heard a cautious footstep in the gallery above. He stopped instantly and looked up; but the ill light showed him nothing, nor was there another sound, though for some instants he waited. Only he fancied that he detected a disarrangement in the tapestry over the gallery rail as if some one had leant there and drawn hastily back.

"Beware of the Jesuits and the French," the King had said. Bab remembered the words, hot to think his speech with the Princess had perhaps been spied upon, and he himself already marked out as a victim of French intrigues.

Lightly and quickly he left the hall and passed downstairs without meeting any one, but in the courtyard he saw Monsieur Barillon again, stepping into his satin-lined coach with a shiver for the snow. As the running footmen took their places beside the horses, Bab with the driving storm in his face passed under the window of the coach as the Ambassador was pulling the leather curtain into place.

Bab looked up and the Frenchman looked down, pausing for a second with his hand on the blind-cord. The King's messenger stared into the keen handsome face and stopped for all the heavy beat of snow on his cheek. He thought that Monsieur Barillon would speak. But the Ambassador gave a pointed smile, twitched down the curtain and the coach swung and jolted out of Whitehall gates.

Bab instinctively put his hand to the paper lying next his heart. "He knows," was his instant thought. "Barillon knows."

<hr>

CHAPTER III. THE MINISTER

Baptist Mompesson had rooms in Thryft Street, behind the Duke of Monmouth's great mansion in Soho fields; when he reached them he was snow from head to foot, and the darkness of the storm had merged into the darkness of dying day.

He took off his heavy wet mantle and went shuddering to the fire that welcomed him from the wide hearth. It was so bitter cold that last week's *Gazette* had spoken of a possible fair on the ice. Baptist remembered no such weather since the year of the Plague. He drew the heavy curtains over the view of dancing flakes and began packing his mails. The packet for Holland left the Thames every morning at six; he wished to depart with the next that set sail. He declared to himself that nothing less than a frost that sealed the river should delay him.

By seven of the clock his simple preparations were made. He had written to the Admiralty, packed his luggage, paid his lodging, explained his departure as a visit to his brother in Berkshire, and was ready for Danby and his last instructions.

But my lord was late. Bab became impatient; he flung up the window and stared out at the bewildering circle of snow-filled light his candles threw on to the night, closed it again and re-strapped his portmantles. Close on ten my lord was ushered up by the child who waited on Bab.

"If this storm does not abate you do not sail tomorrow," was his greeting.

Bab, in the relief of his arrival, was warm in welcome. "My dear lord, it will take more than a snowstorm to delay me."

Danby had his cloak off and was by the fire. His orange-silk coat with bullion enrichments and a thick crusted embroidery of glass sequins, his fair ringlets and clear blue eyes, his complexion of rose and white fresh above the black velvet round his throat, dwarfed the modest room to a mere background for his comely courtliness. As he held out his stiff fingers, released from chill gorgeous gauntlets of doeskin, to the grateful fire, his face wore the same anxiety as when Bab met him on the stairs.

"I would go at once—for I think I might be prevented going at all if I delayed," said Bab, looking at him keenly.

"The King holds firm—the King must have the Protestant marriage," answered Danby strongly.

Bab snuffed the candles that stood between them. "Monsieur Barillon knows," he remarked.

Danby glanced over his shoulder. "Knows what?"

"My errand—the King's mind."

"Not quite," replied the King's Minister. "Something, of course, he guesses—not all."

"How much?" demanded Bab.

Danby shrugged. "Enough to endeavour to thwart you."

"The Princess Mary knows," said Mr. Mompesson. "She met me below the stairs and entreated me to stay my journey. My Lady Monmouth was with her."

"She will give some trouble yet," frowned Danby. "As wilful a piece as need be..."

"But Protestant," added Bab.

"Yes," assented Danby. "Still her father's instrument."

He turned about, flashing his fine dress. "Look you, Bab," he said earnestly, "This marriage is the one thing to save us all. Temple and Arlington saw that two years ago and brought the King to propose it. The Prince refused the alliance, for it was put in the nature of a bribe and he smelt France behind. But I tell you, if he refuses this time, I and my policy are as good as lost."

"Are you no firmer than that in the saddle?" asked Bab, leaning forward across the table.

"Who is firm in his seat?" retorted my lord, "it is up and down with all of us. England is no passive hack to be spurred and kicked at any man's desire. I dare not, if I would, support the French alliance."

He bit his lower lip and added: "I dare not—I have been threatened with impeachment once. If I go against the Parliament, the people, I may look to a quick end to all my troubles."

"England clamours for a peace," admitted Bab, "and the maintenance of the Protestant interest in Europe—such is the policy of your lordship, I take it..."

The earl looked at him intently. "Such is my policy, the only one I dare to hold; this session roused a wind I thought would blow our heads from our shoulders. The King is most deeply pledged to France, but he was checked by this temper in the people..."

He paused and brought his hand down lightly on the low mantleshelf.

"The Duke is heir and a Papist—that is the unforgivable thing; and if his daughter, Queen of England to be, marries a Prince of her father's faith—we are all on the rocks—not I nor any man I know can pull the Government through the tumult there will be."

"The King sees this?" asked Bab.

"The King is a wise man," retorted Danby. "He observes how far he may go—he will have this marriage and a peace sooner than shake his throne."

"The Duke will never consent."

"The Duke must—his own inheritance is in great jeopardy. Think not of the Duke; King and people consent."

"But—the Prince?" asked Bab thoughtfully.

Danby bit his forefinger. "The Prince must be won—at any cost. In this match he will flout France and win England to the Dutch side; he has aimed at that since '72."

Bab was silent awhile, figuring in his mind these great policies, and my Lord of Danby spoke again impressively as one who strives to enlighten and convince.

"To please the Parliament without whom we are penniless, to please the people without whom we are not safe, the King must throw himself on the Dutch side; the French and Popery are loathed in England, and the Prince of Orange is the hope of all Protestants here. I tell you, I hold myself pledged to that young man; he is third from the throne; if he marries the Lady Mary he is second and a force in the country."

Bab gazed earnestly into the florid worn face of the King's Minister. "My lord, once again, is the King sincere? I can hardly credit it. Has he finished with France, or is this to be, as was the Triple Alliance, followed by a Treaty of Dover?"

Lord Danby did not lower his eyes. "The King could not, if he would, play false."

Bab smiled. "Your lordship knows that there is naught easier. The Prince could be dazzled with the alliance and the marriage, seduced from his allies, led into a peace, fed with promises and forsaken— is that the policy of his Majesty?"

The Minister made no answer.

"If it were," continued Bab, "it would spite me to the heart to be the engine of it..."

Danby interrupted. "The Prince of Orange is not a foolish man; he has proved that."

"He is a hard-pressed one," returned Bab. "The defeats he has suffered in the last campaign would unnerve an ordinary Prince, with De Ruyter slain and the French in Sicily. My lord, flatly, I hold his Highness an extremely brave Prince and should be reluctant to go offer him a rope of sand in his desperation."

My Lord of Danby turned about with some vehemence. "I am not deceiving you; the King will be free of France. Do you think we can afford to see the Spanish Netherlands' at the mercy of Louis?"

"I'll take your word, my lord," said Bab quietly. "I am English and Protestant and I cannot think that your lordship would have made choice of me to fool the cause I admire."

"I made choice of you," returned Danby, "because I held you an honest, prudent man, one who could speak sincerely to the Prince and carry belief. A specious diplomat would but waste his time. I warn you that you will find the Dutchman extremely obstinate, and that you must go carefully in matters of conscience."

He sighed wearily on the ending of his speech, and pushed his fingers up into his hair. "There are times, Bab," he added irrelevantly, "that I wish I was in the Tower and done with it."

"Yet your lordship would do a great deal to avoid being clapped up," smiled Bab.

"I stand or fall by the Protestant Marriage," said my lord gravely. "And others than I will go to ruin if it fail, for if the Parliament refuses supplies we are thrust into French arms and England is in a turmoil..."

He came up to the table where Bab sat. "Do your best for the sake of us all. In that paper the King gave you I have put some heads of various matter that you may use to persuade the Prince; the rest I leave to you. Live privately and avoid Sir William Temple, whose vanity is like to have a sore cut at being left out of this business."

Bab rose. "One word. If Monsieur Barillon knows the King's resolve to this match, which I think he does, am I not like to have some difficulty with his spies and agents?—for he is a very knowing man in intrigue."

"The Prince endures no Frenchman at the Hague. Your fine wits should suffice you to defeat secret designs." My lord went to the window and lifted the curtain. "What of your journey? The packet-boat leaves Gravesend at six, and the barges will take a great while down the Thames this weather."

Bab opened the window and looked out. "The storm is not near so fierce—it shall not do me the disservice to delay me. I start tonight."

When he closed the window he turned to find Danby with a half-reluctant air counting out gold pieces on to the table.

"Here are twenty pounds English," he said, "and a draft on a banker at Amsterdam for fifty. I'll send you more."

He sighed and picked up his cloak. "Make the Prince the finest offers in the world," he said, "so he consent to this match."

"Will your lordship be guarantee for the performance of these same offers?" asked Bab.

Danby held out his hand. "If I be not in the Tower," he smiled.

Baptist Mompesson grasped the still cold hand of the King's Minister and looked squarely into the steady blue eyes.

"I'll serve you well," he said simply.

The house was dark, the people being abed, and Bab took up a candle to show my lord down the steep, narrow stairs. When the street door was opened he looked anxiously up at the sky, where the snow-clouds were beginning to thin about the moon. At the corner of the square waited my lord's coach, the horses with white flakes on their harness and the feeble radiance of a street lamp showing the colours on the hammer-cloth. Danby waved his black-plumed hat, smiled and turned rapidly up the street. Bab mounted silently to his room, flung himself in the deep chair beside the fading fire and, taking his brow in his hand, mused over the mission he was embarked upon. He could not avoid falling into some exultation that he had been entrusted with an errand so nice and so important, and his apprehension, that he was to be the mere ignorant instrument to delude the Prince, had been largely removed by my Lord of Danby, whom he had known all his life and did not believe a guileful man. Besides, his own shrewdness showed him that the King had pushed the French interest in England as far as he durst; and unless he could disown the connection with Louis and placate the people with a Protestant marriage to the Princess Royal matters were like to be driven to a crisis Charles would be as reluctant to face as my Lord Danby.

And Baptist Mompesson's thoughts touched a nobler level: the King was the King, and of England; might he not in all honesty wish to aid his own blood, his country's faith? Bab thrilled at the contemplation of the struggle in the Low Countries which had been sustained four years against such unequal odds. He was not proud of the part his country had played and eager enough to see it redeemed by a change of policy; he disliked France and the arrogant King, who wished to cast the shadow of his sceptre over Europe.

Defender of the Faith!

The words haunted Bab's imagination; his Puritan blood hated the growing tyranny of Rome; his good English sense revolted at the subservience of the King to any foreign Power. He opened the window again, heedless of the chill breath from the snow-clouds above the roofs, where a faint moonlight glittered in the crystals, and gazed up into the spaces of dark blue with a fine uplift at the serenity and mystery of the scattered stars.

When he drew back into the room again he found the fire a mere heap of ashes, and one of the two candles guttered out in the draught. His eye was caught by my Lord of Danby's glittering dole which lay in a little heap on the letter of credit beneath the solitary candle.

He picked the pieces up, one at a time. "Clipped coin," he thought almost unconsciously as he looked at the uneven edges. The King's saturnine face smiled from a defaced blank.

CHAPTER IV. THE SICK PASSENGER

The child's cradle packet-boat for Holland left Gravesend in a bitter cold wind that turned strongly to the south-west at the Hope, and put a day between that and Margate.

A brisk change to better weather sent them upon the coast of Holland, and Bab was in good hopes of landing on the third morning when a thick fog rose up with great swiftness and kept them stationed in the icy waters of the North Sea.

The packet carried the mail and one passenger beside Bab. He was an English clerk in employment at one of the great Amsterdam houses and had been to England to attend the death-bed of his father. Bab was quick to get this much from the captain; he had a lurking fear of Monsieur Barillon and his agents. The Englishman had not been seen since their embarkation at Gravesend; he lay in his cabin in the torture of seasickness and Bab had the ship to himself. Walking the deck in the fog that isolated them as completely as if they had been a thousand miles from land, he cast up his chances of success, all he had heard of the Prince to whom he was sent, all the arguments he should use, the care he must take to keep himself, quiet, free from curiosity or malice.

His tense thoughts were broken by some one stumbling forward on the spray-washed deck and catching his arm.

"Your pardon, Sir—but has the ship stopped?"

It was the other passenger. Bab looked at him keenly. He was a tall man, very plainly dressed in a mourning cloak of camlet, middle-aged, long-jawed, of a ghastly sallowness in the complexion, wearing a short peruke, and an old-fashioned hat.

"Certainly, do you not observe the fog?" Bab answered rather dryly.

The stranger groaned and clung to the taffrail as the ship lurched sideways into the white expanse of mist.

"I am no sailor," he confessed. "I have a great disease and sickness when on the sea."

"So it seems." Bab was concise. "Yet, having your employment in Holland, you must needs cross often."

"Not often," said the other feebly. "I forgo my country sooner."

It was all the converse they had, but Bab kept his eye on the man as he moved away up the deck.

In a few hours the fog lifted and a pilot came out in a rowing boat, and took them to the Brill. At Maaslandsluys the two passengers took a barge for the Hague, and in the unfriendly light of a dull afternoon were steered by two silent Dutchmen through the waterways of Holland.

Bab was reserved through design, and his companion through sickness; they sat wrapped in their cloaks with never a word between them till they reached the frozen canal where they had to leave the barge for a traineau. Then there was some question as to the transfer of their baggage, and Bab turned sharply to the stranger, "You must know the Dutch; will you speak to these fellows?"

The other discovered none of the confusion Bab had half expected; he addressed the porters in their own language, and so proved his advantage over Bab, who had neither Dutch nor German. As the traineau sped forward down the long canal the King's messenger almost decided that the sick passenger was no more than he declared himself to be, a clerk from Amsterdam.

Windy sea-clouds were blowing over the Hague as the Englishmen entered it, the trees were hung with snow, and the houses and churches were clear as a painting in the cold atmosphere.

Bab paid his way in the clipped English gold, and received a handful of heavy Dutch money in return. The town seemed very quiet, almost sleepy, not at all like the theatre of great events. A few boys were skating, a few people passing to and fro. When Bab stepped out of the traineau and found himself in the long neat street, a sense of depression overcame him; he seemed unaccountably far from the beginning of his mission and hopelessly far from its accomplishment.

My Lord Danby had given him the address of a house well used to accommodate English and Scotch refugees, but Bab, utterly strange to the town, resolved to stay the night, at least, in the modest hostel opposite the spot where the traineau landed him. This, it appeared, was also the intention of the other passenger, who declared himself far too sick to proceed that evening to Amsterdam. It occurred to Bab as strange that he had not travelled at once thither, without touching the Hague, and his doubts of the fellow rose even when he crept up to his room and was seen no more.

The inn was small, dark, slumberously quiet and notably clean; the black furniture in the parlour shone with a wax-like polish, and the brass about the fireplace where the pine logs blazed was of a silver paleness. The host was polite, quiet, able to speak French and a little English, and disposed to be friendly.

Bab, during his dinner of dried fish, cheese, cock-ale, and Deventer honey-cakes, obtained from him, under cover of the curiosity of an ordinary traveller, much information. The most important point was that the Prince ('Stadtholder,' the host called him, and the title sounded strange to Bab) was not at the Hague but at Dieren, a country seat of his outside Arnhem. He might return any day to attend the sitting of the States, but his movements were uncertain, his journeys unheralded. Since the close of the last campaign he had been mostly at Dieren or Honsholredijk, Bab was told, save the one week he had spent in Amsterdam in the endeavour to raise money for the war from that opulent but republican city.

The host spoke of the Prince with intense respect and affection; the losses of the last campaign he passed over as nothing to be set against the salvation of the country which the Prince had secured by his diplomacy and his valour. Bab, probing as much as he dared, was surprised at the power the Stadtholder appeared to enjoy, and the strong position he held in the United Provinces. The host said that his Highness was consulted in everything. He had remodelled the constitutions of the three provinces he had rescued from the French, and put the bridle even on Amsterdam; no one durst or wished to oppose his will. The East India Company had given him grateful presents, and Gelderland had offered him the sovereign title, which, however, was refused by a prudent Prince, who needed not the name when he had the power.

In return, said the host with animation, his Highness had made great sacrifices for his country: all the emoluments of his offices he had given the States for their defence, and his immense private fortune he was devoting to the same end; he had refused to conclude treaties for his own advantage, and his one thought and aim, since the ghastly year of '72, had been the deliverance of his country and his faith.

Bab was fired by this talk of the young Prince he had always admired. He thought of starting at once for Dieren, but considered that it might be wiser to wait at the Hague, and, since the dreary day was closing in and he had no object to serve in going abroad, he went to his room and read over the Lord Treasurer's instructions. The paper contained little he had not been told; the words of the olive-faced King remained his chief guide.

As he was opening his mails he heard a footstep outside the door. He paused instantly, put out his hand and quenched the one candle that dispelled the dusk. The handle was cautiously turned, and the face Bab had been expecting to see peeped in—it was that of the sick passenger.

The King's messenger kept still and silent, and the tall dark figure advanced into the room. When he was well over the threshold Bab sprang up from beside his portmantles.

"You are very clumsy, Sir," he said angrily.

The stranger gave a start. "Your indulgence," he answered feebly, "I have mistaken my room."

Bab Mompesson crossed over and turned the key in the lock. "You have mistaken your man," he said briefly.

"What do you mean?" quavered the stranger.

Bab had a pistol on the table; he placed his hand on it as he answered. "You are the Duke of York's spy, Sir," he said quietly. "You have been sent by his Highness to watch and circumvent me—and you were making a good beginning tonight by endeavouring to steal my papers."

The other hesitated, then laughed. "Very well," he answered in an utterly changed voice. "If you are the agent of one brother, may I not be the agent of the other?"

"I serve his Majesty," said Bab grimly. "I am glad you are so recovered of your sickness."

"Light the candles," suggested the stranger calmly, "and we will talk...You may take your hand off that pistol for I am unarmed. My name is Thomas Carew. I come from Berkshire—your county, I think, Mr. Mompesson."

As he spoke he seated himself in the cushioned chair by the glowing tiled stove, and smiled up at Bab, who lit the candles and placed them on the table. "You were doubtful of me from the first, were you not?" he asked. His manner was easy and pleasant; his heavy plain face held an expression of authority and composure. Bab disliked him intensely.

"You carry it off very well, Mr. Carew, but you have set yourself to a difficult game. If you know so much of my errand as to wish to circumvent it, you know that its success is the wish of the King and the people." He took his place behind the lights that gave a glowing fairness to his blunt Saxon features and rested his elbows on the table.

Mr. Carew fixed him with keen light eyes. "You have come to arrange a Protestant marriage between the Princess Royal and her cousin," he said in a low tone. "And I dare assure you, Mr. Mompesson, that you will never bring it about."

Bab set his lips. "Desist while you may and spare yourself some pains," continued Mr. Carew with weight.

Bab laughed shortly. "You waste your breath, Sir. Does his Highness of York carry such weight in the councils of Europe that he can prevent what England has resolved upon?"

The other's look deepened in meaning. "Behind the Duke of York is the King of France, and he will have the countries of Europe shaken like peas in a pan before he will permit the heiress of England to be united to his greatest enemy."

"Permit!" repeated Bab. "What do you, an Englishman, with such words? It is for King Charles and the Prince of Orange to say yes or no to this bargain, and if they cry quits and England is pleased, no other shall interfere."

He rose impatiently. "I know your intentions and you mine," he added, "and further speech does us no manner of good."

Mr. Carew looked at him over his shoulder. "You are resolved to go on'?"

"I am resolved to obey my master," was the short answer.

"Well," Mr. Carew rose with a little smile on his thin lips, "I think you are a very proper engine for the King's purpose, and I will tell my employer so."

Bab was slightly baffled by this. He eyed the other suspiciously. "You to your business, I to mine," he said grimly. "And I would be sorry to change with you. You are one of those who would catch us all in the French net, and make us slaves to the Pope of Rome."

"I am of the Romish faith," replied Mr. Carew, and his eyes showed angry; "so is the King's brother."

"So is not the King's niece," retorted Bab. "And remember we are in a Protestant country, Mr. Carew. The Prince, I take it, is not one to endure treasons and intrigues hatching in his dominions!"

"Would you care to speak of me to the English Ambassador'?" interrupted Mr. Carew.

Bab was taken aback by his knowledge of Danby's instructions to keep everything secret from Sir William Temple, but he put a bold face on it.

"I would speak of you to the Prince himself," he said.

Mr. Carew seemed amused. "I judge the Prince no more eager than the Duke for this match," he remarked, "and with *both* sides unwilling you are like to have a difficult task."

Bab was further angered that his adversary should also know the mind of the Princess Mary. "Your sly Papist talk will get no more of me," he said. "Only I warn you while we are on this soil I have a bit on you and shall not fail to tighten it."

Mr. Carew looked sourly. "If you would not be at cuffs with common sense, Mr. Mompesson, do not threaten one who has that behind him which is beyond your meddling."

Bab unlocked the door. "Get to your chamber," he said. "Neither you nor I make profit out of this talk."

The Romanist passed into the corridor and so, slowly, with a glance backwards over his shoulder, up the stairs.

Bab made the door secure, and went to the window to ease his temper by the cold sea wind on his brow. He was more annoyed than seemed reasonable to his own common sense at this instant discovery and espionage. He blamed the King for allowing his brother to so accurately plumb his intention; he blamed Danby (whom he had always considered a reckless politician) for some looseness that had disclosed his design to Barillon. Hampered at the very onset by an enemy at his heels, Bab's mind began to give audience to depressing fears and doubts. If the Prince was cold, the Duke unwilling, France inimical, the King lukewarm, and Danby tottering before the blast of an enraged Parliament, what chance had he of bringing to the ripening those schemes that he was entrusted with, the policies with which Charles had flattered his patriotism? Peace in Europe, the end of a disgraceful subservience to King Louis, succour to Holland, and the Protestant marriage to seal this and secure the future of the true faith.

Staring out over the various gables and roofs of the Hague, fast being blurred from his vision by the misty descent of night, Bab foresaw himself making a feeble and ineffectual figure in contradiction to the importance of his business, did he not exert all his wits.

He decided his first object must be to gain the Prince, and his cheek flushed as he recited in an under voice to the windy evening some of the powerful arguments he would place before his Highness, and the terms in which he would make clear to him the state of England, a country at odds with itself, outwardly corrupt, but true at heart.

The peaceful clear chimes of some great church Bab could not see broke the frosty stillness of the motionless town. Bab closed the window, walked about his room awhile, and finally unbolted the door and thrust a challenging head and shoulders on to the blackness of the corridor. The household was seemingly abed, and though Bab swept the darkness with his fat yellow candle he saw no trace of Mr. Carew. As he stood there, silent, it occurred to him with sudden force that for a man of astuteness it was a very foolish thing to make that almost open attempt to enter the room of the person supposed to be deceived, and still more foolish to suppose that one on such an errand, in a strange place, would leave about anything worth the endeavour to steal.

This reflection discomposed Bab; he felt that there was some meaning deeper and much more subtle than any apparent as yet in the behaviour of the sick passenger.

CHAPTER V. IN THE WOOD

By the middle of the next day Bab had left the "Panier d'Or" and taken up his lodgings in the quarters mentioned by Danby, a fine house in the Princengracht, kept by one Mevrouw Vanderhooven, the Scotch widow of a Dutch merchant, who let chambers or offered asylum to such of her countrymen or others of the true faith who had fled the persecutions in the Scottish Lowlands or elsewhere.

Bab was given a room at the top of the house, looking on to the trees and the wide canal, now frozen, that ran out of the town toward Ryswyck. It was a pleasant apartment, the windows clear as crystal, floor and walls polished to an amber hue, curtains and bed hangings of white checkered with blue, a big stove of painted tiles and fresh linen covers to protect the seats of the shining chairs.

Mevrouw Vanderhooven was friendly if stern. She spoke sharply but with good intention. She was stout, forty-five and plain; her cap and collar were of a whiteness so glossy and pure that her brick-dust complexion and red hair glared by contrast; her course hands were deft at woman's work; her large feet nimble about the house. She prided herself upon having no weaknesses, "vanities" she called them, but she tolerated a fat grey cat that had no pretensions to respect, and she had been know to sit up all night with a one-eyed, asthmatic parrot her husband had brought home from Jamaica twelve years before. Her real and unobtrusive charity gave shelter to a sour and precise minister, named Fear-the-Foe Gibbons, who had been at his glory under the Lord Protector;' a Flemish jewel-worker and his daughter, ruined by the French occupation of the Spanish Netherlands; one of Cromwell's former officers in delicate health, who gave lessons in fencing; an old woman from Overyssel, who had lost her family in '72; and an English adventurer, exiled for his remarks on the King of England.

These people, who all seemed to Bab disagreeable and uninteresting, occupied the lower part of the house under the strict government of Mevrouw Vanderhooven, who checked with a firm hand their quarrellings and arguments, endured their complaints and joined in their endless prayers, toiled for them and obtained little thanks.

The upper part of the house was let to an old man who was one of the elders at the Groote Kerk,3 single and reserved, a young widow who did fine needlework, and a German gentleman, at present in Berlin. In the attics where the servants slept was a room that led to a small tower on the roof; this was occupied by a wrestler or tuner of stringed instruments, who owned a beautiful clavichord. He dared play only when the rest of the household were out of earshot, they being unanimous in declaring it an ungodly device.

Bab, having discovered this much of the people under the same roof, laughed inwardly at the motley crowd he found himself among, requested his meals might be served privately, and left the house with the key of his room in his pocket.

The sharp eyes of Fear-the-Foe Gibbons followed him from the tall lower window, and the Huguenot jeweller squinted from behind the gaunt shoulders of the Scotchman. Bab, glancing hack, gave them a smile that was not returned, and passed on to the left, toward the centre of the town. The wide streets, the handsome houses, the trees and open spaces, the shining windows with their outside mirrors, the clean steps and polished handles of the high doors, were a cause of marvel to the Englishman used to the crooked thoroughfares and filthy by-ways of London and Paris.

The people were well dressed though with a markedly quiet taste, the shops fine and numerous. Bab saw no sign of the effects of the war that had threatened to ruin the country four years ago, though he marked various figures such as he had seen in Mevrouw Vanderhooven's house, refugees showing more or less pride and poverty, wounds and rags.

There were several skaters on the canals, sledges for business or pleasure, drawn by ponies, and little ships blown along the ice by the wind in their great sails.

Bab came to the very centre of the town, saw for the first time the Binnenhof, the Buitenhof, and the Gevangenpoort, buildings stately and sombre and built round the Vyverberg lake, where now the swans walked slowly on the ice. Passing under the dark archway of the prison he came out into the Plaats, and so down the Kneuterdyck Avenue and into the Voorhout, filled at this hour with carriages and fashionable people, moreover in itself the finest street with the most lordly houses that Bab had ever seen. Among the passers-by he discerned Mr. Carew, the Papist spy, walking leisurely, and at that sight hastened his steps and so got out of the press through the Tournooiveld into a quieter street, having no desire to be under the observation of his enemy. A few steps brought him to a street of fine villas, white-fronted, planted with very tall trees; beyond the houses spread a large park or wood.

Bab crossed and followed the road. A great gate stood open on a wide drive, and a little group of gentlemen on horseback were talking to some men at the entrance of a small lodge or guard-house. It seemed to Bab to be a public garden. He turned through the gate and passed unchallenged down a beautiful double and lofty avenue of fine trees. The ground was thick with brown dried leaves, the path hard with frost; the thousand branches that mingled together against the grey sky were delicately outlined in snow, which also lay in patches here and there among the undergrowth.

Bab walked briskly, enjoying it; where the avenue ended he took one of the many paths and came into a portion of the wood in its natural state. Holly grew among the dried ferns; firs and yews made patches of green-blue of velvet softness against the burnished and dead hues of bare branches and faded foliage; a quantity of rooks clamoured harsh converse, and small birds flew across his way with a startled stir of wings.

Presently the clouds broke and clear silver-gold rays fell across the beech-boles and glittered in the snowdrifts.

Bab, following his path, found himself on a bank overlooking a lake that curved out of sight. A graceful beech, hung with moss, drooped above the frozen water, on which the curling gilt leaves fluttered above the sparkling rime; beyond this a group of high trees bounded Bab's vision. It was so solitary, so still, so pleasing that Bab almost unconsciously slackened his steps, and finally, becoming impatient even of his own footsteps, seated himself on the stump of an ancient tree, twisted with reddened ivy, and gazed at the sweep of ice, the silver-green trunks, the twisted, shrivelled bracken, the whole dead and lovely scene.

So remote did the place seem that he was startled when the distant chimes of the Groote Kerk reminded him of his vicinity to a town, and unreasonably surprised when a young man skated suddenly round the bend of the lake. He instantly reflected, however, that this must be a common resort, and wondered he had not seen more skaters.

With the curiosity of the idle, Bab noted the stranger's appearance as he approached through the pale sunlight under the shadows of the beech-trees. He was slight, of the middle height, and carried a large sable muff; his face was concealed by a leaf hat with a plain buckle; he wore a claret-coloured coat, fur-lined, and high soft boots. As he turned toward Bab he held the muff up to his face as a screen against the sharp wind.

Bab was struck by something heavy and foreign about the stranger's dress, then by the perfection of his skating, and he debated if he should give him greeting, and get into speech with him, seeing they were alone in the quiet landscape, when the new-comer lowered the muff and raised his head.

Observing Bab he stopped instantly and said something in Dutch.

The Englishman shook his head and smiled. "Good day," he answered pleasantly. "And if you know no tongue but that we should not hold a long converse."

The other took a half-turn about the ice and came to a stand below the spot where Bab sat. "What is your business here?" he asked in English, marked with only a slight accent.

"None at all," replied Bab frankly. "I had time on my hands and came here for pleasure, Sir. I am a stranger to the Hague."

"English?" asked the skater briefly.

"As you see."

"How did you get in?"

"Into the park?" smiled Bab. "Through the gate."

The young man reflected a moment while the light wind fluttered his hair and cravat. "Are you skating?" he inquired at length.

"No," said Bab, who thought him dry beyond politeness.

"Can you?"

"No," said Bab again.

For the first time the stranger looked up at him. "These are private grounds," he remarked, "and you have no manner of right here."

Bab was taken aback, but composed. "I'm sorry," he said. "Is this your land, Sir?"

"I come from the house."

"Where is it?" asked Bab with interest.

"Near—through the trees there." As he spoke he sat down on the bank and unstrapped his blade skates that glittered strongly through the clog of snow.

Bab rose. "I had no wish to trespass," he said good-humouredly. "I thought it public like the Mall. I only came to the Hague yesterday."

The young man, with the skates in one hand, sprang lightly up the bank and stood beside Bab. "What business have you in Holland?" he asked gravely.

"My own," said Bab quietly.

"Your reserve discovers prudence," returned the other. "Is your affair as weighty as it is secret?"

Bab looked at him closely. He had a majestic and manly countenance, remarkable eyes and thick curling hair of a dark brown; a likeness in the face to someone he had known troubled Bab.

"I am a mere traveller who comes to the Hague out of curiosity," he replied.

"Curiosity!" returned the other scornfully. "Who journeys to Holland out of curiosity!"

"I, certainly," said Bab; then with an attempt to shift the conversation; "You speak English extremely well, Sir."

The compliment did not seem to please. "My mother was English," was the indifferent answer. "Are you long for the Hague?"

Bab made a light response. "Until my curiosity is satisfied."

"Are you known to Sir William Temple?"

"No, not at all," replied Bab, half annoyed at these repeated questions.

"He is at Nymegen now," remarked the other, "attending the Peace Congress the King of England holds there. I though it might be that you waited his return."

"No—my residence here depends not on politics," said Bab, wondering why a stranger should take interest in his movements.

The young gentleman shivered. "Let us walk on," he said, fastened his skates together over his arm and thrust his hands deeply into his muff.

"Your weather is extremely cold," remarked Bab as they followed the narrow path above the bank, "but in London it has been worse."

"Yes, the packets have been delayed," was the brief answer.

Bab did not quite know how to continue. He judged his companion a gentleman, perhaps an officer of some rank, and imagined an acquaintance with him might prove useful; but he found him difficult to talk with.

"You live at the Hague?" he hazarded.

"Yes—where are you staying?"

"In the Princengracht."

"Ah, at the house of one Widow Vanderhooven."

Bab assented, surprised. "You know the place?"

"I know it as a house frequented by English and other refugees."

"A strange gathering," laughed Bab.

"Not a house an ordinary traveller was like to hear of," remarked his companion dryly.

Bab reddened. "You appear to suspect me of some far-reaching design," he returned.

The other was silent, and the King's messenger glanced doubtfully at his delicate and haughty profile. He thought the young man not more than twenty-four or twenty-five, yet the gravity of his expression and the stateliness of his manner were not in keeping with youth; he had an unfriendly air of gloom, yet the arresting attraction of composure and authority. Bab felt that this talk was not purposeless, that he had some design in his action, and so came quietly.

The path curved suddenly round the water and Bab saw, at the end of a short avenue, a white house with a high flight of steps shaded from the winter sun by the bare boughs of the snow-glittering trees.

The young man stopped and turned his clear, deep glance on Bab. "If your affair is what I think it," he said shortly, "it is ill served by delays and misunderstandings." He paused, coughed, and gave a half-resentful glance at the snow-clouds that were obscuring the sun. "You are Mr. Baptist Mompesson," he continued, "my Lord Danby's private agent."

Bab flushed and stared at the speaker. "How can you possibly come by that knowledge?" he demanded.

The young man answered brusquely: "I am the Stadtholder I came back from Dieren yesterday. This is my house; if you will come in, I will look into your business."

———————————

CHAPTER VI. THE MIND OF THE PRINCE

Bab was so amazed that he stammered like a startled child and stood foolishly.

"I perceive that you are not a very accomplished courtier," said the Prince, "but I think you do not come on an embassy of compliments."

Bab uncovered. "Your Highness had me unawares," he said simply. "Sure, I cannot mind me in a moment of my wits."

The sun was now completely veiled in sullen glooming clouds. The Prince turned down the bare avenue. He said no more to Bab, who followed, his hat in his hand, by no means pleased with this sudden and informal audience and overawed by the quiet haughtiness of the Stadtholder, whose manner showed no friendliness.

William ascended the steps slowly, and Bab came behind him into a small vestibule with a marble floor, where a clock ticked primly and dark portraits showed conspicuous on the light painted walls. The Prince put down his skates, his hat and muff on one of the chairs; the same silence that filled the wood was over the house. William opened the door to their right and Bab followed him into a small room very plainly furnished.

"You may wait here," said the Prince, and was leaving, when at the door he turned. "You have your papers."

Bab handed Lord Danby's letter, the Prince gave it an indifferent glance and returned it, departed and closed the door. Bab felt that the King of England's messenger might have had a more gracious reception; he was prepared to dislike the Prince. The room in which he waited had the air almost of a dissenting church, it was so prim, so neat and severe. The only picture was a large, sober, stormy landscape that occupied the whole of the chimney-shaft; the chairs had leather backs and seats fastened with brass nails; the wall was panelled half-way up in a linen pattern of carving, above the moulding it rose plain to the ceiling, the large crossway beams of which were finished by little shields bearing the arms of Nassau.

Bab contemplated these details with an unfriendly eye; his father had been a Puritan, but his own instincts were not for severity. The Prince was different from what he had fancied him, different from any one he had ever spoken to, and the strangeness and foreign atmosphere of master and house depressed him. He sat glaring at the vista of leafless trees through the polished window against which a few flakes of snow were falling.

It was half an hour before the Prince returned accompanied by two gentlemen as silent as himself, one young and noticeably handsome, the other very grave and older.

"Mynheer Bentinck and Mynheer Dyckfelt," said the Prince briefly. "And now, Mr. Mompesson, we will hear what you have to say," Bab had risen on their entrance. William motioned him back to his seat.

The two Dutch nobles and the Stadtholder took the stiff chairs at the table; Bab eyed them with a sinking courage. "Your Highness will understand..." he began.

William interrupted. "Make not your discourse a chime of empty words, Mr. Mompesson; we are so pressed with great business that we are wishful to come to the heart of this matter."

Bab bowed. "Yet I must be so bold as to ask Your Highness to allow that no business can be greater than that I am charged with."

William glanced at Bentinck, who gave a slight shrug. Bab was nettled.

"I am King Charles' messenger," he said, "and I was bid ask a private audience."

"These are my friends," replied the Stadtholder. "His majesty would not be secret from them, I think, but from the States." He had a slow impressive manner of speech that carried great weight, and a soft voice though it sounded weak and strained. Bab, observing him now without his beaver, thought he looked fatigued to the point of sickness, though he was not pale but had a clear, tanned complexion and eyes marvelously brilliant and alert; as he spoke he took his brow in his hand and rested his elbow on the table. "Why did my Lord Danby choose you for this mission?" he asked suddenly.

"It is difficult to say, Sir," returned Bab frankly. "Before my lord grew to such a height we were something friends, being both on the King's side, though Protestant and I of a Puritan family—but, more than that, my noble lord, his Majesty said to me: 'As you are an honest, plain dealing man who believes in God, I will trust you to convince his Highness better than a glib courtier.'"

Mynheer Dyckfelt smiled across the table at Mynheer Bentinck; the Stadtholder moved his head so that the thick chestnut hair concealed his countenance from Bab and answered quietly: "What was the bottom of his Majesty's desire in this journey of yours, Mr. Mompesson? Sir William has my full confidence. There has been many a messenger going to and fro King Charles and me since this weary war began, and none of them has wrought any good."

An earnest look sprang into Bab's blue eyes. "Sir, I have it greatly at heart to carry through the King's wish, for it is the wish also of Parliament and of England."

The Prince did not move, even by a little. "Would my uncle have peace in Europe?" he asked quietly.

"He *must* have peace," answered Bab. "The Parliament presses and the people clamour. Is it to our advantage to see France striding across the continent, our faith whipped with fire and sword?"

The Prince looked up, he was suddenly pale, his large eyes dark and glittering. "Does my uncle see that, at last?" he asked with a proud bitterness. "At last! He is afraid of France, would patch a timid peace—but that will not help us. I tell you, Mr. Mompesson, had my uncle aided me, even with a thousand men, in '72, he had not need to dread France now." He spoke with a force, an emotion that held Bab silent; with yet a deeper passion in his contained voice he continued: "I speak very freely to you, Sir, for I doubt not you know the mind of the King, therefore it is as well that you should gauge mine. In my desperate extremity, England held back from me and leagued with my enemies—I have been pushed to the very verge of despair and only by God's grace am I sustained—and it is always my uncle who has dipped the balance against me. Now, fearful of France, fearful of his people, he would force a peace, but we who have endured so far can endure to the end, Mr. Mompesson."

He paused in an exhausted fashion and pressed his Frisian lace handkerchief to his lips.

"The King has done with France," said Bab warmly. "I am no courtier, Sir. I loathe the King's policy. I would he had helped you in '72—but it is not too late."

"It is very well to talk of peace," returned William. "But on what terms?"

"With England on your side you could make the terms," answered Bab. "This is the main object of my embassy—to offer Your Highness, as guarantee of the King's faith, the hand of the Princess Royal."

Bentinck looked at the Prince, who kept his glance fixed on the table.

"That proposal was made me by my Lord Arlington in '76," he said.

"Affairs have changed since '76, Your Highness."

William shot him a long look. "You mean that then I had not been beaten so often by the French? It does not make me any easier to be bought, Mr. Mompesson."

"Not bought, Sir—it would be the triumph of your policy, a blow in the face for France."

"And the price?"

"Peace, Your Highness."

"On the terms of France," said the Prince. "Mr. Mompesson, I stand alone in what I do. Doubtless my task seems impossible and the King's offer brilliant, but I should be the most miserable man alive if I should accept it. I am pledged to my country, my allies, my conscience to continue this war until death or justice end it..."

"Justice!" Bab caught at the word. "The King will see justice done."

The Prince's eyes were contemptuous and Bab flushed. "*England* will see justice done," he amended proudly. "England admires and loves Your Highness—England would stand by you against Papist Tyranny."

"Assure me that and Europe is saved," said William.

"This match will assure it to Your Highness."

"Is the treaty or the wedding to come first?" asked the Stadtholder.

The King's messenger could not mistake the disdainful curve of his mouth.

"Your Highness does not trust England nor me," he said. "I will ask you reflect a little. My Lord Danby has pledged his position on this policy."

Bentinck spoke for the first time. "Her Highness is heiress of England. What does her father the Duke think of a Protestant match for her, when he desires to establish his own faith?"

"The Duke's will would bend to the will of the nation, my lord."

The Prince's face softened into a half-smile. "What does my cousin think of this bargain?" he said irrelevantly.

Bab was so unprepared for this from the Stadtholder's gravity that he replied awkwardly: "Her Highness is very youthful—her mind is still changeable."

"Which means she likes not what she has heard of me," said William calmly. "I recall her as a wilful child some seven years ago when I was in England. I think a lady from my uncle's house is scarce like to favour me. But this is early talking only; all else aside, I have a fancy to marry where my liking goes and should wish my wife to be of that mind."

In his heart Bab thought the fair and headstrong Princess, untaught and lively, was not likely to be attracted by this austere young man. It seemed to him that small happiness for either would lie in the match, but the domestic aspect of the affair was not his concern.

"This marriage would bring Your Highness one nearer the throne and give you immense weight in England," he said eagerly. "To one of already such power in the Councils of Europe that must have weight..."

The Stadtholder looked at him intently. "Mr. Mompesson, this is not a personal matter. I could have made separate treaties to my own advantage any year since the war began. What is my advancement compared to the great issues involved?"

"Does not Your Highness desire peace?" asked Bab tentatively.

"On just terms, yes."

"What terms?"

"The Peace of Munster established the balance of power in Europe. When France will return to that I will sign a peace."

"France never would," was surprised from Bab.

"Then let the war continue."

"To what end?" asked Bab. "Your Highness can scarce have ultimate success."

"Men have said that to me before, Mr. Mompesson," said the Stadtholder calmly. "It were an ill symptom in me if I listened to these discouragements."

"My sentence was incomplete," answered Bab. "I would say, Sir, that you can hardly come to final victory without the aid of England."

"I may achieve my end by the grace of God and my own will," returned the Prince. "What are outside aids compared to inner strength?" He rose abruptly, and the others got to their feet.

"Your Highness makes a scorn of my mission," said Bab mortified.

The Prince glanced at his friends and smiled quietly. "We must talk on this subject again, Mr. Mompesson. I have to see some of the

States, now, privately," he said. "I have writ to his Majesty that you may have my reply in a few days—wait upon me again shortly."

Bab felt that he had so far failed; he had a sense of unfriendliness and prejudice on the Prince's part. Even the King's warnings had not prepared him for this unmoved distrust of England; he was overawed by the Stadtholder and resented the two silent Dutch nobles, who bent such odd glances on him. He bowed, accepting his stiff dismissal; William gave him the briefest nod, and crossed to the window with his back to the room.

As Bab closed the heavy door he heard the Prince laugh maliciously, as if he had discomfited one he disliked, and make some remark in his own language that Bab took to be a slighting stricture on himself. The Englishman was humiliated and genuinely cast down; he stood for a moment in the light-vestibule forcing his composure.

Opposite the door that opened on to the steps was another, placed between two little stairways that led to upper apartments. As Bab was leaving, this was flung wide and a young man in a plain green coat came out. Before he closed the door Bab had a glimpse of a magnificent hall painted from floor to ceiling with richly coloured figures, and a large window looking on to an ornamental garden.

The young man softly turned the handle on these splendours and smiled at Bab. "Ah," he said in French, "the English gentleman from the Princengracht. I saw you this morning—I am the wrestler from the turret."

He had such a pleasant engaging face, eyes so deeply blue and friendly that Bab was moved to admit him into instant comradeship. "This is a strange house," he said, lowering his voice confidentially. "Are there no servants?"

"Only a cook and a valet—half the place has been shut up since the Princess Amalia died. The Prince returned only yesterday." The glance of each turned to the door that concealed that potent personality.

"Is he in there?" asked the young wrestler dubiously.

Bab assented. "You come here to look after the instruments?" he asked.

The other nodded and drew the string of the velvet bag he carried.

"There is a beautiful clavichord in the Orange Hall that I am mending and wresting into tune. I have been coming here for the last week. It can hardly be quieter in the grave. Do you walk home with me?"

"Why, yes," said Bab.

They left the palace together.

CHAPTER VII. RAMON DE LA ROSA

"You are French?" asked Bab as they trod the frozen paths under the bare beeches.

"No," smiled his companion, "Spanish—Protestant Spanish who has never seen Spain. I come from Brussels, Sir. My mother was Flemish, my father was slain at Seneff and our lands are fallen a prey to the French, hence you see me at the Hague, wrestling clavichords." He glanced down at the little purple velvet bag of tuning forks and strings he carried and added on a laugh: "It is a strange life in Mevrouw Vanderhooven's turret with those fanatics for company."

"I would sooner have gone to the wars," said Bab.

"Perhaps you do not know the wars," returned the other. "A penniless gentleman may find scant employment there—yet the next campaign I might join the Prince."

"The Prince," repeated Bab thoughtfully. "What opinion have you of the Prince?"

The young Spaniard replied with a counter-question. "Have you business with him?"

Bab instantly reflected he could not, if he would, disguise that he had access to the Stadtholder, and that since his mission was already known to France and the Romanist, there was little to be gained by cloaking it with too great mystery. "I come here on English affairs of moment," he answered.

"I can be discreet," was the quick answer. "My name is Ramon de la Rosa—nothing to you, but in Brussels it used to count for honour. I would ask no questions, only I was moved to marvel you should have seen his Highness when few knew even that he has returned from Dieren."

Bab was frank; he liked the young Spaniard. "I met the Prince by chance."

"And did not know him?"

"No—yet I thought him like some one—and now I recall that his countenance holds a resemblance to a Stewart Prince who died, the Duke of Gloucester, and his own mother. Their paintings are in Whitehall."

"He is a particular brave Prince," said Don Ramon, "and a man to be feared. He was educated a Republican—you have heard it?"

"Yes, he had a sour youth."

John de Witt (1625-1672). Painted by A. Blooteling, after le Barri.

"He was very little thought of till the war broke out, and then he rose at once to such a pitch of wisdom and courage that he is absolute in these States and renowned in Europe. He holds the strings of a great alliance and gives such a clog to the wheels of France, they can scarce make progress."

They had cleared the park, passed through the gates and were out again in the now twilight streets.

Bab lowered his voice. "Yet think you he can maintain the conflict single-handed much longer?"

Don Ramon shook his head. "The States, it is whispered, have a great mind to a peace; the taxation is enormous; the allies, too, would close with France tomorrow if it were not for the Prince, but he will not be persuaded that King Louis can be brought to reason—any way but by the sword—so the adamant resolution of this young man keeps Europe in arms."

"We of the true faith must admire him," said Bab.

Don Ramon smiled. "We of the true faith, yes," he answered softly.

They were crossing the Voorhout, which was now almost empty of carriages and people; such a gust of cold saltish wind swept up it that Bab drew his camlet cloak close about him.

"Yet,"—he spoke following out his reflections—"one may doubt the Prince's policy. A peace would bring much good to Europe."

They turned down the Kneuterdyck, bending their heads before the wind.

"Ay," assented Don Ramon. "One man thought so. Do you mark that house?" He pointed out a mansion to their right, of pink brick with wreaths of stucco flowers adorning it, standing at the corner of a narrow street down half of which ran the garden wall. It was a fine dwelling and seemed to be empty since every window was shuttered and door and steps ill kept.

"That was the house of John de Witt," said the Spaniard, "who for twenty years ruled this country according to honour."

They paused and gazed at the deserted mansion that suddenly held a horrid interest for Bab. "Only four years ago, was it not'?" he asked under his breath.

Don Ramon observed him with something of cynicism in his bright eyes. He slipped his hand under Bab's mantle and drew him on. "John de Witt was a man who loved peace, and did his duty by all men. He made mistakes—and here he paid for them."

Two minutes had sufficed to bring them out on the Plaats, facing the gloomy prison of the Gevangenpoort, with the frozen Vyverberg to their left. Don Ramon pointed up at the largest barred window of the prison.

"From there John de Witt looked out on the crowd below—under that archway he and his brother were dragged to death, he in his velvet mantle, Cornelius in his night-shirt, for he had been under torture, and here where we stand they were hacked to pieces by the mob."

He smiled, cruelly it seemed to Bab. "I have met a man who bought one of John de Witt's fingers for two sous and a mug of beer, and who saw the heart of Cornelius bleeding on a pot-house table. Well, what of honour and gratitude? Come on, it grows cold."

"It was a black deed," said Bab strongly, "and I like not to think on it. Four years ago—faugh!—the place smells of blood."

Cheerless and leaden the day was shortening; scanty flakes of snow fell reluctantly from the pall of clouds that hung low above the tourelles and roof-lines of the Binnenhof; the twisting black boughs of the trees shivered mournfully in the harsh icy wind.

"How often he passed here," said Don Ramon in a very quiet voice, "when he came from the Binnenhof to his home; with what varying, what anxious, what uplifted thoughts he must have trod this spot where he met the final agony."

They silently traversed the tunnel-like arch of the prison; it was so obscure with shadows that they could scarcely see each other.

"What hand had the Prince in that deed, think you?" asked the Spaniard suddenly.

Bab shuddered despite himself at the confining blackness of the walls that had enclosed such horror. "If one judges by circumstances he knew somewhat," he returned; "if one judges by character he is innocent."

"I would give much to know," said Don Ramon intensely.

Bab was glad when they came out into the sombre daylight of the

Buitenhof. "Were you a friend of John de Witt?" he asked. "You seem to feel his fate."

"Any honest man may feel that," replied the young wrestler. "It was a thing almost beyond credence—horrible."

Bab looked at him as they crossed the square of the Buitenhof. He had a strong face, under-jawed, dark-skinned; his hair was a tawny colour, in showy contrast to his blue eyes, his nose aquiline and his mouth wide and finely curved. When he felt Bab's candid gaze on him he flashed round a quick glance and laughed. "I speak with force," he said in a half-explanation, "because thoughts grow in strength by brooding, and I have so few to listen to me."

The melancholy that seemed to lurk behind his gaiety touched his last words with sadness. Bab grasped his arm warmly. "Give me your friendship. I am glad I met you. The spring comes surely and with it undreamt-of hopes."

He felt affectionately toward the exile with the engaging face and soft manners. Don Ramon returned the pressure of the honest hand that had slipped to his under the green mantle. "I will play you the clavichord," he said, "one day when the others are at church. They are good people, but they pray too much."

It was dark when they entered the house in the Princengracht. Don Ramon smiled brightly at Bab and went instantly upstairs with the obvious desire of avoiding the other occupants of the house.

The King's messenger was following to his room, when a lean hand caught his coat. "A word with you."

The formal tones belonged to the Scotch minster. Bab looked round into the hard countenance of Fear-the-Foe Gibbons.

"On what subject, worthy Sir?" he asked, none to eagerly.

For answer Fear-the-Foe drew him into the grim front parlour, which gave Bab an instant sense of depression. The walls were oak half-way up, whitewash above; the table and the stools were of black wood polished until they appeared coated with transparent wax; the stove was plain white tiles; next it stood a heavy press, so large, dark, and solid it looked as if it must contain something more foreboding than mere clean linen. Near the window hung the old one-eyed parrot in a black ring; his gaudy feathers were ruffled, his tail drooping; he looked as misplaced and lonely as a cardinal in a dissenters' meeting-house.

"Where is Mevrouw Vanderhooven?" asked Bab, who fancied some protection in that lady's presence.

"She makes walnut water for the young Fleming who has sore eyes," said Fear-the-Foe. "With squinting at keyholes, I doubt not," he added spitefully.

"Squinting at keyholes!" laughed Bab, "what should she see through keyholes in this house?"

The Scotchman frowned on him, marking with a disapproving eye his cravat of Bruges lace, his breeches fastened below the knee with rose-velvet ribbons, the silver braid on his black coat and the pink silk rosettes on his square-toed shoes. "You are not clothed as if for a godly mission," he remarked. "Those who would start on the Lord's path must first unload themselves of fripperies and vanities."

"Why, I am sure you are right," said Bab good humouredly. "What would you speak to me of?"

The Covenanter seated himself at the table on which burnt a single candle that reflected its entire length in the depths of the polish. He lifted a knotted forefinger at Bab. "You have not been two days in the house," he said, "and already you are junketing with the profane young man from the turret."

Bab was annoyed by this espionage and interference. "The poor young Spanish gentleman?" he queried.

"Yes—the wrestler of worldly instruments."

"I like him," returned Bab. "What have you against him, Sir? He is of the true faith and has suffered for it."

"All is not truth that is told," said Fear-the-Foe pursing up his leather-like features. "The Prince of Darkness often gilds cracked and broken vessels."

"What do you mean?" asked Bab straightly.

The Covenanter's dull eyes blinked across the candlelight. "Trust not that youth," he said sternly.

"What right have you to say that?"

"I have the right to say whatever seems to me to the service of the Lord."

"Well, what object?" demanded Bab impatiently.

"I would turn your feet from snares and your eyes from darkness," returned the preacher. "If Mevrouw Vanderhooven had listened to me," he added on a note of personal bitterness, "the Spanish youth had left the house a year back."

"A little charity, Sir," commended Bab. The words of the Scotchman served to further increase his interest in Don Ramon. He could easily perceive that the one amiable person in a house of soured fanatics would be likely to have an ill time; his only wonder was that one so youthful, gallant, and pleasant should remain under the same roof with these warped, disabled, and embittered unfortunates.

"Scorn good advice," retorted Fear-the-Foe. "Listen to the words of the enemy rather than the councils of the friend—it is the way of wild and wanton youth."

"Come, Sir," smiled Bab. "I am not a child—able at least to choose my friends." He crossed over to the parrot, who roused from torpid meditation to greet him with something like a curse.

The ill-nature of Fear-the-Foe took another turn. "I cannot conceive how a God-fearing woman can endure that heathen abomination. If the devil, its master, had not endowed it with such a beak I had sent it back to Tophet long since."

Bab forgave the parrot, since he saw that its militant attitude was defensive rather than offensive, and that its bad temper served to save its neck.

"Well, good night, Sir," he said. "There are some letters to be written—I will ease you of my company."

Fear-the-Foe deigned no answer; his lips moved in pious ejaculations. He produced a worn calf-skin volume from his pocket and seemed, on opening its covers, to be at once sunk in holy meditation.

Bab went up to his room and lit the candles; he heard the rest of the household going down to prayers, but Mevrouw Vanderhooven did not concern herself with the consciences of the lodgers who paid; stern observance of religious exercises was only exacted from those whom her charity supported. As the strong sound of prayers that seemed rather to command than entreat rose up the stairway, Bab sat down to write a letter to Lord Danby.

His expressions of success were doubtful; he drew a discouraging picture of the attitude of the Prince and spoke resentfully of Mr. Carew; but he bid my lord say little to the King as yet, for he surely hoped to be more forward in his mission before he next wrote.

When he had finished his letter, cast it into cipher and sealed it, he bethought him of seeking out Don Ramon, who was not likely to have joined the conventicle in the parlour. With this object he took up a candle and went to the foot of the narrow staircase that led to the attics. A faint and lovely sound slackened his steps; he paused listening. The soft notes of a muffled music floated down the mean stairway; an aria from Monteverde's ancient opera of "Orfeo," full of such caressing regret, such pleading sadness, such low complaining of gentle heart-break that Bab stood mute and, still leaning against the dark wood panelling, absorbed in the melody.

He had no doubt that it was the young Spaniard who played, and so personal did the slow notes sound that he would as soon or sooner have disturbed the prayer-meeting below as go up to his new friend now.

Half guiltily, with the step of an eavesdropper, he returned to his chamber, as the clavichord of Ramon de la Rosa changed into the minor key and seemed in languishing numbers to celebrate regretted joys and unforgettable tragedies.

CHAPTER VIII. TERESA

The next morning was changing from a bitter pale snowing into a crystal cold and bright sunlight when Bab left the house in the Princengracht. Before he had descended the winged steps Don Ramon had overtaken him.

Their greeting was cordial. "I have already been to the *Huis ten Bosch*, as they call it," said the Spaniard. "The palace," he explained. "The Prince's retinue arrived yesterday, and he is to go open the States today."

"What is your journey now?" asked Bab.

"To see this same procession of the Stadtholder. Have you aught on your mind for this morning?"

Bab, who had already sent off his letter, confessed to idleness.

"Then come with me," said Don Ramon. "I go to the only friends I have at the Hague. They own a villa near the wood and will rejoice to see you."

Bab came willingly. Don Ramon was composed and blithe; it was difficult to associate his gallant presence with the sad strains of last night. There was no melancholy in his manner now, he conversed in an easy and lively fashion as they crossed the town, which Bab admired anew in the winter sunlight. There were a great number of people abroad all going toward the Binnenhof and the streets through which the Prince would have to pass.

"He is most popular," said Don Ramon, observing the crowd. "They would give him a public entry again and again, but he ever refuses."

"Why?" asked Bab, who after the English court found the Prince too severe.

"He has not the temper for display," answered the Spaniard. "And when the people are so laden with taxes it were ill they should spend money on pageants."

"Yet if it would please the people it were good policy," said Bab, mindful of the tactics that kept King Charles on his throne. "Indulgence will gain more friends than justice. While his Majesty dines in public and has a smile for every corner he may with impunity interfere with the charters of our liberty."

Don Ramon laughed. Bab had an unreasonable feeling that he did not like the Prince although he spoke of him in tones of such deliberate, measured admiration.

They crossed the Plein and came out on the long road that ran by the wood belonging to the palace; the sun was high, and sat throned in a glory between imperious banks of clouds; the air had a steel-like quality of bright coldness.

"I must tell you of these people I take you to," said Don Ramon. "They are a Portuguese gentleman, Don Ambrose Lacruez, and his daughter—he is a retired merchant of some means. I came to know them," he added simply, "through the mending of Dona Teresa's lute."

As he spoke he stopped before one of the handsome houses that stood along the right-hand side of the road. "This is their villa."

Two large lime-trees and a narrow strip of garden divided from the highway a red brick mansion mortared with lines of white; the frontage rose in step-like divisions culminating in a single stone on which was written *'Lust en Rust'* [Delight and Rest] in deep-cut letters. The upper windows had small balconies, the lower ones mirrors on jointed arms; from all white shutters opened out against the brick. Bab had a glimpse of rich sombre rooms through the shining glass as they stepped up to the small portico.

Don Ramon entered without ceremony. A maid in peasant costume, pretty and curious to Bab's eyes, was polishing the panelling of the hall. Don Ramon spoke to her in Dutch. "Is your mistress within?"

"Upstairs, Mynheer."

The girl rose and stood respectfully with lowered eyes as they passed up the smooth, dark-hued stairway. On the first landing Don Ramon paused before a tall door and softly opened it. Bab followed him into a large room with two long windows, furnished simply but finely with Eastern pieces and the beautiful Dutch furniture. A fire burnt on a hearth of bright-painted tiles, and a lady rose from beside it as the two entered. She was young, delicate in face and figure; she had slow movements and an air of calm stillness; her eyes were Eastern eyes softly cloudy, her pallor of a white rose fairness; her locks were smoky brown, black in the shadows, and were gathered by a coral comb into a fall of ringlets at the back of her small head. She wore a dress with a tight bodice and full skirt of a stiff satin, white checked with blue and enriched with silk flowers in green and pink round the hem and across the breast; over her shoulders was a scarf of fine black lace with a silver border. She held a resplendent lute glistening with a mosaic of gold and mother-of-pearl; the ivory neck lay on her shoulder beneath her coral earrings.

Don Ramon stepped forward to meet her, and Bab saw by the look that passed between them that there was love for each other in their hearts. By her words he knew that it was unconfessed, for she said formally in French, "How goes it with you, Don Ramon. Is this your friend?"

He presented Bab and the lady's eyes made barely disguised scrutiny of his appearance.

"I am honoured that you have come," she said.

"I hardly know by what right I am here," he answered smiling. "I must be utterly unknown to you, Madam—I am at the Hague on the musty business of politics."

"You must not suppose that I take any interest in those matters," said Dona Teresa. She laid the lute across a Chinese table painted in gold, and drew the lace scarf closer round her shoulders. "It is cold away from the fire," she added. "I will tell my father you are here, and then we will go on to the balcony to see the Prince pass."

She left the room gracefully and gravely. Bab was rather surprised that she should have been prepared for his coming and also that a ruined refugee like Don Ramon should be on such terms in a house obviously wealthy. He could understand the daughter, but not the father.

Don Ramon opened the long window and stepped out. Above the trees of the wood the clouds were piled in shapes of splendour burnished to copper-gold about the disc of the sun; the yet unmelted snow sparkled in crystals along the roadway where the growing crowd gathered. He gazed at this prospect till in a few moments Dona Teresa, wrapped now in a blue velvet mantle, returned with her father, a man still young, hawk faced and of suave and pleasing manners. He was affectionate to the young wrestler, who re-entered the room to greet him, and graciously courteous to Bab. The four stepped on to the balcony, Bab next the lady, who was muffled to the chin in folds of velvet, and, even then, shivered a little. Bab good-naturedly felt himself in the way, but since that first ardent glance she had taken no notice of Don Ramon, and the Englishman concluded a pretty romance from their reserve, imagining the pride and poverty of the Spaniard and the filial obedience of the lady caused them to seal their lips, if not their eyes, to love. Glancing at the manly figure of Don Ramon with added interest, the fresh fineness of his black garments, the silver buckles on his shoes, the delicate needlework of his tie and ruffles struck Bab as unusually costly for one in his position. Almost unconsciously the harsh words of Fear-the-Foe Gibbons slipped into his mind, but he at once dismissed them with an inward laugh at himself for even remembering them.

As the chimes of the Groote Kerk struck half-past twelve the expectant crowds made way; a party of halberdiers in blue and pink with blue tassels fluttering at their weapons rode briskly past, the hoofs of their horses striking pleasantly the frozen road.

"Look," said Dona Teresa to Bab. "Now the trees are bare you can see very well."

"Is this the Prince?" he asked as an ornate coach with four horses appeared through the bare trunks.

"Yes," she told him, and the shouts that arose confirmed her. The coach was going too fast for the liking of the people of the Hague. It was surrounded by running footmen in white, carrying half-lemons at the ends of canes; the horses were very handsomely caparisoned in blue and gold; the hammer-cloth was powdered with the billets and lions that were the arms of Nassau, and the curtains at the windows were of fine turquoise-coloured silk.

Bab had an instant impression of these details, a glimpse of the high arched nose, thin cheek and curling hair of the Stadtholder, who was leaning back with no notice at all of the people, and the equipage swept out of sight. Another coach and a further detachment of the halberdiers closed the procession.

"He goes to open the States with a speech in favour of war," said Don

Lacruez, "and they are mightily inclined to peace. It remains to be seen how the people will take it."

"He has made himself absolute," said Ramon on a strange note of bitterness.

"Not quite," answered the lady, without looking at him.

"I do not think the States will stand another campaign." She appealed to Bab, "Do you, Sir?"

"Why, I do know nothing of your politics, Madam," he returned. "The Republican party, the Loevestein faction of John de Witt, is dead, is it not?"

"No," she said with some vehemence. "It lives yet, though no man would dare say he belonged to it. Amsterdam has never been wholly in the Prince's interest. They say France has more weight than his Highness in the councils of that city."

"By which I perceive you are a very pretty politician after all," smiled Bab.

She slightly flushed. "No, no," she vowed. "Shall we go in now?" The little party moved into the austere room.

"Have you seen the sights of the Hague?" asked Dona Teresa. She idly picked up the lute and fastened a broad black ribbon to the neck; below the blue velvet mantle showed the hem of her skirt bright with the multitude of silk flowers and her small pink shoe. Don Ramon was talking to her father in the farther window and she spoke directly to Bab.

"Why, no," he answered, "it is an extreme fair town, Madam."

"A village," she smiled. "Do you not know it has no charter?" Her black eyes rested a second on his face then sank to her lute. "You are here on business to his IIighness?" she asked.

"Yes," said Bab. "But it does not take me all my time."

Dona Teresa seemed to be considering. Bab regarded the heavy curls on her delicate neck and the movement of her fine fingers on the ivory neck of the lute with a kindly pleasure. "You must come with us this afternoon," she said at length without looking up. "We are going to the galleries of Mynheer van Courvenhove, who is one of our wealthiest merchants and a director of the East India Company." Again her cloudy glance sought his eyes. "I dare assure you, you will find very fashionable people there, maybe the Prince himself, and you may see all the treasure from China and India and have the pleasure of drinking the new tea at a guilder a cup."

"It is very amiable of you, Madam," said Bab, rather surprised at her kindness, "and I shall be joyed to come."

At this Don Lacruez crossed to him and inquired in a courteous tone if he was fond of birds.

The lady gave a slow laugh. "My father demands toll on the patience of any who comes here," she said to Bab. "He has, you must understand, Sir, an aviary full of rare parrots and macaws, and now he would beseech your admiration of them."

Bab, discovering an immense interest in birds, quickly assured Don Lacruez of his particular desire to behold this collection, and so, following his host, left Don Ramon and the lady alone. As the door closed she roused herself from her attitude of indifference and looked slowly over her shoulder at the Spaniard, who stood by the hearth.

"Have you mended the Prince's clavichord?" she asked softly.

"Not yet," he answered.

She shifted her mantle from her stiff satins and stood up. "Who is this Englishman?"

Don Ramon lifted the bright azure eyes at her question. "A Berkshire esquire sent by Danby with the King's consent to bring about a peace and a marriage between the Stadtholder and the Princess Royal."

Dona Teresa caught her breath. "Why did they choose such an instrument?" she exclaimed.

"That was the King's guile to convince the Prince by the simple honesty of his agent."

She crossed the room with delicate steps, holding the lace shawl together on her bosom. "Did he tell you this?"

"No—I had it from Father Constant."

"He is at the Hague again?"

"Yes, he followed this man from London."

"Ah—you saw him recently."

"Yesterday. I met him on the Voorhout. He calls himself Thomas Carew and is staying at the Tanier d'Or."

A pause broke the quietly uttered converse. A long slanting sun-ray discovered tangled gold in the depths of Dona Teresa's clustering locks and lit Don Ramon's curls into tawny fire. They each looked into the dying flames on the hearth, she very still and he with a slight shudder and a flush in his face. She let go her hold on the lute and it slipped up her arm on the black ribbon, jangling the strings into broken sweetness. "He—he knows not?" she asked in a hushed voice.

Don Ramon raised his head with a startled expression in his wide eyes. "No, no," he answered.

Another silence, during which her tense breathing was a marked thing.

"You alone know," he said almost harshly.

"Sancta Maria!" She cried quivering. "I alone!"

"Teresa!" he muttered and turned his face away.

She put her hand tightly to her throat as if to ease the throbbing there. "May I," she whispered, "now we are alone—just once? From me, sweetheart; when it comes from my lips you can find music in it."

He turned about and smiled, but in his eyes was extreme anguish. "Anything from you, child," he answered simply, "for you hold the key of my soul."

She went swiftly pale. "Cornelius!" she said in a breaking tone, "Cornelius!"

CHAPTER IX. THE LAC CABINET

The galleries of Mynheer van Courvenhove were always liberally attended in the afternoons, for there might always be seen the latest curiosity from the East, the finest furnishings of wealth and the most elegant forms of fashion, in china, silver, carpets, spices, lacquer, and bronzes; here there might be heard the last news of the war, discussions on the newest book published at Amsterdam, of the gossip from Paris and London; here the biting pamphlets of the more decent order and the news-sheets of the United Provinces could be read and commented upon; here also tea, so costly that to drink it was a distinction, was served by pages from the Indies in turbans and coloured scarves.

Today an even larger number than usual crowded the rooms, for his Highness, who had a patriotic interest in the East India Company, had announced his intention of a visit. The talk of all was engaged by the subject of politics. It was known that the Stadtholder had spoken for two hours to the States, persuading them to a continuation of the war, and that their High Mightinesses were reluctant to embark on another campaign. It was whispered that Mynheer Gaspard Fagel, Grand Pensionary of Holland and entirely in the Prince's interest, had been heard to declare that it would be impossible to raise another war budget and dangerous to suggest fresh taxations. Enormously wealthy as the United Provinces were with all the commerce of the world almost under their control, they could hardly bear the expenses of a costly war and the burden of subsidizing the allies much longer. They did not now fear actual conquest, and present comfort seemed of more value than future security; only the immense influence and unshaken resolution of the Prince had prevented them from making a peace two years ago. It was generally believed at the Hague that the Stadtholder had been invited to a marriage with the niece of King Charles, and some resentment was discovered that this brilliant offer was not immediately closed with.

Bab Mompesson moving here and there among the varied crowd gathered hint of this, and that which made him think the feeling of the United Provinces was as much for peace as the feeling of England. He began to perceive that only the personal coldness of the Prince to the bargain proposed prevented the success of his embassy, and he resolved to seek out Gaspard Fagel, as representative of the States, rather than be toiled in his, and his country's object.

When his reflections had carried him thus far from the costly monsters and elaborate abortions of India and China exposed in the galleries of Mynheer van Courvenhove, a gentle touch from a grey gauntleted hand recalled him to himself. "The Prince comes," said Dona Teresa in his ear.

Bab turned about swiftly and beheld the Stadtholder coming leisurely down the galleries. Mynheer Bentinck was with him and a number of other gentlemen. He talked to Mynheer van Courvenhove, who answered very slowly, and stopped now and again to examine the objects that crowded the walls and floor. Even in the bazaars at the Royal Exchange Bab had not seen anything more rare and fine than the Eastern treasures amassed here: rolls of painted silk with gorgeous designs of plum branch and willow, bamboo and tree-peony, porcelain cups of pulsating blue and scarlet, shining yellow or deep purple, silk pike carpets from Manchuria, satin panels mounted on ivory rollers and enriched with threads of gold, Canton embroidery laded with heavy lotus blossom and flying swallows, woven silk coats and mantles in a thousand hues, ornaments of silver-gilt filigree, of jadeite, amethyst, amber, coral, and pearls, basins and vases of bronze and translucent enamel, rose-water sprinklers with long necks glittering with polished gold, incense-burners of cloisonne enamel, little dishes of coloured glass, shaped like a plum blossom, an egg, a peach, a lotus leaf, snuff boxes of white jade carved with black bats and mystic symbols, figures of gods, kings, and priests in ivory-white porcelain or carved in green-tinged rock-crystals, fishes and birds in red and white agate, rosaries of pearl and corundum beads. Models of temples, palaces, pavilions, and terraces carved in ivory and wood, screens painted and embroidered, wine vessels in bronze parcel gilt, and statues of marble and stone made a resplendent confusion among the inlaid furniture, the mirrors, cabinets, chairs, and couches that stood against the dragon and phoenix-painted hangings concealing the wall.

As the crowd moved aside at the Prince's approach, Bab saw these exquisite things more clearly. He was pleased with their beauty and moved to admiration at the thought of what they represented in sheer worth of money. He stepped aside beside a bronze Buddha decorated with diapering of gold and tinkling with little bells as the Prince came up. Dona Teresa lifted her silk skirts out of dangerous proximity to vivid-hued porcelain and cloudy glass bowls and rested her hand on Don Ramon's arm.

Close to the three of them stood a particularly handsome cabinet in buff-coloured and vermilion lacquer, powdered with gold and enriched with a thousand details of fantasy and luxury in jade, lapis lazuli, turquoise, and amethyst.

Directly before it the Stadtholder paused and the crowd stopped about him. "You have a fine piece there, Mynheer," he said to Mynheer van Courvenhove. He seemed not to see Bab though he stood so close.

The merchant bowed. "Would Your Highness wish to observe it nearer?"

"If you please, Mynheer," answered William. Something to the surprise of Bab, he was affable and gracious as if there were no such thing as war abroad and opposition at home. He wore a State dress of white, purple, and black brocade, with a gold sash and violet ribbons below his knee; he carried his black velvet hat under his arm, and held a long cane with a porcelain handle. Mynheer Bentinck was also resplendent in grey satins and a coat lined with sable. Bab found neither of them as austere as he had imagined.

The red lac cabinet was displayed for the Prince's inspection. It opened with a pure gold key, discovering a multitude of little drawers each furnished with a handle in black, yellow, or red jade, amber, mother-of-pearl, rock-crystal or agate in the form of a fish, a bat, a dragon, a phoenix, or a blossom. The flap was encircled by a border of peonies and grasshoppers in lapis lazuli and ivory; the lustrous coral lacquer back and legs were carved into openwork foliage of lotus and plum, among which crystal and topaz blossoms showed; the feet were twisting dragons encrusted with mother-of-pearl and wearing gilt collars; the whole cabinet was shot with flecks of gold in the lacquer that gave it the glittering appearance of the gorgeous plumage of a shining-breasted bird.

The Prince genuinely admired it; he shared his countrymen's taste for Eastern furniture, and had a fine collection, but he owned nothing so choice as this. "This must needs be a high price, Mynheer," he said.

Then a thing happened that appeared very extraordinary to Bab. The Prince lifted his eyes from the cabinet and saw the three standing respectfully among the bronze figures and painted screens.

Bab bowed. The Prince gave him a half-glance and fixed his eyes on Don Ramon.

Neither said a word. The Spaniard bent his head and Dona Teresa curtsied; but Bab had a quick sense of some tense and powerful emotion passing between the three of them.

The Prince stood arrested as he had turned; in his face was a strange expression of mingled horror and anger, the look of some one who is startled, repelled, and enraged. So quickly did he regain command of himself, so instantaneous was the expression, so calmly was he the next moment talking to Mynheer van Courvenhove that Bab would have believed that the Stadtholder's emotion existed only in his own mind had he not chanced to glance at Don Ramon and seen his countenance transformed to white hideousness with such a glowering of savage hate that Bab felt an instant sick aversion to him.

"Sir," he whispered, "what is it?"

Don Ramon moved away. He pulled out his handkerchief and pressed it to his lips with a half-shuddering laugh. Dona Teresa retained her hand on his arm, imploringly it seemed to Bab.

"I have seen a man who once did me a great wrong," he said thickly. "Someone in the Prince's retinue."

Bab was baffled, not enlightened.

"Come away," said Teresa, drawing him through the crowd.

The blue flame in his eyes faded as he looked down at her; he hastened his step. Both seemed to have forgotten Bab, who heard him mutter in half-explanation, half apology; "It is the first time that I have met him face to face."

Puzzled and a little annoyed, Bab returned to where the Stadtholder still stood before the lac cabinet. The Prince did not seem to have noticed his departure nor his return. Mynheer van Courvenhove was explaining the symbolism of the carvings—how the bat stood for happiness, the peach for long life, the blithe looking grasshoppers for winter—and his Highness listened pleasantly.

As Bab came up, the Prince spoke in his decisive accents. "What is the price of the cabinet, Mynheer?"

The moment the merchant had been evading was no longer to be put off; he paled in agitation. "Your Highness would not think of buying it?" he asked humbly.

"Why not?" smiled the Prince. "Yes, I will buy it, Mynheer."

"Alas!" answered Mynheer van Courvenhove in unfeigned distress, "the piece is bespoke for the King of France."

Every one made a little stir, and the Stadtholder flushed with displeasure. "Why did you show it to me?" he demanded.

The merchant stood like a guilty man. "Your Highness knows that we must trade with our enemies as well as our friends. This piece was ordered a year back for his Majesty's apartments at Marly."

"What is he paying for it?" asked William.

"Five thousand guilders, Your Highness."

The Prince turned away. "I am not rich enough to compete with his Majesty—as yet," he said haughtily, and Bab thought the words referred to more than the lac cabinet.

This instance of the power of the King of France, who was able to thus indirectly humiliate his rival in his own country, caused whispered comment as it flew from one to the other. It was generally considered tactless of Mynheer van Courvenhove to have the cabinet in sight: the unfortunate merchant thought so too now, but who, as he asked himself bitterly, could have guessed his Highness would take a liking to that, of all others?

Whatever chagrin the Prince felt it was soon effectually concealed; he looked at this and that and was universally gracious. Bab followed him with the others, since Signor Lacruez had also disappeared with his daughter and Don Ramon, and the Englishman had no one to consider but himself. He intended, if possible, to gain speech of the Stadtholder, and found his opportunity as William, on taking leave of some ladies, wives and daughters of the States, in velvet, turned again into the long gallery.

Bab stood unmistakably in his path and the Prince addressed him, "Who were your companions, Mr. Mompesson?"

Bab was rather at loss. "Spanish Protestants, Your Highness," he answered. "The lady is the daughter of a merchant here." He felt it disloyalty to their kindness or he would have added what was on the tip of his tongue—that he knew nothing about either of them.

"Spanish," repeated the Prince, slowly bending his great eyes on Bab. "Spanish, did you say?"

"Yes, my noble lord—the lady, I think, is Portuguese?"

William did not deign to explain his interest in the insignificant strangers. Bab thought that he would pass on without another word, but after a second's silence he spoke again. "I shall look to see you in the afternoon tomorrow, Mr. Mompesson."

"I thank Your Highness."

William gave him a straight by no means friendly glance, took Mynheer Bentinck's arm, and so left the galleries, bowing right and left in acknowledgement of the salutes he received.

Bab watched the purple and black brocade out of sight and was turning to leave also, when a little incident again attracted his attention to the red coral Foochou cabinet. An elderly and mean-looking man, wearing an old fashioned habit and spectacles rimmed with horn, touched Mynheer van Courvenhove on the arm as he returned from escorting the Prince from the galleries. Bab, who was directly before them, turned sharply at the stranger's question.

"How much is the King of France giving for the red lac cabinet."

Mynheer van Courvenhove looked perturbed; he had no desire to renew the subject of the ominous piece of furniture that he feared had cost him the favour of his Highness. Bab, amused at this comedy round a cabinet of Foochou lacquer, listened unabashed to the conversation.

"The King of France is giving five thousand guilders," said the merchant. "It is, you will observe, a very fine work of art—the legs being carved cinnabar lace from Soochow, and the body, the admired Foochou, most delicately painted..."

The other interrupted. "His Highness the Stadtholder would have bought it, would he not, Mynheer?"

"You heard," answered Mynheer van Courvenhove, who had indeed noticed the insignificant old man standing among the crowd quite close to the Prince, "but his Highness cared not to go above the price."

"Well," said the stranger dryly, "I will buy it."

Mynheer van Courvenhove reddened with agitation. "It is bespoke for the..." he began.

"I will double the price," put in the other calmly; "ten thousand guilders, Mynheer."

The merchant was silent with confusion and astonishment.

"Perhaps you think that I cannot pay?" asked the old man. "My name is Balthasar Bree, and if you have inkhorn and quill I will write you a note on the Bank of Amsterdam."

The name meant nothing to Bab but a great deal to Mynheer van Courvenhove. It was that of a famous wealthy Jew of Amsterdam, who was believed to have more ships at sea and more gold in the bank than any trader in the United Provinces.

"Certainly I can find another piece for the King of France, since it would be far from prudence to refuse your price—but his Highness..."

"Never mind to think of his Highness—send me that cabinet tonight. I am staying in the Spui Straat," said the Jew. "Do you wish the letter now, Mynheer?"

"Your name is enough," answered the merchant, "but his Highness the Stadtholder..."

The Jew turned off with a little bow and never a glance at his purchase. Bab, amused and interested, followed him out of the galleries into the cold darkening streets. In the doorway both paused. The King's messenger was so curious he almost asked his silent companion what his object was in securing the cabinet as such a cost.

Mynheer Balthasar Bree turned up the collar of his mantle, adjusted his spectacles and set off at a brisk pace down the street. Bab, with a little sigh, dismissed the incident and took his own way "home"—as he had already begun to call the austere house in the Princengracht. He thought of Mevrouw Vanderhooven, of her guest, of her parrot, and even of Fear-the-Foe Gibbons with kindliness, but in a certain strange inversion of feeling his mind dwelt on Don Ramon, whom he had so quickly liked, with a not-to-be denied sense of distrust.

CHAPTER X. GRAND PENSIONARY FAGEL

When the coach of the Stadtholder cleared the Hague, and was rolling down the smooth avenue that led to the *Huis ten Bosch*, William roused himself from the reverie he had been sunk in since he left the galleries of the East India Company and said to his one companion, Bentinck, "What became of the sons of Cornelius de Witt?"

The question was so sudden, so abrupt, so unexpected and referred to a subject that the Prince was always so silent upon that William

Bentinck flushed and started. "The sons of Cornelius de Witt?" he repeated foolishly.

"Yes, my lord," said the Prince, rather sternly. His face showed pale in the twilight glimmering in the coach, and he leant back in an exhausted fashion.

"I hardly know," answered Mynheer Bentinck. "They died abroad—one at Venice, of the plague, I think—in truth I am not sure."

"Both dead," said William sombrely. "I thought so too."

Mynheer Bentinck—always inclined to the reserved part on these matters of delicacy—held his peace.

The Prince soon spoke again. "What think you of Baptist Mompesson?" he asked serenely. "Is he Danby's tool or Danby's dupe?"

"I think Danby sincere," said Mynheer Bentinck.

"An Englishman!" The Prince's tone was eloquent of infinite contempt.

"Sincere, surely," persisted Mynheer Bentinck. "He has staked his policy on the Protestant alliance—all news from England makes that clear."

"I had a letter from my loving uncle this morning," said William. "Peace, peace is his cry—the Parliament forces him; he threats me with his authority and recommends me to hear Mr. Mompesson—his authority!" The Prince laughed and added: "My lord Sunderland has been at the pains to write me that if I would be prosperous at the English court I must send the King more flattering and respectful letters. He even recommended a canting note of compliments to the Lady Portsmouth."

"Good advice, I believe," said Mynheer Bentinck.

"I cannot bring myself to it," replied the Prince shortly. "She can scarce work me more mischief than she has done already."

"If you spite her, she will prevent this match."

"You know," answered William strongly, "that I do not wish that marriage."

"But Holland does," said Mynheer Bentinck softly. "And would not Your Highness make some sacrifice to gain the English alliance?"

The steady jangle of the harness was the only sound that filled the darkening coach for a few moments, then the Prince spoke. "I would sacrifice myself any way but that. This girl—this child—Anglican, almost Papist, brought up to hate me—to favour the French, frivolous and foolish, what woman is other at Whitehall? No, even if the offer was sincere, I would rather pay some other price..."

Mynheer Bentinck was slightly amazed that the Prince took such a personal view of a political marriage. Devoted adherent as he was to the interests of his Highness, he in his heart considered it reckless folly to chaffer with such a match as King Charles offered. William appeared to feel this lack of sympathy, for he said no more on that matter.

"I shall have trouble with the States," was his next remark. "The burden of the war begins to gall the people." His voice was full of concern and feeling. "If I could lighten it, Bentinck—how lack of money clogs endeavour!"

"Alas!" said his friend, "How will they bear another campaign?"

"They show an inclination to deal separately with England. Mynheer Fagel is in despair," remarked the Prince. "He thought the

States not much persuaded by what I said today—he fears I may become unpopular."

"Gaspard Fagel is a knowing man," returned Mynheer Bentinck.

The Prince ignored that. "If Gaspard Fagel grows timid, he goes," he said. "I have enough difficulties without adding to them by using instruments that bend in my hand."

"Then," asked Mynheer Bentinck hesitatingly, "you will in no way change your policy in deference to this opposition it causes?"

"In no way," said William shortly.

The coach stopped before the steps, white in the twilight, of the *Huis ten Bosch*; the Prince and his companion passed into the palace and entered the little chamber where Bab had his first audience. The candles were not lit, and the fire was half out. A repellent air of discomfort was over the sombre room, the stiff furniture, the tasteless arrangement of chairs and table. A great change had come over the house since the death of the Princess Amalia a year ago. She had left the palace and its furnishings to the Prince, and he, preferring it to his other great residence at the Hague, lived there the few months he passed in the Capital. He spent twice what his grandmother had on the establishment and lived with a mere modicum of the comfort. Tonight his gloomy humour noticed the dreariness of the place. "It seems we are ill looked after here," he said. "The room is chill as the grave."

Mynheer Bentinck put on more logs and rang the bell. "The place needs a mistress," he said. "The lack of ladies makes us something between a monastery and a camp."

The servant entered and lit the candles; a flame spurted up on the hearth. The Prince looked discontentedly round trying to discover the cause of his dissatisfaction.

"There are the rooms in the other wing," suggested Mynheer Bentinck.

"The Princess Amalia's rooms," returned William. "How could we live in them? The place is well enough," he added, "since we are half the year at the war."

"The war will not last forever, Highness," said William Bentinck cheerfully.

The Stadtholder gave him a sharp glance. "I believe you, like all the others, are for peace," he answered. He flung his gloves down on the table and pulled broodingly at the tassels on them.

"For a just peace," amended his friend.

"Will you get justice from France or from England save with the sword?" demanded the Prince bitterly. He coughed and looked round at the severe walls, the stormy painting over the mantleshelf, the straight line of the red curtain over the tall window.

Mynheer Bentinck turned his bright face toward him. "You are out of humour, Highness."

"I have a headache, forgive me," the Prince smiled in a quick softening. "How those people talked today. Then this morning I was with the moneylenders—I have not told you yet."

"No." Mynheer Bentinck looked reflectively into the fire.

"I wished to see what I could get on the German estates and what mortgage I could raise on the revenues of Orange. Ten million guilders would carry on another campaign, William."

"But you would cripple your fortune mercilessly, Highness."

"They offered me five million on my personal credit," continued the Prince. "They said the Bank of Amsterdam might do the rest, but I care not to go there; they would make it no more, saying my estates were so hampered already and that it was like casting money into the sea to spend it on war."

Mynheer Bentinck was silent.

"One reminded me," added William, "that my Uncle Charles owed me a great sum my father lent him. I told him I had been to England on the matter once to no purpose, and that his Majesty was not likely to refund the money, even if he had it, knowing, as he does, what use I should make of it."

"What will you do for the next campaign?" asked Mynheer Bentinck, in no very hopeful tone.

"One might farm out the revenues of the admiralty—" The Prince broke off. "Some way we will get the money, whether the States grant supplies or no."

"But these are desperate expedients."

"It is a desperate situation," said William earnestly; "as desperate as it was in '72, for all the enemy is not knocking at our door. If we cry peace now France will see she dare do what she will, and while we are growing stupid in false security, she will arm for the final assault on the liberties of the world. It is known," he added, "that Louis aims at no less than that, the conquest of Europe."

Before Mynheer Bentinck had time to reply, a quiet usher entered and announced, "The Grand Pensionary." To both these young men the title still brought a thrill, a vivid memory of the man who had last borne it, who had, under that name, been ushered into their presence only a few years ago.

"I will see Mynheer Fagel here," said the Prince. "Will you stay?" he asked his friend.

"No," answered Mynheer Bentinck. "It only offends Mynheer Fagel." He left the chamber in rather a depressed fashion a little before the Grand Pensionary entered.

The Prince, without rising, greeted him with an even kind of civility. "Is there more to say since this morning, Mynheer?" he asked, and pointed to the chair at the opposite side of the dark table.

Gaspard Fagel, pompous, alert, self-confident, capable, was tonight a little agitated; he bowed over the Prince's hand and seated himself. William leant back in his stiff chair; his eyes were heavy lidded and shadowed underneath, his face pallid under the tan of exposure; he continually pushed the heavy hair back from his forehead in a restless way.

"Your Highness, I have been talking to some of the States," began the Grand Pensionary.

"So I supposed," said the Prince dryly.

"I find them horribly inclined to peace."

"Have you not been able to convince them of their folly?" asked William sternly.

"If any man could it would have been Your Highness. I still believe that you are powerful enough to continue the war for at least another campaign, but it will be a severe struggle."

Gaspard Fagel (1634-1688). Painting by Johannes Vollevens."

The young Stadtholder leant forward, the candle-light catching in the gold threads of his brocade coat and the diamonds, his impatient difficult breathing heaved on his cravat. "Mynheer Fagel," he said. "The States must hold out, there can be no talk of peace yet. I will stake all my influence, risk my reputation, my fortune on preventing a peace now."

The intelligent brown eyes of Gaspard Fagel narrowed on to the resolute face of the Prince. "It was difficult enough two years ago, Highness; now, it is twice as hard."

"Why?" demanded the Stadtholder.

"The Loevestein faction raises its head again; the King of France stirs up all that may turn an ill handle to Your Highness' interest; the city of Amsterdam is obstinate—and the people begin to desire a respite from a costly war."

"All this I know," said William. He rose, crossed to the hearth and stirred the fire-consumed logs into sparks with the toe of his shoe. "It makes no difference," he added, "this opposition must be overcome as we have overcome opposition before. The war continues."

Mynheer Fagel moved uneasily in his chair. "What further adds to the strength of these contentious faction is the knowledge that England wearies for a peace." He paused, then continued: "It is believed, Highness, that King Charles would renew the offer of the hand of the Princess Mary."

The Prince's hazel eyes showed slits of agate brightness under the drooping lids. "In all public matters I am the servant of the States," he said. "I make no private treaties, I have no secret understandings. The States know everything—save in the business of my marriage. There I have the right to please myself, yet, for your own satisfaction, know that I do not think of this English match."

"It has been offered, then?" asked Mynheer Fagel.

"Yes," said the Prince shortly.

"That is a tremendous thing!" exclaimed the Grand Pensionary. "If Your Highness had told me sooner..."

William cut him short. "Mynheer Fagel, will you look to domestic matters, where you are admirable, and leave foreign policies to me?"

Gaspard Fagel was silent, as always, under the Prince's rebukes. He did not even resent them. He had neither thoughts nor ambitions outside his place. His one fear was to displease the Prince, not from any servile dread of losing his position, though he was proud enough of the rank he held, but from an honest sense of duty to the man whom he blindly believed in. He was a perfect civil servant and a very loyal follower; he did not know and never could have been brought to see that the Prince was so unreasonable as to despise him.

After a moment the Stadtholder spoke again in a less severe tone. "The States must be managed, Mynheer. I will speak to them separately myself. And as for these discontents the King of France causes with his intrigues, I do not think they go very deep anywhere save in Amsterdam, and if that city offended me too far I shall know how to reduce it to obedience." The tone was more that of a King than that of the first magistrate of a Republic, but it did not jar on the ears of the Grand Pensionary.

"There is so little excuse, Highness," he said, "for continuing a war that is no longer defensive. Your Highness has driven the French from the country, restored the lost Provinces to their liberty, brought France to wish for peace, and England to ask for it. In the eyes of the people that is sufficient."

William flashed him an impatient glance. "Are you so shortsighted that you do not see that a peace now would be on the terms of France—a triumph for Louis? We should be cowed, not satisfied, and with the Spanish Netherlands at his mercy, Spain deserted, enfeebled, Germany overawed, England in his pay, the continent would lie easily in his grasp, and we, with ships dispersed, armies disbanded, alliances dissolved, we should be helpless as we were in '72."

Gaspard Fagel had no answer. If he did not contradict he did not respond, and in the pause of his silence the young Stadtholder felt the isolation of his own loneliness like a sword sweeping between them. Gaspard Fagel did not understand. The Prince's thoughts flashed back to the last Grand Pensionary, John de Witt, his tutor, guardian, opponent, the man on whose fall he had risen, the man who had been murdered in his name by his followers. The personal differences between them had been forever effaced in William's mind by that final tragedy. He remembered John de Witt as his enemy but as a great man, the only man who had opposed him, strength for strength, principle against principle. Thinking of John de Witt, who had fallen but never bent, the Prince felt contempt for this patient, faithful instrument of his, Gaspard Fagel, and scorn of all the men about him who did not understand—did not understand. With an effort he forced himself into speech.

"The only question is that of the supplies for the next campaign, which I do intend to open in April. The allies, as you know, have promised to take the field by then. I have told the States the great necessity for a powerful army. As they seem so slow to move it must be repeated." The distaste and impatience with which he spoke did not escape Mynheer Fagel, who rose.

"I will not trouble Your Highness any more tonight," he said humbly.

"Come to me again tomorrow. I hope to return to Dieren next week. Good night, Mynheer."

When Gaspard Fagel had gone the Prince took a deep arm-chair by the fireplace, leant forward a little and stared into the shadows that ringed about the light cast by the candles on the stiff table. Even his undaunted courage had to admit a profound depression. The odds had always been great, now they threatened to become overwhelming. In his heroic stand against the infamous onslaught of France he had been helped by the enthusiasm, the endurance, the self-sacrifice of his countrymen. He had saved the United Provinces and driven out the conqueror; he had gained fame, admiration, respect from Europe. At Seneff he had proved himself a hero and won praise from Conde. He had justified himself in what he had undertaken. His vigorous intellect, his steadfast courage, his unshaken faith in God, and his unwavering resolution made him the hope of the lovers of liberty in England, Germany, and even in Spain and Austria. His diplomacy had gained allies, his home policy had been beneficial. At twenty-four he was absolute in his own country and feared abroad. But now it seemed that the tide was turning. No one would be patient long enough, neither his allies, nor his people, nor even his friends. They could not see as he saw; they wanted peace. The burdens of the war were terrible. The country was safe. Charles was willing for, Louis not averse to, an end of the combat. Spain was decaying, Austria engaged in a long struggle with the Turks, Germany distracted. Peace on any terms was becoming the cry of Europe.

William of Orange felt himself standing almost alone in his opinion. He could still count on the loyalty of the States, but he was risking it; he could still count on the affection of the people, but he was training it. The offers of Charles had made his position more difficult as that King had intended they should. Even Bentinck blamed him for not accepting them. But the cause of liberty was not to be served by these specious means. The English marriage was a trap, the English King's talk of peace deception to fool his own people. France was behind them and William knew it. He knew also that neither Louis, Charles, nor James of York intended that he should become the husband of Mary Stewart, and he meant not even to dally with the bait he had once before refused. He was aware his decision would be misconstrued. Already the Loevestein faction was whispering that he wished to continue the war because it made him of greater importance to the States. This did not trouble him, for he had never guided himself by the varying and conflicting opinions of men, but he could not fail to be affected by the tremendous nature of the stake he was casting down to back his immovable conviction—the trust, confidence, and affection of his country, his heritage, so hardly regained, his position in Europe, so essential to the safety of his faith, the very existence of the Protestant estates themselves—he was risking all this on the hazards of war.

As he stared into the inscrutable shadows that veiled the rigid chamber that was all he had of home, he could not but be weighed down in spirit with a keen sense of the responsibilities he assumed. Never for an instant did he waver from his firm decision, but he almost doubted his own powers to carry his immovable purpose to completion. The odds were so tremendous, and if internal discontent was to be added to them, if Louis was to carry his intrigues into the very heart of the United Provinces, what chance had he—what chance? Even as he formed the bitter question he checked it as blasphemy to the high faith he held. He clenched his hands and rose. To doubt was to doubt God and destiny. He put aside all thoughts of failure. The war must continue.

In the tense stillness of the house and the wood beyond it, the young Stadtholder's strained senses seemed to hear the confused sounds of gathering conflict, to see the panorama of battle unrolled. He walked about the confined room. High endeavours, bitter struggles, large issues, memories, and forebodings blurred the thoughts usually so clear. He did not see the bare-legged furniture, the precise walls, the great painting of storm, the logs dying in pale ashes, the candles guttering with tall blue-edged flames, but a great battlefield spread in the Low Countries, the French cavalry, the sun on the muskets and the bits, the blue standard powdered with lilies, the red-coated English battalions, behind them a great fortress rising up...

The opening of the door caused him to turn with a start. It was William Bentinck. The Prince hesitated, it was in his mind to confide his mood, his depression and resolution to his friend. He was bound by the tenderest ties to Bentinck, whose devotion and self-sacrifice had saved his life last year in the terrible illness which all had declared would be his end. Bentinck loved him, and he was loyal to that and grateful. Nothing could ever come between their friendship, yet in his soul William knew that Bentinck understood as little as Gaspard Fagel. He stood by the table looking rather wistfully into the fair fresh face of the young man who waited inside the door. He did not speak.

"It has a disconsolate air here," remarked Bentinck lightly. "It does no good to brood in the half dark and cold."

The Prince smiled gently. "You are right, William," he said, and left the chamber with his friend.

CHAPTER XI. THE END OF BAB'S MISSION

Bab Mompesson met Don Ramon on the stairs of the house in the Princengracht. The young Spaniard was smiling and serene. He carried his velvet bag of tuning instruments, and a hat with a long feather. "I am going to the *Huis ten Bosch*," he greeted Bab, "to finish the Prince's clavichord."

Bab had not seen him since the hurried exit from the bazaar. His friendliness been unaccountably cooled by that incident; he did not say that he also was bound to the palace for an audience of the Stadtholder. "The clavichord takes a long time," was his answer.

"A difficult piece of work," returned Don Ramon. He lifted his calm blue eyes and looked steadily at Bab. "Dona Teresa asks if you will not wait upon her soon. Her father will give us both dinner if we go this evening. What do you say?"

Bab could not perceive any reason in asking a stranger to join so intimate a party, nor how it was that Don Ramon could so utterly ignore the circumstances of their last parting. Curiosity and complaisance mingled made him accept however. They took leave of each other, Don Ramon leaving the house and Bab turning into the parlour that he might avoid the awkwardness of overtaking him, since they both pursued the same route. He found Fear-the-Foe Gibbons and the parrot in sole possession of the gaunt room.

The Scotchman gave him wry greeting, "Junketing with the ungodly again!"

Bab went up to the stove. It was a cold day and his room unheated. He was glad to warm his hands.

"How did you know?" he returned pleasantly.

"I heard your voices on the stairs, and saw the youth go forth decked with gauds and knots and trappings of the scarlet woman!"

Bab was not so disposed to silence this gossip as he had been before. "What have you against Don Ramon?" he asked.

The Covenanter pursed up his pale mouth. "Does a clavichord take so long to mend?" he demanded.

"Why—what do you mean?"

"He goes almost everyday to the palace of the Prince," answered Fear-the-Foe solemnly. "And he goes for no lawful purpose, being no better than a spy of that man of abominations, the King of France."

Bab was considerably startled. "Have you proofs?" he exclaimed.

"The proofs lie in my own senses," returned the other sourly.

"Have you told your suspicions to Mevrouw Vanderhooven?"

"She prefers to believe the glib tale of the youth to the simple words of honesty."

"Well, I cannot credit your doubts either," said Bab. "I think your judgment gets a little warped, Sir, sitting there and considering your neighbours from morning till eve."

Fear-the-Foe darted him a glance of unutterable scorn, folded his hands together and turned his face to the window by which he continually sat that he might observe the doings of the street in the reflectors that projected from the frame.

Bab half laughed, picked up his hat and left the house. He believed that malice and bigotry were the motives behind the Covenanter's speech, but, nevertheless, he could not deny that a slight aroma of mystery clung to both Don Ramon and Dona Teresa.

It was crisp, bright weather. The dry snow crunched under foot and glimmered on the branches of trees and on roof-tops as the pale sunlight parted the heavy, distant clouds. When he arrived at the palace, Bab was informed that the Stadtholder was abroad; but even while he lingered in the light vestibule, William returned, accompanied by several young noblemen, armed with guns and carrying game.

The Prince at once noticed Bab. "Ah, Mr. Mompesson." He handed his gun and the wild ducks he carried to a servant, took off his hat and fur gloves, and held out his hand to Bab. His manner was distinctly gracious. Bab's hopes rose. He followed the Stadtholder with a lighter heart than he had known since his last audience.

William, after a word or two to his companion, passed before the King's messenger into a room to the left, one of the Princess Amalia's suites and infinitely more elaborate and elegantly furnished than the chamber Bab had seen before. The white walls were ribbed with gilt and painted with flowers. A drawn silk screen stood in front of the fire-place. The furniture was French, pale wood and delicate tapestry. Save for a certain chill air of desertion, the place was charming. Above the mantle was an oval portrait of a young man in armour wearing an orange scarf, a blue Order, and carrying a baton. Bab thought it represented the late Stadtholder, father of his present Highness.

William moved the slender chairs awkwardly, as if his surroundings were not familiar to him and as if he felt that his severe hunting dress and high boots stained with snow were out of keeping with the feminine luxury of Amalia of Solms. He took his seat on a low sofa by the window, and looked rather absently at the long avenue of bare trees without, and the rooks that continually crossed the tumultuous clouds.

Bab remained standing, his fine presence and grey coat with rose points, his fair, thick curls and wind-flushed face illuminated by the blithe leaping firelight that found its way above and beneath the screen.

"Be seated, Mr. Mompesson," said the Prince at last, without looking round. "I think our business will not take very long."

Bab took the chair nearest the Stadtholder. "I do hope," he answered earnestly, "that I do find Your Highness better disposed toward us."

"I have heard from my Lord Danby this morning," answered William, ignoring that. "His letter largely touched the affair you have come on, Mr. Mompesson."

"What does Your Highness think of my lord's arguments?"

The Prince turned and gave him a straight glance. "I have written to my lord and to his Majesty," he said. "I think it was hardly necessary to trouble you with this mission, Mr. Mompesson."

"His Majesty trusted that I should not make a failure of it," returned Bab, deeply mortified. "As yet Your Highness has given me no chance to explain..."

William interrupted. "Not the messenger, but the message is wrong," he said calmly.

Bab flushed. "Will Your Highness give me leave to speak on these policies?"

"I think," replied the Stadtholder, "that it would waste your time."

"My noble lord," said the Englishman, "you are pleased to make a great mock of me...You do not use me as one who comes from the Majesty of England."

"I use you as one whose errand I mislike," answered William. "No doubt you are a good servant to your master."

Bab was daunted and dismayed by this attitude on the part of the Prince. He felt himself unable to advance any argument against this calm of dislike and preconceived resolution. "What answer am I to take to my Lord Danby?" he asked with some dignity. "What am I to tell his Majesty?"

"I will not dissemble with you," said the Prince calmly. "My answer to you is what it was to my Lord Arlington. With all sense of the honour done me, I do decline these offers. I take the field in April."

Bab flushed brightly. "Will Your Highness listen to me no further in this matter?"

William faintly smiled. "Indeed, Sir, you will not move me."

Bab rose. "Maybe, my lord, my poor reasoning is not like to change your resolution, which is based on some bottom you think fit to conceal from me. I do not understand Your Highness."

The Stadtholder made no attempt to interrupt; he was looking at Bab curiously and intently. Goaded by his failure, and inspired by the cause he had at heart, the Englishman continued, "It is strange that a Prince of Your Highness' wisdom, patriotism, and foresight should so briefly refuse to enter into negotiations so manifestly for the benefit of your country. To persist in these desperate straits instead of concluding an honourable peace, looks more like obstinacy than courage."

"You speak very plain, Mr. Mompesson."

"I feel very warmly, my lord."

"On the subject of this peace?" asked the Prince quietly.

"On the subject of my Lord Danby's policy: the casting off of France, the Protestant marriage, the Protestant alliance, the raising up of England to her old place, which is what Your Highness might do if you would put your hand to it."

William still regarded him earnestly "You speak like an honest man, Mr. Mompesson," he said. There was a change in his manner, the coldness Bab had found so repellent had vanished, though he was very grave. "You speak like a man who believes in the truth of his mission."

Bab looked startled. "I had this offer of the Princess Mary her hand from the King's lips."

"I perceive," said the Prince, "that you are sincere in what you have undertaken, and that to you it seems headstrong wantonness for me to refuse these proffers." He put his hand in his pocket. "Now I will read you some passages from a friend of mine, who is a great man at the court of England, and keeps me well informed of affairs there. He is one you must know well, but I may not reveal his name." With this the Prince took several letters and papers from a silver-clasp pocket-book, selected one and opened it to the light.

"This was sent me a fortnight ago," he remarked.

Bab stood astonished and bewildered, while William in a low voice read from the letter he held, "'Among other things, I must acquaint Your Highness that there is another attempt to be made to draw Your Highness into a peace which shall be wholly to the advantage of France. Very fine offers are to be made Your Highness, who must judge for yourself what they are worth when I tell you that Monsieur Barillon, the King, and Danby made a bargain last week, by which we are pledged to help France, who is to pay us enough to enable us to dispense with the Parliament. This is like to have very ill consequences if Your Highness stands not firm in the matter of the peace, which it is intended you shall sign before ever the marriage, which is likelier to end at Paris than the Hague. Your Highness understands what I mean. Therefore, with submission to your better wisdom, I do entreat Your Highness not to be misled or beguiled by these flatteries—but I have not enough apprehension of your being caught to press any more in this train.

"'The King sends a man little known at court to Your Highness, Mr. Baptist Mompesson, and a Romanist priest, Father Constant, who passes under the name of Thomas Carew, and is deep with the French agents at the Hague.'" The Prince paused and looked up at the Englishman.

Bab stood motionless, his head hanging, his hands open at his side. "What can I say?" he asked bitterly. "What can I say?"

The Prince folded up his papers and returned them to his pocket-book. "Who wrote that letter?" cried Bab, raising his head desperately.

"I said 'a friend of mine,'" replied William laconically.

"One who knows so much!"

"A great man in England."

Bab said one word, "Sunderland!"

"The writer matters not, Mr. Mompesson—it is the substance of the letter I would have you note."

"I have been duped very sorely," said Bab, the blood rushing to his fair face. "I am utterly undone and amazed. I do entreat Your Highness to believe it..."

"Had I not thought you a sincere man, Mr. Mompesson, I should not have been at the trouble of reading you that letter."

"I am ashamed...that Danby..."

"Mistake me not," interrupted the Prince. "I do believe my lord sincere. He sees that a peace is the only means to secure him from Parliament, but he has gone too far in commerce with the French to disavow them."

"Oh, what is this?" cried Bab. "Where is any manly virtue left? Faith and honour are gone out of England...'Defender of the Faith', the King quoted to me, and the while deceived me. Now I do in truth see why men do so cherish and look to Your Highness in admiration, for it seems that you are the only single-minded Prince in Europe, the only one who looks not after his private interest. But as for me, I have been flattered and duped and stand a figure of naught before Your Highness."

William rose and approached the Englishman, who was the taller by half a head yet seemed of an inconsiderable stature in his humbled discomfiture, compared to the princely carriage of the

Stadtholder. "Intermeddle not with politics, Mr. Mompesson," said William kindly; "they are no matters for plain-dealing folk. I do now perceive that you are an honourable man, no mere tool such as at first I thought you; therefore, if I put any slight on you, I am sorry for it."

"The suspicions of Your Highness were just," returned Bab. "I have no word to say. I have been fooled..."

"It is no discredit to you, Sir. You must tell my Lord Danby that you found me well informed on the subject of English politics, and to his Majesty—what you will."

Bab was silent. In his keen disappointment and humiliation he felt an impetuous desire never to see the friend who had fooled him, the master who had lied, or the country where these ruled again. He was collecting his angry thoughts to take a grateful leave of the Prince, when a little sound interrupted their discourse and gave a singular turn to the end of Bab's mission. It was the whining and scratching of a dog. William went to the door and opened it on a magnificent boarhound from the Russians, with yellow eyes, who greeted him with extravagant joy. As the Prince, with the door open, was stooping over the dog, a sudden full chord of music broke on the silence of the palace.

"That comes from the Great Hall," said William, alert instantly. "Now who plays there?"

Bab, through his own bitterness, remembered Don Ramon, who had said he would be at the *Huis ten Bosch* today. "It is the young Spaniard, Sir, I think," he said, "who was with me yesterday. He wrests the clavichord of Your Highness."

The Stadtholder looked at Bab sharply. It was obvious that he had not known of this. He took the boarhound by the collar. "Come, Sir," he said, "we will visit this friend of yours."

Bab, too absorbed in his own concerns to greatly care about much else, followed the Prince across the vestibule and through the small door from which he had seen Don Ramon issue the first day that he had met him. He found himself in a large and splendid hall, with a cupola and walls painted from floor to ceiling with richly painted and glowingly coloured figures; processions, portraits, gorgeous costumes, flowing robes, fair faces, and eager children were blended into one fantasy of allegory and decoration by the lavish art of the painter. A large window faced the door and showed a prospect of garden. There was little furniture save a few chairs with covers on, but before the window was the clavichord, a large and noble instrument, enriched with gildings and carvings, at which sat Don Ramon playing. The unfriendly white of the winter day was full on his powerful, finely moulded face; heavy locks of tawny hair hung on his low forehead, and his blue eyes were fixed sternly before him.

The click of the latch and the light step warned him of some one's approach. He looked up, and seeing William holding the white dog inside the door and Bab just behind him, he rose and stood by the clavichord.

William crossed the bare polished floor. "You are a tuner of musical instruments?" he asked in Spanish.

Don Ramon answered in the same tongue. "Yes, Your Highness. I am mending this clavichord, which is very fine, though neglected."

"You do not," said William, regarding him steadily, "speak Spanish as if it were your native tongue."

"It scarcely is, Sir," replied Don Ramon calmly. "I have never been to Spain, having lived all my life in Brussels."

Bab looked in vain for the emotion he had seen in both yesterday; each was now composed, serene and unmoved. Save that they looked at each other very keenly, and Don Ramon bore himself with more haughtiness than was consistent with his position, there was nothing remarkable in the manner of either.

"Who," asked the Prince, "procured your services for this clavichord?"

"Mynheer van Both," answered Don Ramon instantly, "one of the secretaries of Your Highness, whom you left at the *Huis ten Bosch* during the campaign."

"It is very well, Mynheer," said the Prince, speaking now in Dutch. "Is it nearly mended?" He touched the instrument with his fine fingers.

"Very nearly, Highness," replied Don Ramon. "But the tones still jar. I have had to replace the strings, which is a delicate matter."

"You speak better Dutch than I have ever heard a foreigner use," remarked the Prince. "My compliments, Mynheer." He smiled, and an instant's gleam flashed from the Spaniard's blue eyes as he bowed, and the Prince turned away with the great elegant dog at his heels. Bab followed, with a half-smile at Don Ramon. He had not understood the conversation, which had been held in two languages unfamiliar to him, nor was he greatly interested now in anything save his own affairs. Still it flashed into his thoughts that he should warn the Prince of what Fear-the-Foe had said of Don Ramon, yet his instinctive good-heartedness forbade him.

William took leave of him in a grave kindly fashion, gave him his hand and smiled, but the King's messenger was weary of soul as he left the *Huis ten Bosch* with his mission ended in such miserable failure.

———————

CHAPTER XII. A JEW OF AMSTERDAM

The Prince returned to the room where he had interviewed Bab, sat down at the table near the window and wrote in pencil in his pocket-book, "Mynheer van Both, one of my secretaries, is to go in the train of Mynheer Dyckfelt on his forthcoming embassy to Brandenburg. Mynheer Dyckfelt to be warned that this man is not to be trusted."

When he had put up his pocket-book he leant forward languidly and propped his head in his hand. The headaches that he had always known had become more cruel since his late illness, his cough had settled into a perpetual asthma, his already delicate health was shattered to such an extent that his enemies hoped and his friends feared he could scarcely endure the fatigues of another campaign. He thought of that now as he sat glooming across the room. On the tulip-wood table near the fire was a heap of letters and papers he had cast there that morning—accounts from the army contractors, bills for guns, fusees, shoes, forage, letters from the Paymaster of the Forces, from moneylenders, from his cousin Waldeck, from his agents in England, Germany, and Austria.

Frederick (William) the Great (1620-1688), Elector of Brandenburg.
Engraving by Jeremias Falck.

He looked at this pile of correspondence with distaste and was
making an effort over himself to rise and attend to them when his

subdued usher entered. "Your Highness, there is a man craving very strongly to see you."

"Who is he?" asked the Prince indifferently.

"He gave no name. He bade me tell Your Highness he was a Jew of Amsterdam."

William reflected a moment, then said: "I will see him."

As the usher left, the Prince crossed over to the fire. He loathed the cold; even in summer he could not get warm enough. He shivered now, for all his fur-lined coat. The white boarhound, who had been asleep by his chair, rose and followed him to the hearth. The door was opened and an old man, wearing a brown coat with a little collar of marten fur, and holding a cap of the same, entered. He stooped slightly; his beard and hair were silver-gray, his face thin, his eyes concealed behind horn spectacles.

"Good day, Mynheer," said the Prince with some curiosity.

The other clasped his worn cap on his breast and bowed very low. "Has Your Highness," he asked in a soft voice, "leisure to hear me for a little space?"

"If you will enlighten me as to your name and business, Mynheer."

"I am known as Balthasar Bree," replied the Jew humbly. "A merchant and a director of the Bank of Amsterdam."

William had heard of him and of his wealth. "Are you come to complain of the taxes?" he asked. "I have had many here on that errand."

"It is not mine, my noble lord."

"Will you be seated, Mynheer Bree?"

As he spoke the Prince took the chair by the fire. The Jew bowed again. "It is more fitting that I should stand. Will Your Highness deign to answer a question your humble servant shall put?"

"Why, I will give you some manner of reply," returned the Prince.

The old merchant gave him a steady, earnest glance. "Does Your Highness intend to continue the war?"

William, inured to opposition on this subject, replied briefly. "Yes, Mynheer."

"Your Highness will not make peace with France or England?"

"No."

"There is much opposition to this resolution of Your Highness?"

"A great deal, Mynheer Bree."

"Your Highness meets with very hard usage from your people."

"They do not understand," replied the Prince quietly.

"Your Highness will take the field this spring?"

"If God be willing."

Mynheer Bree answered in the same low, even, respectful tone. "Yesterday I spoke to a Jew of Tangiers, who told me that Your Highness had come to him for money."

"It is very true," said the Stadtholder rather grimly.

"And this man made difficulties?"

"I have so far mortgaged and hampered my fortunes that I cannot raise the sums needful on my personal security any longer," said the Prince frankly. "These men would have me pawn my word for a higher rate of interest than I am like to be able to repay, and I must sooner go without the money than undertake what I cannot perform.

"What is the sum necessary, Your Highness?" asked the Jew softly.

"For the next campaign and the debts left from this—ten million guilders."

Mynheer Bree raised his dimmed eyes to the strong face of the young man. "I will advance Your Highness fifteen million guilders."

The Stadtholder swiftly flushed. "What security will you take for such a sum?" he asked.

"The word of Your Highness."

"And what interest, Mynheer?"

"None. If Your Highness overcomes in this struggle you have undertaken I know that you will repay me—if Your Highness fails, the loss of the money will be the least of my misfortunes."

William rose. "Why are you doing this, Mynheer?"

The old Jew answered simply: "From the great respect and admiration I bear Your Highness—from love to the most tolerant country in Europe, which has so long sheltered me and mine."

The colour still lingered in the Prince's face. He fixed his brilliant eyes on the old man's placid countenance and spoke with emotion.

"Mynheer, I cannot accept this offer—cannot so far put myself in your debt..."

"It is I," said Mynheer Bree, "who am far in the debt of Your Highness. You saved my life, my fortune, as you have saved that of every man and woman in the United Provinces. You have made this land a shelter for the oppressed, the miserable, the persecuted of all nations. You have ruled tolerantly and with wisdom over men of all creeds. You have respected conscience and fought for liberty. You go now, putting aside discouragements and temptations, to expose yourself for your people against great odds. All I have is yours. What use is it lying in the Bank at Amsterdam when it might be feeding your soldiers, building your forts, helping, even by a little, in the high endeavour of Your Highness?"

"Mynheer," answered the Prince, "you do encourage me. Amid much opposition which attends all I do I am glad to know of one who believes in me, even though he overpraises. For yourself, you have spoken very nobly, but reflect that if I cannot get supplies from the States I am never likely to be able to repay this great sum."

"What would become of my money if King Louis conquered?" answered Mynheer Bree. "Would I not rather have it in the hands of Your Highness than in the hands of the French?"

"You are a patriotic man," said the Prince warmly. "Your sentiments do you honour. I would there were more of your mind."

"There are very many of my mind, my noble lord; thousands who pray earnestly for the safety and success of Your Highness, who, alone in Europe, does stand for toleration and liberty. My faith is not the faith of Your Highness, but I would help you to the last guilder, because you are just to all faiths." A faint colour touched the old man's cheeks. "Your Highness does accept my offer?"

The young Prince held out his hand, "With gratitude from my heart."

The Jew went down on one knee and raised the slender fingers to his lips with such dignity that he honoured himself as much as the man he reverenced.

"Nay," said William raising him, "I have, alas, done nothing to deserve this. I am a very poor thing to be God's captain, but if endeavour will do it, I shall succeed."

"May He," answered Mynheer Bree, "reward your princely heart, your noble courage, your generous wisdom with all happiness of victory."

"If I fail," responded the Stadtholder, "I will, if I have life, nevertheless repay you this money."

"Your word," said the Jew, "is better bond than the elaborate pledges of others; they but seek a chance to escape. Yet think not of the money at all, and take it not as a debt. It is not given to Your Highness but to the cause of liberty, of which you are the guardian, and I, humble as I am, may still be of yet further use to your noble lordship." He paused a moment, then added in his slow, humble fashion: "I do know makers of arms and guns, fusees and carts, who would supply Your Highness on credit, if I told them that I, who am reputed cautious, had lent Your Highness this money, also the contractors for provisions and clothes—this might be of some service to Your Highness."

William gave him a deep glance of gratitude. "No service could be greater. I will not dissemble from you that upon the success of this campaign depends my power to resist a peace—and upon the proper furnishing of the troops largely rests my chances." The Stadtholder spoke with warmth and animation in a manner very different from his usual reserve. In truth, this offer of help, coming when he was most beset with opposition and detraction, had wonderfully heartened him. No intriguing Prince could have been more pleased with some personal gain or victory than this young man was with the easing of the burdens that hampered him in his single-minded endeavour to serve his country and his God.

"Mynheer Bree," he said, "you have put me under a great obligation. That you have served me is a little matter, but it is a great thing that you have been of help to your country."

The old Jew bowed. "Tomorrow I will wait upon Your Highness with the bills and the names of those men who may be able to supply Your Highness at cheap rates." With that he bowed again and took his leave. William accompanied him, pressed his hand graciously, and, with the courtesy of his rank, escorted him across the vestibule to the outer door.

"God be with you, Mynheer."

"God be with Your Highness."

The slight figure of the old Jew disappeared down the steps into the still twilight of the wood; the clouds were parted about the horizon over long glimmers of yellow sky against which the trunks and branches of the trees rose black and mysterious. The Prince closed the door and noticed with something of surprise that it was quite dark in the house and the candles already lit in the hall. He crossed to the door of the Orange Hall, turned the handle gently and looked in. The young wrestler had gone, the dark shape of the clavichord showed before the light space of the window. William paused in the vestibule. He heard Bentinck and another nobleman laughing in the room right of the door. He had no desire for their company. The passionate wish for action that would scarcely allow him rest, irked at the confinement of the house. He picked up his hat and gloves from the chair where he had flung them and quietly left the palace.

The air was shudderingly cold; a few stars, points of crystal half obscured in trailing vapour, showed here and there through the trees. Behind William rose the dark outline of the palace and the yellow lights in the window; before him the encroaching shadows lurked in the long avenue, and half hid the paths and undergrowth. The Prince passed along the wall at the side of the palace that bounded the private garden and so presently came out of his own grounds into the flat open country looking toward Delft, above which the night clouds were gathering, changing slowly in a little wind. He walked steadily along the high road until he came to a bridge over a wide canal, and there he paused, for it was becoming very dark. As he stood there, believing himself alone, and utterly absorbed in his hurrying thoughts, he was startled by the sound of voices speaking softly in French.

"You think he knew you?" asked one—a woman's voice, very low.

William looked over the bridge and saw the figures of a man and a woman standing by the side of the canal in earnest converse. Both were wrapped in cloaks and in the deepening twilight it was impossible to see more than their uncertain outline.

"No," replied the man after a little "he did not know me or I had not been here now, Teresa. How should he know me?" The voice was that of the young wrester. The Stadtholder recognized it instantly.

"God keep us through it all!" cried the woman tremulously.

"Van Both said he was resolved upon the war—well, who knows? A chance bullet, a stumbling horse, the fever...I will wait."

"Thank God for that!" cried his companion.

"So much concession to your fears," answered the man almost fiercely, "but if he survive this campaign nothing can stay my hand.

"Hush, hush," she entreated. They moved slowly along the canal. William could still overhear what they said had he cared to listen, but he turned away and retraced his steps toward the palace. He was scarcely within his own gate before he met Bentinck carrying a lantern.

"Out alone and so late, Highness," Bentinck remonstrated; "and the Hague swarming with French ruffians who would put a knife between your shoulders for a pistole..."

The Prince grasped his arm and laughed excitedly. "I have the money for the campaign," he said. "And who knows—a chance bullet—a stumbling horse—if I should die that way, who would serve the turn of Holland?"

"What do you mean?" demanded Bentinck startled.

"Nothing...Mynheer Bree will lend me fifteen million!"

"He will? And, Highness, the cabinet, the red cabinet bespoke for the King of France, has been bought by this same Jew and sent but now to you—it is in the dining hall."

They turned sharply, and saw the lit windows of the *Huis ten Bosch* to their right.

"There are some that love me," said the Prince. "This old man it seems."

"What of me, Highness?" asked Bentinck reproachfully. He held the lantern low to light their steps, so could not see the Stadtholder's face. He heard him laugh again in the breathless, excited fashion.

"I have refused the offers of King Charles," said William, "and have staked it all on this campaign. God defend us!" He spoke solemnly and Bentinck thought that something like a sob followed his unsteady laugh as he repeated: "God defend us!"

PART II. THE PRINCESS

"...la tout puissance de l'homme dont le caractère est avant tout une volonté invincible."
(The power of a man of character is above all an invincible will) —
Saint Beuve.

Mary Stewart II (1662-1695).
Engraving by John Smith, after Van der Voort.

CHAPTER I. DEFEAT: AN EPISODE OF THE WAR

A stormy evening was closing over the plains of Brabant. About the horizon thunder-clouds gathered; an occasional flash of lightning disturbed the sultry air. On the ramparts of the little fortified town of Gembloux two officers were standing gazing over the darkening prospect. They were both Spanish. Now and then they spoke to each other in a whisper. One had a spy-glass in his hand which the fading light rendered useless. Behind them the sentinels tramped steadily to and fro. At rare intervals patches of the wide landscape before them were illuminated with a sullen glare of red, and the sombre stillness was broken by a dull boom. Watching with straining senses for this the two men became so motionless they might have been figures carved out of the ramparts. They knew that these glares of red were the fires of the French harassing the retreat of the Dutch and Spanish forces from Charleroi, and that under cover of the August evening the remnants of the allied army was falling back on Brussels.

A campaign that had begun in defeat was ending in defeat. Louis had swept his boundary-line from Cambrai to Valenciennes; his flaunting successes had never before reached the height of this campaign of 1677. At Cassel, before St. Omer, he had gained bloody victories. Cambrai and Valenciennes had fallen. The Spanish Netherlands, the bulwark of the United Provinces, lay under the shadow of France.

A clock in the belfry of Gembloux struck eight. The officers moved and walked slowly along the ramparts. It was so hot that they both loosened their cloaks and flung them over their arms. A soldier came up silently and lit the lanterns hanging at intervals on the battlements. Once or twice a horse's hoofs clattered from the dark town below; then some one began to sing and stopped abruptly. Little sparks of light leapt up in the windows of the houses; very few closed the shutters because of the heat.

The two officers went into the guard-house over the town gate. It was a stone chamber with two open windows, one looking on the town and the other on the country. Above the fireplace hung a painted figure of the Madonna. Two tallow candles burnt on the rough table, and guttered furiously in the cross-currents of air. A man lay along a bench asleep; another sat by him smoking. On the floor stood an earthenware pitcher of water; the lip was broken and the water had spilt over the floor. On the table were a handsome blue Flemish tankard and a pack of playing cards. A great quantity of flies circled languidly round the room and buzzed in and out of the thunderous night.

The new-corners nodded at the others. Weary apathy seemed to have taken the place of strained energy. They continually yawned; none of them had been to bed for two or even three nights.

"No message?" asked the man with the pipe.

"None," came from the younger of the two officers who had been on the ramparts.

"Do you think he will come to Gembloux?" questioned his companion.

They all looked at each other and shook their heads. "He will fall back on Namur," said the first speaker.

"You said that five days ago."

"Well, I meant it."

The young man went to the window overlooking the open country. He was very fair, and slight, and comely. "How they fight, those

French devils," he cried with sudden animation. "Luxembourg has swept the Netherlands without a check. I would like to serve a man who can do that. It is intolerable here."

He turned impatiently back into the room. The smoker remarked languidly: "I have writ for leave of absence."

None took any notice of this remark. A flash of lightning plunged like a sword into the midst of the darkness.

"Waldeck's division must come up soon."

"That is Waldeck out there." His companion made a large gesture toward the hidden distance.

The other denied it warmly. "Then where is the Prince William?" he demanded.

"At Charleroi."

"He will never take it."

"He cannot do anything against Luxembourg," put in the smoker.

"He is no great general," said the youngest with the swift judgment of youth.

The two older officers laughed. "It is not his fault," one said. "What can he do against France?"

"I am sorry for him," cried the second one. There was a pause; then the sleeper groaned and woke. The lightning again and a clap of thunder shook the silence.

"This means a peace," remarked the smoker irrelevantly.

"What about peace?" exclaimed the man who had just awakened, "is there any water?"

He got to his feet. He was shivering and burning with fever; his eyes had the glazed look of delirium. There was a great deal of silver bullion on his dress, tarnished to a dingy colour. He took a glass from the table and staggered to the pitcher; as he tipped it clumsily, the water ran over the dirty floor.

"I have had such dreams," he said thickly. "I thought that I found a stiff corpse in my bed at home...quite stiff with the arms up praying...I had to break the elbows to get them down...Why do we die praying?"

He gulped the water greedily and lurched to the window. "These carrion flies!" cried the youth, keeping them off with his glove.

"There will be a peace by November," said the smoker sagely.

The sick man leant his head against the mullions. "Why do we not fight?" he asked vaguely. "The Danish want help...How can they keep that position?...Those new guns have burst, we have only two left..."

"Come, Diaz," said the young officer kindly, "your wits are scattered and you..."

A stab of lighting cleft the obscurity, the thunder broke his speech; as it died away they heard another sound that brought them all alert to the window. A vague sound of movement beyond the earthworks of Gembloux. With straining eyes and curses for the dark, they peered across the blackness. The rain was falling in heavy warm drops that splashed on the rough sill. The young officer and his companion ran out onto the ramparts again. They picked out a little group with swinging lanterns coming toward them. The rain increased into a powerful downpour. The lightning showed the line of the ramparts, the irregular shape of the town, the faces of the men with lanterns. One of them was the commander of Gembloux. The two officers from the guard-room saluted. All stopped, bending before the heavy rush of the rain. The commander had heard from the outposts that some Dutch regiments were approaching, unheralded. He wished his men to receive them.

"They have been defeated?" asked the young man on a gasp.

"Yes—a three day's fight before Charleroi. This is the end of the war."

The words passed quickly. The summons of a trumpet rang out between the thunder. Drenched with warm rain the soldiers descended the steps in the wall and reached the streets of Gembloux. There they dispersed, shadows in the storm. A clatter of arms and horses' hoofs told of men assembled. The sick officer came and stood foolishly by the gate, hatless and swordless. The commander appeared again, on horseback now. Flambeaux and lanterns scattered the darkness; the rain hissed in the torch flames, some sank out. The gates cumbrously swung open, there was a riding to and fro, a shouting of commands in the sharp Spanish, little glints and trails of colour, of uniforms and trappings in the shifting, changing cross-lights and a cavalcade came at a trot from the outer night.

A great crash of thunder interrupted their reception. The Spaniard called out "Who is in command?" unheard.

The new-comers drew rein. The officer dashed forward. "Who is in command?"

A slim rider in a red cloak answered. "His Highness Prince William of Orange, Captain General of the United Provinces, Commander-in-Chief of the Spanish Forces." The great yellow lamp over the gateway fell on the owner of these titles, who held his horse in a pace before the rest, and showed him to be a haggard young man in dark armour.

"The Prince!" The Spaniard uncovered.

The young Captain General touched his hat. "You are the Marquis las Torquas in command here?" he asked.

"Yes, Highness."

"You did not receive my message today?"

"No, Highness."

"He was killed or taken then," said the Prince. "How is your garrison?"

"Well, Your Highness, but we have had the fever among us."

"Thank you, my lord. I wish to see the burgomaster—will you accompany me?"

The horses were touched and the cavalry swept through dark streets. Windows were flung open, people came to their doors despite the rain; many had snatched up arms, as quick fears told them this was the dreaded French at last. The burgomaster was at supper. It was his daughter's name-day, and the fine dining-room was full of guests. He left them silently, and came out to the Prince and officers in the ante-room with his napkin in his hand. Dripping rain from cloaks and trappings stained the polished floor. The Prince alone had flung off his mantle in the hall. He stood bare-headed. A gold chain and a jewel hung over his black cuirass, which was rusty in places. His boots and spurs were wet with mud, his white cravat soiled. The arm that had been shot through at Seneff hung rather stiff at his side, with the other hand he held his gauntlets against his breast.

As the Fleming entered, the Prince spoke at once. "Mynheer the burgomaster, the French will be here by tomorrow. Can the town hold out?"

The thunder was rolling into the distance, monotonous was the swish of the rain against the diamond casements.

"I can leave you five hundred Spanish—no more. What will your townsmen do?" demanded the Prince curtly.

"Defend themselves, my lord," answered the burgomaster.

"You are well provisioned?"

"Yes, Your Highness."

"Marquis, you can trust your men?"

"I do think so, my lord," replied the Spaniard eagerly.

The dark eyes of the Prince flashed again to the Fleming. "I am falling back on Brussels. If you can hold out it makes the capital easier to save. Send your families to Liége."

"Can I do anything for the army of Your Highness?" asked the startled yet resolute burgomaster.

"I thank you. Supplies are to meet us at Landen. If you have to capitulate, Marquis, destroy the ammunition, the French are hard put to it for guns." He spoke in a tone of decisive authority and resolute composure. The fact that he had been defeated for the sixth time since the opening of the campaign from which he had hoped so much, that he had left his men reddening the plains of Brabant, that he had that day heard the joy-bells in Charleroi as the French entered, that he carried with him a letter from Gaspard Fagel, saying the States were resolute to end the war, made no difference to his unmoved fortitude. His behaviour ever roused his men to a rapture of enthusiasm, and these about him now felt a great admiration inspire them, though none of them knew the bitterness of the mental agony his courage concealed.

"Will Your Highness rest here a little?" inquired the burgomaster.

"No, I thank you, Mynheer. I have to meet the army at Landen." He held out his hand and the Fleming kissed it with trembling lips. "You must hold council for the best means for your defence. The place seems to me well fortified."

So he went out on to the wide head of the stairs, his grasp on his sword, and so down the flambeaux-lit stairs, while the hushed girls and young men crept out of the dining room in festal silks, and peered over the stairs at him as he caught up his wet mantle and the hat with the white feather, and passed into the narrow streets where the rain fell heavily from the eaves and ran thickly down the gutter.

The burgomaster stepped on to the carved balcony to see him ride away with his guards about him. While the clatter of their going rang out yet upon the cobbles, the Fleming spoke to the awed guests gathered beside him. "Think that he has neither father, mother, nor wife, that Prince! An Emperor would be glad to call him son. He is one among a world of men. He said not one word of discouragement—not one word."

The Spanish marquis rode back from the farther town gates with a hurry of emotions at his heart, while through the town filed the Dutch soldiers, silent, grave, weary, with matchlocks set and drums beating through the violent rain. Fugitive lights appeared at windows, doors, at corners of streets; the people were astir in the houses; bells clanged perpetually from a convent in the heart of the town. In the guard-room on the ramparts the officers assembled again. Two of them, with unconquerable southern laziness, commenced playing cards. They had received no orders and felt no concern; only the very young man and the sick man were restless.

"Did you see him?" demanded the first impatiently.

"Who?"

"The Prince!"

One of the players raised his eyes. "Yes, a frail, worn young man on a great horse, haggard with fatigue."

The youth answered quickly. "He has a heart of fire! Did you note his eyes—undaunted eyes, even now! I would rather serve him than Luxembourg after all!"

The older man looked at his cards. "He is certainly most to be feared when he is defeated," he remarked. "They are stubborn stuff—these heretics."

"Sancta Maria!" cried the fair young officer in a rapture of excitement, "could we hold out—here in Gembloux? If the day would break!"

"It is not midnight yet," yawned the other player. "Why do we not go to sleep. Look at Diaz there, pacing about like a prisoner waiting torture."

The fever-stricken man caught his name and stopped by the window where the broken lances of the rain fell out of the darkness into the pale, glimmering candlelight. "Get ready," he said hoarsely. "Did they not say Luxembourg? We could beat the French once— not now I think."

He clutched vaguely at his sword, shaking the tarnished silver on his dress, and sank foolishly on the bench. His staring eyes and glazed lips, his dishevelled hair and burning cheeks made him a wild and pitiful object. The two at the table were indifferent to him, but the young man crossed over to his side. "You will be off duty soon, Diaz."

The other sat forward. "I wish," he said in an ordinary voice, "you would stop those people crying—they have been crying all night, and I cannot sleep at all."

The youth looked at him in silence, and muttered a little prayer to the Virgin, then turned away to the window and gazed out on the stormy blackness while the rain smote his eager face and the bravery on his laced coat. His thoughts were with the defeated general riding away on the dark horse in the dark armour, with the jewel glittering in the centre of a rusty cuirass, and the brilliant eyes in a weary face; he was dominated by the thought of the lonely courage that held its way untroubled by disaster. These are the men who make nations, he thought, and wished that he too had been born a Prince.

"Lost!" cried one of the players and flung down his two last cards with a hand shaking from fatigue. The other rose and dipped up some water in his glass from the pitcher; the soft bubbling sound and the splash of the overflow on the stone was grateful in the sultry stillness.

The sick man began to laugh, rolling his head against the wall. "And this is the war!" he cried.

CHAPTER II. THE LOVERS

On a peaceful afternoon of the month that saw William of Orange beaten back across Brabant a young man and woman landed from a barge in the quiet town of Leyden, and walked slowly along the shady, silent streets. Warm breaths of languorous perfume stirred from the lime-trees with every touch of the delicate breeze; the shadows of the thick leaves lay over the straight fronts of the houses; in the patches of the sun the red bricks and white mortaring showed brightly. The University was closed for the summer, the town half empty, and now, at the most solitary hour of day, seemed utterly deserted. Many of the windows were shuttered, many had the white blinds drawn behind the shining glass. The sense of lazy stillness, of soft peacefulness was like a drug to fevered thoughts and excited imaginings. The man and woman walked beside the canal, under the trees, and did not look at each other. They came soon on to the Rapenburg with its shops for the students, shops for books, for swords, for printing, for ribbons and brocades. Most of these were now closed. The sunshine and the shadow of lime and wych-elm trembled over their neat doors and shutters, and over the signs hanging above the porches. Where the little bridges crossed the canal they were mirrored below in a dark semicircle that broke the long clear reflection of the trees that was only divided by a clear line of blue down the centre. Birds were twittering unseen; their clear notes emphasized the sunny sleepiness of the ancient town. Soon their seemingly aimless progress brought them out by the University, full in the sunlight, with the trees like a bodyguard, before, behind, and either side.

They paused on the farther side of the canal and he remarked, in a low voice: "It is strange to me that I ever worked and laughed and was thoughtless within those very walls!"

She looked up at him in a kind of terror. "Why did we come here?" she asked. "Why did you bring me, Cornelius?"

"Why?" He smiled wearily. "It does not sadden me, Teresa. It is gone, wiped away like mist off a glass, those days...I wished you to see Leyden, with me. Let us go to the Kerk of St. Pieter; it is a place that I used to love exceedingly."

She made no answer, only gave a wistful look at the solemn building of the University. As she had just heard it was a place where he had been happy, she would have liked to gaze at it awhile and kiss its stones, but she came obediently. They turned down the narrow Kloksteeg, where the high houses excluded the sun, and came out into St. Pieter's Kerk Plaats with the splendid church rising up above the trees into the upper stillness of the light. Quiet stately houses surrounded the close of the church, which was planted with great elms and limes, and one chestnut with giant leaves drooping downwards, and under the deep fresh shade of this tree a bench was placed. Don Ramon led the way to it and they seated themselves silently.

The thick leafage and clustering shade concealed them from the surrounding houses; but they could see the church, with the sun on its towers, through the open spaces of the foliage. Dona Teresa sat motionless, her hands folded in her lap. Her dark loveliness was obscured in a deep blue hood and mantle which fell away over white muslin embroidered by her own needle in garlands of coloured flowers; transparent shade rested over her entire figure save on her foot and the border of her gown, where the quivering shape of a chestnut leaf wavered on a gold patch of sun.

Don Ramon began speaking in his usual pleasant voice. He called her attention to the sound, harsh yet melodious, of the birds in the higher branches, and to the great brightness of those flecks of blue to be seen here and there among the boughs and leaves. She did not reply and indeed scarcely heard; her ears were straining and her heart beating for him broaching of the subject he had brought her here to discuss. It had been his wish to speak to her away from the Hague—that was a town of horror to him—and she had curbed her anguished impatience until it was his pleasure to open his lips on the matter that so burnt upon her heart.

With tender and saddened eyes she glanced up at him as he sat, profile toward her, leaning a little forward and watching a slim bird hop across the sun-flecked gravel. He wore a brown coat something the hue of his long bright ringlets, and a cravat of point lace from Venice falling to a green sash; his dark-complexioned face, his vivid eyes, the serene level brows and firmly curved mouth wore an expression of half-scornful self-control. He had taken off his hat and the occasional breeze stirred the stiff waves of rich-coloured hair on his low brow.

"Well?" he said at length, not looking round.

"I am patient," she answered.

"You know all," he said with an air of reluctance.

"Not all."

"Your father has told you."

"No."

"You have not asked him?"

"You would hear it from me, Teresa?"

"Did you not," she replied, "promise to tell me here today?"

He looked at her now with earnest, affectionate eyes. "That is true," he admitted. Their converse was very low, scarce breaking above a whisper, hardly more than a murmur in the stillness.

"My Dearest," said the lady quietly, "tell me what you have resolved upon."

They gazed each into the other's grave face as he answered, "The Prince returns to the Hague in, perhaps, a month's space."

"When the campaign is ended?"

"The campaign is ended now—with his failure to take Charleroi. He will come to the Hague, Teresa, unhurt by wound or fever."

She quivered and murmured, "Yes?"

"We have our plans."

"So I believed."

"All this spring and summer, Teresa, they have been formed."

"I know."

"I am glad," said Don Ramon sombrely, "that he was not slain in battle."

Dona Teresa shuddered. "I wish that God had ordered it that way," she returned.

"No," he said strongly, "for this way he dies as *they* died, violently."

"Oh, hush." She laid her hand on his cuff. "Speak lower—who knows what spies may encompass us?"

"Our voices do not travel beyond the chestnut shade," he answered her softly. "The details I will not break upon you now—enough that I am to do it."

"How?" she asked faintly.

"Not in the cabinet—no murders with the knife. He goes often to the sea with but one page or so, and rides up and down the sands—that will be the time."

"And afterwards?" she faltered. "Your safety?"

"There is to be a boat there—French—but my safety..."

She checked him "I know what you are going to say. Spare me."

He bowed his head. "Nothing can much matter—afterwards," he replied gently.

"Not even me?" she asked in a strained voice; then before he could answer, "forgive me—that is weak and foolish—I meant it not. I am prepared and quiet, see, Cornelius—tell me more, indeed I will talk no more folly."

He pressed the fair hand that lay in the fold of her blue mantle. "You remember Baptist Mompesson? I saw him yesterday. The Prince gave him an ensign in his guard and he was at the war—back at the Hague now and at the palace. He will be useful. He suspects nothing. Van Both being gone we have no spy at the Prince's court." He moved his square-toed shoe in the gravel and then said awkwardly: "I want you to return to France first, Teresa."

She turned on him vehemently. "Oh no!"

"My Dearest, it would so hearten me to think of you in safety."

Dona Teresa flushed and trembled. "You know me too well to press this, indeed you must say no more of it. An obscure little plotter like myself is well used to look after herself. When you are safe from the Hague, I follow, not before."

He sighed and was silent; he sat droopingly, the bright locks flowing over his breast.

"Cornelius," she said again in accents touched with anguish, "will you not allow me, in some way, to be of help to you?"

He did not reply to that; in an absorbed voice he said, "I went to see my mother last Friday and told her. She was quite calm; she neither urged nor restrained. She goes about her household duties and thinks of *him*. She blesses me and said *his* murderer might know a sharper punishment than sudden death. Her brain is broken."

"Yet you told her," whispered Teresa.

"She would not speak under torture," he returned proudly. "She prays God to let her die, but sometimes He is hard."

"Yet," said the lady, "her fate is happier than mine, for she loved him twenty years before she lost him."

Don Ramon turned sharply with an expression of agony on his face. "Do not," he said unsteadily, "remind me that I have brought you nothing but regrets."

Her eyes gleamed through a thick veil of tears. "Ah, no—I would not give those regrets for a lifetime of happiness."

He was silent again, looking long and sadly into her eager face.

"Does not this," she asked at last timidly, "this resolve—bring any satisfaction to you, any peace?"

He unlocked his lips on broken passionate speech. "It is the other men—they who do it for money or ambition—*he* is the Prince—a hero called, though I must not think that—and they so small!—intriguers merely—just for a place or a pension..."

"My father is one," she said, "and I no better till I met you." Her lips were pallid and the dark eyes wet.

"Your father is your father," he answered. "I speak of these others—King Louis' men."

"We are no better," she persisted. "And do you not take their means?"

"I know." His low voice was thunderous. "I have become enmeshed in petty things—I thought over it, brooded too long—it should have been at once—alone, *my* vengeance, *my* hand, *my* life to pay!—not this, the instrument of others, with ignoble planning for safety—afterwards." He bowed his head and she sat looking at him, dismayed and shivering.

"If you could forget!" she murmured.

"No," he said in calmer accents, "I cannot forget—and this distaste, this weakness, is but a temptation to draw me from my path. It shall be this year...I would it could be this fatal month, the very day they died..."

"Cornelius," said the lady in a voice that strove against her passion, "I have never sought to persuade you or argue this matter—I have been very quiet though it has been such despair...I will not speak of that...I have been amid desperate affairs all my life—but this..." She paused to control herself.

"Teresa," he whispered gently, looking at her with his blue eyes half veiled by the tawny lashes.

"You know," she said with great sweetness, "that you ask a tremendous thing of my love."

He was mute.

"I am aware," she continued, "that you will soon be lost to me."

He made a protesting gesture of his hand to hers.

"No," she went on, "I am certain that you will be too proud to live—your French boat is but to deceive me—you will give your life for what you do."

So clearly had she read his intention that he could not bring denial to his tongue; he was strangely glad too that she should not believe him capable of ignoble flight of the common ruffian.

"You see," she cried in torn accents, "I know you, and I make for you the greatest sacrifice in the world—a more tremendous sacrifice than you can realize, Cornelius—for you do not think much of me—now."

"My Dearest..." he said impetuously.

She interrupted. "Why should you think of me, close to such a thing? I do know that I am too mean a creature to ask consideration from you. Hush—let me speak. I am so grateful, Dear, that you should have looked on me—at all. I know that before you met me you had a resolve and purpose in your heart that left little space for other thoughts...I am content to have it so, I will be very patient, I will not trouble you—only in one thing indulge me—let me be of use to you now."

"You are everything to me—there is no one else to whom I can talk as I talk to you."

"More than that," she replied passionately, "give me more than that, tell me everything, confide in me—I shall not tremble nor weep. Think, I shall have all my life lonely and useless, and if you do not give me something to remember, to be proud of, how shall I bear it?"

"You do shame me," he said. "I am utterly yours. There is only one thing I put before you, and that is this inward oath and passion which drives me to remember, and to avenge, the dead." They both sat mute and the brown bird hopped almost to their feet; the shadows of the chestnut leaves were lengthening, and the sun on the walls of the St. Pieter's Kerk brightened to a ripe crimson gold.

Don Ramon spoke again. "I will confide to you my most vague, most dreaded thoughts. Oh, Teresa!"—he broke out into subdued but tense emotion—"sometimes it seems so idle and so vain, so long ago and dead and I a silly drifting fellow. What would *he* have thought of this? I am fallen away from ancient honours and become as mean as my broken fortunes—and this man, my enemy, does great actions and is blessed by the people—yet that is all weakness and I do not really falter. I will strike at the Prince and so at the country, and *both* shall pay."

Dona Teresa shook off her hood from the black hair that the straying sunlight glinted into dusky gold; her face was so colourless, the fine brows seemed dark as ebony, nor was it all the sickly hue cast by the trees that gave her this fainting look of pallor, but the deep anguish she was not weak enough to utter. "You must do what is in your soul to do," she said, "as God directs."

"God!" He caught up the word with a half-scornful emphasis. "Do we not cheat ourselves with God? *They* served Him, and to what end? The Prince serves Him and shall it save him from human passion and vengeance? I tell you, Teresa, there are good men and wise men who believe in God, either of Romanist or Calvinist thinking, for that, were He there, He would have it all so different."

"I am not learned," she said, "and this seems to me blasphemy."

"If you have faith you are very rich, and I a wanton fool to disturb it," he answered. "My mother has faith—even after all."

With the setting of the sun an even greater peace had come over the ancient town, the great church, the quiet houses, the luxurious trees in the silent cloister. A deep lingering sweetness was in the long shadows, the still sunlight. In the uppermost blue beyond the leaves Teresa could discern two butterflies, white and gilded. She had a great desire to get to her knees and hide her face and weep.

"Come," said Don Ramon, "let us go home." He rose and put her mantle about her in silence and they left the Kloksteeg with hushed feet.

There was no sun in the Rapenburg, darkness lurked in the water and lay on the fronts of the houses. "A new moon," said Don Ramon and pointed it out, faint in the light sky.

"And by the time it wanes?" she breathed.

He smiled, composed again and stately. "The roses will be over," he answered. "What else?"

"Do not deceive me," she said. "Two great men will be avenged and a proud Prince dead."

He still smiled. "I hate him so, I would he was a meaner man in deed and spirit."

CHAPTER III. A MARRIAGE OF CONVENIENCE

The lodgings of Sir William Temple at Nymegen had a pleasant sober garden, well filled with rose trees cut into glossy hedges set with white, pink, and red blossoms. There Sir William, representative of England at the long ineffectual congress King Charles held in this town with the object of making peace between France and the United Provinces, walked in the pleasant October sunshine, his soft handsome face rather perturbed in expression, and there beside him walked the Stadtholder in buff coat and riding-boots and wearing a little black scarf, his face sad and serious, and speaking with that abrupt energy he used when in passionate earnest.

"Are you not yourself tired of this comedy of a congress? Now this dispute, now that, and all to no purpose. We did not take these means to bring England to a peace in '74—and they will not bring France to reason."

"I do think," answered Sir William gravely, "that the congress will achieve its purpose now. The States will have a peace despite all that Your Highness can say or do."

"You have been listening to Gaspard Fagel," returned the Stadtholder.

"I saw him—yes. He said that there must be an immediate, even a separate peace—that Flanders must be abandoned to the French, on whose forbearance Holland must henceforth depend."

"That is desperate counsel," said the Prince briefly. His eyes seemed to laugh with anger.

"Mynheer Fagel appeared desperate—he looked sick and despondent, and added there was not one man in Holland who was not of his mind."

The Prince answered warmly. "I know one and that is myself, and I will hinder it as long as I can."

The Englishman was silent; for his own part he thought that King Louis would get any terms he liked from the States, and that no further effort on the part of the heroic Prince would suffice to prevent a quick peace.

"It is useless," said William again, "to persuade me to a separate treaty with France or one that leaves our frontiers in her hands. I will not abandon my allies by whose aid I have preserved the independence of my country, and I will never sign a peace that leaves King Louis stronger than before. You, as my friend, must know I am sincere in what I say."

"I know," replied Sir William with his eyes on the roses, "the courage and resolution of Your Highness. But I fear that the Dutch are so disheartened with the ill success of the war, the slowness of the allies in coming to terms, the damage to their trade, that they are resolved to clap up a peace on any terms—and that Your Highness must be brought to fall into the same opinion as the States on this matter."

The thin cheek of the Prince flushed. "You think an unfortunate general and a governor whose people are not with him might take another tone from that I hold," he said. "But if I had ever let ill success weigh with me I had given up life itself, long since." He paused and they walked up and down the narrow path in silence. "You know what this has been," continued the Prince after a little, "a year and a half of letters, intrigues, meetings, and no end arrived at...Last year my uncle sent me a messenger with secret offers—I told you of that, you recall?—and asked you of the lady's person and if my friends in England would care for the marriage, though the man, who was a poor, simple fellow, I sent back with a refusal at once."

"Lady Temple took two letters of Your Highness to the King and the Duke—you have not told me the replies."

"The Duke wished all talk of it postponed until after the peace, but I do think that the King and Danby are frightened by the heats in Parliament, and would be willing. Still it ended. I was not eager, nor am I now."

Sir William answered with some warmth. "I dare assure Your Highness this match is my dearest wish. If you would make this peace and seal it with this marriage..."

The Prince interrupted. "I will make no peace by which we lose a yard of ground. King Charles wishes the advantage of the French, and would make us little better than a country conquered, but that shall never be."

"I do not know," answered Sir William with something of dismay, "how ever King Charles and King Louis are to be brought to the terms Your Highness desires, seeing the eagerness of the States for a peace, the strength of the Loevestein faction, and the late successes of the French."

William paused before a bed of carnations and herbs that grew at the turn of the rose hedge. "I must go on and take my fortune," he said quietly.

Sir William looked at him earnestly. "Despite everything?" he asked. The firmness of the Prince seemed to him almost incredible.

"Why, yes," answered William simply. He coughed, then added: "I did this morning see a poor old man tugging alone in a little boat, with his orders, against the eddy of a sluice, upon a canal, when, with the last endeavours, he was just got up to the place intended, the force of the eddy carried him quite back again, but he turned his boat as soon as he could and fell to his oars again, and thus three or four times while I watched him." He raised his brilliant sincere eyes to the Englishman's face. "This old man's business and mine are too like one another. I ought, however, to do just as the old man did, knowing nothing of what effort will succeed, any more than what did succeed in the poor man's case."

"Perseverance will accomplish all things, I do believe," said Sir William, who, however, owned an easier creed, a less stern philosophy himself, "but in the present case it is difficult to see how all these stubborn contentions may be settled."

"King Charles," said William, touching the heads of the carnations absently with his riding-stock, "must induce France to restore Franche-Comté and return to the terms of Aix-la-Chapelle, or those differing but little. Unless he will do this, as I have writ his Majesty, the war must go on and God Almighty must decide it."

"I think the King will not go so far. Cambrai must be ceded to France."

"I would rather," the Prince declared passionately, "charge a thousand men with a hundred than consent to a peace on any such terms."

Sir William answered quickly, "Your Highness is in the right, but the right is a difficult matter to enforce..."

"Do you think," interrupted the Prince, "that if I went to England I could persuade King Charles to my way of thinking?"

"Does Your Highness contemplate that journey?"

"Yes," said the Stadtholder. "Bentinck has been there since June. He writes that the Parliament, the people, Danby, and some way Arlington are eager for the King to declare war on France."

"I do wish with all my soul," said the Englishman, "that his Majesty could be brought to this view and so become a glorious King and make England a great nation once more—and I think that if any man can do it, Your Highness is he."

"I can make the endeavour," answered William. "At least I will bring England to induce France to a more reasonable peace."

They walked leisurely between the rose hedges into a wide path set with all manner of late summer flowers. Sir William reflected a little within himself, then said, very courtly, "And what will Your Highness do with regard to this marriage I have at heart?"

"Why," replied the Prince, "if I like the lady I will have her—but not as the price of any concession—before the peace, not after."

"That will be a difficult matter, Highness, but I do think you are more like to influence the King than he you." Sir William smiled in his lazy, pleasant fashion, and added: "As for the person of the lady and her dispositions, I have had nothing but good reports of her, as my wife will have told you."

"I know," said the Stadtholder gravely, "that it would scarce pass in the world for a Prince to care about these matters, but I have confided to you that it does weigh with me what manner of lady my cousin is—for the ordinary sort of Princess is what I could not bind myself to, and the ordinary life of courts one I could not lead. Were I to have trouble at home it would be more than I could bear, for I am like to have enough abroad for the rest of my days."

"I think she will give no trouble to any man, this Princess. She is supposed of an extreme sweet nature and has lived quietly at

Twickenham all her days with Dr. Compton for her governor, who is an honest if not a learned man."

"Well," said the Prince, "I will take these reports of yours as encouragements, and if she be as you say I must take her and make the best of it, though God knows, if I were not pressed to it, I would not marry at all with my fortunes in this state."

The cold and practical view of the young man, his questioning as to the qualities of his proposed wife, as anxious and no more, as inquiries after the worth and value of Genoa velvet or Milan armour, roused a faint, half-amused protest in the equable mind of Sir William Temple. "Highness," he said smiling, "do not despite good women because there are so many of them—a worthy wife, yea, even one penniless, brings her husband more content than a kingdom."

"You speak in a romantical strain," returned the Prince calmly. "If she looks after his house and minds her own affairs she may save some trouble, but she cannot be valued with great things."

"I speak from what I have known," said Sir William. "My lady has been so vast a blessing to me that no words could express it."

"Your marriage," said the Prince dryly, "was not a marriage of convenience."

Sir William assented warmly. "But Your Highness might find the like comfort nevertheless. A lady of wit and charm may be a companion..."

"A companion!" the Prince smiled. "Do you conceive me, my friend, making a companion of a woman?"

Sir William was silent. He felt that in some things his Highness had yet much to learn, and he wondered if Mary Stewart could teach him. He admired the Prince as he admired no other man, but he was a little sorry for the lady. They turned back into the richly scented rose garden. Sir William spoke of indifferent things, of what the house had cost him and the difficulties of obtaining supplies from Arlington, the humours and passions of the various Ambassadors assembled at Nymegen and the anxious monotony of the life there. "Do you," he then asked, "return to the Hague, Highness?"

"No. I have written to England asking permission to journey there, and till the answer comes I shall be at Dieren hunting."

"God-speed and all manner of good wishes," said the Englishman on something like a sigh. "Trust Danby. I think him honest though engaged against his will secretly to France. Beware of Sunderland, who is a subtle knave."

"But might be a useful one," returned the Prince. They went into the cool spacious house and into the large front room, darkened by the quiet shadows of the yet deep green tree in the courtyard. The Prince went to the window and looked out. With a half-absent gesture he pushed back the dark auburn hair and pressed his hand to his brow. "I am so weary of it all," he said with deep languor. "I would sooner die than undertake this journey."

Sir William put his hand affectionately on the buff sleeve. "There are new and splendid prospects opening out before Your Highness."

"God knows. So hampered, so hedged about, it is hard to act. This campaign was an agony! It was God's will to humble me and I was in the dust! Defeat after defeat—swept from Brabant! I think they must have laughed at me, the French. I was a fool before Luxembourg, before Conde, before Turenne. Ah, to be so inadequate to one's desires!"

Sir William's real love for the Prince was greatly moved by this sudden unveiling of mental anguish, the more so as the Englishman knew what a face William had put upon his misfortunes, how he had taken every fall with no slackening of energy and borne his unprovoked disasters with the unconquerable courage and haughty single-mindedness that had made him a hero in Europe. "The greatest captain and the bravest soldier can afford to talk in this style," he said. "Your Highness has done great things—none greater than the nobility with which you have taken these crosses."

"You ever flatter me," replied William. "It is a pleasant fault in you." He smiled faintly. "I must go on even though I do not see a step ahead, for did I falter now the country is as good as lost." He added some words of leave-taking and the two left the chamber and crossed the wide hall into the courtyard, where the Prince's grey horse and his page waited.

Beyond the far-flung shade of the thick-leaved tree the sun blazed on the white gravel, the open gate, the quiet street beyond.

William mounted and rode slowly out of the shadow, the Englishman, bare-headed in his elegant velvets, at his stirrup. As they reached the gate, the Prince looked keenly down the sunny street. A single horseman on a white steed was leisurely passing. He was a lean dark man wearing a prune-coloured cloak. He gave the Stadtholder and his companion a long look over his shoulder, put spurs to his horse and galloped out of sight.

"Who is he?" asked Sir William half idly. "I have seen him more than once in Nymegen."

The Prince shaded his eyes to gaze after the departing cavalier. "He thought I did not know him," he remarked. "He is some agent of France. He comes here to consult his Ambassador, I do not doubt."

"How does Your Highness know him?"

"He was at the camp—with the Spaniards. I broke him for disobedience."

"There are too many of these saucy villains abroad," said Sir William impatiently.

The Prince gave him his hand; they took warm farewells and parted. The English Ambassador was not a religious man, but he put up a short prayer as he watched the lonely figure with the little page gallop away down the quiet street of Nymegen, a prayer for the honour and safety of England, and the life of the young man who stood for these things.

CHAPTER IV. BAB AND THE CONSPIRATORS

The man in the prune-coloured cloak stood inside the door of Signor Lacruez's upper chamber, bowing to the company. It was late afternoon and the whole air mellow with thick sunshine. Dona Teresa sat by the open window with a white cat on her knee and a book in her hand; the master of the house and Don Ramon were talking together; all three turned and looked at the new-comer with some surprise.

"I sent no herald. You are a little astonished that I have gained the Hague so soon?"

Lacruez answered in his usual gracious manner. "Indeed, Mr. Fairfoul, I was expecting you any day now the army has gone into winter quarters." He offered a chair and the visitor took it, directing a keen glance at Don Ramon, who stood silent, and, it seemed, displeased.

Dona Teresa rose, the cat in her arms. She wore a dress of a gold colour, and coral round her throat, and about her shoulders a filmy shawl of a hazy blue. Mr. Fairfoul looked at her as he unclasped the prune-hued cloak. "Time away from you is time ill spent, mistress...You make me forget set speeches."

She averted a face of frowning pallor. He laughed. "Come, you have known me long enough to forgive that compliment." He turned to the two men. "Do you want to hear my adventures at the camp?" He lifted his head and his smiling eyes were insolent. He was well favoured in a hard black manner, Irish, clever and infamous. Under the coloured mantle his dress showed stone-gray velvet, trimmed with silver ribbon and knots of violet.

Lacruez considered him. "Are your adventures of importance?"

"To myself, yes." The black eyes danced. "I have discovered matters worth your hearing also."

"To speak very frankly," returned the other, "we are in great need of clear information, being tormented by many false reports."

"My first news then—the Prince will not come to the Hague. He lies at Dieren and after that goes to England."

Dona Teresa looked at Don Ramon, who, without turning his head, remarked: "We can wait."

"Oh, yes," said the Irishman, "we can wait—but if the marriage fails and..."

"The marriage?" questioned Teresa.

"...of the Prince and Mary Stewart—if the marriage fails and the King Charles binds him into a peace, I have sure news from France that our business will be unnecessary."

Don Ramon looked round now. "You mean," he said, "that France will not require the life of his Highness if she can accomplish his discomfiture?"

"I do—we are thereby excused from a dangerous service."

"It makes no difference to me," answered Don Ramon disdainfully.

"Ah, I had forgotten," said Mr. Fairfoul smoothly. "You cherish some private vengeance that we are not to know of." He smiled. "But your private vengeance is no matter to France."

Don Ramon answered quietly: "You speak as one in the pay of France. I do not serve that country but my own motives in joining this plot."

"Let that go," said the Irishman lightly. "If the Prince makes a triumph, marries the heiress and hinders the peace, we are to do as we arranged. I wrote you, Don Ramon, the particulars of that plan."

The swift colour passed over Dona Teresa's features. She seated herself again, and the white cat jumped from her slack embrace.

Lacruez spoke. "You made an attempt at the camp, Father Constant said. Why?"

"Because Monsieur de Louvois considered the time good. King Louis was very hopeful of his successes, but the energy of the Prince made them dear bought. Those were very bloody victories, and the Prince out of the way, Flanders would have fallen in two days. I was in the Spanish guard and said I would take my chance. If I had succeeded I should have been a peer of France." He laughed, looking from one to another of his three listeners.

Dona Teresa closed the window. "Speak lower," she said.

His voice sank. "There were opportunities enough, but I had to think of my own safety. He, the Prince, was about everywhere. It was astonishing that his body could support such fatigues. It was reviews by daylight, torchlight, starlight—always at the head of his men, reprimanding, rewarding, listening to this, to that..."

Don Ramon interrupted, "I do not wish to hear of the virtues of the Prince of Orange," he said harshly.

Mr. Fairfoul, sitting easily back in his chair, smiled maliciously. "Not virtues, qualities—a different matter. Well, after the fight outside Ath, I had, I thought, my chance. The troops were all broken, dispirited and worn out. The Prince thought of giving battle on the morrow and rode privately among his men that night to observe the chances of fortifying the ground...I heard of his intention and slipped away from my company and laid myself behind some poplars where he must pass to his tent. "It was a darkish night and very still, and I had my carbine ready and thought the thing done. He came up with two officers; he was riding unarmed. I had reckoned on that, for I knew he had the courage of the devil. One of them held a flambeau and I saw his face, his cravat, and his breast with the blue ribbon."

Dona Teresa shuddered. Mr. Fairfoul marked it with some amusement.

"He was looking straight in my direction, but could not see me for the darkness. I had my carbine levelled when he pulled up his horse and was still—a fair mark. Now I could have done it, but a kind of confusion came over me. He seemed so certainly to be looking at me. Then he spoke to one of the officers and smiled, and chance had it that the other cast the torch forward and I was revealed, not recognized. I cast down the carbine and fled. My officer broke me for leaving my post. Since I was out of the army there was none in it to do the business, so Monsieur de Louvois has to wait."

"You made a clumsy affair of it," said Lacruez with some scorn.

The Irishman's black eyes narrowed. "I have done good business elsewhere—my gifts do not lie in the direction of murders. I think we have Amsterdam so in the French interest that the Prince will not be able to raise another penny there. French money has so been spilt in Spain they will throw over the Prince for a lifted finger. Father Constant has returned to London to take the King the report of how things stand here, and to concert with the Duke of York means to prevent the Prince's marriage."

"We make progress," said Lacruez. "The Loevestein faction grows daily stronger and the Prince daily more unpopular. If he fails in this matter of the marriage and a peace is concluded in spite of him I know not how he will hold his place."

"The Loevestein faction lacks a leader," said Lacruez. "If John de Witt was alive we might see Holland a Republic again."

"As it is—take away the Prince, and she slips into the lap of France and we make our fortunes out of it," smiled Mr. Fairfoul.

Dona Teresa opened the window. "It is so hot," she murmured.

The Irishman was quick to catch her remark. He rose. "My talk wearies you?"

"It was not addressed to me," she answered coldly.

He laughed and shot a glance at the contained face of Don Ramon. "I will relieve you. I always wish to pleasure you, Dona Teresa. I have sordid matters to discuss with your father. Adieu." He took Lacruez by the arm and drew him from the room.

"God Almighty be pitiful!" murmured Teresa as the door closed.

Her lover looked round at her and smiled sombrely. "Am I like that man, Teresa? Yet we are working together for the same object..."

"And your life is at his mercy."

He gave that no thought. "If John de Witt was alive—if my father was alive—then I might be a happy man!" He pressed the palm of his hand to his brow and shuddered.

Desperately she pulled at the ends of the blue scarf and broke into disturbed speech. "This Irishman is a coward too. Why did he not do it then, when he had the chance. He left it to you, because he was afraid!"

"Do not talk of him," said Don Ramon. "Let us go out—I am stifling here...when will *he* return from England? Not later than November when the States assemble...Come out, Teresa, into the air."

She came at once, obediently, bare-headed, her hand timidly on his brown sleeve, her dark eyes meekly and anxiously searching his face. He said no word as they passed through the garden, then suggested they should walk along the country road, lovely with autumn sunlight and autumn colours in the trees. Then he was silent again, breathing deeply and often looking on the ground, nor did she dare to speak though her very heart-beats were hushed with anxiety. As they passed beside the princely woods that encircled the palace they met a young officer of the Stadtholder's guard, walking leisurely.

"Mr. Mompesson," said Teresa quickly and would have drawn Don Ramon aside, being in no mood to meet anyone, but he looked up quickly at her words and hailed the Englishman. The three maintained an even if not intimate acquaintanceship; since the return of Bab from the war they had met once or twice casually. Bab, out of favour with Danby for plain speaking, employment in England closed to him if disgust had permitted him to accept it, had found congenial service with the Prince, and in less than a year had become very fond of Holland.

Don Ramon greeted him eagerly as if he found his easy company welcome distraction. The three paused in the centre of the golden-shaded road. "I hear the Prince comes not to the Hague," remarked Don Ramon.

"He did—yesterday, privately, and left this morning for Dieren. He sat up all night making note of his furniture at the *Huis ten Bosch*. It is exceedingly rich."

"He means to sell it?" asked Dona Teresa.

"Yes, Madame. The Princess Amalia had everything she touched of pure gold, even the keys and the bottles for water, besides ewers, cups, and services of plate, and now it must all go to help pay the debts of the campaign, notably to one Mynheer Bree, whom the Prince would not have lose."

"He goes to England soon?" questioned Don Ramon.

"I do believe it." Bab fingered the end of his scarf thinking of his hopeless mission.

"Think you he has much chance of success?"

"Why, very little, though he has my Lord Treasurer Danby on his side and, as I do think, Sunderland—the people too, but against him the King, the Duke, the Princess—the French!" Bab screwed up his face and laughed, then added gravely, "It would be greatly to the honour of England could he bring them back to the policy of the Triple Alliance."

Don Ramon smiled. "Do you know when he will return?"

Bab shook his head. "But I heard Mynheer van Zuylestein say they could not stay a great while—not more than a month I think. Are you still in the house of Mevrouw Vanderhooven?" he added pleasantly.

"Yes."

"And the old Cameronian?"

"He has gone back to Scotland. He heard the Saints were being persecuted and went to share their fate."

"These fellows do not lack courage," returned Bab. "I hope Fear-the-Foe will not fall into Lauderdale's hands. But I interrupted you sadly—I must take my leave. May I wait on you soon, Madame?"

"Yes, naturally," she assented, and they were taking informal leave when Don Ramon asked with some abruptness: "What do you think of the Prince?—you must have seen something of him."

Bab seemed rather at a loss. "He has the greatest courage of any man I have met," he answered at length; "the sort of Prince one would die for, I suppose." He smiled, lifted his beaver, blithe with blue feathers, and they parted, he going toward the Hague, Don Ramon and the lady slowly in the opposite direction under the embowering shade of the deep-hued honey-yellow, russet-red trees.

"My Dear," said Teresa softly, "you are very ill at ease."

But the brow that he bent on her was serene, the blue eyes calm. "What is to become of you, Teresa?" he said sadly. "What will become of you?"

A faint gleam came into her tender eyes. "I can live—as your mother lives."

Some deep thought held him silent awhile; a few scattered leaves caught in the folds of her gown and fluttered on to the faint blue gauze about her shoulders; the full curls were blown back from her wide brow by the western wind that was rising with the setting of the sun.

"Teresa," he said at last, "you believe in God—and if I should die—do not tremble, there is nothing terrible in death—if I should die I would like my wife to pray for me—but dare my selfishness ask you to become the wife of a man pledged to what I am pledged?"

Her bosom heaved, and a pale flush rose under her eyes. "My lord, you are of too noble a name to marry such as I—I will not hamper you. I can be faithful without oaths."

"One might think," he answered, "that you mock me. The utmost honour my name can obtain is that you should share it."

She was silent. Her love, an impersonal thing, showed her herself insignificant, meanly born, and him stooping from the glory of shattered greatness to this last seal of ruin, a secret and ignoble marriage. She felt that her very adoration wronged him, pulled him down to smaller issues than the great ends that were his heritage. "I have had sufficient advantage of your misfortunes," she said humbly; then with a hidden passion beating behind her words: "I do wish I was of some wealthy, noble house that I might put it all by to go into exile with you!"

The level rays of the sun struck through the straight trunks and made the air dusky with lavish gold. To their right the country lay flat and green to Delft, whose church rose a noble distant shape above the even level. Their steps slackened and paused. They had left the houses behind them; above their heads were mounting clouds ribbed with crimson, obscuring the blue.

Don Ramon looked about him on the land quiet in the wealth of rich sunshine. "My country," he said on a little gasp, "for which my father died." He took off his hat as always at his rare utterance of that name, and stood straight with frowning brows and eyes, bright and deep, as another of his name had stood before cannonade, the rack, the bloody death.

Teresa felt herself swept aside with other useless things. She shivered, feeling beyond his thoughts. Unavailing folly of protest faded on her lips. The sunshine grew chill and the west wind stung as she pictured her devotion standing unheeded outside the gates of his proud agony. She touched the hand that held his hat, and he smiled at her as he might have smiled at a wayside maid who offered him flowers—this, at least, to her passionate fancy. "Cornelius," she said with a trembling, breaking tenderness. She caught at the thought of the nearer tie to make her one with his wrath and sorrow. "Cornelius—let me be your wife."

CHAPTER V. NEWMARKET

The very flower and utmost splendour of a handsome nation setting a high value on beauty and grandeur, bodily strength, and the lavish display of wealth, was gathered at Newmarket for the finish of the October races. Versailles might show great elegance, more pomp of ceremony and laudation of kingship; it could not boast any such gathering of opulent loveliness, careless-handed magnificence open gorgeous idleness and pleasure-seeking, such universally fair faces in men and women, such merry speech of unshackled freedom, such wanton good-nature as made Newmarket dazzle in these festival days of autumn.

Today, the squires, dons, yeomen, and clergymen, who had come to see the court, were departing, for the races were over. The King, more slowly, was leaving the heath with his brother and the great nobles. Some went to the cockpit or the tennis court. Charles, who loved walking better than either of these diversions, came leisurely, lingering in the open. With him, beside his grace of York, was my Lord Treasurer, my Lord Buckingham, my Lord Arlington, my Lord Mulgrave, all handsome men and tall though none of them reaching to the great height of the King and his brother, who in grace, carriage, and splendour dominated the gorgeous group. A little apart from them but obviously of their company walked William of Orange and William Bentinck, different in dress, manner, and bearing.

The King laughed, talked, yawned; the nobles argued over their dogs, their horses, their cocks, their bets. The Duke gloomed in silent displeasure. The Prince, talking quietly of home affairs to his companion, kept his eyes cast down and saw everything.

Through the confusion of light converse the King whispered to his brother: "My friend, you are expert in indiscretion."

"What now?" asked the Duke sullenly.

"I see that Father Constant of yours on the racecourse in a very thin disguise. Do you think our nephew does not know that spies are about him?"

"The man is in the service of your Majesty as much as in mine," retorted James.

"He is not here by my orders."

The Duke was silent. He had been discontented, and with some reason, ever since his return to England in '60. Now, with this project of marriage for his daughter to the champion of a religion he had forsaken and detested, this suggestion of sacrificing himself for his brother's convenience, his discontent reached bitter anger. The King looked at him with unconcerned eyes and paused, making a little gesture with his hand to the Prince.

William came instantly and stood before the group of Englishmen, the slightest in stature, the plainest in dress of any there. The King wore ruby-coloured velvet and a hat with a buckle of brilliants; he carried a cane with a knot of violet ribbon. The Duke was in scarlet fringed with gold; his curls waving to his black sash and over the wine-hued satin knot on his left shoulder. The two standing side by side, both of great height, dignity, and fine presence, the elder darkly attractive, the younger aristocratically handsome, made a regal pair to represent the Majesty of England, well supported by the graceful figures and fair Saxon faces of my lords behind. The court might be corruption at the heart, but it had a very haughty, gorgeous seeming. The power and charm of the Stewart blood was well displayed in the persons of these two Princes.

"Nephew," said the King kindly, "will you not go to the cockpit or the tennis court, or play basset or comet in the house?"

"I would rather," answered William, "be on the road to London, your Majesty. Since I came to England for business I may not linger in it for pleasure." He flushed a little as he spoke, being well aware of the opposition, enmity, and ridicule of the men behind the King, of the dislike of the King's brother, perhaps even the King himself.

"We go to London tomorrow," said Charles, fixing his black eyes on the slim, quiet young man with an expression between amusement and malice, "and you shall see your cousin Mary. James will give you warm welcome, eh, my lord?"

The Duke bowed stiffly; Buckingham laughed and whispered something to Mulgrave; only Danby looked grave, perhaps anxious.

"Then for tonight," returned William, "I beg your Majesty to excuse my attendance. I have no skill in house games and there is some pressure of business I must attend to." He bowed and stepped aside. James gave him a haughty look; Charles smiled. The nobles whispered and laughed so loud that the King good-humouredly reproved his favourite, Villiers, "Come, George, we must be serious and mind our manners when we have guests."

The Prince, some paces away as they all moved toward the town, knew perfectly well that these men laughed at him with the Englishman's scorn for the foreigner and the courtier's scorn for the man of action. He was aware that they were all in the pay of France and so therefore bitterly opposed to his marriage and a peace favourable to Holland; that they had great weight with the King, more with the Duke, and, being powerful men, made a frontage of enmity difficult indeed to overcome. His friends, the

Whig lords, were not there; the Opposition did not attend the races; they had in any case little influence against that of Monsieur Barillon and his paid supporters.

William had foreseen these difficulties before he undertook the journey, and now what had seemed hard to do at Dieren seemed almost impossible on Newmarket Heath. Prince of the blood as he was, renowned in Europe, a favourite with the Parliament, the dissenters, even the Church of England, admired by men like Halifax and Temple, his position in the English court was worth nothing. Even the King lent his aid to the subtle conspiracy to make him feel that whatever he might be in his own country, in England he was overshadowed, powerless, and no great man. William saw this clearly and bore with serenity the signs of it in many little acts of insolence. He knew Monsieur Barillon behind that policy, and behind him his master, Louis of France, and he was neither baffled nor angered into forgetting that he was the pivot round which all these intrigues centred, that on his firmness in resisting an unjust peace half Europe was relying, and that for his discomfiture the other half was eagerly waiting. He said as much now to console Bentinck, who had been smarting under English insolence since June.

"My Lord Sunderland is your hope," answered his friend. "He is very quiet, but more powerful than you would believe and inclined to us."

The Prince glanced at the resplendent group a little ahead, then down again at the low gorse-bushes with their coarse yellow flowers, and said nothing. When they had almost reached the town, my Lord Danby openly left his companions and crossed the heath to the two Dutchmen.

William gave him a quick look from under the dark beaver. "Are you of my party?" he asked abruptly.

This honesty of expression for a moment confounded Danby, who was used to dealing in very double speech; he coloured and paused. "I have been assured so many times," said William slightly smiling; "and that you, my lord, do hate France."

My Lord High Treasurer rose to sincerity. "It is God's truth," he said, "and I will serve Your Highness any way I can."

The Stadtholder answered gravely. "I thank you, my lord, and I am glad for the sake of Christendom and your country that you have resolved upon a manly course."

Danby thought this dangerously plain speaking, and a severe censure on the French party, almost on the King, but he was not lacking in courage and with all his heart he detested the thought of subservience to any foreign Power. "Your Highness will have to go carefully," he warned.

"I have been doing that," answered the Prince, "all my life."

"The difficulties in the way of a good peace are tremendous."

"I am well used to difficulties," said William quietly.

"Your Highness must rely upon the people and the Parliament."

Almost unconsciously the three had quickened their steps and were now almost up to the royal party. The King called out to Danby: "Are you plotting treason, Tom?"

"He has joined the Opposition," said Rochester, turning his sharp flushed face.

"The winning side, I hope," returned the Lord Treasurer, and so pledged himself to the Prince.

"My Lord Arlington looks sourly," remarked Bentinck. This nobleman had lost all manner of credit with the Prince in his mission of '74 and was, through jealousy, the enemy of Danby. Once he had been in favour of the Protestant marriage and half leant to it now, but constant to nothing long save his devotion to the person of the King, he wavered in obscure intrigues and could not be trusted even by the most sanguine.

"Those gentlemen about his Majesty are very pretty puppets," said William, "but cut the strings that are being pulled at Versailles and you have only harmless lumber. Ignore, them, my lord, and strike higher."

This boldness warmed Danby; he felt himself venturing on a dangerous policy, but he was pleased with the part he had chosen.

"I," continued the Prince, "must be at the Hague again in a short while. You will understand, my lord, that I have no time for ceremonies or delays. The King must decide immediately."

"I will tell you," said Danby frankly, "there is a great momentum of public feeling against the French Alliance. The marriage of Your Highness to the Princess Mary would be very popular, and would ease the minds of the people with regard to the faith of her father. It is this that forces the King's hand; of himself he would rather stand well with France."

"So would the lady, I think," put in Bentinck. "She has shown me a very great coldness which looks ill for the reception she will give Your Highness."

"The disposition of the Princess is no matter," said Danby impatiently. "She does what her father bids and what her uncle countenances. Your Highness has more serious oppositions to encounter than the caprice of a girl."

James II (1633-1701). Painting by John Smith.

They entered the town and made their way through the block of coaches and chairs in the narrow crowded streets. The royal party had entered their carriages and driven to the King's lodge. William made no pretence of paying court to his uncle, and Charles was scarcely at the pains to play the attentive host. The large issues that were to be fought out at Whitehall were suffered to lie in abeyance at Newmarket. But Danby dined with the Prince at his lodgings, and talked with the passion he had too long suppressed of the disastrous policy of the King and the humiliation England was under. Encouraged by the presence of a sincere and courageous leader, he had resolved to pledge himself to the bold policy of a war with France. England and Holland backed by Spain should speedily reduce that proud power to her proper place in the continent she now dominated, and Charles would realize the dreams of the old Cavaliers and become a great King. To accomplish this end Danby wished to propose terms of peace so arbitrary that Louis would refuse them haughtily, upon which England could declare herself tired of the profitless office of mediator, and resort to force instead of argument to bring France back to the articles of the Treaty of Westphalia.

The Prince listened keenly to this unfolding of a plan of action that so closely followed his own views. "This is not the King's wish?" he asked.

Danby was frank. "No—the King's wish is to get from Your Highness a peace that will please France, to, if possible, prevent the marriage of Your Highness to one so near the throne as the Princess Mary, and to end the war by crippling Holland and satisfying King Louis."

William's brilliant eyes flashed at the Minister. "You have courage, my lord."

Danby bowed. "Your Highness has more—if Your Highness will stand firm we may yet succeed."

The Prince looked thoughtfully round the plain lodging with a gaze that saw other things beside the dark furniture and smooth walls. "Why," he asked, "did the King offer me this match—twice?"

"To please the Parliament, and in some way to bribe Your Highness."

"His Grace of York and I do not love one another," remarked William. "He is not the Prince I would choose for a father-in-law."

"His daughter is heiress of England," said my Lord Treasurer, "and you may well overlook dislike to the father for the sake of her dowry."

The young Stadtholder answered gravely: "There is no such temptation in a crown to me, my lord, least of all in a crown that comes through a wife. If England can be brought to her proper place and to league with us against France I would as soon go without this marriage, which, I tell you plainly, will not be liked in my own country, where there is a great jealousy of England and a great distrust of the Stewart name."

"In that way Your Highness plays into the hands of your enemies. The lady will be married in France, and the influence Your Highness might have had on English politics goes to some French Prince."

"I will speak further on this matter when I have seen the lady," said the Prince guardedly.

Danby, who had heard Charles laugh over his nephew's determination to see his future wife before he pledged himself, hastened to speak praises of the Princess. "She is called a beauty," he said.

"That may be a disadvantage," returned the Prince briefly.

Danby slightly lifted his brows. "She is pious..."

William interrupted. "It matters not for her qualities if she is malleable, easily taught, quick to obey. Now, as for this peace, draw up the draft to be put before the King, my lord, and we will discuss the articles in London."

Danby rose, a gaily careless figure in appearance in his white velvet, blue ribbon, fair curls and racing favour, frowningly anxious in the face, flushed and excited. "If I could rouse the people!" he cried. "We have fallen on such sloth, folly, indifference—if I could make England great again!"

"The people!" said William. "The people are always the same, material waiting for the hand to shape it. It is the great men who count in the history of a nation." His deep eyes brightened as he added: "England was mighty under Cromwell, and could be mighty again."

Danby started at mention of that name and the Prince noticed his surprise. "You think that a strange thing for one, half a Stewart, to say—but you know it is true. Where was Macedonia but for Alexander, the Western Empire but for Charlemagne?"

"Or the United Provinces but for Your Highness," said Danby with sincere admiration.

The Prince slightly flushed. "You must not put compliments upon me, my lord," he answered. He was silent awhile, then asked, half smiling: "Why did you send to me Mr. Mompesson?"

"Because there was no one about the court I could trust to make any impression upon Your Highness. I had long knowledge of him, and his Majesty approved the design to send you one fresh from intrigue."

"It lost his Majesty a servant and gained me one. I have given him an ensign in my guard. Since your lordship cast the poor gentleman out of his employment in the Admiralty he was in sad straits."

"Why did Your Highness do that?" asked Danby.

"It is always good policy to put an honest man under an obligation," answered William. "And he did his duty very well. He was more like to have persuaded me than your other envoys; Mr. Laurence Hyde, for instance, who wasted a great many words to no purpose."

"He was the advising of Sir William Temple—no fault of mine."

William looked at him steadily, still slightly smiling. "Why did you send your Priest at Mr. Mompesson's heels to spy on him and me and intrigue with the States?"

Danby coloured hotly.

"I do think it poor, witless statecraft," said William, "to never be sincere."

"I am forced to a double game," answered the Lord Treasurer bitterly. "It was never a wish of mine to deceive Your Highness—or do harm to the Protestant faith..." In his heart he a little marvelled that the Prince was so well informed of the doings of his enemies.

"Well," said William quietly, "you have now the chance to prove your sincerity and friendship, my lord. If you stand by me now, you may rely that when I have the power I shall not lack the will to be useful to you—and you may remember that the interests I ask you to serve are those of England, Liberty, and the Reformed faith."

CHAPTER VI. BLINDMAN'S BUFF

Twice the Prince of Orange had waited upon his uncle of York at St. James' Place in the fields beyond Westminster; neither time had he seen the Princess Mary. The excuses were obvious, first a headache, second her devotions that must not be interrupted. The third time his Highness came backed by the King's command and was received instantly with a deference that made him suspect further humiliations.

The Duke was not there to present his daughter; the Italian Duchess was at Windsor; the Princesses held a revel to celebrate the name-day of one of their ladies. Chance, improved by Papist cunning, had thus prepared an elaborate slight for the Prince, who, with his thoughts engaged by the destinies of nations, found himself the butt for the delicate scorn of a frivolous and alien world.

He was ushered into he ballroom overlooking the lavish English garden, announced and left. His name fell unheeded into a laughing crowd, for the Princess and her ladies were playing blindman's buff. Mingled with them were the Romanist gentlemen of his Highness of York, and some young nobles of the French faction.

The Prince paused inside the door. He had Frederick van Zuylestein' and William Bentinck with him; both these, familiar with the English court, suspected a concerted insult in this reception.

Mynheer Bentinck whispered his suspicions to the Prince. "I know," returned William. "Again—France?"

The room was lofty and hung with a Flemish arras; the long windows stood open on October flowers and October sunshine, distant trees and a blue sky veiled with faint clouds. In the deep window-seats, on the chairs against the wall, were fans, lutes, boxes of bonbons, bouquets, and books. About twenty ladies and as many gentlemen moved swiftly and laughingly out of reach of a fair girl blindfolded; not one of them took any heed of the new-comers standing against the door.

"Which is the Princess?" asked William of Mynheer Bentinck.

"She who plays blindman," was the answer. "But what behaviour is here?" he added hotly.

The Prince did not answer; he saw France behind this as behind all the humiliations, defeats, and agonies of his life. His enemy dealt him a stroke as surely under cover of a girl's caprice as he had ever done on the battlefields of Brabant, and the Prince's spirit was braced to a defiance as dauntless as he had flung back after every French victory, every French threat.

The merrymakers ran to and fro on the long polished floor, the women with full silk and satin skirts they lifted gracefully from shoes with gleaming buckles, bare shoulders and flowing curls, brilliant eyes, white chins patched with black stars and pearls round smooth throats; the men with late roses among the heavy lace of their cravats, little gold and silver rapiers at their side and brocade coats sparkling with threads of bullion, all handsome in the fair English fashion and laughing among themselves with aristocratic haughty freedom.

The Prince looked among the careless crowd for the lady who pursued them, and saw her, in a white satin gown, with loose waving chestnut curls and a lace handkerchief tied over her eyes. She laughed as much as any, in a breathless, excited way, moving slowly with outstretched hands in pursuit of the quick figures that eluded her, pausing now and then, bewildered and laughing the more. The Prince watched her gravely. He might love England in theory, be pleased to talk his mother's tongue, and proud of Stewart blood, but now among them he felt himself foreign indeed, in everything as different from these men as was the Princess different from the women of his own country. Mynheer van Zuylestein touched his sleeve, and demanded how long he would endure this.

The Prince asked silence. He was very pale with mastering the imperious pride that burnt like flame in his blood when he was angered; he leant against the doorpost and followed the movements of Mary Stewart with narrowed eyes. To interrupt the mazy game, save by raised voice or violent action, was impossible. One after another the Princess' guests ran by with no heed of the three within the door, yet it might have been supposed by the very pitch of their gaiety and perfection of their self-absorption that they were perfectly well aware who watched them. One indeed betrayed herself. A lady in a blue robe as she passed shot a quick glance of curiosity from the Prince's friends to the Prince himself. Mynheer van Zuylestein made a half movement forward. The lady fled. Close after her was the Princess, her skirt caught up for safety off silver shoes. William stepped suddenly across her path; with a laugh of triumph she flung out her hand and caught his sleeve.

The game ceased instantly; everyone stopped where he stood, turned and stared. The Princess, instantly aware she had touched a stranger, released her clasp, and was drawing back but he took her right wrist and held it firmly. "This is an informal audience, Madam," he said.

At the unfamiliar voice, terror, confusion, and annoyance flushed the Princess' cheeks. "Who are you?" she stammered, knowing well, since his name was still ringing in her ears.

"Your cousin," he answered. "I do think his Majesty advised you of my coming. Did he desire you to entreat me thus?" He looked from her round the company. "England," he said, "has taken much from France, scarcely, it seems, her mode of courtesy."

They had to endure this thrust in silence. He was a royal Prince, and they did not know how far the King was committed to him. The gentlemen bowed, the women curtsied; the governess of the Princess, Mrs. Villiers, was humble in her excuses for the mistake; hollow protestations were ill amends for a studied slight. The Prince suffered the lady to run on. When she had finished he made no reply, but turned again to the Princess, who stood foolishly, with the bandage about her eyes and her wrist in his grasp.

"Madam," he said, "you know what has brought me to London. Is it your wish to receive me like this?—for if this is the manner of treatment I am like to get, I can easily resolve to return as I came."

The Princess trembled and paled. "I think I am of no great account in your visit, Sir; merely a thing you hang on the skirts of business."

He freed her hand. "This is the third time I have waited on you, and you still are pleased to behave with no manner of courtesy. Will you not at least uncover your eyes, Madam?" He was angered to the quick that she did not dismiss the smiling whispering crowd who were enjoying his discomfiture. At this last request, some of the ladies laughed outright and the Princess stepped back.

She laughed also, but in a forced and trembling fashion. "The game is not finished, Your Highness," she said. "I touched no one—Your Highness is not of my guests." In truth she found it as difficult to untie the bandage and look at the man before her as if it was iron clasped and locked to her curls.

For a second the Prince paused. He kept his eyes off the people before whom he was forced to speak as a man will keep his hands off his enemy. The sun from the rich garden caught the heavy folds of the Princess' dress, and fell on his slight figure in the violet coat and the thick hair so much the hue of hers. He looked on the ground as he answered: "I will no longer interrupt your play, Your Highness."

She curtsied. "I shall look to see you in Whitehall, Sir," she said in a feeble voice.

The Prince bowed to her in his stiff military fashion, foreign to the English beaux and therefore matter for laughter, only half suppressed, among the clustered gallants. Not all his command could keep the outraged colour from his cheeks; he turned on his heel and left the chamber with his two friends, taking no heed of the rest of the company.

As soon as she heard the latch click into place the Princess pulled the bandage from her eyes and faced round on her court. "I have been extremely uncivil," she declared. Her glance sought out her governess. "I do hate you, Mrs. Villiers, that you have put it into my head to behave thus."

"Oh hush, Highness," cried that lady, a little disturbed lest she had indeed gone too far. "It was a mistake..."

"A very well-prepared one," returned the Princess with dignity. "And I have been to blame to countenance it. Ladies, my lords, this revel is at an end and you may leave us." With a haughtiness beyond her years she dismissed them, checking by her own gravity, comment and smiles at her discomfited suitor. When she was alone save for her sister, her governess, her three ladies, and the Lady Monmouth, the handkerchief that had been over her eyes was pressed to trembling lips and her cheeks flushed with approaching tears.

"Oh, fie!" cried Lady Monmouth, casting herself into the window-seat.

"Can you never do a spirited thing but your softness must immediately repent it, Moll?"

"His Highness had a reception that should teach him to abandon his suit," said Anne Trelawney, the lady whose birthday had proved so convenient in the schemes of the Papists. "And you know, Highness, that you hate the man."

"How can I know that," demanded Mary, "when I have never seen him?"

"You had your chance," smiled Mrs. Villiers. "How were we," she added, "to know that you were so tender in this matter when you have a thousand times declared that you would sooner anything than marry the Prince of Orange?"

"That is a very different matter to hating him," returned the Princess. "He said I was discourteous, and though I do wish him back in Holland I like not to give him pain." Her soft eyes, over brimmed with tears, she turned hastily away to conceal them from the unsympathetic glance of Mrs. Villiers, and made an appealing little movement to the Lady Monmouth. "Will you come out into the garden?" she asked; "and you also, Anne?"

Miss Trelawney, fair and tall, with a heart-shaped patch on her rounded chin, followed languidly. Once in the garden the Princess burst out passionately: "I do detest this scheming—I was weak to let this happen!"

The other two ladies exchanged smiles. "You never did anything savouring of unkindness, but you did not repent it, Highness," said Miss Trelawney in accents more of contempt than admiration.

The Princess, clinging to Lady Monmouth's arm, was silent. The three slowly paced the walks between the bushes of late roses and the proud blooms of hollyhocks, the clusters of herbs and yellowing leaves. Before them a hedge of yew opened in an arch onto the fruit garden, where peaches and plums hung behind nets on the mellow red wall, beyond which were the harvest fields and the high outline of elms. The sunshine was deep coloured and resplendent over tree, field and the old front of the palace, and gave to all it touched that lingering sweetness of home-sickness and regret that comes with the light of autumn afternoons. The air was heavy with the scent of a late hay harvest, the stinging perfume of herbs and the bitter fresh aroma of sweetbrier, blossomless but still brightly green.

The Princess sighed, dried her eyes, and looked half sadly round the rich quiet of the garden.

"You would not care to leave this, Highness," asked Miss Trelawney, "for the marshes of Holland?"

"Indeed I shall not," answered Mary hastily. "I could not, oh, I could not leave England," and even at the thought her tears started afresh.

"It is a common fate for Princesses—to leave their countries," said Lady Monmouth. There was a pause. A fine breeze swelled the silk skirts back from the delicate waists as the ladies walked slowly, and stirred the heavy curls escaping from the coronals of pearl-sewn ribbons.

The Princess twined her fingers into Lady Monmouth's hand. "What was he like?" she asked.

"The Prince?"

"Yes, of course."

Miss Trelawney laughed. "Why, Highness, why did you not look for yourself?"

The Princess again entreated. "Anne, dear Anne, what was he like?"

"Like his mother," answered the Duchess.

"As if I could remember her!"

"You know her picture in Whitehall—I go by that."

"Ah, yes," said Mary doubtfully. "Dark then?"

"Hair the colour of your own, Moll, but hazel eyes..."

"Not handsome," interrupted Miss Trelawney, "and short—he scarcely topped Your Highness."

The Princess heaved a sigh of dismay.

"Take no heed of her, Moll," said the Duchess. "The gentleman was well enough—he was different from our men, but what of that? We have many beautiful faces at court that disguise folly and falsehood." She thought of her own lord and smiled scornfully.

Mary faintly flushed. "He had a grave voice," she remarked.

"And wonderful eyes and thin hands. Do you wish me to make a catalogue?"

"I shall see him myself tomorrow at the ball," said Mary with an affectation of indifference. "What were they laughing at in him?" she added.

Miss Trelawney raised her brows. "I don't know! He made a foolish figure. His dress was old-fashioned, I think, strange at least, and he had such a stiff air..."

"You should not have laughed at him, and I do not like these comments," said the Princess unreasonably.

"You asked for them, Highness."

The Duchess spoke gravely. "Their own folly caused them to laugh. The Prince was in a cruel position, and any man who stands alone makes an easy butt; he has a manly bearing and a soldier's carriage—would look a Prince in any company. Were he of the appearance of a devil for ugliness and my suitor I'd take him knowing his history."

"You talk like Mynheer Bentinck," said Mary, "who would, when I would permit, talk hours of the great things the Prince had done—yet what were they? Any man will fight."

"Not for such objects," said the Duchess. "Do not plague me, Moll, the man is a hero—he *does*something—has made his own fortunes and the destiny of a nation. Imagine to be the wife of such a one!" Her vivacious black eyes flashed at the girl's soft beauty with a half-mocking envy.

"But if your hero does not love you?" said Mary plaintively.

"No matter for that if you can be of use to him—*do* something, help a little." She smiled, checking herself. "We useless ones always talk like that. Being an idle fool I would wish to direct a nation..."

"I would rather be peaceful with one I could care for, and who thought only of me," answered the Princess. "That is not out of fairy tales," she added defiantly, "but what one might hope for when one is young and not hideous, Anne." She paused and bent over a great bush of yellow roses whose blossoms were wide open on their hearts.

"The Prince will never be that manner of lover," said Miss Trelawney decidedly. "Great deeds or no, I think he would be clownish with women."

"Peace, child," replied the Duchess. "You are a little Papist and poison poor Moll with your talk. If this Prince is her fortune, let her make the best of it. A wife will find no fault if her husband be cold with women so she can win him to be different with her. 'Tis the soft manner covers the indifferent heart."

Miss Trelawney pouted.

"Oh, my two Annes," cried Mary, slipping an arm round the waist of each. "I do not want to be married at all—I would like to wait—

some one might fall in love with me," she added with a blush. "And I'd write him letters despite old Mistress Villiers, and he'd reply with verses—not a word of State affairs and wars. Would that not be monstrous divine, Anne?"

She appealed to Miss Trelawney, who responded: "Yes, but men of spirit do not write verses."

"Not his own," said Mary, "the pretty lines that Mr. Waller writes."

"You have had verses," smiled the Duchess. "What of Mr. Dryden's poetry when you danced before the court in the masque—'Two glorious nymphs of your own god-like line...' Something that rhymes with that, then, 'Whom you to suppliant monarchs shall dispose, To bind your friends and to disarm your foes.

"The Prince is not a 'suppliant monarch,'" answered the Princess. "And if I went to Holland I should never dance in masques. Say you do not think I shall go, you two Annes, do!" The last brilliancy of the sun was full on her rich yet childish loveliness, the silk gown, soft locks, liquid eyes and gentle lips.

"No, you shall not go!" cried Anne Trelawney.

"I think you will," said the Duchess. "You must ask Dr. Lake's prayers. And now come into the house; you may catch a chill any moment once the sun sets."

"A little longer," pleaded the Princess. "See what a charm it has, the ending day." She stood a-tiptoe to see beyond the yew hedge and farther fruit wall, away into the glorious distances of sunny field and foliage. "England!" she whispered and caught the arm of the Duchess. "Dear heart, I love it very much." She mused awhile then said: "Is he like my uncle or my father?"

"The last a little, yes—but moustaches a la royale and shorter—no not like, I think, scarce a Stewart at all. But do not take my judgment, Moll, see for yourself."

Mary spoke as if she had not heard. "That rose—is it not a perfect colour of crimson?"

"It will be the last or near it," said Miss Trelawney: "the bush has no more buds."

"Then I will have it," smiled the Princess. She delicately broke the bloom from the stem and held it up with a little laugh of delight, but as she gazed at it the petals fell and left the bare stalk in her hand.

The other two ladies smiled but the Princess paled. "Oh!" she exclaimed in a tone of dismay. "Why did I do that—why did I pluck it?"

"What is the matter, Highness?" asked Miss Trelawney carelessly.

"You know that if a rose falls in the grasp it means you will die young," said Mary wistfully. "My grandfather Claredon taught me that and bid me beware October roses."

"Oh, fie!" cried Lady Monmouth, "would you listen to such things?" But the Princess was strangely saddened. She moved away gravely with the stripped stem held tightly, and the reluctantly departing sunlight making a red radiance in her hair. "Perhaps only a few years," she said. "But what have we any of us—such a little time?"

"A strange remark, Highness," smiled Miss Trelawney.

Mary looked at her with absent eyes, then turned, a lonely lovely figure, toward the palace.

———————

The Prince, returning to Whitehall through the fields, the Mall, the walk with St. Evremonde's aviary, past the archery enclosure, the bowling-ground and the old tilting-yard, well-dressed people about him and the autumn glow lighting up the smoke that rose from the city, saw and valued England whose alliance was essential to his country and to him, for what she appeared to him, a nation free, luxurious, easy, impatient of little crosses, slow to move in large decisions, careless, cold, ungrateful, insincere, insolent, loving show and splendour, superficial in matters of the spirit, superb in bodily accomplishment, of much levity in expression yet great by reason of her independence, her shrewd judgment, her immemorial courage, her immovable pride; the very arrogance that made her hated made her gorgeous, the very lightness that disdained to be serious even at an extremity, gave her a poise of power and greatness even when, as now, her hypocritical policies touched infamy.

William did not love this country, scarcely liked it. Prince of her blood royal, still she called him alien and his pride hardened at her insolence, her dishonesty, but he hungered after her power, the strength of the fair-haired men, the wealth of the extravagant city, the fertile country, the contained townships. Here is a country might be raised to the very pinnacle, he thought; here a people to hurl against France—if I could get them, if I could lead them!

He was so deeply wrapped in a flame of high musing, his thoughts were so far from personal matters, that Mynheer Bentinck had to speak thrice before he heard and then he turned absently.

"Highness," said Mynheer van Zuylestein, "we were talking of the lady."

William had utterly forgotten Mary. "Ah, the Princess," he answered. "She is little more than a child." He reflected a moment, then added; "They were uncivil—but she is an unwilling instrument, I do think."

"You laid so much on the seeing of her," said Mynheer Bentinck, "and now you seem to make very little of it."

"She has a greater loveliness than I thought to see," replied the Prince seriously. "She made me ashamed that I should have been brought before her in so ill a light that she could be led to flout me—and I do feel twice ashamed to press on her a suitor she dislikes, but I must have England, Bentinck."

"Then you will formally ask for this lady's hand?" questioned Mynheer van Zuylestein.

"Yes," said William wearily. "It will be an up-hill fight," he repeated strongly, "but I must have England." They entered the vast buildings of Whitehall, crossed the galleries of loungers waiting for the news, an audience of a Minister, or a word with the king, and took the stairway to their own apartments.

On the first landing a gentleman of great beauty entirely dressed in rose brocade stepped very softly out of a gilt door. His appearance was most noble and winning, his features delicate and sensitive, eyes and mouth long and smiling, nostrils finely curved, a low brow and thick fair brown ringlets, a figure slight, tall, and supple—a very lovely Englishman.

Seeing the Prince he paused and bowed most lowly in an exquisite homage of courtesy that topped even my Lord Danby's deference to his Highness. William stopped and glanced at Mynheer Bentinck, who whispered: "Sunderland."

The Prince caught the low-breathed name. "Does your lordship know me then?" he asked keenly.

The Earl answered in a voice marred by the affectation of a court drawl: "We have no other of the quality of Your Highness at Whitehall that we should mistake you, least of all I who have looked so long for your coming." The words, the tone, the manner held the very essence of flattery. William straightened. "I am pleased to meet your lordship," he said briefly.

Sunderland raised to his heart a white hand almost concealed in the Venetian point lace at the wrist. "Your Highness," he said, "has no more loyal servant in England than I do hope to prove myself."

"I hold myself fortunate," answered William in an impassive tone, "in having thus the good-will of your lordship."

My lord raised his slumberous, long-shaped eyes and looked into the straight gaze of the Prince. "Would Your Highness deign to speak with me a few seconds? This cabinet is empty."

William gave his friends a little nod, and followed my lord through the gild door into a small chamber furnished with an overpowering richness of silk, gold, silver, paintings, and crystal; the atmosphere was scented, caressing, indolent, like my lord. The Prince took a stool by the window and sat erect and alert with his hat and gloves on his knee.

Sunderland remained standing in an attitude of respect, conveying admiration, deference, obedience; everything about him was soft, his voice, his movements, his smile, his glance. "Your Highness received my poor letters?" he asked.

"I must thank your lordship for them," said the Stadtholder briefly. "Be seated, Sir."

The Earl took a chair delicately.

"My one desire was to serve Your Highness," he protested, "for whom I have the greatest admiration in the world."

"Come, Sir," said the Prince bluntly, "What is the matter in hand?"

Sunderland brought the light touch of his perfumed fingers to his heart. "The marriage of Your Highness." He smiled gently.

"You mean to help me in that?" asked William.

"In everything."

Even the astute Prince could read nothing but a steady sweetness in the beautiful eyes and charming mouth. "You have protested yourself my friend," he answered. "What then is your advice to me in this affair, Sir?" Sunderland's low voice was even more hushed. "Be firm, Your Highness."

"In the matter of the peace?"

"Yes."

"There I would not be weak," smiled William.

"Be cautious," breathed the Earl.

"I think that is my nature," replied the Prince.

"Whitehall is set with traps; they mean to have Your Highness in one or other of them."

"I shall have my eyes open."

Sunderland leant forward across the handsome table. "There is hardly a man of any weight at Whitehall not paid by France to thwart Your Highness."

"I can believe it," exclaimed William bitterly.

"Even my Lord Treasurer Danby," said Sunderland softly.

"I do think him pledged to me," declared the Prince.

"So he is—sincerely—yet taking money from Monsieur Barillon," the Earl added impressively, "and he has not wit enough for the double business."

William frowned. "Lord Danby uses the word you would take, Sir, and calls himself my friend. If you would have me respect that title in you I may not abuse it in him."

"Your Highness is, as ever, right. Do not think I would discredit my Lord Treasurer in your eyes." The Earl drooped his long lids and added gently: "His Majesty, the Duke of York, and my Lord Danby have driven a bargain with France for two million livres, the price that Parliament shall remain adjourned till April next."

The Prince could not repress a quick exclamation. "The Parliament and the Opposition is, Your Highness, your one hope of bringing England to an alliance," said Sunderland quietly. "And until the session opens affairs are in the hands of the court party, which is to say, the French."

"What," asked William on a quick breath, "is then my uncle's object in treating with me at all?"

"To beguile the people and bring Your Highness to a peace, for which France would pay well."

"The King is then to force on me the terms of Louis?" demanded the Prince.

"Yes."

"And they..."

"Are what Your Highness would never consent to."

The Prince was silent a moment, endeavouring to fathom the meshes of the net his enemies had about him. Sunderland watched him with half-veiled humble eyes.

William, when he spoke, used a cold tone. "You are of the Privy Council, Sir, why do you speak against the policies of your party?"

Sunderland smiled softly. "What interest could my motives be to Your Highness?"

"It seems that you betray your master," said William.

There was no change in the Earl's charming face. "I serve Your Highness," he answered calmly.

"Many men have said that to me; sometimes it has little meaning."

Sunderland bowed. "Has it not been my great fortune to have been of some poor use to Your Highness already, in my accounts of parties at this court?"

The Prince looked at him steadily. "I cannot see, my lord, why you should favour me; my policy, I think, is scarcely yours."

"The policy of Your Highness is what we shall all come to," answered Sunderland. "France and England will not pull together long. When the split comes, the moment will be yours to shape. This King holds together his intrigues by every expedient; after him, what? The Duke is a Papist, clumsy—dull after the Duke," His voice fell pleasantly. "Your Highness follows. It is but a few years before you may command England if you are helped to this marriage now."

"I had never skill in dreams," answered William; "it is of the present I must think."

The Earl was still smiling. "You will not see much of me in Whitehall, Your Highness, but I have more influence with the King than any man."

"And yet would be the friend to my desires," answered the Prince.

"As I will prove. If Your Highness will stand firm you shall have this marriage before any talk of a peace. Danby has angered the French by his championship of the Protestant interest, and they mean to ruin him by disclosing his dealings with them to the next Parliament."

"Sure," exclaimed William, "here is a coil of base infamy!"

"Danby," continued Sunderland unmoved, "will be abandoned by the King, the Tower will render him useless for a while if not for ever, Arlington will rise, the French party will be supreme, and who at this court will represent the interests of Your Highness but myself?"

"You work underground, my lord," answered William, "and in ways I cannot follow. You know what I stand for and what my wish was in this journey—if you will give me your help I must be grateful."

"I think your gratitude," said the Earl, "will come to be worth much, Your Highness."

"Is that your motive in serving me?" asked the Prince.

"You imagine," smiled Sunderland, "that I am utterly base."

"I do not understand you."

"I do yet hope to merit some little esteem from Your Highness."

"You cannot deserve it better than by inducing the King to leave France and unite with us against her."

"Your Highness thinks that difficult?"

"I know it so."

"But Your Highness has never recognized defeat."

The Prince replied quietly: "While I bear a constant mind I cannot know it."

Sunderland mused a little with soft eyes downcast. "Let Your Highness speak plainly to his Majesty, relying only on your own wisdom; press your power with the Whigs, which is greater than you realize. Do not speak of me or my words."

"I have some discretion," said William. He rose. "I will see the King tomorrow."

"There is a ball in the evening." Sunderland was standing with his air of graceful deference. "Obtain an audience of his Majesty before that, Your Highness. Monsieur Barillon sees him in the morning."

"Your lordship knows everything."

Sunderland did not deny it. "My knowledge is at the service of Your Highness."

William looked at him shrewdly, but the delicate placid features did not betray themselves by a quiver. "I think, my lord," said the Prince, "you are one of the cleverest men it has been my fortune to meet."

The Earl raised his eyes and for a second they shone. "You and I together, Sir," he answered, "could make something of England."

"Perhaps we should have different desires as to what to make her," said William a little haughtily.

"Had I a master like Your Highness, I should have no thought but to fulfil his wishes." He bowed till the fair curls concealed his face. The Prince, with no relaxing of his steady gaze, offered his hand and Sunderland kissed it with exquisite homage. "Will Your Highness make some chance to speak to me at the ball tomorrow?"

"I shall not forget."

Sunderland opened the gilt door, stood at it with bent head as the Prince passed out, and on a further bow closed it silently. As the Prince stepped on to the landing he saw Sir William Temple coming up.

The two friends greeted each other warmly; then Sir William glanced at the door of my lord's cabinet. "You have been closeted with—Sunderland?"

"Yes."

"The most powerful man in England," whispered Sir William, "and the most shameless."

The Prince faintly smiled. He had never told even Temple of his secret correspondence with his Majesty's Secretary of State. "A clever man," he said.

"But infamous," maintained Sir William. "You saw his furnishings? All bought with French gold."

"Ah, I suspected it," answered the Prince with scornful lips.

"The French spend a revenue on him. What had he to say to Your Highness?"

William took his arm and drew him slowly along the corridor. "French gold," he said, "has bought other things in Whitehall beside the knick-knacks of my Lord Sunderland—methinks among others the conscience of the King."

"Sunderland has spoken!" whispered Sir William eagerly.

"He will help me," returned the Prince.

"What has Your Highness paid for that help?" asked the Englishman.

"I have never in my life bribed any—my lord helps me out of his own policy."

"I do wonder," said Sir William with a touch of the vain jealousy he affected to disguise under indifference, a pardonable accompaniment to his warm nature, "that Your Highness cares to use any such man as my Lord Sunderland, who is as close as may be with the Lady Portsmouth, Monsieur Barillon, and all the enemies of Your Highness."

"If he who would accomplish great things is nice for clean tools he will lose his object in the search for them," answered William. "Base men may be turned to great ends if properly managed; heap enough dust together and it will help you to mount to a star; so I, using these little mean men, will work the general good."

CHAPTER VIII. THE WILL OF THE PRINCE

"I have talked," said the King, "with Danby, Arlington, and Temple till mine ears buzz, and now it seems I must go over this ground again with you." He looked at his nephew, who sat immovable in the shadow, then unlatched the window that opened onto the gardens of Whitehall, the river with boats going by and the fine autumn rain pattering on fallen leaves. He himself was in the window-seat, sitting carelessly with a serious face and black eyes watchful.

"There need be but few words on the matter," answered William. "It is only for your Majesty to say—yes or no."

"To what question?"

The Prince rose, crossed to the window, and rested one hand on the frame of the embrasure.

"Will your Majesty break with France and make an alliance with us, and will you, as an earnest of this, give me the hand of the Lady Mary?"

"That is put bluntly," smiled the King. "But you came to make a peace and this sounds mightily like making a war."

"Peace is a pretty word," returned William earnestly, "yet sometimes it has but an infamous meaning. As your Majesty is a King, and would deserve well of your people, you must come to see that war only can now secure the repose of Christendom."

Charles smiled. "The repose of Christendom is a big matter; we had better leave it to God, who is better able to manage it."

"God," said the Prince, "works through His instruments; we do His will when we perform our loftiest duties."

The King raised his thick brows good-naturedly. "That is God according to John Calvin. I am glad that He has revealed Himself to less earnest souls, the Pope of Rome for instance, who said we poor mortals need not trouble ourselves about these matters as long as we pay the priests."

William flushed. "I will not encroach on dogma," he answered gravely. "God is in faith that is truly obeyed—and conscience is His realm, and one where I would not intermeddle. The peace of Europe means universal liberty or it is an ignoble thing."

Charles turned his fickle unconcerned eyes on the young man and seemed to be considering him very curiously. The Prince was pale, looking tired and ill; oppressed by the London stench and smoke he coughed constantly; the expression in his eyes was as if he controlled incessant pain.

"I cannot conceive why you should kill yourself for a parcel of rogues and boors who will be anything but grateful," broke out the King softly. "What are the States to you that you should toil to give them security? In what is one form of religion better than another, that you should sacrifice your ease for it? Believe me, there is nothing in the world worth the discomfort you put yourself to. Go with the tide—if you strive against the current you will sink, but you will not alter the course of the water."

Mary Stewart I, (1631-1660). Mother of William III.
Painting by Bart van der Helst.

William scarcely heard the words so fixed was he on his own way. He shifted his argument onto ground where they might meet with a common interest. "Sooner or later you must have war with France, Sir. Your people are not of a temper to endure to see another nation conquer Europe—and now is the moment to strike while you have allies, the country with you, and before the French are too strong."

"Sooner or later," repeated Charles. "I have enough wit to make it later and not enough energy to concern myself with the repose of this earth when I am tasting the delights of another sphere."

"Have your people no claim on your Majesty?" demanded William.

"It is plain," smiled the King, "that you have been bred a Republican. If those good burghers had given me your education I would have taught you that the people are the last thing that should trouble the mind of a King. They will not thank you for thinking of them save in little things, such as fireworks and a bad example, which will make you popular enough to keep your throne."

"Your country, then?" asked William.

Charles shrugged his shoulders. "What is my country? France was kinder to me than England, and though my grandfather was Scotch they used me hatefully—and I can scarce play the patriot for Wales and Ireland."

"Your country is the country you rule," said William. "Surely your Majesty does not remember private pique in royal politics?"

Charles straightened himself in his seat and looked at the Prince with a half-amused reproach.

"How comes it that you, my sister's son, make yourself the champion of the common people and a plebeian faith?"

"I owe something to my father," answered William with an instant flush; "the House of Nassau ever put a high value on these things your Majesty rates so lightly."

"The House of Nassau," said the King softly, "left you a despoiled and broken heritage, the House of Stewart may leave you a crown."

The Prince drew back a half-step and fixed his glowing eyes with an almost painful intensity on the King's heavy-featured face.

"Listen to me," continued his Majesty earnestly. "My niece Mary is heiress to this throne, her husband will stand second to the kingship of England...You know my brother is a bigot, and stupid. How long do you think one such will hold this country? You are already the hero of the dissenters—the party that put Cromwell in Whitehall would gladly put you there..."

The Prince interrupted, rather breathlessly: "What is the bottom of your Majesty's meaning in this?"

Charles answered instantly: "That the hand of Mary is a gift that is well worth some consideration on your part."

"What consideration does your Majesty require?"

Charles glanced thoughtfully out at the rain descending on the yellow trees and leaf-covered paths. "An immediate and separate peace with France."

"No," answered the Prince sternly. "I will make no terms in that direction, peace must please me, and please Holland before I sign; nor will I have this marriage the matter of any condition, neither will I forsake my allies that they may say I sold them to buy me a wife."

Charles smiled and finally laughed. "Sir William warned me of this humour in you."

"It is said," answered William with strong passion behind the even words, "and it is meant; any who know me, Sir, will tell you I do not lightly change my mind. I would rather go back the subject of

French laughter with nothing accomplished than patch up a dishonourable peace to gain a personal advantage."

The King's dark skin faintly flushed. "You speak very boldly, nephew," he said with some heat; "you are under an obligation to me as the head of your family."

"Of my mother's family, Sir," replied William. "I do not found my fortunes on the distaff side, and of my own house I am the head!"

"You are an obstinate Dutchman," said the King, "and I think I shall do nothing with you; yet reflect that you have not been so successful in the war that you can carry it with too high a hand now."

The Prince answered with barely concealed pride.

"We have maintained the fight against tremendous odds for five years; we have driven the French from our territory and we are able now to treat with them on equal terms."

The King rested his dark hand on the window-sill and looked out at the rain. "But you cannot keep it up any longer," he answered quietly. "Your case is worse now than it was two years ago. I have a sure knowledge that the States are not with you, and you had best conclude peace while you can make any terms at all."

His low lazy voice was meant to cloak and disguise the harshness of the words, nevertheless they stung the Prince into a passionate answer. "Your Majesty took that tone to me in '72, and by God's help I have survived those dangers as I shall survive these."

Charles appeared pleased that he had roused so much feeling in his contained opponent; he looked at his nephew smiling. "I speak as your friend. You are on a dangerous course. I should not wish you to end life as I began it."

"You do not understand me, Sir," replied the Prince quickly. "I am not here to bargain for my future fortunes but to build a peace or a war that shall secure my country. As I have told Sir William Temple, I would rather have a few towns in Flanders than all the personal advantages you can offer me."

"Louis must have Franche-Comté and Cambrai," said Charles.

"Never—we return to the peace of Westphalia or the war must go on."

"And I," said Charles, "can say that if I get no peace you shall have no English marriage." There was a gleam of anger under the smooth pleasantness of the King, and a contained passion behind the quiet bearing of the Prince. The opposition between them, which had been growing for years, now reached the fierce point of personal encounter, the clash of temperaments, desires, and wills. William, every whit as imperious as his uncle and exasperated by treachery, double-dealing, and falsehood, held himself under a strong curb not to speak to Charles as he would have spoken to Gaspard Fagel, and the King, meeting for the first time since he came to the throne a fearless and outspoken defiance of his wishes and a firmness that he could neither evade nor quell, had it in his heart to silence William as he had often silenced Danby.

"You," he continued, "came to England to obtain a favour from me—you must be a little prepared to bend to my desires."

The Prince kept his eyes on the view of Whitehall Gardens. "I came to England because you, Sir, held out hopes to me that I might win your alliance. This marriage was in the first place of your offering, not of my asking."

The King was silent.

"Doubtless," continued the Prince in a tone so controlled as to be almost expressionless, "your Majesty's aim was to deceive and confound me. I can well believe that you never intended I should have the hand of my cousin, and that your wish was to make me serve the object of France by inducing me to forsake my allies and sign a peace to King Louis's advantage—but I pray your Majesty to believe that in these things I am immovable."

Charles rose impetuously, roused and angry. "You are not addressing your Dutch burghers," he said haughtily.

But William had long since worn out the language of deference to his uncle; weary years of compliments, flatteries, and concessions had produced no results, and he had little to gain now by submission.

"I know very well to whom I speak, Sir," he answered steadily. "I think it is your majesty who does not know me. I have come to England and I will not leave now without the Princess. These shuffling policies become a child's folly, and I will not be the sport of them."

The King's black eyes widened; he stood to the utmost of his great height, his hand on his breast. "What *will* you do?" he asked quietly.

"Your Majesty may guess I have some power in England. Your subjects are disaffected, your Parliament antagonistic, you yourself say that a Papist ruler would not be tolerable to your people. I have more friends in this country than your Majesty knows of, and if I choose to lead an opposition I can give some trouble."

"Ha! you talk of rebellion!" cried the King.

"Since I am not a subject of your Majesty, I cannot be rebellious—but I would remind you, Sir, that you are not the Czar of Muscovy, and there are Englishmen most averse to the policy of your Majesty."

"You talk very boldly," said the King, half curiously. "You threaten me with intrudes among my disloyal subjects?"

"I warn you, Sir, that England is behind me, not behind you."

"It's true," exclaimed Charles, "you have been well trained in republican impudence!"

William smiled bitterly. "There was a time, Sir, when I was at your feet, when a word of encouragement, a regiment of men from you would have made me your servant. You could then have gained me, my country, and have prevented the crisis you are face to face with now. But since you choose to join with my enemies, to do all in your power to crush me, since I have stood utterly alone without any help from you, since my country owes you nothing, why should I now hold humble language to you?"

"You choose to be ungrateful..."

William caught up the word passionately. "Ungrateful, Sir! Holland sheltered you at bitter cost and you strove to destroy her. My father did his utmost for you and you forsook his son...It is your Majesty who has been ungrateful."

They faced each other for a moment's silence, the insolent black eyes and the steady hazel exchanging quiet challenge; then the King dropped again into the window-seat and propped his chin on his palm, his elbow on the window-sill, in an attitude of careless indifference. The Prince put his hand to his brow, coughed and moved a little away; as soon as he was turned from the window the King gave him a quick side-glance.

The rain was slowly ceasing; above the yellow grey length of the river, a ragged silver break showed in the clouds; some birds commenced a lusty song in the trees near the window. William took a half-turn about the room and paused before his uncle again.

"It comes to this," he said, speaking in his slow fashion. "Your Majesty may have me for a friend or an enemy, and I entreat you to think which will be the better for you and your realm."

Charles looked round sharply. "What manner of answer do you expect to that?" he demanded. His eyes were narrowed and he fondled the black curls on his breast.

"I expect," said William coldly, "that you will, Sir, answer according to your own interest."

The King fell on to a silence hard to interpret; his eyes had a smouldering look of wrath, but round his expressive mouth was a faint smile.

"An enemy or a friend," repeated the Prince firmly. "Yes or no, Sir. We have dallied with this issue through too many weary foolings."

Charles raised his head and gave the Prince a flashing smile; then he broke into a laugh of charming good-fellowship and rose, composed and dignified, gracefully master of himself.

"You are an honest fellow," he said, "and you shall have your wife."

CHAPTER IX. MARY STEWART

Sir William Temple held Mynheer Bentinck with a whispered word. "The marriage is to be announced to the Privy Council tomorrow."

The Dutchman was startled. "How is this?"

"The Prince spoke to the King this afternoon. Sunderland moved in our favour."

"But the Duke of York?"

"Overruled. Danby is exultant." They parted discreetly, going their several ways in the rich ballroom, each elated with the final triumph of that policy they had maintained through so many disappointments and reverses. To Sir William it meant the ultimate success of the spirit of the Triple Alliance he had planned with John de Witt ten years ago, to William Bentinck hope for his country and mortification for the oppressors of his country, the French.

The light of a thousand candles flashed back from mirrors wreathed with flowers and filled the great hall with a bright, tremulous and glowing illumination; long tapestries of silk in tender and soft colours draped the walls, brocade curtained the windows and the atmosphere was heavily scented. My Lord Sunderland, the handsomest man even in a company that contained the Prince James of Monmouth, kept, as always, in the background and was seated beneath the musicians' gallery, with his beautiful lady, playing with a monkey held by a black page in amber coloured velvet. There Danby, more sure of himself, less fearful of a sudden fall than he had been since his elevation to power, made his way through fluttering fans, spreading skirts, and gilded rapier scabbards. Sunderland looked up smiling, his soft hand still on the monkey. He was dressed far more richly than any gentleman in the room; his coat was encrusted with an embroidery of costly jewels and at his throat was a sapphire clasp Danby had seen on the table of Monsieur Barillon.

"We have to thank the good offices of your lordship," said the Treasurer, who had not till now known an ally in this statesman.

Sunderland looked down deprecatingly.

"His Majesty," continued Danby with his rather rash frankness, "assured me that you had advised him his safety lay in this marriage."

"I told him," drawled Sunderland, "that the Opposition was mighty strong."

"My lord," put in his wife, raising languishing eyes, "thinks the Prince of Orange one who has the right at heart and the true faith, and therefore would do him what poor service he can."

She was an exceedingly fair woman, glimmering like a golden pearl in her white gown with her pale yellow hair falling in loops on to her bare shoulder; she had the modest deportment of a nun, the downcast glance, soft ways and speech of my lord himself, but her appearance held splendour and allurement.

"The Prince is fortunate in having your ladyship for an advocate," said Danby.

"I do," she answered humbly, "admire him greatly, in so far as a silly woman may understand what he has accomplished."

Sunderland again lifted his long eyes from the monkey. "You must permit me, my lord, to express my great joy at this triumph of your diplomacy. You are, surely, a proud man tonight."

Danby flushed under the grave flattery. He was so exultant that he could not refuse to credit the compliment. "Sir William too," he said generously, "has had a great hand in this."

"Sir William," protested my lady, "is a person for whom I have the liveliest esteem. I am more than ever rejoiced at this new honour he has acquired."

Danby bowed very low and passed on. Sunderland was entirely occupied with the monkey that leapt round his hand and climbed up his arm and chattered in his ear; my lady unfurled a great fan laden with gold, and over the half-circle of it watched the changing crowd. The King was there, looking haggard and serious, in a black coat with his blue ribbon and a couple of bow-legged little dogs flopping after him and a couple of women trying to amuse him and getting silence for their pains. Buckingham was there, heavy-eyed and restless, reckless in talk and over-dressed; Arlington, noticeable by the black plaster that concealed the scar on the bridge of his nose, sour because of Danby's eclipsing triumph; Sir William, placid and pleased; and the Prince of Orange, talking to no one, but standing by the fireplace with the air of a man who endures rather than likes his company.

Monsieur Barillon came up to my Lord Sunderland. "I hear some rumour," he said in an abrupt French whisper, "that this marriage is resolved upon."

Sunderland lifted a baffled face. "I know nothing—nothing!" he answered in the same tone and language. "The King will not disclose anything to me. I was on my knees to him beseeching him not to give his consent..."

Monsieur Barillon interrupted. "What is the other influence at work?"

Sunderland answered in an even lower whisper: "Danby—he is openly pledged to the Prince. You must get rid of him. I have warned you before to be aware of him..."

Monsieur Barillon looked through the crowd for the fair head of that unconscious cavalier, gave a suppressed exclamation of anger and moved away. Sunderland returned the monkey to the page and looked at his lady. For one second their eyes met in a flash of amused understanding, then they both rose. His Highness of York, heavily magnificent in purple and gold, was approaching them. Lady Sunderland sank to the ground in the deference of her curtsy; my lord's bearing was humility itself.

"So," said James harshly, "your wits have failed this time, eh, my lord?"

"What is my poor influence, Your Highness, against the weight of my Lord Danby and Sir William Temple?"

"They are both impudent fellows," declared the Duke wrathfully.

"Yet, Your Highness, a little caution would serve us better than anger. Since Your Highness must consent, use this as the opportunity to confound your enemies, who say you would subvert the State religion, by letting them observe how signal a proof you give of a tolerant mind." This, given breathlessly in the lightest of whispers, was heard and pondered by the Duke, who clumsily ogled Lady Sunderland's shrinking beauty the meanwhile.

"Well, you have done your best," he conceded, and swung off, biting his forefinger.

The Earl looked sharply round the now crowded chamber, then said to his wife: "Anne, I do not think the Prince of Orange will come to us—we will go to him." The lady, who appeared so perfectly in sympathy with her husband as to understand him without any explanation, came meekly, page and monkey in her train. They discovered the Prince engaged in what seemed a very one-sided conversation with my Lord Halifax, for that nobleman was talking in a witty and charming style and his Highness was listening without any very great appearance of interest. At sight of Sunderland, Halifax instantly bowed his leave; there was a quiet and unfailing dislike between them.

William looked at the Earl with inscrutable eyes. "You have a fine company here, my lord," he remarked.

Sunderland presented his wife. The tuning of the violins rose above the talk and movement, and then the sound of the King's laughter, caused by some jest at his brother's gloomy face, it seemed.

The Prince was taken aback by the splendour of my lord's wife as he had been by the splendour of my lord's cabinet. It was all one with the astonishing dazzle of wealth and beauty England made that women such as the Countess should be as common and as little regarded as roses in June. The Prince was courteous; she was almost the first lady he had spoken to in England. He found in her that quality he had been conscious of in her husband; some fascination that made dislike impossible. She spoke, naturally and charmingly, of the Princess Mary, who had not yet arrived, and her praises were very discreet and well chosen, her words picked so nicely that the Prince found himself more interested in his promised wife than he had ever thought to be. Sunderland, gleaming from head to foot, stood quiet and self-effacing, with veiled watchful eyes and a smiling mouth.

The Queen arrived with a train of ladies; there was a stir, a changing of the groups. The Princess Mary entered with Anne Trelawney, Sarah Jennings, and their governess. Among general loveliness these three were still noticeably lovely, very young, slim and delicate, with the wide English look of frank pride.

The King went over to speak to his niece, and Lady Sunderland, with a prompting too delicate to be resented, almost to be noticed, brought the Prince to do the same. Charles looked at William, smiled and presented him with careless good-nature.

"My Dear, this is the cavalier who is to be your husband—and you—" he had his eyes on the Prince, "you must remember that love goes ill with war."

Mary curtsied, swept a wild, timidly bold glance over the person of the Prince, then stood dumb.

"You do not remember me, Madam, when I was last in England?" he asked.

"No," she said. Her timid voice was lost in the rising and falling murmurs. She withdrew among her companions instantly and

William made no attempt to follow her. He stayed with the King, who was in silent humour and, it seemed, cynical.

The violins played a pavan; the floor cleared and two couples swept from the gathered glitter to the dance. Charles took his seat; the Prince was one side, the Duke the other; a dry conversation passed between the three. William pulled the long ears of one of the King's ruby-coloured dogs. The obvious strain between him and the Duke that even the King's easy indifference could not disguise was matter for amusement to men like my Lord Halifax, but the cause of some anxiety to my Lord High Treasurer.

More couples joined the pavan, among them Mary Stewart and Lord Buckingham. Her mood had swung round to desperate gaiety; dancing with her was a passion. She was fond of company, of music, of admiration. It seemed to her that never had Whitehall looked so entrancing as it did tonight, never had the homage of smile, glance, and whisper been so delightful, the music so full of a glorifying excitement, her own step so light, her spirits so high. She thrust into the background of her thoughts the terrifying image of the grave young man whom her uncle had made known to her with such ominous words; her joyous youth would not believe in such sudden and stern ending to all delights of home and liberty. That very morning her father had encouraged her to defy the Protestant marriage, and Monsieur Barillon had found occasion to whisper flatteries about the homage of the court of France. Entrenched behind these hopes she danced with a high beating heart and eyes that shot defiance at her uncle and the stranger cousin who, her cheeks burnt to note, was watching her intently. She was, perhaps, the finest dancer in the court and had besides a fresh pleasure in it, being new to balls from her childhood at Twickenham, that gave an added grace to her stately youth.

The pavan over, she danced the minuet with Monsieur Barillon and smiled at him and suffered his compliments, and turned her eyes no more to those about the King's chair. The Frenchman conveyed a triumph in the fact that he had her for his partner, seeming thereby to utterly ignore the Prince and his claims. James, observing him, became less gloomy; Danby fretted; Buckingham started a laugh at the expense of William. The Princess, as if ignorant or careless of these striving wills and passions of which she was the centre, moved through the minuet with a proud step, flushed cheeks and sparkling eyes, looking very noble in her rose-coloured satin with great pearls round her slim throat and in her waving hair. When the minuet was finished she swept past the Prince on the arm of Monsieur Barillon, her smiling eyes fixed on his vivacious face, glowing now with the thrust he dealt his master's enemy, and so brought William after her as surely as if he had been her jealous lover.

"May I lead you out for the next dance, Madam?" he asked, looking not at her but at Monsieur Barillon with great haughtiness.

Fear as well as dislike urged a plain refusal she did not dare utter. Her fingers tightened on the Frenchman's scarlet sleeve as she answered on a compromise: "I think I will dance no more, Highness."

"You dance too well to dance so little," he answered, but not in the tone of a compliment.

Mary did not look at him. "Indeed, I would rather not," she said.

Monsieur Barillon glanced at the Prince like a rival. "I think the lady's wish is clear enough, Your Highness," he said pleasantly.

"So is mine," answered William. "I wish to speak to my cousin. If she will not dance, it makes no difference." He used a tone there was no evading.

"I perceive," remarked Monsieur Barillon with something of a sneer, "that Your Highness is resolved to carry the differences of the battlefield into the ballroom. France and the United Provinces enjoy a truce, which I, at least, am wishful to remember."

"The peace," answered William significantly, "is neither made nor resolved upon, and courtesies between me and the Ambassador of his Christian Majesty are futile."

They faced each other with unconcealed dislike and bitterness; Monsieur Barillon pompous and gorgeous, William undauntedly quiet and stern—the vexed Princess between them.

The Frenchman finally bowed. "Since Your Highness is so resolved to remember the war," he said, "may I wish you more success"—his eyes flickered to Mary—"in your present endeavour then rewarded your gallant attempts in the last campaign."

"Monsieur Barillon..." began William dangerously.

The Ambassador waved his handkerchief to his lips and interrupted with a light laugh. "Hearts are easier to win than towns—to some men,"—his smile was very pointed—"though it is possible Your Highness may find the first as unattainable as the last."

Unexpectedly the Princess flashed into words. "Monsieur Barillon, I think your business is neither love nor war, but politics. Should you not keep to what you know?" The moment she had uttered this, the harshest and most daring speech of her life, a painful blush stained face and brow and neck. The impulse had been formed and the words spoken before she had time to realize her own brazenness. Now it seemed to her a terrible thing to have done. She stood her ground courageously but only by a fierce effort of pride.

Monsieur Barillon, hit both as regards his bravery and his gallantry, had some ado to conceal his mortification. He had thought he was pleasing the Princess by following her lead in discomfiting her unwished-for suitor; but, as he bowed himself out her company, he reflected that a young simple girl was the one unaccountable thing no diplomat could manage.

The flaming blood still burnt in the cheeks of the Princess; she kept her eyes down and bit her full lower lip desperately.

"Madam," said the Prince, in a pleased tone, "you are the first person at Whitehall I have heard rebuff Monsieur Barillon."

"He was not civil," she answered unsteadily, "but I suppose I should not have said what I did."

"I like to think that you have the spirit to silence insolence," he returned, "yet I do fear that you agreed with Monsieur Barillon rather than with me."

They stood in a deep window embrasure, a little apart from the company. The Princess had no excuse to go and no wish to stay; she was frightened, distressed, and angry; her eyes remained obstinately downcast as if the fact that she could not see the Prince was some protection.

"I understand none of it," she answered, and her fingers closed on her fan till the ivory sticks cracked.

William spoke gravely. "You understand something of the issues between the King of France and myself?"

"I know nothing about it," she replied. "I am stupid and I have not been interested in these matters."

"Not," he asked, "in your own country or your own faith?"

Never had she been spoken to so gravely, even by Dr. Compton; she felt herself foolish, like a rebuked child. "I am glad to be English," she said, "and of the Protestant religion."

"Then you would also be glad to do something for England and the Protestant religion, my cousin, would you not?"

Her anger died in an increased confusion; she made no reply.

"Being royal," insisted William, "you must have considered these matters. Why then do you put slights upon me to please the French? You must know what prompts you there."

His calm words reduced her motives and actions, she felt, to chaos and folly; with instinctive honesty she thought of her main reason and with a trembling bravery expressed it. "I do not want to leave England."

William glanced round the costly hall and fine company. "You enjoy—all this?"

"Yes," she said with some defiance.

"My country"—he touched the words with most loving pride—"has not these splendours to offer. I fear you would find it dull in my houses after this, but there are other things even a woman"—his settled contempt of her utmost was in that—"might find pleasure and profit in."

"I am not frivolous," protested Mary. "I have read 'The Whole Duty of Man' and understand it—but..." She stopped in dread of the betraying tears that hung on her lashes; she felt dimly that, being a woman, she had no right to find fault with her fate and that her complaints were mere promptings of an evil heart, yet even more dimly she wondered why if women were never to have a choice in anything they were given the spirit to rebel.

"I fear you dislike me," said the Prince.

Quick courtesy swept her into a denial. "Oh, no, Your Highness," she added with an effort, "I do regret that I was uncivil yesterday."

"I thought," he answered, "that my reception was not of your designing—but now, as then, you will not look at me."

The pink satins trembled with her agitated breathing; still he was nothing but a voice to her, for she kept her eyes resolutely away.

"Madam," he said with some humour, "you had best look at me. I am plain-featured enough but your imagination will soon paint me an ogre."

"I do respect Your Highness," she answered, seeking refuge in a compliment. "Mynheer Bentinck has told me..."

He interrupted. "You must not listen to Mynheer Bentinck. He is my friend, my best friend, and always flatters me."

The dance and the music were at full height; no one appeared to be noticing them. Mary felt something of the courage of the early evening return. "Sir," she said, "do you never dance?"

"I used to."

"It is one of my prettiest pleasures."

"You must remember that I asked you."

"I am tired now, Highness," she said quickly.

He turned to draw nearer to him the gilt chair behind, and her eyes took instant note of him. Calvinistic, Puritan, sour fanatic he had been called to her, but these forebodings were not justified; at least he wore his hair in curls, his clothes were rich, he had an easy bearing. With some indignation she rejected Anne Trelawney's estimate; if not as imposing as the gallants of Whitehall, he was, as Lady Monmouth had said, well enough. Pale he looked and tired, haggard for his age. He was neither very tall nor showy, yet certainly of a stately and remarkable appearance. Some women, she decided, would call him handsome.

As he placed the chair for her she kept her glance on him and for the first time their eyes met. His gaze was curious, hers shy. More than anything she felt that he was different from any one she had met; there was some repulsion in this and some attraction; her glance dropped again to the fan on her knee.

"My mother's name was Mary Stewart," he said gently. "I think you are like her, and that surprises me, for I never thought to see again a face as fair as hers."

"You pay a fine compliment, Your Highness," she answered.

"Believe me, I have never done so before."

She was silent, not ill pleased. She did not know if she liked him or not, but she felt a strange pleasure in the fact that he *was* different from these others, all fair speeches and fair looks. At heart she was serious herself. She half responded to this austere gravity. And had he ardent eyes...

He said no more and she did not know what to talk about. His hand rested on the side of her chair and she noticed it, thin and aristocratic, lying slackly now, but power and strength in the curve of the long fingers; it prepossessed her in his favour. There was about his whole person this air of power and refinement, a hidden ardour behind a contained delicacy. He was no longer looking at her, but at Monsieur Barillon, who talked to the King. Suddenly he made a quick excuse and crossed the floor to his enemy. She thought he looked to advantage among the other men, who had, to her eyes, a certain coarseness in their ruffling magnificence, and the knowledge that he stood alone there against them appealed to her interest in him. Yet he was very serious; she was afraid of him. She did not want to go to Holland. After all, had he said a word of that? Her hopes rose. Perhaps something had happened to break the marriage off. In that case she was prepared to like him.

Mrs. Villiers and Anne Trelawney came up to her. "It is all over, Highness," said the elder lady, "your marriage is to be announced to the Privy Council tomorrow."

Mary rose. "Who told you that?" she demanded faintly.

"Your father, Highness."

Mary's lips trembled and her bosom heaved.

"Poor thing!" said Miss Trelawney. She gave the Prince a glance of aversion. "Why, they might as well have given you to some Colonel of Puritan cavalry left over from the Rebellion."

Certainly he was now hateful to Mary also, but she checked her lady with a piteous dignity. "Anne, you must not speak so of my—my cousin." She paused a moment to control herself, then added: "Mrs. Villiers, I am going home." She left Whitehall with no leave-takings and cried all night in a hopeless and open grief.

CHAPTER X. TEARS

The Prince looked from the windows of his apartments at Whitehall on to a garden bare of leaves, lying under a cloudy sky; it was chill even for early November and sad even for the end of autumn. Lord Sunderland was speaking in an insinuating fashion of the intrigues of the English court; William listened with an air of lassitude. Whitehall, London, had become as nothing to him. Before his inner vision was his own fiercely beloved country and Flanders, battlefields, towns, and fortresses where her liberties must be defended. He longed to be home again in the clear air under the cloudy skies amid his own people.

Outwardly his mission to England had been successful; he had achieved by sheer force of will what had seemed impossible. England was rejoicing that tomorrow would see him united to the heiress of England. Monsieur Barillon was confounded, the Duke of York sullenly submissive. Charles had been edged on by Danby, Sunderland, and himself into forming a treaty that Louis was to accept and into promising to show fight in case of a refusal, but William's heart was weary with that self-discontent that renders all success tasteless. Doubt of his own powers, distaste of the long labour of it all, disgust almost of life itself, sat heavy on his spirit. He saw that Danby was marked out for ruin by Louis for his bold championship of his policy, that there was no trust to be placed in Charles, who was, with more or less graceful good-nature, merely going the way he was forced and that he had done himself little good by an alliance that his enemies would use against him in his own country. The King, ever pressed for money, was giving his niece the dowry of a noble's daughter, less than what he owed William, and the Prince, who could be magnificent upon occasion, had sent her, through Bentinck, jewels to the full amount of her jointure, so that his marriage brought him no wealth. Nor was it a soothing reflection that she was weeping herself ill at St. James's because tomorrow was her wedding day.

A passionate impatience took him to set her free, have done with the false King, wash his hands of the English, return and continue the fight alone. But there he was tied. The States, his allies, were anxious for a peace; no one would support him. If he lost England he must make what terms he could and be thankful if he saved his country's mere independence. His marriage and his influence with men like Halifax, Danby, and Temple, was his one chance against the overweening power of France, and to keep and improve this chance he must take silently, if not patiently, the fickleness, the meanness of the King, the dislike of James, the tears of Mary, the insolence of the English court—all of which things were unutterably hateful to him. He felt galled and downcast as he had not done since he was helpless under John de Witt.

Sunderland, ever observant and tactful, observed this temper in him and strove to shape his discourse on soothing lines.

"Monsieur de Duras," he said, "is to go to Paris with these terms..."

William interrupted. "My lord," he said, "Monsieur de Duras will come back with a refusal. What will the King do then?" His eyes flashed a pent passion and his lips were openly scornful.

"His Majesty," said the Earl softly, "will call a Parliament and declare war on France."

"I wonder!" exclaimed the Prince. "I have been amused with these tales so long, my lord."

"Danby is pledged to it."

"Danby! Danby will go like chaff before the wind if the King changes...What of your free Parliament? Monsieur Barillon will bribe the Opposition to pull Danby down and declare for peace."

Sunderland was considerably startled that his Highness should show such a sure knowledge of what, in his own opinion, was most likely to occur. He preserved a calm silence, however, and a serene face.

"And I," continued William grimly, "shall be betrayed again."

"I fear Your Highness is not satisfied," said Sunderland softly.

"How can I be satisfied," broke out the Prince, "when on all sides I see weakness, falsehood, paltering? And a little strength would make it all so easy!" he flushed with the energy of his speech. "Do you not think that if the King showed a firm front now, if he built his ships, poured his troops into Flanders, defied France, he could not get the terms of Westphalia or Aix-la-Chapelle again from Louis? If I had a free hand I would do it tomorrow." His eyes shone in an agony of passion; he held his heart and coughed. "You," he added vehemently, "know that I speak the truth, but the King does not care. I and Holland might be dead and lost if he had the money for his pleasures."

He paused a second, then added bitterly: "What can I do? I am always cabined within the compass of some other man's weakness."

Sunderland shot a keen glance at his passionate face. "I would stake a kingdom on Your Highness," he said quietly. "If the King were a cleverer man he would do the same, but I tell you this—you will have England yet—England and France. It must come to that issue, and Your Highness will be the man of that crisis."

William stared gloomily out of the window. He had lost much of his reserve, his calm. Sunderland had that strange fascination in his very presence that he could charm men into unconsciously revealing their true emotions and even William's inmost soul was bared before this man he yet knew to be in the pay of France.

"I am so sore and beaten with their intrigues!" he cried. "Buying, selling, betraying, and what weapons may I take against these things? My own countrymen tire, my allies are disheartened, I am become a mere puppet in ignoble events, and I do wish I was dead, as it would be better for me to lose my life than my honour."

The Earl answered in his low, almost tender voice. "It is November now and stormy weather, but we are not so far from May when it will be blue over Europe. Your Highness, who has so long shown wisdom and courage; will not now despair."

"Despair!" repeated William mournfully. "I have forbidden myself to think that word, yet sometimes I do imagine that God has put upon me more than I can perform."

"He who inspired will sustain Your Highness," breathed the Earl. "Remember what the resolution of Your Highness stands for, what renown and admiration you have got, what safety for your country, what glory for your name."

William did not appear to notice the meaning of the words. "I am very tired," he said irrelevantly; "the air of London is death to me." He leant back in an exhausted fashion and frowned out at the English skies as if he hated them.

"Your Highness," said Sunderland, "has some good friends in England, Halifax..."

"He," interrupted the Prince, "is a man not of his own times and one who will not be very useful to any party."

"Temple..."

"Sir William is so disgusted with court employment, scarce getting his postage from Arlington, that he retires among his flowers at Sheen and I shall obtain little more from him."

Sunderland smiled. "I am ever at the court and at the King's ear and I shall do my utmost to serve Your Highness."

William looked at him sharply and curiously, then he too smiled. "I do believe you will, my lord."

"You are not satisfied," said the Earl softly. "Well, the work you are on is slow, Sir, and there are many cunning turns and twists in the road to success. What if the Parliament was to suggest that no Papist could sit on the Throne of England and the Duke of York was to be excluded from the succession?"

"Whose scheme is that?" asked William quickly.

Sunderland lifted his shoulders modestly. "Do you not think it a fine stroke?" he asked.

"Not one that his Majesty's Minister could deal," returned the Prince.

"There are," suggested Sunderland, "indirect means,"

"Your policy," was the answer, "is, methinks, of sufficient complication already, my lord, and I do confess that the domestic politics of England are difficult treading for me. The one thing I have a mind to is this alliance against France and the rest may go."

Sunderland spoke on another subject with the same pensive face and caressing voice. "I hear that Your Highness has been asked to a banquet by the city—now it would be wiser if you did not go."

"They are my friends and I will not slight them," answered William briefly.

"It will anger the King."

"There is no great need that I should please the King. What he does is through force and not love of me," said the Prince sternly.

The Earl sweetly administered a reproof. "I think a softer temper in Your Highness would serve you well—some effort to please, a few compliments such as are loved by the lesser sort, more deference to the King and the Duke, more compliance with the King's favourites, for I do think the haughty demeanour of Your Highness will be some hindrance to those great designs you have at heart." He smiled deprecatingly, having spoken as no one else had yet dared to speak to the stern Stadtholder, and took a pinch of snuff out of an enamel box with a display of a fine right hand.

William looked at him without resentment. He liked any form of courage, and the unblushing courage of the knave that my lord certainly possessed and his personal charm were such that he took from him what he would not have taken from Fagel, or even Bentinck. "I am not here to command myself into complaisance with people who dislike me," he said, "but to obtain a certain thing—and I do tell you this, my lord, that the lewd bearing of your English is such that I, used to plainness but courtesy, do find it intolerable, and, not being by nature meek, I could with great ease be rougher than I am."

The thought behind Sunderland's serene look was: If you ever come to be King of England, there will be an end of rakery in Whitehall and I must learn to kneel devoutly at my prayers. Aloud he said: "This coarse humour in our English I do deplore; they will ever leave the large conjunctures abroad to devote themselves to the small follies at home. There are not," he added with perfect gravity, "many of what Your Highness would call godly men at Whitehall."

"My Lord Mulgrave now," said William, lured on to greater openness, "comes to me yesterday, and I not moving from my seat, as I never would before a man of his quality, he laughed insolently, and said, 'It seems Your Highness cannot rise before anything less than a town.' Now we call ourselves a republic, but there is no man in the United Provinces who would so dare speak to me."

Sunderland committed this to memory to tickle the ears of the King with and answered: "His Majesty himself will take these quips and so these gentlemen grow over bold."

"I cannot use greater courtesy to these spaniels of the court to whom I should use a whip," said the Prince with some anger.

"Your Highness is a soldier and used to the obedience of the camp— in England we are grown insolent with freedom and foolish with levity. Pass these things by and gain the warm opinion of the crowd by a pleasant humour, Sir, for with the common people the manner is everything."

William took this good-naturedly. "I have not had to court popularity at home," he said, "and am stiff in the ways of it."

The Earl rose and picked up delicately his cloak lined with rich fur, his muff, his scented cane, his gloves fringed with bullion and his diamond-buckled hat. "It is noticed," he said smoothly, "that you pay but little attention to your Princess at the ball and the play."

"She will thank me for it," interrupted William quickly.

"If she hated you," answered Sunderland, "which God forbid!—she would still be pleased that you should not neglect her. Remember, Sir, she has about her father's people, and no man but yourself can win her from them."

"What can they do?" frowned the Prince, rising.

"Make more mischief than you will ever know of," returned Sunderland. "Forgive me, Highness, but if your wife does not grow to care for you she will become your great enemy, and when you have set her up in your house to work evil for you, you will know what a woman can do, for I think at present you despise them too utterly."

He took his graceful leave on that and left the Prince with a new thought. What if this soft weeping girl with her chaplain and women did come to hate him and intrigue against him? It was gall to think that in his own country, in his very house, he must set up those who were in sympathy with his enemies, under the influence of the Duke of York and of Louis' spies and tale-bearers, insolent English! "I have," he thought bitterly, "done myself no good turn with this marriage." He remembered with the unreasonableness of pride that the mother of Mary Stewart had been *his* mother's waiting woman and her grandfather a mere commoner. Upon reflection this brilliant marriage was not brilliant from any point of view save that of the lady's ultimate claim to the throne of England, a distant and perilous honour.

The Prince clapped on his hat discontentedly and went out into the gardens. The rain had ceased but the day was leaden and lowering; the trellises, stripped of their last roses, showed bare and gaunt above the paths sodden with dead leaves. Here and there a few yellow bushes gleamed palely; purple swollen dog-berries and a few clusters of ash, scarlet and drooping, showed amid the bare boughs. A boat with vast sails was going down the river; the fields on the opposite bank lay hidden under a damp vapour; dimly to the right rose the towers of Lambeth Palace.

William disliked the garden, the weather, the grey bulk of the palace, the dull and sullen river. His exquisite and critical senses were fretted by the smoky atmosphere, the close odours of a great town, noticeable even in Whitehall Gardens, and the raw undercurrent of the east wind. As he continued his walk nearer the river he saw two ladies; one he knew at once for Miss Anne Trelawney.

He accosted her. "How is the Princess?" he asked. "You are, I think one of her ladies, Madam."

Miss Trelawney knew him but was surprised that he should know her. She was a little frightened, yet her answer was barely courteous. "The Lady Mary is very well; the Lady Anne is sick and gives her Highness distress."

"Sick?" questioned William.

"The smallpox, methinks, Highness," said Miss Trelawney calmly.

"At St. James?"

"Yes, Sir."

"It were better, Madam," he suggested, "if the Princess Royal moved to Whitehall."

"Oh Sir, she would never leave her sister; they are vastly fond of each other."

"She must, Madam," he answered firmly, "leave her soon."

"That is what we are all breaking our hearts over!" exclaimed Miss Trelawney flippantly. "I do not know how the Princess will endure it."

William ignored that. He asked with a calm that put Miss Trelawney out of countenance: "In what does the Princess spend her time?"

The lady curtsied as she answered maliciously: "Tears, Your Highness."

To her surprise the Prince smiled. "If you think to come to Holland, you must leave this mode of speech at Whitehall, my child." He touched his hat and turned on his heel, leaving her with flushed cheeks murmuring "Clown!" indignantly to her companion.

At the end of the walk set with laurels still green, William met Mynheer Bentinck. "A letter," said the gentleman. "The post is just in—they were delayed in Calais Roads."

"From Mynheer Fagel," remarked the Stadtholder. He tore it open and glanced over the pages. "Trouble in Amsterdam, a conspiracy suspected at the Hague, wishes I would return. And so I will, with the first fair wind."

"There is other news," said Mynheer Bentinck with the air of one who has ill tidings. "Sunderland did not tell you?"

"Sunderland told me nothing. He gave me advice. It is surprising how I listen to that fellow, Bentinck, when I know he is a knave."

"Well, then," Mynheer Bentinck gave it bluntly, "the Italian Duchess had a son this morning at Windsor and the Duke says you can have his daughter gladly now."

William stared at his friend. Mary Stewart was no longer heiress of England. There was no reason nor advantage now for him in the match for which he had so striven and to which he was beyond withdrawal committed. "France will be pleased," he said on a sharp breath. He added quickly: "have you waited on the Princess this morning?"

"Yes—she seems dutiful. She tried to conceal her tears from me." "Always tears!" exclaimed the Prince impatiently.

"She took the jewels humbly," continued Mynheer Bentinck, "and wished me to say she thanked you—not much else. Her women are charming. Miss Villiers, the governess' daughter, is an entrancing creature."

"And the Duke of York has an heir!" mused William. He looked at Bentinck and laughed.

CHAPTER XI. CLOUDS

Don Ramon and Father Constant (in the neat dress of a merchant) were walking the flat fields outside the Hague beside ice-locked canals. Before them the land lay a mere strip, above them the sky was heaped with cold and noble clouds that made all humanity beneath appear insignificant. Don Ramon had a smile on his lips as if he pondered some secret satisfaction; the Englishman was speaking. "The Prince and his wife returned but yesterday, yet it is believed that they will go at once to Dieren."

"I know," said Don Ramon. "I am sorry," he added, "that he has a wife."

Father Constant gave an impatient wave of his hand. "It is now more than ever necessary that the heretic be removed," he answered, "since he hinders our design. These two men, he and Lord Danby, are in the way. King Louis has nothing to fear once they be gone."

The smile of the younger man deepened; he looked with curiosity at the priest. "What is your motive in this?" he asked almost indolently.

Father Constant answered instantly: "To establish the Roman Church in England."

"A good motive in its way," said Don Ramon. "If you believe in—anything—why, you cannot spend your life better than by striving for it; all else is a rudderless course, long and purposeless."

"You," said the priest quietly, "are as ever ready?"

"As always—yes."

"The opportunity must be found soon."

"From Mr. Mompesson I can learn when the Prince is likely next to go to Scheveningen."

There was a minute of silence, then the priest spoke half hesitatingly. "I do not quite trust that Irishman, Dermot Fairfoul."

"Why?"

"He is a clever man. He sees that you have no manner of care what happens—afterwards—to yourself, and I believe that he fears for his own safety."

"You think he might betray us?"

"Why," answered Father Constant, "I have thought him not the man for a dangerous enterprise. He failed outside Ath."

"It was not meant that it should be he," said Don Ramon in a tone of contempt. "Why did you ever engage such an obvious rascal to our schemes?"

"He is a clever man," repeated the priest. "He has been of great use in distributing the money of France in Amsterdam. Mainly by his arts the whole country is riddled by French factions that would, at the given signal, rise up..."

Don Ramon interrupted. "Why then do you suspect him?"

"The Hague is well policed. I think Mynheer Fagel has some inkling of a plot and that Mr. Fairfoul knows it."

"If he is afraid, let him leave the country."

Don Ramon spoke with some impatience and the priest answered quickly. "I spoke but on a surmise." He paused, then laid his hand tenderly on the young man's arm. "I do wish that you, who are about to do so much for us, were of the true faith."

Don Ramon looked at the clouds. "I do this thing because of my own desires and no thought of any God touches me at all. Let that be."

The priest sighed. Dry frost-crystals lay on the short stiff grass, broken flags and reeds bent above the frozen intersecting canals. A few farms, white, red, and bright green, rose against the sky-line, breaking the even level of the flat country. The two companions slackened their steps and finally parted with a few words as to their next meeting; they were never seen together in the Hague.

For a while Don Ramon wandered along the hard paths bordering the narrow water, and watched the clouds, then his unnoticed steps brought him back to the town again, into one of the smaller, quieter streets with which he was but little acquainted. A milk-cart with glimmering brass cans was rattling over the cobbles, and a cart of frozen vegetables drawn by a dog and driven by a peasant in a fur cap. There was no one else in all the long narrow street. When he reached the end of it Don Ramon found a little shop for the sale of swords, pistols, muskets, and articles of warfare of the cheaper kind. He paused before it, looked at the sign, the weapons in the window, cleaned and neatly arranged.

While he lingered the vegetable cart drove up and the housewife came to the door and bargained over onions and turnips. When the purchase had been concluded they fell onto less personal talk. Don Ramon heard them discuss the new Princess with very little friendliness. The prudence of the Prince in not giving her a public entry was applauded. She had worn pearls in her ears, a French hat and a low gown in the coach, had a black page, a monkey, a worldly English chaplain, and a retinue of ladies no better than herself. She was to be considered a vain young woman with no godly notions in her head, and it was lamented that the Prince had not done better.

The gossip over and the little cart gone, Don Ramon stepped up to the woman of the house. "I could get a pistol cleaned and mended here?" he asked.

"Yes, Mynheer."

"And a sword handle tightened?"

"Yes, Mynheer, will you come in?"

He followed her through the low doorway into the narrow passage and so into the little shop with its whitewashed walls, polished beams and floor, long counter and rush bottomed chairs. An elderly man in horn spectacles was removing the rust from an old-fashioned helmet inlaid with gold; he rose and bowed at the entry of Don Ramon. The woman with the vegetables in her checked apron left them.

"Good day," said the young man with his serene smile.

"Good day, Mynheer."

"I have here a pistol, out of use and something broken." He took the weapon from his side and laid it on the counter. The gunmaker looked curiously at the gentleman who carried these arms and then at the pistol, which was most beautifully damascened and wrought with gold.

"An hour will set that right," he said after an examination.

Don Ramon unbuckled his sword. "This also is in need of repair; seeing your sign minded me—the hilt turns in my hand." He laid it in its scabbard and hanging straps beside the pistol, and again the old man glanced from the rich weapon to the tawny-haired young man with the calm and bright blue eyes.

"This is a very valuable sword, Mynheer."

"Yes—fine steel of Toledo," smiled Don Ramon. "But the hilt, as you see, is loose."

"It is easily mended, Mynheer, as the pistol. Shall I send them to your lodgings?"

"No—I will come again, in a couple of hours' time or less. They will then be ready?"

"I can promise it, Mynheer."

Don Ramon turned to leave when his eye was struck by a bright object at the back of the shop among the rows of bandoleers, Turkey-blade swords, muskets, and lined and stringed head-pieces. It was a large fragment of velvet of a peculiar shade of soft red, very much torn and hanging like a flag from the staff of a pike. Don Ramon stood arrested; the door handle slackened in his grip. "What is that, Mynheer?"

The gunsmith looked up. "What, Mynheer?"

"That velvet..."

The other turned quickly and stared up at the stuff. "Ah, that," he repeated with some embarrassment, and adjusted his spectacles.

"Well?" asked Don Ramon. He closed the door and returned to the counter slowly.

"Tell me—where did you get that fragment?" he demanded.

"Hush, Mynheer, it is a thing not to speak of too loud." He paused, then added; "I have had it there for years, and you are the first to remark it."

"Has it," asked Don Ramon, "a dangerous import that you are so slow to give me the meaning of it?"

"No, Mynheer." The gunsmith looked keenly at his questioner, then said: "That is a piece of the mantle of John de Witt as it was torn from him on August 20th, 1672. You remember?"

"Yes—I remember."

"Well, Mynheer, I, who had lived so long under the government of Mynheer de Witt and always considered him a great man, preserved that as a memorial of him."

"How did you obtain it?" asked Don Ramon steadily. "I also admired John de Witt."

Thus encouraged the gunsmith explained. "It was the artist..."

"The artist?"

"Upstairs Mynheer, he lodges over the shop, and has done for a great while."

"Well—he brought you that—relic?"

"Yes, Mynheer."

"He—he was out that day?"

"Yes, Mynheer, in the evening. You were not there?"

"No."

The gunsmith peered at him with some curiosity. "He brought that home; he was very furious against that hateful black deed. With all submission to his Highness I can call it no less."

"His Highness," interrupted Don Ramon fiercely, "is no master of mine or of yours. I am a Republican."

"This is a Republic, Mynheer."

"Not while William of Orange is at the head of affairs."

"Hush, Mynheer."

Don Ramon smiled bitterly. "You disprove yourself. Were this a free Republic should we need to choose our words?" He held himself still a moment, then he said: "I knew Mynheer John de Witt, that is why I questioned you."

The gunsmith was respectful and sympathetic, though more than a little afraid of this tall, stately, and bold-spoken young man.

"Would you desire to see the artist, Mynheer?" he suggested.

"Why?" asked Don Ramon abruptly.

"Only that he was there—that he could tell you more than I." He hesitated. "I think also he has something that belonged not to Mynheer John."

"To whom then?"

"I think to Mynheer Cornelius." The cold yet brilliant light in his eyes startled the old man. "I do not know," he added hastily. "Will you not come upstairs?" He came round the counter and stood with his hand on the door.

"What thing is this your artist has that belonged once to Mynheer Cornelius de Witt?" Don Roman asked steadily.

The gunsmith opened the door. "Indeed I do not know, Mynheer. Will you not come upstairs?" he repeated. Don Ramon followed him silently up the clean narrow stairs to a small landing that contained three doors, one of which led to the studio of Mynheer van Oost. As Don Ramon stepped into the little, brightly-lit room he saw the artist seated before an easel painting on a small panel of wood. Before him on a shelf against the wall a clear brown glass, a peach, a bunch of grapes, two striped carnations and a vine-leaf were arranged in elegant disarray. He rose up instantly at the sound of the opening door and stood with his palette on his thumb. He was a small man, very neatly dressed in grey with a courteous quiet air of self absorption.

The gunsmith began some explanation; Don Ramon cut him short. "Mynheer, if you will spare me a few moments I will tell you what I interrupt you for."

The painter bowed. He thought this young man had some commission for him. He motioned to the gunsmith to withdraw, offered Don Ramon a stool and returned to his work placidly. "Well, Mynheer," he said, screwing up his glance on to the peach, "you will forgive me if I continue my painting, but this time of the year the fruit and flowers are so costly and last such a little while."

Don Ramon made no answer. He looked with a strained and absent gaze at the white-washed walls, the canvases, goblets of gold and silver standing on the floor, the two doves in a wicker cage by the window, the porcelain stove whose warmth made comfort in the bare room. Mynheer van Oost, a little surprised at the silence, glanced over his shoulder for a clearer impression of his visitor. He saw a young man of a rich handsomeness, a port sombre and contained, well dressed in black, weaponless, and holding on his knee a plain hat with a long white feather. The precise confined lines of the neat room threw into the relief of contrast a dark-complexioned face, ruddy leopard-coloured hair, eyes darkly blue and a figure of slack magnificence that the painter was quick to appreciate. "You are a patron of the arts, Mynheer?" he inquired, knowing that he spoke to a gentleman of quality.

Don Ramon glanced at the exquisite marvel of jewelled colour on the easel as a man might glance through the portals of another world. "Ah, yes, you paint," he said. "Who for now, Mynheer?"

"The Prince," answered Mynheer van Oost. "I have, with many others, to thank the kindness of his Highness, who, despite the great expenses of the war, ordered near a hundred pictures a year for his galleries at Dieren and Soestdyck."

Don Ramon frowned. "I also have been employed by the Stadtholder," he said. "I am a wrestler of stringed instruments."

The surprise on the painter's face was hardly concealed. "A wrestler!" he repeated.

"I was once in this employment to the daughters of John de Witt," continued Don Ramon. "I had great favours from him and from...his brother."

Mynheer van Oost laid down the palette glistening with wet pigment and listened, impelled to attention by something intense and painful in the manner of the other.

"I was in the shop below, having my sword mended. I saw—I mean the man told me he had a fragment of the mantle of John de Witt...It roused memories of a great man, his goodness to me...I was told that you had brought it, and that you had some relic that belonged to...Mynheer Cornelius de Witt."

"I do perceive," returned the painter gently, "that you were much attached to these statesmen. I also, Mynheer had cause to be grateful to Mynheer the Grand Pensionary. I went out on the evening of his most bloody murder."

"Do not, I pray you; recite me what you saw," said Don Ramon hoarsely.

"Then what did you want with me?" asked the painter mildly.

"This—this thing that belonged to the elder brother—something he had that day—something of his you bought in the streets?"

Mynheer van Oost rose, gave his visitor a look full of curiosity and went to the deep cupboard in one corner of the room. "You knew Mynheer Cornelius?" he asked.

Don Ramon got to his feet. "Yes, I knew and...loved him." The words were calmly spoken yet echoed like a sob in the little chamber.

"Well," said Mynheer van Oost, "I have kept it sacredly and you will be the first to whom I have shown it. If you knew him (which I never did) you have more right to it than I, and perhaps you would have the courage to return it to Mevrouw Maria de Witt, which I never have had." With this speech he brought from the dark press a handsome box of inlaid wood, black, polished and the insets of ivory and silver.

Don Ramon said nothing. He fixed his deep glowing eyes on the box as Mynheer van Oost unlocked it and raised the lid.

"Vanitas! Vanitas!" murmured the painter with a little sigh as he placed the open casket in Don Ramon's hand. It contained a silver case of an unusual and ominous shape. A swift cold touched Don Ramon's soul and body; his blood seemed numbed in its course, his breath stilled on his lips.

"Mynheer," he asked in a sharp voice. "What have you here?"

The painter answered reverently: "The heart of Mynheer Cornelius de Witt."

A sound like a rushing sob broke from the young man. He sank into the window-seat with the box clasped to his bosom, and the disturbed doves in the wicker cage raised a pretty noise.

"I bought it from a jeweller who saw it on an inn table."

"Enough! Enough!" cried Don Ramon. "If there is a God he will bless you for this," he added passionately.

"It might cost me my favour with the Stadtholder," answered the painter, "but I could do no less—since he was a brother of a man who had shown me kindness. The jeweller made the case, Mynheer, and I put it in a box I fashioned when I practiced those arts."

Not one word did Don Ramon hear. He had lifted that dreadful-shaped case from its white silk lining, and held it up in his long fingers and gazed at it with enthraled eyes. It was of plain silver, on the front the three gray hounds, the arms of De Witt, and under that this inscription:

The heart of Cornelius de Witt, Admiral and Ruard of Putten, who was barbarously massacred the twentieth day of August 1672, together with his brother, John de Witt, Grand Pensionary of Holland, between the Gevangenpoort and the house in the Kneuterdyck, by the people of the Hague, who did this murder in the name of William Henry of Nassau, Prince of Orange.

"You think it bold?" questioned the painter. "Well, I was very happy under John de Witt, as well off as under this young man, hero though he be—not that I would say anything against his Highness..."

"I will give you," said Don Ramon as if he broke a silence, "what you wish for this."

Mynheer van Oost smiled. "I do not trade in such things. Since his sons are dead, it should go to Mevrouw de Witt."

"I will take it to her...I...mean the family have sought for this. Forgive me, I have much on my soul."

"Take it," returned the painter warmly. "I have thought that the heart of a murdered man was not of such good omen, but you will know what to do with it for I observe that you loved Mynheer the Ruard."

Don Ramon returned the case to the box, which he locked, and rose. His great stature dwarfed all the little things in the room. He picked up his fallen hat mechanically. "Thank you," he said. "I thank you."

The painter thought him brief and blunt. He marked that he neither offered his name nor his abode, yet it was impossible to doubt he was an honourable man, and one who had been moved by this pitiful relic of a patriot and a martyr.

So Don Ramon went down the stairs and into the street with no word or answer to the gunsmith, who saw him in the passage and called out that his sword was ready. He turned rapidly toward the town, walking briskly as a man with a set purpose; then at the corner of the street he felt the road dip beneath him and the houses sway. He stumbled against the wall and drew a painful breath; he lifted his eyes to the clouds, cold, lofty, piled high to the utmost arc of heaven, and his lips trembled.

The street was shadowed and still, the houses closed and mournful, but behind these clouds was an inner light that guilded their shapes with a steady radiance.

CHAPTER XII. THE TRAITOR

The gunsmith's shop, the artist's room with the glowing stove, the cage of doves, the glittering painting of still life had become to Don Ramon as the distinct yet distant creations of a dream. He remembered them with a kind of horror as he leant against the corner of the house and stared at the box that contained the heart of Mynheer Cornelius de Witt. In his right hand he held the key, which was fantastically shaped of fine silver filigree; as his fingers slackened, it fell with a clear clink to the cobbles. The sound recalled thoughts that galloped wildly to regions fearful to enter. He stooped, caught up the key and in raising his head saw Mr. Dermot Fairfoul crossing the end of the street, and looking at him with a careless yet pointed air of insolence. The blood began to stir in the frozen veins of Don Ramon; he stepped lightly across to the Irishman. "Where are you going?" he asked in a thick tone.

"What is that to you?" demanded Mr. Fairfoul, coming to a pause.

Don Ramon laughed and laid his hand heavily on the other's shoulder. "Where are you going?" he repeated.

Mr. Fairfoul noted dangerous eyes, a reckless bearing, a look that he had never seen on the serene face of Don Ramon before, and he used the instinctive caution of a man face to face with an unusual mood in another. "I am going to the Binnenhof," he answered pleasantly enough.

"I think you spy on me," said Don Ramon with a smile.

"Spy—on you?"

"You are very often in my path."

"Don Ramon, you are not yourself today," said Mr. Fairfoul firmly.

The other laughed. "Come, we always dislike one another."

"What are you seeking to put on me?"

"To the Binnenhof!" Don Ramon loosed his hand suddenly with a movement of utter contempt.

"Well, why not?"

"Who are you going to see there?"

"Who do you think?"

"Mynheer Fagel."

The Irishman flushed. "What is the matter with you?"

Don Ramon laughed as if beside himself. "You are going to betray us all, you poor creature, but not—do you hear me?—before I have killed this wicked Prince."

"You are intoxicated," said Mr. Fairfoul quickly. "You don't know what you say—in the open street!" He lowered his voice and clutched anxiously at Don Ramon's mantle in his effort to silence him.

"Do you think that I could be stopped by such as you?"

"Do you want," demanded Mr. Fairfoul fiercely, "us both to be arrested?"

Don Ramon looked past him with great eyes of dreaming hate. "If I let you go, you will warn him. I know your kind who act for money."

Mr. Fairfoul answered desperately. "If you must talk like a madman, come outside the town."

"Away from the Binnenhof," answered Don Ramon. He added sombrely, "If no other way, I can kill you."

"What!" exclaimed Mr. Fairfoul softly, "we shall see as to that."

They walked in a rapid silence through the glooming streets out on to the fields toward Ryswyck, where Don Ramon had walked with Father Constant in the earlier afternoon. Here by a canal and a clump of alder-bushes, Mr. Fairfoul came to a stand. "Now," he said, "if you are sane and sober, explain yourself."

Don Ramon seated himself on the close-shaven stump of an alder. Behind him a distant windmill with a thatched roof cut the straight line of the horizon; overhead the clouds were changing, submerging into one hard threatening darkness.

"It came to me when I saw you," said Don Ramon slowly, "that you must on no account betray us—because of my wife as well as because of what I have to do."

Mr. Fairfoul moistened his lips and frowned anxiously. "Who," he asked, "gave you this character of me?"

"I know it for myself," said Don Ramon calmly.

Mr. Fairfoul forced a laugh. "Something has turned your brain."

The other ignored all he said with the settled calm of a man absorbed in other issues.

"My life," he said, "is of no value beyond this one use— *afterwards* you might betray me to the scaffold, not before. I will see to it not before."

"Why," cried Mr. Fairfoul, rather pale before this mood, "why do you suspect one who has gone as deep into this affair as any—as yourself?"

"The death of the Prince is nothing to you," returned Don Ramon, "save as you can make money out of it. You know very well that though it will ruin Holland and elate France, it will bring death to those immediately concerned. You would not wish to lose your life for that, would you, Mr. Fairfoul? No, you would rather make a fortune by betraying us all." He spoke with almost painful clearness and slowness and when he finished smiled dreadfully.

The Irishman shivered with anger. "I will leave you to debate these thoughts alone," he said. "I take no heed of your insults, for I do think you mad." He stepped back as Don Ramon rose from the alder-stump. "Mad," he repeated and was turning away. "Since I can get no reason from you, I have no wish to argue here."

Don Ramon was lightly across his path. "If I have to knock you senseless you shall not go!" He put his hand to his side.

The Irishman exclaimed quickly: "You are unarmed. If you force folly I'll not be answerable. Stand aside."

His quick temper flamed up as the other gripped him firmly by the sleeve. "You are unarmed," he repeated on a note of warning.

"I remember," answered Don Ramon, "I left my weapons with the gunsmith. Yet I can prevent you."

"You are a very great fool," exclaimed Mr. Fairfoul, wrenching at his sleeve. "Suppose I wished to betray your fanatic scheme, is this the way to stay me?"

"Yes, this!" cried Don Ramon and had him by the throat.

Mr. Fairfoul swayed. He was the slighter man and animated by no such deep passion; but he kept his footing, struggled himself half free and slipped his hand round to the secret pistol he carried. Don Ramon saw the action, gave a short excited laugh and loosed his hold to grasp the weapon but the Irishman was too quick for him. He brought the butt end down with ugly force on the other's tawny curls where they swept back from the brow.

Don Ramon gave a sick lurch, threw out his hands and fell sideways on his elbow.

"I told you you were a fool," gasped Mr. Fairfoul.

Don Ramon laughed under his breath, tried to rise and slipped on to his face unconscious. With shaking fingers Mr. Fairfoul arranged his disordered clothes, replaced his pistol and picked up his hat. The stern grey clouds were breaking in a smear of dull red behind the windmill; a dreary sunset was closing into a colourless day. Mr. Fairfoul turned briskly on to the high road and so back into the town. He went to an eating-house off the Plaats, had a good dinner and sat over it till the clocks struck six, then he took his way through the cold, lit streets to the Binnenhof. He asked for the Grand Pensionary and after some delay was admitted.

His interview with Mynheer Fagel was brief. It ended in that gentleman taking him in his coach to the *Huis ten Bosch* and demanding an audience of the Stadtholder.

The Prince was at dinner, but the Grand Pensionary sent in a message talking of important business, and William, with his mind ever on the alert for complications of international politics, came out instantly. He found Mynheer Fagel in the white-and-black-tiled lobby.

"What is this?" he asked at once.

"Your Highness," said Mynheer Fagel impressively, "I have a rascal without in my coach who is prepared to give a full account of a plot..."

"A plot!" interrupted the Prince impatiently and with some disappointment. "I thought you came with weighty news."

But Mynheer Fagel stood his ground. "I know how regardless Your Highness is in these matters, but this is a serious affair. The man was with the army and has been employed to intrigue with the Republican faction in Amsterdam..."

The Prince was at once caught by that. "Amsterdam!" he frowned; then, "I will see the fellow and discover if there is anything in this."

"Not alone, Highness?"

"Mynheer Fagel, go and speak to the Princess, who is making a lonely dinner and finding us all mighty dull after Whitehall."

The Grand Pensionary, who had had one glimpse of a lady of a discomposing splendour and foreign richness and was shy of the scorn of royal beauty, endeavoured to excuse himself, but the Prince commanded him into the dining room, and himself gave orders for Mr. Fairfoul to be admitted into the small sombre chamber where Mr. Mompesson had once been received. A few candles were hastily lit and the curtains drawn across the November evening. There was no fire and the Prince noticed it and annoyance clouded his humour; the cold was in his blood and he hated chilly rooms. He stood on the hearth, in his brown dress and black sash, and bent but watchful pose, looking like a haggard falcon, slim, alert, fine fibre drawn taut with acute contained passion and steady compelling eyes of unfathomable meaning.

Mr. Fairfoul entered, and thus found himself, a few hours after his mad encounter with Don Ramon, in the presence of the Prince, against whom that young man had launched his hate. He was quite composed and swept the Stadtholder a courtly bow; but William was at his sternest, and his sternest was an iron humour of freezing gravity against which even impudence spent itself in vain. "Mynheer Fagel," he said, "tells me you have some information you would sell to us."

The Irishman answered with no abatement of his calm. "Not sell, Your Highness. I can tell you of a plot that..."

William broke in with a dry scorn: "I hear of these plots every day. If you come here to amuse me with idle tales you will find it a dangerous game. Who are you?"

"Dermot Fairfoul, Sir, Irish and a Catholic. I was with Your Highness your Spanish forces in the last campaign."

"Plotting the meanwhile against my government, eh?"

"No, your Highness. I was dismissed by my officer for a small fault of discipline, and, leaving the army, fell in with one Lacruez who I had known before, and he led me on to engage in schemes between the French and the Republicans in Amsterdam." He knew the man he spoke to well enough to couch his speech in open and concise terms, and with a quick glance under his lids marked the effect of it.

The Prince was imperturbable in look and voice. "What went wrong with this bargain that you come to me?" he asked.

"Sir, I found myself, to my extreme horror, involved in an inner plot which aimed at nothing less than the life of Your Highness."

"And you thought that dangerous?"

"I thought it infamous."

"And so resolved to betray your accomplices," said the Prince quietly. "Well, go on, Sir."

"What I have now to disclose is of so surprising a nature..."

"Do not trouble yourself about that, Mr. Fairfoul, I am used to surprising things."

The Irishman, slightly discomposed, bowed. "Your Highness will remember that when the Mynheeren de Witt met a just death at the hands of the people, who punished them for the usurping pretenders they..."

Again the Prince's cold voice cut into his speech. "The Mynheeren de Witt were my friends and great men; speak of them with respect, and do not try to put on this vile form of flattery."

The tone was like a whip and even Mr. Fairfoul's brazen cheek flushed; he took up the thread of his discourse with difficulty. "Mynheer Cornelius de Witt left two sons—both of whom went abroad; the young died and the elder caused it to be given out that he too was dead of the plague at Venice—but he returned to the Spanish lowland and lived in Brussels under a disguise. There I met him. He was seized with a fever and became very ill, and one Dona Teresa, daughter of this Lacruez, nursed him..."

"This," said the Prince, "is of no interest to me."

"I must beg a little longer—a few more words. This son of Cornelius de Witt had been a lazy drifting fellow since his father's death, and after this fever he cherished the black design of murdering Your Highness—to whom," added Mr. Fairfoul with some malice, "he attributed the death of his uncle and father."

William turned his head and looked down on the floor so that his commanding profile, with the high arched nose, curved lips and cleft chin, was toward Mr. Fairfoul, who continued with more confidence before lowered eyes: "This Cornelius de Witt became drawn into the French plots at Brussels, and was ever foremost in the intrigues that were to ruin Your Highness. About a year ago he came to the Hague, calling himself a Spanish Protestant and pretended to the tuning of stringed instruments. By this means and through the help of a traitor in your service, he gained access to this palace and was the means of conveying much information to the French. This Lacruez also came to the Hague under the disguise of a merchant, and the two were engaged to encompass the death of Your Highness, which was to be the signal for the rise of the French factions and the overthrow of Holland."

"Go on," said the Prince without looking up. "Finish what you have to say, Sir."

"When it was known that Your Highness would accomplish this English marriage, it was resolved in Paris that you and Lord Danby must go—and this Cornelius de Witt was the man to despatch Your Highness, which he intended to do the first time you rode on the sands at Scheveningen; and I, knowing no other way to prevent a murder, am here to give Your Highness this information."

The Prince did not speak and Mr. Fairfoul continued eagerly: "If Your Highness is apt to disbelieve me I have papers which will prove what I say, and you may search the house of this De Witt, where he lives with his wife, the daughter of Lacruez."

William raised his eyes. "You tell me," he said, "what I have known for a year."

Mr. Fairfoul stepped back and clutched the chair behind him. "Sir!" he exclaimed.

"And I can give you," continued the Prince, "some details that you have omitted—such as that outside Ath you endeavoured to put a bullet through me." He smiled. "Did you think that I did not see you? I have good eyes and a good memory, Mr. Fairfoul."

The Irishman's dark face was flecked with pallor. He pulled himself erect and answered thickly: "Your Highness is mistaken. I have been in no plot but what I was led into by this wicked De Witt."

"You are," answered the Prince, "the very contemptible hanger-on to the sins of better men. What you have told me I know, and will deal with in my own way. As for you—I had better have had you shot outside Ath as I advised."

"I was never near Ath!" exclaimed Mr. Fairfoul. "Your Highness is deceived. If you knew of these plots I was not aware of it. I wished to save your life..."

William took a step forward. "Keep your lies," he said in a cold disdain. "What can you tell me of these intrigues in Amsterdam?"

Mr. Fairfoul measured him with a baffled glance, then said sullenly: "Nothing."

"Ha! you mean you will not. You are to buy your freedom by betraying the more reckless plotter, and will use it to continue to work for France. It is a pretty scheme, Mr. Fairfoul, but one that will not serve."

"What does Your Highness mean to do?" cried the Irishman savagely.

William rang the bell. "You go to Loevestein," he said, "for you are a dangerous-talking man and I will have you silenced."

Sheer thwarted anger and swift hate held the spy and traitor dumb. "One question—how do you know this man to be the son of Cornelius de Witt?"

Mr. Fairfoul saw a gleam of hope in that; despite everything the Prince was interested, it seemed. "He betrayed himself a thousand ways. Among other things he treasures one of the medals struck in '72 and the face on it of Mynheer the Ruard is his face."

The usher entered in answer to the bell.

"Tell the officer on guard," said the Prince, "to get a plain carriage and an escort and take this man to the Gevangenpoort. I will send out my orders."

Mr. Fairfoul gave a furious exclamation. He prided himself on being a clever man and here he had walked, like any fool, straight into the trap.

He began some incoherent speech, but William silenced him. "Any disturbance now will not help but damage your case. The soldiers are without. I advise you to go quietly."

Mr. Fairfoul controlled himself. He considered that he had been always careful about documentary evidence, and that once on his trial he might be able to implicate his enemies without betraying himself; and there were so many powerful men whose secret he held that they must, out of self-defence, protect and save him; so he turned and followed the usher without a word.

But the Prince foresaw his line of action quite clearly and had other ideas. He sat down to the desk in the corner and wrote out brief orders that the prisoner, with the greatest secrecy, was to be taken to Loevestein and there kept from all communication with any one. There was to be no trial. In these matters his Highness was absolute. As he sealed up the paper and sent it to the officer, he smiled rather grimly at the thought of the pretty plan of vengeance he was spoiling for Dermot Fairfoul.

CHAPTER XIII. THE WIFE OF THE STADTHOLDER

Don Ramon sat up, shivering, and looked about him on a glimmering world. A steady sleet was falling and the pains of fever shot through his limbs. He dragged himself on to his knees and fell over again with a cruel ache in his head. Before him the windmill stood black against a flat silver sky; he realized that this was the dawn. Old horrible fancies that had not touched him since his illness in Brussels crowded upon him, and so powerful was their spell that he began to imagine himself still lying in the bed with the red canopy, through long nights and days, fighting disembodied terrors with still feet and powerless hands. He knew he was cold, yet it was as though a blanket of ice had been flung over burning limbs, for he felt his blood run hot despite the sleet. With a broken call and a mighty effort against these swarming terrors, he struggled on to his elbow and tried to rise.

As he moved he saw lying in the wet grass a black and ivory box. Instantly he recalled everything. He stretched out his hand for the dear object and snatched it to his bosom and lay on his side holding it so between his heart and the bare earth. He remembered now what had happened and the incredible folly of his behaviour; the unthinking impulse that had led him to interfere with Dermot Fairfoul when he was unarmed and beside himself with a fierce passion. By now, the Prince knew; the traitor must have gone straight to him. Don Ramon kept repeating that to himself. "By now the Prince knew..." Teresa must be already under arrest. Poor soul, how she would have waited for him last night. He must go and see...

Again he tried to rise. The sun was strengthening and the rain had ceased, the added brightness was added strength. He clutched hold of the smooth alder-branches and got to his feet, but he found that one of his ankles was agony beneath him, having been twisted in his first fall. He was so near the high road that he could see it, lying long and white between the level wet fields, and he knew that he was not far from the town; yet to walk there seemed as impossible as to walk to Amsterdam. His movements had shaken the warm blood through his matted hair on to his brow. He wiped it out of his eyes with his sleeve, set his teeth, held the ebony box tightly to his breast and made painful progress to the roadside. After a few steps he fell to his hands and knees and dragged himself desperately that way, his thought now that once on the high road some passer-by might assist him to the town; but when he reached it, he fainted again and lay prone with his head across the stones that bordered it.

The next thing he was aware of, was the sound of a coach that thundered through a heavy dream. He opened his eyes on to bright sunshine and had a confused impression of an equipage with four white horses coming toward him. He cried out incoherently; a beautiful face appeared at the coach window; voices struck strangely in his ear; the horses drew up, the coach door was opened and a lady appeared on the step. The sight of her cleared the brain of the wounded man. He summoned all his strength and sat up, raising his head. "Madam—if you would send some one..."

The lady came impetuously toward him and gave an instinctively horrified exclamation at his appearance. He had an open cut on his temple, a torn bruise on his cheek; his hair was thick with blood, his clothes wet, clinging to him and stained with mud. That he was a gentleman was obvious and added to the terror of his condition.

She spoke to him in French. "Is this highwaymen, Sir?" Then impulsively: "Will you get into the coach?"

He saw that she was driving from the town and answered with difficulty: "It is no matter—if you would send one..."

Another lady had joined her. The two whispered together a second then approached him, both very pale and agitated.

"We will take you back to the town, Sir," said the first speaker. She turned to the immovable footmen and ordered them to lift him into the coach.

The other made some protest. "Do you not think that we should leave him here and send some one?" she whispered.

"Indeed no," was the swift answer. "How could we?"

"Not in your coach, Madam," murmured Don Ramon, "indeed I am not fit." Her footmen had helped him to his feet and he was painfully aware of the wretched figure he made before her pitying eyes.

"Oh, poor gentleman!" she cried, approaching him. "Could we not do somewhat to stop the bleeding?" She snatched her handkerchief from her bosom and gave it him. He was glad to clap it to his face that he might be of less offence in her sight.

With some difficulty he was lifted into the satin-lined coach and placed on the seat facing the horses, that he might, said the lady, be less jolted. She gave her orders and stepped in after him, followed by the fair-haired girl, who seemed half frightened, half amused.

Don Ramon perceived the dark lady to be a very lovely creature, delicate as a blown flower, spiritual and eager like a fine flame of white fire. Her earnest and soft brown eyes were large and narrowed, long ringlets of chestnut hair fell from under her beaver hat. She was dressed in furs in a costly and foreign fashion and had a silken grace and a shy tenderness about her beautiful to behold.

He forced himself to speak as he felt the coach turn round. "Madam," he gasped, "I incommode you. I am only..."

She interrupted. "You must remain quiet. I fear you are very badly hurt. If I had some water—Indeed you put me to no trouble."

As the coach swung round on its leathers he was swayed forward almost against her silk skirts; she put out her hand to support him and caught his arm with a little sound of pity on her lips.

He was striving with thoughts of Teresa, his one object being to find her, at once.

"Where shall we take you?" asked the lady.

He could not speak, the motion of the coach was agony; groaning he slipped forward unconscious. They sprang up and supported him on the seat.

"What have you done, Highness?" cried the fair lady half reproachfully.

"I should have at once asked him where he lived," said the Princess. "I am so stupid! Now we must take him to the palace."

"There are hospitals at the Hague," suggested Miss Trelawney.

"You could not take a man of quality there," answered Mary. "How it makes me tremble to see that gash on his head. Do you think it was highwaymen?"

"Mynheer Bentinck," said Miss Trelawney, "told me that there were no highwaymen in Holland."

"He has no sword!" the Princess bent over him in a shy pitying curiosity. "And there is a ring still on his finger!"

Miss Trelawney began to laugh in an excited fashion. "Don't you think him very handsome, Madam?" she asked.

"Yes—he might be English," said Mary half wistfully.

"Oh!" cried Miss Trelawney, "but this is an adventure!"

The Princess was supporting the wounded man against the satin lining of the coach his blood was staining. She could not bear to look at him; her bosom heaved in agitation and her lips trembled. "Tell them to drive to the palace, Anne," she said.

Miss Trelawney put her head out of the window and spoke to the footmen; by now she was enjoying the episode.

"You—you don't think the gentleman is dead?" asked Mary.

Her lady was scornful. "Men don't die so easily.

"What shall we do when we get home?" murmured the Princess. She had been her own mistress such a short while that recollections of the authority of Lady Villiers still haunted her. She could not realize that she was free to do as she pleased.

"Why, I suppose you are the mistress here," said Anne Trelawney, "unless you wish to commence by being a cipher at your own court."

Mary blushed. "I don't understand these people," she answered, as if excusing herself. "I don't wish to offend. I am afraid that they none of them like me as it is. I wish," she added timidly, "there was some lady to put me in the way of what I should do."

"You defer too much to everyone," said Miss Trelawney. "You should, Highness, remember that you are a Princess of England and carry yourself as such."

Mary sighed. The coach rolled through the streets of the Hague and the unconscious man sat huddled in the corner as if asleep next the Princess, who gave him now and then a fearful glance. She did not dare to express her conviction that he was dying, nor her fear of what their reception at the palace would be, to her calm and unsympathetic lady.

When they arrived at the *Huis ten Bosch* she alighted with a horrid mixture of relief and dread and gave faint orders that Don Ramon was to be carried up the steps to the vestibule. When she saw him there, a ghastly-looking figure on one of the stiff chairs against the neat wall, her fear broke her reserve.

"I am sure he is dead!" she cried. "What *shall* we do, Anne?"

"I suppose there is some manner of physician to be discovered," answered Miss Trelawney. At this moment Mynheer Bentinck entered the lobby and the Princess turned to him with unfeigned pleasure. He was the person she knew best at her husband's court, and in the first loneliness of her exile almost a friend. She gave him breathless explanations.

"Surely I know the fellow," said Mynheer Bentinck, looking at him. "He is badly hurt—a cowardly blow, too."

Mary sent Miss Trelawney for wine, which was the extent of her knowledge of any remedy. "Who is he?" she asked.

"I do not know him, Highness, only his face seems familiar."

"A gentleman," said Mary. "It must have been robbers."

Mynheer Bentinck looked at her in some amusement. "What does Your Highness mean to do with the cavalier?"

"Indeed I know not," she answered shyly.

Miss Trelawney returned with the wine and a glass. Mynheer Bentinck rejected this as no manner of use, and fired by the gaze of two pairs of beautiful eyes, looked to Don Ramon himself with the skill learnt at the wars. A page was sent for linen, cordial, and water. Mynheer Bentinck washed and bound up the wound that Mary could not look at. Miss Trelawney held the basin and encouraged with grateful glances.

"You are very clever," she murmured.

He disclaimed all skill; but the Princess gave him the sweetest thanks, and he did not hasten over the task which made him the object of interest to these English ladies.

"My muff to put his head on," suggested the Princess, "the seat is so hard..." She handed it as she spoke. They were standing very close to the wounded man, Mynheer Bentinck kneeling between Mary and Miss Trelawney. The cordial had its effect; a little colour came back into Don Ramon's face and he moved his lips.

"You see," said Mynheer Bentinck triumphantly, "he is not dead."

"Oh, I thank you," answered Mary, blushing and glowing. "I do thank you."

Miss Trelawney smiled. "Is he not handsome, Mynheer Bentinck, now the stains are washed from his face?"

Mynheer Bentinck lifted his blue eyes. "It is a matter of taste." Then he laughed, and Miss Trelawney laughed too and snapped open her pomander, which was of foiled crystal and held four divisions of different perfumes, and put if under his nose with fine fingers. "In case you feel faint," she suggested, and Mary joined in the laugh, which was silly, meaningless, and delightful—the first thoughtless moment she had had since she left London.

Their mirth was short-lived. A door opened sharply and the Prince's pastor, in black and bands, a figure of terror to Mary, stepped into the lobby. He beheld a curious picture: Mynheer Bentinck, the most worldly of the Stadtholder's friends, dressed in a suit of London fashion, on one knee beside a chair on which a pale man with a bandaged head was resting; the Princess in her silks and furs bending over the back of the same chair; and that fair flaunting girl, Anne Trelawney, thrusting her pomander on Mynheer Bentinck while all three laughed like children.

"Madam!" cried the pastor sternly.

The laughter died instantly. Miss Trelawney drew back and Mynheer Bentinck rose. The Princess blushed painfully. "We are endeavouring to revive this gentleman," she said timidly.

The Calvinist gave her a look as if she had been the scarlet woman herself, then cast an equally withering glance on the disorder of bottles and bandages disfiguring the neat vestibule. "Who is this gentleman, Your Highness?" he asked grimly.

"I—don't know," faltered Mary, and stopped frightened. Mynheer Bentinck answered for her—gave a brief explanation.

The pastor was in no way mollified. "I trust," he said with bitter disapproval, "that you Highness was well advised in bringing into the palace one who may be a dangerous character."

"I think he is not," answered Mary with some dignity; "but a poor gentleman I could not leave to die on the road..."

Don Roman drew a sigh and half lifted his head. The sharp eyes of the Calvinist rested on his face. "I do know the man," he said coldly "He is one Mynheer Fagel has had under his observation some while. He pointed him out to me but the other day in the Voorhout." He approached and the Princess drew back in dismay. "This may be the means of bringing a villain to justice," he added. "For I do think this is the man who was in a plot to attempt the Prince's life."

Mary was white and speechless, but Miss Trelawney had her answer ready. "Sir, how can you know the fellow again in this state?"

"His face seemed familiar to me," admitted Mynheer Bentinck.

"I am sure," said the Calvinist earnestly, "that I do not make a mistake."

The Princess spoke now. "Do you not think, Sir," she said pleadingly, "that we should wait and give the gentleman a chance to explain himself when he recovers?"

"Your Highness," was the stern answer, "is over-generous."

"I am sorry," murmured Mary. She felt that she had acted foolishly and was ashamed of her action before this unfriendly judgment; her unhappiness and loneliness redoubled on her; the tears started to her eyes. Miss Trelawney tapped her foot impatiently that the Princess should take this attitude and that Mynheer Bentinck (of whom she had had some hopes) should allow it. "Here is a fuss over nothing!" she cried angrily, and tossed the fair curls that were a peculiar offence to the Dutch pastor.

"Is it a slight thing," he demanded stiffly, "that the house of his Highness should be made the refuge for such a one as I do take this man to be?"

Mary stifled the silly tears. "I am sorry," she said meekly. "Mynheer Bentinck, can you not fetch some one to end this one way or another?" As the appeal left her lips, she looked round to see the Prince and some gentlemen carrying guns enter the vestibule from the door on the right. It added to her confusion. She had thought that he was abroad. She stood like a culprit with pale cheeks.

William glanced at the little group and stopped. "What is this?" he asked briefly.

Mynheer Bentinck explained. "Now we hear," he added, "that her Highness has brought home a dangerous conspirator."

"Let me see him," commanded the Prince. Miss Trelawney stepped aside and he approached and bent over the figure of Don Ramon.

William looked at him long and intently, then drew back with something like a sigh. "Mynheer," he said to the pastor, "as it happens, I do know this man very well. He is a harmless Spanish gentleman who is a wrestler of musical instruments."

The Princess gave a gasp of relief; the others looked incredulous. "Is Your Highness sure?" asked the Pastor.

"Yes," answered the Prince curtly. He added to Mynheer Bentinck: "I know where this man lives"—he gave the street and house—"see him taken there."

Don Ramon was moving and murmuring like a man in a tortured sleep.

"Say to his wife," continued William, looking at him, "that I knew him and sent him back to her."

Mary recovered some spirit. "I am glad that he was not a villain," she said. "I do hope that Your Highness will forgive me for this trouble—but I could not leave the gentleman to die."

William looked at her shrewdly. "It is curious," he said, "that you should have been the one to find him. Where was it?"

"On the road outside the town, Sir, where we had gone to take the air."

"Well," returned the Prince, "if you would keep within the grounds, Madam, you would run no risk of these unpleasant adventures." With that he touched his hat to her and left the house with his friends and dogs, leaving her stung by what she could not but regard as a public reprimand. She did not wait to see Don Ramon carried away, but hurried into the dark little room the Prince had just left, followed by the indignant Miss Trelawney.

"Oh, Anne, Anne!" she cried from a bursting heart, "I am so unhappy." Fresh tears rose to the eyes already misty with weeping for England. "He hates me," she added. "And I cannot like him and I cannot bear this country. They are all against me and I am afraid of them."

Anne Trelawney, instrument of the Duke of York and the French, improved her opportunity. "It is monstrous," she said. "No woman of spirit would endure it, you must write home how intolerable it is here. Dr. Hooper sees for himself already what manner of place we have got into."

"Dr. Hooper," returned Mary, "makes matters no better by continually urging discontent on me. Since I am here I must make the best of it." But her tone was doleful.

"Remain in the grounds!" quoted Miss Trelawney. "Is this a nunnery?"

But the Princess was not to be roused to open indignation, nor drawn into open rebellion. "I hope the Spanish gentleman will recover," she said evasively, repenting already of having said too much.

CHAPTER XIV. THE FAIR ON THE ICE

It was after Christmas, cold, fine, and merry at the Hague. Fairs were held on the ice, on the Plaats; there were balls, dances, and theatres in the town, but the sombre routine of the *Huis ten Bosch* was unaltered. Miss Trelawney, searching for her mistress one January afternoon, found her alone in the chamber that had once belonged to Amalia of Solms but now was largely stripped of its beautiful furniture. She sat in the window-seat watching the blue sky between the interlacing bare branches.

Anne Trelawney asked where the other ladies were. The Princess answered languidly that they had gone out with Dr. Hooper, but the Prince having a strong dislike to that clergyman she was forbidden to accompany them. "Where have you been, Anne?" she added.

Thereupon that lady confided to her that she had discovered some relief to the general dullness in the shape of Mr. Baptist Mompesson, the English officer in the Prince's guard. Mary remembered him, also her first meeting with him in Whitehall. She sighed. "Do you like him, Anne?"

"Oh, I don't know. But I am very thankful for him here."

"I thought you liked Mynheer Bentinck," suggested Mary.

"Mynheer Bentinck is ever tied to Miss Villiers' skirts," was the answer.

"Most of the men are," said the Princess. "She is clever."

"But so plain!" cried Miss Trelawney scornfully.

"Yet clever," insisted Mary. "She can talk to men on the things that interest them. I am so stupid." She changed the subject rather quickly. "Well, tell me about Mr. Mompesson."

"There is nothing to tell, Highness, except that he wishes to take me in a sledge on the ice to see the fair. May I go?"

"Oh, Anne, ought you?"

"I suppose not," admitted Miss Trelawney, "and that is why I want to go."

"When?" asked Mary.

"This afternoon—now."

"Yes, Dear, of course you can go," smiled the Princess, "It will leave me rather dull," she added wistfully.

"Highness"—Miss Trelawney pressed her hand—"it will be monstrous fine on the ice after being shut up here so long, and Mr. Mompesson is such good company—it would be quite like the old days when..."

"Why, what do you mean, Anne?"

Miss Trelawney fondled the small hand in coaxing fashion. "I want you to come too, Highness!"

"Oh, Anne!"

"You know you would like it," urged Miss Trelawney, "though you say 'Oh, Anne!' in such a frightened manner!"

"I could not, indeed," answered Mary. But the temptation was strong; idleness tormented her like a plague. She had been to church twice, read her pious books, worked a collar in cross-stitch, played cards and looked out of the window till these things were unutterably stale. She had not had a single diversion since she came to the Hague, and her spirit drooped within her through sheer monotony.

"Why should you sit moping here?" cried Miss Trelawney, "when every other lady in town is enjoying herself? Why, you may die of weariness if you don't find some amusement for yourself."

"I wish we could go to Dieren," said Mary. "But these State affairs that keep the Prince here seem unending."

"The Hague is well enough," answered Anne Trelawney. "It is the palace that is so intolerable."

"Dear Anne, indeed I can't go."

"You must, it would do you a monstrous deal of good!"

"Don't urge me."

"Well, I won't go without you. What is there in it if we both go?"

"But what would Mr. Mompesson think?" breathed Mary.

"Mr. Mompesson suggested it."

"Oh, how vastly bold of him!" Mary looked shocked.

"He *is* bold," admitted Miss Trelawney, "but then, Highness, you owe him some courtesy. He is the only Englishman here."

Mary shook her head. "It is really impossible."

Miss Trelawney was undaunted. "Who is to know? We can wear masks."

"It is sure to be discovered," said Mary with a sigh. "And truly, Anne, I don't dare to risk it."

"You are afraid of the Prince," said Anne Trelawney hotly.

Mary was silent. "He does not give you so much of his own company he can object to you finding some other," added her lady.

"He is very deep in affairs," said the Princess, looking out of the window.

"It seems to me he has not said two words to you since we came to the Hague."

Mary was again silent.

"Where is he now, Highness?"

"He and Mynheer Bentinck went out some time back."

"With Miss Villiers, I'll swear!"

"Yes," said Mary unsteadily. "She was with them."

Anne Trelawney looked at her mistress keenly. "The Prince is too often with Miss Villiers. If he has time for her he has time for you."

"She is brilliant," answered the Princess. "She can speak to him about his business. He will not open his lips to me knowing I am ignorant and silly."

"Betty Villiers is a designing piece," declared Miss Trelawney. "I never would believe any good of a woman with a squint like an ogre.

"I do rather wish," said the Princess ingenuously, "that I had left her behind."

"I wish you had," agreed Miss Trelawney warmly, "but if she throws her ogre's glance on Bab Mompesson I shall say what I think of her ugly face!"

"Oh, hush, Anne!"

Miss Trelawney returned to the attack. "Well, will you come, Highness?"

Mary blushed, laughed, and rose. "I do believe I will."

"There!" cried Anne Trelawney delighted. "You'll thank me afterwards!"

"I have been so cooped up I have been like to die of spleen," said the Princess in self-excuse. "And I should dearly like to see a fair on the ice."

"Well, let us make haste, Mr. Mompesson is waiting—and, Highness, he knows that cavalier we found wounded, and where he lives, so we might go and ask how he progresses and get a peep at his wife."

"Indeed we will," said Mary, animated already. "And, Anne, what shall I wear?" She was very splendidly dressed; her clothes were the one pleasure left her, and she took a great joy in them. Her gown was pink brocade with a long tight bodice and sleeves very plain in shape but embroidered all over in flowers of white silk and gold thread.

"That will do." answered Anne Trelawney, who was gorgeous herself in blue Genoese velvet. "I will get your mantle and mask. I am sure it is cold—but Mr. Mompesson has a lovely sledge." Still chattering gaily she drew the Princess from the room, and a few minutes later the two, with hushed, guilty laughter, crept out of the palace at the back and so down to the canal, where Mr. Mompesson waited with his sledge.

His grateful air of homage and frank gallantry was pleasing to the Princess, reminding her of England and the world she had moved in there, of the time when she had been flattered for her position and praised for her loveliness, not ignored and forgotten as she was now, a mere pawn in an ardent game.

There was a white horse on the sledge and Mr. Mompesson drove skilfully. It was impossible to resist the sense of exultation given by the keen air, the blue sky, the gold sunbeams.

"Do you remember," whispered Miss Trelawney, "when we escaped from Twickenham and Mr. Sidney took us up the river?" Mary blushed beneath her mask and drew closer to her companion. She laughed delightfully. It was impossible for her to remember she was a great lady with a stately dignity to maintain when it was so pleasant to be young and free.

On one of the big canals they stopped, and Mr. Mompesson left the sledge in charge of the man at a booth for sweets and led the ladies round the pavement that edged the water, as it was impossible for them to walk on the ice.

"I wish you would teach me to skate," cried Anne Trelawney in the best of spirits.

"Why," answered Bab, "the ice would be gone before you had learned."

"Oh, I do not consider it difficult," said Miss Trelawney.

"I saw Miss Villiers on the ice in the park yesterday."

"But she had two cavaliers to support her, Madam," answered Bab thoughtlessly.

Mary's attention was instantly distracted from the engrossing sights of the fair. "Who were they?" she demanded rather breathlessly.

Mr. Mompesson was covered with confusion. Miss Trelawney's eyes shot scorn at him for clumsiness, though she herself had set the trap.

"One was Mynheer Bentinck," he said, "the other, Madam..."

Mary put an end to his hesitating embarrassment. "The other was his Highness," she finished with dignity, "was it not?"

Reluctantly he admitted it, and cursed himself for a fool not to have remembered how women took these things.

"Because," said the Princess quickly, "Miss Villiers told me she wished to go on the ice and I—suggested—that they should take her."

Miss Trelawney knew, and Bab guessed, that this was a gentle lie and the trivial episode poisoned their enjoyment. Miss Trelawney suggested the wounded Spanish gentleman and Mary agreed. She was the first to recover her spirits and seemed soon absorbed in a childish pleasure at the people and things about her. Mr. Mompesson, hearing her sweet laughter and seeing the lovely grateful joy she showed for his little attentions, wondered in his heart that the Prince should deny himself the happiness of giving delight to a creature so loving and innocent, and not have honoured his wife with his company in the little time he gave to lighter things, instead of finding his recreation in the conversation of the bold and witty Miss Villiers, whose masculine understanding was, to Bab's mind, a poor substitute for the soft charms of Mary.

They reached Don Ramon's little house in a quiet side street, and the ladies remained without while Bab entered. He returned in a moment, after a few words with Teresa, and gave his report to the Princess. The gentleman had been in a fiery fever but now lay with hopes of life, though he was extremely weak.

Mary was sincerely pleased. "Does his wife—" she altered the word, "is she fond of him?" she asked as they moved away.

"To a passion, Madam."

"And he of her?" inquired Miss Trelawney.

"It would seem so," answered Bab briefly for fear of another false step. He mistrusted the vivacious maid of honour.

Mary took the arm of Anne Trelawney. "How these stones hurt my feet!" she exclaimed. "But did you ever see such fine houses and all so clean and beautiful!"

"There are," said Miss Trelawney, "a great number of beggars and poor people."

Bab explained. "There is a vast deal of misery at the Hague, Madam, because it is the asylum for the oppressed and wretched of other countries, being the most free place in Europe, and these people that you see are unfortunate Protestants fled from persecution."

"Cannot something be done for them?" asked Mary impulsively.

"His Highness, Madam, does a great deal. That is his life-work—to make the whole of Europe as free as Holland."

Mary was silent.

Bab continued with a man's instinctive admiration of the actual achievement of another. "The Prince is the sole hope of these people and of the different classes they represent. There is not one of them who does not bless his name every time they say their prayers."

"It is something to be proud of," said Mary simply. She had no money with her; but she ran into the debt of her companions in indiscriminate charity to every forlorn object they passed on their way back to the ice, where the fair was beginning to gather huge crowds. The puppet shows, the roasting oxen, the booths decked with coloured flags, the ships on the ice were all new to Mary, as was the bright, and to her eyes curious, dress of the peasants with their handsome jewelry and fur garments. Something foreign and different about her and Anne Trelawney attracted attention as they made their way through the press, but through sheer unconsciousness she was quite at ease, and the other lady rather enjoyed the sensation their progress made.

Not until the purple of evening was staining the clear sky did they turn home. Mary sank into the sledge with a sigh of regret and fatigue and Miss Trelawney demanded triumphantly: "Was it not worth it, Highness?"

"It was," answered Mary, "wholly delightful."

When they arrived at the palace gates she thanked Mr. Mompesson in a pretty manner of gratitude that caused him to flush to his side curls, and entered the palace in the most light-hearted mood she had known since she left England. Miss Trelawney was elated too. They returned to the drawing-room and laughed at each other.

"Oh, la! what a hoyden you are!" cried Mary. "But I should be dead of dullness without you, Anne!"

"What is this?" asked that lively lady, snatching up an inlaid box from the couch.

"I do not know," answered the Princess, "it was found in a coach—*my* coach they called it—and sent it to me. It is not mine and it is locked."

"Heavy, too," said Miss Trelawney, weighing it in her hand.

"Put it away," smiled Mary, "some one will claim it—into that little Chinese cabinet, Dear. And now look what I have brought home." She opened her pink silk skirts and showed them full of silly trifles bought at the fair: fancy paper bags of nuts, little wooden dolls, models of windmills, and horns of sweets. Miss Trelawney began to pull the same assortment of articles from the depths of her muff.

"Would you dare eat that?" challenged Mary, holding out a bar of deep brown substance.

"It is only sugar," answered Miss Trelawney, smelling it, "but we could try it on the monkey."

"Oh, no," said the Princess. "Besides," she added, "that would be no proof of its quality since he will eat anything."

Miss Trelawney arranged her purchases along the top of the painted harpsichord, and Mary rose with hers gathered in her skirt. "You have a doll like mine, Anne," she laughed; "one that moves its legs and arms. I do love dolls." Her sentence ended in a little gasp for the door had opened with a startling suddenness and the Prince entered. Their laughter was so dead it seemed that they knew not even how to smile: there was not a word between them.

"You have been out, Madam?" asked William, glancing at their mantles and masks cast down on a chair.

"Yes," said Mary faintly.

"Where?"

"In the town, Your Highness."

"Who with?"

"Miss Trelawney."

He gave that lady a look of dislike. "Alone with her?"

"No—that is—" She trembled excessively and gave Miss Trelawney an appealing look.

"Well?" demanded William mercilessly.

"I wanted to see the fair, Sir," she got out desperately.

"Who took you?" he insisted, and she felt that she had never known how afraid she was of him until this awful moment.

"One of Your Highness' officers," she faltered.

Miss Trelawney was not so delicate. "It was Mr. Mompesson, Sir," she said. "And no harm would have been thought of it in England..."

"This is not England," answered William with a dreadful coldness. "And will you, Madam, allow that Princess to reply for herself?"

"You must not blame them—Miss Trelawney nor Mr. Mompesson I mean," trembled Mary. "It was I..."

The Prince took no heed of her; he interrupted sternly: "Miss Trelawney, will you light the candles?" and went to the window, coughing, with his back to them.

Anne Trelawney murmured at this servant's work, as she thought it, but she did not dare to disobey. As the pale flames scattered the twilight the Prince turned and dismissed her haughtily. She went swiftly and with a bitter flush. Mary stood motionless, holding her stiff skirts full of the follies that had given her so much pleasure a few moments before, and staring at the row of silly little toys Miss Trelawney had placed in triumphant array on the harpsichord; forlorn, lonely, and childish they looked now, like the Princess herself.

"What was the reason of this behaviour?" asked the Prince shortly.

"I was dull," answered Mary, turning away her face.

"Have you no means of employing your time that you must fill it with these indiscretions?"

"I am sorry," she whispered. "I did not mean to disobey or anger Your Highness. I thought it—a proper thing to do..."

"My mother," he returned with some passion, "would not sit to table with a commoner, and I should be sorry that my wife who has her name should not have her dignity."

"I was very moped," pleaded Mary.

The Prince was scornful of her excuses. "Is there not plenty to do in the world?" he demanded. "My countrywomen find enough to employ themselves with."

She thought him unjust and it gave some spirit to her reply. "I see no one—I am not used to living without company or diversion..."

"The amusements of Whitehall," he answered, "would not be tolerated in my house, Madam, nor is the license of England possible at the Hague. In future you will take your pleasure as I direct, and what you do not do in my company you will leave alone."

She heard that he was really angry and shivered before the most masterful will she had met. "I get so little of your company," she choked on a sob. "I did not know you cared..."

"Do not think because I see so little of you that I am, Madam, indifferent to your behaviour, or that I will permit you to conduct yourself as you choose because I have no time to give you."

She thought, with flaming cheeks, that he found time to give Miss Villiers, Mynheer Bentinck, his shooting, even his dogs, and her breast heaved with misery.

"I fear," continued the Prince, "that you have not been brought up to consider serious matters, but I would have you understand that an idle frivolous woman is a thing I would never brook." It was the first time that he had spoken to her intimately or at any length, and his wonted distant stateliness gave an added weight to this reproof now. She lifted a timid glance to his composed face and the powerful brilliance of his eyes caused hers to sweep down again in confusion.

"While we are on this matter," he said, "I would tell you several things that do displease me. I would not have you so often with Dr. Hooper. I have sounded him and do find him narrow on affairs of religion. Prayers are not piety and I will have no dogmatic ritualism at my court. A bigot in any faith is detestable, and you must learn, Madam, that there is good in other creeds and that the Church of England is no more infallible than the Church of Rome."

Mary was taken aback by this. "I do respect Dr. Hooper," she exclaimed.

The Prince went on, unheeding: "Miss Trelawney is too much your confidante. I think she does intrigue and she is a light-minded woman."

"She is my friend."

"I wish you to choose others—and I would have you spend fewer hours at cards and gossip and such abuses of the time which render you a subject for contempt."

Mary's head drooped, she began to cry.

"Neither is your dress such as is suitable," continued William. "The wife of a Prince engaged in the business I am in would gain more respect if she forbore gems and silks."

"I have always dressed like this," sobbed the Princess, with her handkerchief desperately to her eyes.

"I do not like it," he answered coldly.

"The ladies of my uncle's court wear these garments," came almost incoherently from behind the handkerchief.

"Would you," he flashed, "make them your example? I would have you in more modest gown. Let me not speak of this again."

The Princess wept vehemently and her unrestrained tears further irritated his mood.

"Do you wish me," he said, "to think that I have a thing of folly to my wife—fit only"—his eyes were scornful on the trinkets in her lap—"to play with toys?" All his vexation at his useless marriage among his enemies, the smouldering annoyance of having united himself to one who was alien to him in everything, were in the tone in which he spoke these words.

Mary made a quivering effort to stifle her tears, which she felt were doing her no good service. "It is difficult for me," she murmured wretchedly.

He came nearer. "I have not," he answered, "had such an easy life myself, Madam, that I can greatly pity those who fail before difficulties."

Again as on the occasion of their first meeting in the ballroom at Whitehall, she had that sense (she was sensitive to delicate impressions) of secret power and ardour behind his reserve. She felt he was not cold at heart but passionate and disguising himself from her. She rose impulsively and the toys in her lap fell unheeded to the floor.

"If Your Highness would only help me." There was a deep note of pleading in the formal address. She dared to look at him and clasp her hands on her breast with a childish gesture of entreaty. The Prince gazed at her curiously and hesitatingly with an expression of arrested judgment. She flushed, and added sweetly: "If only Your Highness would be as charitable to me as you are to others"—she thought of Mr. Mompesson's words about people who blessed him daily—"it would give me heart to try and please you better."

He admitted to himself that youth, gentleness, beauty, and meekness, though among the things he despised, yet had a value of their own. She had dignity through her very simplicity. He could not disregard her as a fool, though hitherto he had thought of her as little better. He had the impulse to say warm words that would have brought her to his feet, but thoughts of her Roman Catholic father, her perfidious uncle, and her sneering English chaplain restrained him. She was the puppet of his enemies, that was the unforgivable thing.

"I do hope," he said, "soon to go to Dieren, where you can have the company of Mevrouw van Zuylestein, who will instruct you in the manners of this country."

He left her abruptly, and she, who had hoped more from his silence, fell again to tears to ease her unhappiness, while the candlelight flickered in the gold and silver flowers on the beautiful gown and cast little shadows from the piteous row of the toys from the fair standing neglected on the harpsichord.

In the vestibule the Prince met Miss Villiers and Mynheer Bentinck coming up from the garden. The lady held some letters.

"Your post, Your Highness."

She was charming and very demurely gowned in grey. She was, as her mistress had said, a clever woman, clever enough to know that even the sternest heroes like flattery of some kind, if it but be delicate and apt enough.

William took the letters, stepped under the lamp and broke open that from England with impatient fingers. Elizabeth Villiers waited with as much breathless eagerness for his news as did William Bentinck, and the Prince gave it as naturally to her as to his friend.

"God be praised! Monsieur de Duras has returned with a refusal of the terms from Paris and King Charles will declare war!"

His whole face, his whole bearing changed. This was success, this at least some fruit to all his labours, not an ignoble peace, but war with England for his ally. He forgot his wife, crying in the room behind him over her dolls, and all other vexations; his eyes flashed to the admiration and understanding in the flushed face of Elizabeth Villiers.

"Now I am a happy man again," he declared.

"And before all the world a great Prince," smiled Miss Villiers proudly.

PART III. THE PEACE

"Lorsque l'on se propose un grand objet dans sa conduite, on peut suivre d'humbles chemins, pourvu qu'ils soient les plus courts; le but ennoblit les moyens." —MARQUIS DE VAUVENURGUES.

Amalia of Solms (1602-1675).
Wife of Frederick Henry of Orange and Grandmother of William

CHAPTER I. A WOMAN'S POLITICS

In July, Mr. Laurence Hyde came to the Hague on a double mission. His first design, which was to persuade the Stadtholder to an immediate peace, he was unable to pursue, for his Highness was at war; his second, which applied to the Princess of Orange, was easy to accomplish. The lady was at the Hague and anxious to see him. Mr. Hyde waited on her the day after his arrival in the town, for he was due instantly at Nymegen, there to join Sir William Temple, who was still engaged in the endeavour to bring about a peace that would be glorious to the English, acceptable to Austria, the Spanish, and Sweden, fair to the Dutch and pleasing to the Prince, a check to the French and honourable to himself.

It had been a warm spring and now the heat had grown to a heavy languor of long cloudless days and breathless purple nights. The Hague lay under the steady blaze of noon when Mr. Hyde went to the *Huis ten Bosch*. The very leaves in the wood hung motionless in the bright air, and the reflections in the thick stagnant waters of the canals were clear as if thickly painted on glass. A great company of birds were singing loud and carelessly, and the thin dragon-flies with rainbow wings sailed silently above the dry sedges. Round the palace it was quiet with an almost painful peace. An aching loneliness seemed to lurk behind the still sun and shadow on the modest house with the tall windows. After Whitehall Mr. Hyde found it the very desolation of rural peace. Within the palace there was much alteration since he had last been there endeavouring to move the steadfast mind of the Prince. Then it had been like a barracks for darkness, stiffness, and formal arrangement; now he found himself in a room, light and pleasant, with open windows, pale curtains, flowers in wide bowls, the covers off the chairs, more pictures on the walls, a parakeet in a ring, books, embroidery on the table, and a tapestry frame in one corner. The blinds were drawn over the windows and the sun on them turned them to a golden colour and filled the room with close amber light; as they stirred in the hot breeze they disclosed vivid glimpses of the bright green and golden dazzle without. Lilies, roses, gillyflowers, and pinks in the fine china beaupots gave forth lavish perfume. The sense of noonday heat without and sheltered noonday stillness within rested like a spell upon the senses.

Mr. Laurence Hyde, in black watered satins and a crimson mantle, curled, powdered, and composed, bearing evidence to the costly thoughtless richness of Whitehall, put up his glass and surveyed the room with interest. His own dark fashion of languid good looks, long black eyelashes, elegant features and heavy dense ringlets was alien to his surroundings.

He was not left above a moment alone. The Princess entered with a smiling excuse for this delay in his reception. It was not six months since he had seen her blooming at Whitehall, yet he for a second stayed his greeting thinking he had mistaken her person. She was gowned very plainly in cotton, with fine pleated linen covering her bosom to her chin, and little embroidered ruffles to her wrists; her bright hair was gathered up and concealed under a small cap of lawn stitched with black silk, and her sole jewels were a few articles of use that hung by fine chains from her waist. Her face was changed by a greater expression of gravity. The large eyes were set in an earnest look and the lips were very sweetly calm. She was taller too; in every way more beautiful.

She blushed at his instant's hesitancy. "Do you not know me, my uncle?" she smiled shyly.

Mr. Hyde kissed her hands. "You have forgotten England, Highness," he accused her, as he gave her some letters from the English court.

The Princess looked them over, saw one from her father and blushed deeper with pleasure. "I do not hear often from his Highness," she remarked wistfully.

Mr. Hyde knew that the Duke did not allow her a penny and that he had not sent her a gift, scarcely a compliment since her marriage. He waited for some complaint of this obvious neglect, but she said no more on that subject, exclaiming affectionately: "But I keep you standing, my uncle. You are the first I have seen out of England since I left it." She took the little settee by the window and Mr. Hyde a chair opposite. He balanced his Malacca cane across his knee and looked at her curiously.

"I am come to Holland on a diplomatic mission, Your Highness," he said.

"Yes," replied Mary, "I was advised of that."

"You," he smiled, "used not to have much interest in politics."

"Now," she answered, "I do understand them a little more."

"Who taught you?" he asked.

The Princess coloured. "I have learnt from mine own observation," she said.

"It makes my speech the easier, for I am charged to speak to you seriously on matters of import."

Mary paused a moment as if gathering her courage. She stared at the bowl of roses at her elbow and he waited indulgently. At last she spoke. "I shall take it very kindly if you will speak clear and simple, for I do get confused with many words."

"Do not think," answered Mr. Hyde, "that I come to frighten you with momentous talk. My main business is with the Prince of Orange, but since I am your mother's brother and in the confidence of your father, I thought I might with the more grace take it upon me to talk to you as a countryman and kinsman."

Mary fingered the watch, pomander, and scissors lying in her lap. "I do not pretend to wit," she said shyly, "and in truth cannot get your aim."

"Why," said Mr. Hyde, "you have a position you scarce know of. Now the little Prince is dead, you are Lady Royal of England."

"I am not," answered Mary, "of so vain or so careless a temper as not to have thought of the responsibilities that may fall to me, though I would bless my God did He think fit to spare me from the exercise of them."

"You did not used to be so grave," said her uncle shrewdly.

She replied in a low voice. "I am thankful that I have been able in some sort to change with my fortunes. Sure, it would be an ill thing if I remained the silly wretch I was."

"You remain, I hope, loyal to his Majesty and to your father."

"I have still that grace to keep my duty where it is due," answered the Princess timidly. "Why, my uncle, do you ask me these things?"

The large black eyes of Laurence Hyde fixed on her intently. "Your father may find occasion to command your duty."

She looked frightened. "In what manner, Sir?"

"There are many ways in which his heiress may serve the Duke."

"I cannot follow you," said Mary slowly.

"You know that I am here to make this long-protracted peace which the restless ambition of the Prince of Orange delays."

Mary half raised her hand in protest. "I have," she said, "no influence whatever with his Highness."

"You might," he answered quickly, "have a great deal against him."

She looked at the chinks of gold between the blinds and was silent.

"It is known," he continued easily, "in London that Your Highness has no enviable position here, at a dull court among heavy people with a lord continually at the wars."

"I make no complaint," said Mary quickly.

"Nevertheless, his Highness your father has you often in his mind, and would not wish estrangement to come between him and you."

"Should he not have weighed that when he married me to a Protestant Prince?" asked Mary gently.

"That was political expediency that no man regretted more than his Highness the Duke. He is sorry that you should bear the ill fruits of that necessity."

Mary drew a deep breath. "I cannot see," she said, "what good this talk performs."

"Your father would wish to feel he had an ally in his daughter."

The Princess turned her eyes on her uncle. "But I am married to one whose policy is not that of my father."

"Does the Prince of Orange claim your whole duty?" asked Mr. Hyde lightly.

"He is my husband."

Lorry Hyde smiled. "Highness—even in Whitehall it is rumoured Miss Villiers has more influence than you."

To his sincere surprise the Princess interrupted unsteadily, and with passion. "I doubt not a vast deal is rumoured in Whitehall. I have spies about me, and tale-bearers, and mischief-makers. I would I could think my father did not set them on! Sure it is an ignoble thing in him to endeavour to put strife between me and the husband he gave me to!"

"Why, Madam..." began Mr. Hyde.

She caught him up again. "As for Miss Villiers, if the Prince chooses to entertain himself with her converse I bear her no malice for it; but that it should give a handle to ill-natured talk does exercise my patience."

"You cannot," said her uncle calmly, "pretend that you are happy, Madam."

Mary looked at him with eyes dashed with tears, but she answered with dignity: "Sir, for what purpose do you come? I am very lonely and in a difficult position, and I do not take it kindly that you further strive to harass me."

"We want you, an English Princess, to stand for England in this foreign land."

Mary flushed. "I do fear, my uncle, you wish me to join my husband's enemies, and become the centre of the malcontents in this distracted country, betraying my lord his interests to my father."

Mr. Hyde was surprised at the shrewdness with which she had very accurately gauged his meaning. "You have no cause," he retorted, "to fall in with the designs of the Prince of Orange."

"Save that he is my husband," she answered. "And God who joined us cannot mean that we should live ill together. Oh me!—it would be a wretched part for a woman to play to work against the man she swore obedience to."

Well! thought Laurence Hyde, if the puritanical Prince has not converted her! he looked at her critically and said: "You are very young, my lady niece, to be so serious."

"I am very young," answered Mary wistfully, "to have to decide and resolve upon so much alone."

"You are left too lonely; you can have seen very little of the Prince this year."

"He has been at the war since April."

"And he does not acquaint you of his designs, Highness?"

"No."

"Nor write to you?"

"No."

"Nor in any way consult your desires?"

"I pray you," said Mary, "what purpose can there be in this?"

Lorry Hyde smiled. "I only wondered, Madam, what return his Highness made you for your loyalty—in the circumstances, unusual loyalty."

Mary looked troubled. "I only do what any woman would, Sir."

"Forgive me—I do not think it. It never seemed to me the Prince was one to attract a young and fair woman."

The Princess kept her eyes away. "Perhaps for all your cleverness, uncle, you do not understand a woman. You think," she added with some force, "that we care only for men with their heads feathered inside and out, and that we are mightily taken with pretty popinjays whose compliments do not even deceive us. If there be any such simple fools among us, I am not one. I can admire the Prince."

"For what?" he asked, marvelling.

"For what he has done." She glanced at her uncle and flushed. "Do you not see in him that we must applaud?"

"I see a Prince who has kept Europe in a broil these five years with his turbulent ambition."

"And I," said Mary simply, "see far more. I see a man who has pursued the work of God through great and terrible obstacles, in the face of overwhelming difficulties, in desolate loneliness, in sickness, in defeat—one who cares nothing for little things but sets his face to a distant goal—a man who does what there is no other to do in the whole world—one who is the champion of those whom there is no other to champion or defend."

Mr. Hyde laughed. "His Highness has well instructed you in his policy."

Mary answered proudly. "*You* do not understand. His Highness has never said one word of what he does, but I, living here among these people, cannot fail to see—to understand a little."

"You did not take this view in Whitehall, Highness."

"I was very ignorant—I bless my God that I have come to give value to higher things than those that occupied me in Whitehall or St.

James." Her eyes flashed through tears. She trembled and clasped her hands tightly in her lap. Lorry Hyde was at a loss to read her.

"As for this peace..." he began.

"The Prince is against it," said Mary, "therefore am I also."

"This is a woman's politics," smiled Mr. Hyde with his black eyes very keen on her sensitive countenance, "and the politics of a woman in love, Highness."

The blood rushed painfully to her face. She pulled out her handkerchief and pressed it to her lips and laughed unsteadily. "I know nothing of politics. I think I speak but according to my bare duty."

But Mr. Hyde had seen enough. Of all things unexpected this was the most astonishing; that she who a few months before had entered with reluctant tears into this match should now be so under the influence, indirect influence too, it would seem, of the stern young man she had disliked and dreaded. "Well, you have given me a pretty lecture," he said. "And I must beg your pardon for meddling in a devotion I was not aware of."

Mary paled. "You are pleased to be cross with me, my uncle, but indeed I would go far not to offend you. I think," she added trembling, "you do mistake—not devotion—but duty."

"I will give over this argument," said Mr. Hyde, rising, "and leave you to your peace withal."

Mary rose also. "You will not stay to dine with me?"

"I cannot, Highness. I must even start for Nymegen tonight."

She stood looking at him as he waited before her, a little cold, a little angry, the sunlight straining through the curtains glimmering in his black curls and the jewel-work of his scarlet sword-belt. In his stately, blithe, sumptuous appearance he reminded her keenly of that world she had wept to leave, England, her home, and the gallant men of her house and the bright ladies who had been her friends.

"I will write to my father," she said at last. "You must tell him..."

She stopped and he finished the sentence for her. "I will tell him that I found Your Highness a very complete Calvinist."

"I am in the faith I ever was," answered Mary earnestly. She glanced wistfully at Mr. Hyde, then added in a confusion: "Are you to see the Prince, did you say, Sir?"

"At his house at Soestdyck."

The Princess hesitated and drew her brows anxiously together. "Though I do not pretend to intelligence," she said slowly, "I could not be pleased to be known for a fool; therefore I pray you, leave me and what I have said out of your converse with his Highness."

Mr. Hyde looked at her, baffled. "There is no fear that the Prince would dislike your discourse," he smiled.

Mary answered with dignity. "My politics are the politics of a woman, as you said; leave them out of the talk of men."

Mr. Hyde bowed. The Princess melted at once from her instant's stateliness and took a loving leave of him, loading his memory with messages for her friends in London.

He walked homeward through the wood in a vexed mood. He did not understand his niece; in her way she was as difficult to manage as her taciturn husband. Laurence Hyde was not a man of much tact nor diplomacy; he knew it, and his violent temper was spurred by his own faults. He cursed the United Provinces, their clean streets, neat houses, orderly people, pastors, perpetual services, and immovable young ruler whom he must for the second time strive to argue into a peace. He knew that he would lose his own temper and that the Prince would keep his, and he wished in his irritation that Sir William Temple had recommended some one else to this tiresome honour.

Half-way through the wood he met Miss Trelawney in a blue gown walking with the Prince's white boarhound; a pretty figure under the luscious green amber of the slender beech-trees. They saluted each other with the greatest of pleasure; the lady, for her part, broke into a passion of complaint and question. "Mr. Hyde! if you had to earn your bread in this fashion! Dull is too mild! I am moped to death! And London—is Miss Jennings married?—and what is this about a Papist plot?—and will my Lord Danby lose his head?"

"I shall if you so pelt me with questions," he laughed, falling into slow step beside her. "But you may read all that news in the 'Gazette.'"

"You'll read of me," answered the sprightly lady, "that I have drowned myself in one of their hideous canals. I tell you," she added seriously, "that no life in an English parsonage could be so strait-laced as this court."

"I did observe a change in the Princess," he said. "What is at the bottom of it?"

"I don't know," declared Miss Trelawney pettishly. "She is always thinking of prayers and charity, and holy meditation, and her duty. I do believe she will become like those Scots ministers who do consider a white pocket-handkerchief an immorality and a laced tucker one of the deadly sins!"

"Is the Prince to blame for this?" asked Mr. Hyde.

"I suppose so—but he could not have seen less of her. He found her once reading old Hooker and complained of that holy book as too narrow, and looked grimly round the altar steps in the chapel as savouring of idolatry. Beyond that he has not meddled with her, I think, and he has been at the war these three months."

"It must be the air of the palace," smiled Laurence Hyde. "What of Miss Villiers? Is it true that she has an influence with his Highness?"

"Dr. Hooper makes the most of that to set the Princess against her husband, whom he hates," answered the lady-in-waiting, "but his tales are not all lies. Betty Villiers affects the mannish, and exchanges wits with the officers and draws the Prince to talk with her. Dr. Hooper was bold enough to speak to him about that, and this so enraged his Highness that he redoubled his attentions to the bold piece and discussed much of his business with her under the eyes of all of us. But now he has gone to Flanders and who can tell? I swear it is become my chiefest pleasure to watch Betty Villiers bereft of all her gallants, to see her sit nodding over her sewing and yawning over cards and drooping over prayers and scrawling long letters to her servants—and she and the Princess so civil to each other with 'Madam that' and 'Madam this,' and 'If it please Your Highness,' while all the time she is ready to die of spleen, and the Princess would like to pack her back to England."

"This is a dreary life," commiserated Mr. Hyde, laughing.

"It sure is. Were it not for the cross humours we are all curst with, I should think we had got to Heaven, for, sure, it is like the Celestial city, every day the same as the last and all of one sex singing psalms!"

"In London, Miss Trelawney, you said that men were a plague, but it seems that the lack of them makes monotony."

Miss Trelawney pouted. "Oh, Mr. Hyde! You are begging for a compliment and my manners are so rusty with lack of use that I know not how to make one. Come, now I'll not be satisfied until you tell me your news, for I've been ignorant of the fashions and the scandals these six months and have come to believe that all the world wears plain gowns and has a good character, so be the courtier to my silly wench and I'll play the part of rustic miss to perfection, and gape like any simpleton at stories your lady found stale a month ago!" So mingling their laughter they passed under the quiet majestical trees, reviving their native splendour in their speech; while in the palace sat Mary crying over letters from home.

CHAPTER II. CORNELIUS DE WITT

A few days after Mr. Hyde had left the Hague for Nymegen the Princess was driving in her plain little chariot about the country toward Delft, which she loved for its rich woods and low green meadows, when she saw again the young man she had brought insensible to the *Huis ten Bosch* in the first week of her arrival in Holland. He was walking along the shady road, leaning on the arm of a slight dark lady who was dressed with an almost Eastern richness rare at the Hague, and Mary, as her carriage passed them, instinctively ordered it to stop. Miss Trelawney and Miss Villiers looked up from their knotting in surprise.

"It is the Spanish cavalier, Anne," explained Mary; and as she spoke he looked round at the sound of halting wheels and knew her at once. With a flush he saluted.

"You are quite recovered, Sir?" asked the Princess, and he came to the door of the chariot in an impulsive manner of gratitude.

"Believe me, I was grieved that I was never able to thank you, Madam, for your great goodness to me."

His companion raised an exquisite pale face. "Is this the lady I must thank for your life?" she asked timidly.

"You do not know me?" smiled Mary.

"No, Madam," answered Teresa. "I was told some English ladies had found my husband."

Mary was surprised. "I am the Stadtholder's wife," she said simply.

Don Ramon made a movement as if in pain and murmured some incoherent courtesies; burning blood stung Teresa's pallor into colour. They were both grateful for Miss Trelawney's flippant remark. "Have you been ill ever since, Sir?—and are you still weak? Oh, you do look wretched pale!"

"I heard you had the fever," said Mary gently.

"I do thank Your Highness. I have been very ill—it was the recurrence of an old malady. I am better now," he answered firmly but faintly.

"How did you get such a keen blow?" asked Miss Trelawney curiously. "Was it thieves or a private enemy?"

He stood erect, holding his side, the sun full on his rich locks and contained face. He gave the fair waiting-woman his serene smile. "A private enemy, Madam."

"Oh, me!" cried Anne Trelawney. "And what became of him?"

"I have never seen him since," answered Don Ramon truthfully. "He must have fled the country."

"What was the cause..." began Miss Trelawney, but the Princess checked her. "Hush, Anne." She smiled at Don Ramon's wife. "I have not seen you before—in the Voorhout or at church, Madam."

"I never go on the Voorhout, Madam, for I have no carriage, and Your Highness would not see me at church for I am Romanist."

"Oh," said Mary. She found it hard to get it out of her head that this man was a gentleman of quality though she had good assurance that he was not. "You are a wrestler, I think?"

"Who told Your Highness so?" asked Don Ramon quietly.

"Why—it was the Prince."

Miss Villiers, who had resumed her knotting, glanced up for a moment at Mary, then down again.

"You were," continued Mary sweetly, "in the employment of his Highness?"

"Yes—and he..."

"Knew you, Sir, which saved you some inconvenience, for there were some there," Mary smiled, "who vowed you were a dangerous conspirator, and would have pushed it some lengths had not his Highness stood your guarantee."

Don Ramon answered calmly: "I am grateful to the Stadtholder."

"When you are quite recovered," said the Princess, "come to the palace, for I have an old virginal that did belong to my great-aunt which is very much in need of repair—let your wife accompany you."

Teresa curtsied, and he replied. "I am greatly beholden to the goodness of Your Highness."

Mary smiled and commanded the chariot to proceed.

"They were both very stiff and tongue-tied!" exclaimed Miss Trelawney petulantly. "I'll swear he is too good for that little pale creature, who seems to me a person of no quality."

"She is handsome and I should think good," answered Mary, "but you, Anne are always one for finding fault."

Miss Trelawney shrugged her shoulders. "Highness, could we drive into the town. I have to buy those candles my Lady Sunderland wrote me for—those that are six to the pound and burn better than any she can get in England, she says."

"Mr. Hyde can get them," answered Mary.

"Why, he has his hands full of commissions. Besides," coaxed Miss Trelawney, "I want to buy a silk petticoat. It is so pleasant at the bazaars."

"Well, if you will." Mary yielded as she always did, but after the direction was given and the chariot turned toward the town Elizabeth Villiers spoke without looking up. "I should have thought, Miss Trelawney, that the times were of too serious a complexion for you to take such pleasure in trifles."

"What have the times to do with me?" inquired the other lady scornfully.

"The war is sufficient in itself," flashed Miss Villiers, knotting faster.

"Neither you nor I have husbands there," said Anne Trelawney maliciously, "and I for one do not concern myself about the lords of others."

Miss Villiers kept her eyes down; there was no change in her calm face and she did not answer, but Mary blushed furiously. "Anne, you are a giddy creature," she exclaimed. "You know that we must all be concerned in the war."

"I am neither Dutch nor French!" answered Miss Trelawney. "And I do not care which of them is victorious."

Mary's eyes darkened. "You are in my service," she said haughtily, "and you will remember it."

Anne Trelawney was irrepressible. "Am I to make Betty Villiers my example," she asked, "and go four times a day to pray for the safety of his Highness?"

"It is," said Mary, "what we all should do. More prayers would do you good, Anne."

Miss Trelawney darted a sarcastic glance at the grave and unmoved face of Elizabeth Villiers, who would not even give her the satisfaction of blushing. "Perhaps," she said, "his Highness would not take these attentions so kindly from me as he does from Miss Villiers."

The Stewart temper flamed up in Mary; she went pale to her lips, and the instant anger of her face frightened Miss Trelawney.

"Madam, you will leave for England tomorrow unless I have satisfaction for this."

The reproved lady trembled into peace and the three drove through the streets of the Hague in a deep and painful silence. Miss Villiers broke the tension by saying in her low soft voice: "What bazaar is Your Highness going to for the candles of my Lady Sunderland and Miss Trelawney for her silk petticoat?"

Anne Trelawney began to cry; Mary was distressed and agitated. "The first we come to," she said. "Anne, I wish you would not cry—in the open street too!"

Elizabeth Villiers glanced under her lids from one to the other and continued her endless knotting.

"I declare," sobbed Miss Trelawney, "I am so moped I don't know what I say or do."

The Princess accepted this unsatisfactory excuse. "If Miss Villiers will overlook your incivility," she said, "I'll forget it."

"I?" Elizabeth Villiers lifted the brown eyes with the cast in them that was the handle for so many ill-natured remarks. "Why I never even heard what Miss Trelawney said."

Anne Trelawney knew that she had and longed to retort, but managed to restrain her unruly tongue, and the three entered the bazaar in a kind of armed peace.

Don Ramon and his wife, traversing the road slowly, held converse of a different kind.

"I might have guessed it," he said sombrely. "The English Princess—is she not a simple and lovely creature, Teresa, to be the wife of such a cold, stern, ambitious devil!"

Teresa pressed his arm. "Is she not lovely and simple enough to move your pity?" she murmured fearfully.

"My pity?"

"Would you not, for her sake, spare her husband?"

"I do not think," he said sternly, "that she would weep him."

Teresa shuddered and was silent.

"Do you imagine," he continued sternly, "that I should be turned from my purpose because his lady has a fair face?"

Teresa looked up at him strangely. "Supposing she loved him?"

"I think you need not consider that," he answered. "She must, poor soul, be very unhappy."

Teresa bit her lip. They walked very leisurely in silence and presently stopped altogether under the shade of the poplars. "Are you," she whispered, "still resolved to follow the Prince to war?"

"How often have you asked me that," he replied with tranquil tenderness, "and striven to delude me with tales of my own weakness? Anything, Teresa, so that you might keep me from what I have to do!"

She spoke almost fiercely. "It is not easy for me to let you go—to have so ardently brought you back to strength—for this!" She put her hands on his breast and frowned, looking up at him. "Almost I wish that Dermot Fairfoul had told the Prince."

"Would you have had me lose my head for nothing?" he answered smiling.

"We should have been banished—no more—but now..."

He gazed down at her with pensive blue eyes and said irrelevantly: "It was the oddest chance that his wife should have done me a good service—and that he should have stood my guarantee. Also it baffles me extremely what can have become of Dermot Fairfoul."

"He has returned to his own country," said Teresa.

"But that he should not have betrayed us all!"

"He was not the traitor you thought him."

Don Ramon sighed. "I feel very 'tired, Teresa. I have lain too long abed."

She answered eagerly: "Did I not say that you were not yet strong?"

He closed his hands over hers and answered serenely: "But I am strong enough; I have been a poor drifting thing too long. Let us go home."

She had no heart to talk, and he said no more of that subject that was ever in his mind. She knew that he had received a letter from Monsieur de Louvois himself urging him to go to the camp where the Prince was, and put the long-delayed matter through, as the French and Anti-Orange party were now of such a strength that only the hand of the Prince on the reins prevented them from open revolt; that had been the last incentive to his long-cherished purpose, and she felt, as she had never felt before, a desperate and passionate desire to prevent him from this irretrievable act. Her own happiness with him, her glimpse of the Princess of Orange, the meditations she had held with herself when he lay sick, the utter fading of her interest in political matters now she had him, a cowardly dread of the awful fruits of this deed, combined to lend her a thousand eager arguments that he should forego his vengeance; but his understanding had so mastered hers that she did not dare, save indirectly, speak against a passion that was older than his love of her, and, as she feared bitterly, more powerful.

They went home as on any other day, and she opened the lattices of their little house to let the now diminished brilliance of the sunlight into the cool rooms, and put fresh roses in the blue Delft pottery and sang to him the little songs of Spain that he loved. He was gentle, fond, and quiet, and her heart nearly stopped when she thought how almost intolerably happy she would be if there was not behind the sunshine, the flowers, and the music this hideous thing, that grew every day more terrible. She tried not to notice when he asked his servant for the sword and pistol long since fetched from the gunsmith, and looked at them and laid them down on the table where her lute rested. Her song ceased, but her fingers passed lightly over the polished brown keys of the clavichord, while she watched him take from his bosom the great silver medal he wore round his neck by a black cord and smile at it and slip it back.

Presently he crossed the room and kissed her on the brow without a word. Her hands fell from the keyboard. "What are you going to do?" she asked breathlessly.

"Only to write to our friends in Amsterdam," he smiled, and picked up the weapons and left her.

Teresa continued playing. On the open lid of the clavichord was painted a hunt; three cavaliers in a green glade, white dogs and a stream. Something unearthly about this landscape held her fancy always; the blue distance, the melancholy loveliness of the three riders, the clear stream seemed to catch the life of the music and become invested with an elfin reality. Today she thought the cavaliers galloped away like ghosts of happiness with warning glances, that the stream flowed to perpetual twilight, that the tender hills and blue glades were visions of a vanished land that she would tread no more. She ceased playing suddenly and closed the lid on trembling wires and dumb keyboard, shutting from sight the haunting picture, and went to the window and looked over the little garden in which grew a flame-leaved beech with the sun in its upper branches and a great bush of wine-coloured roses. She sat there for a great while in dreaming idleness with a heavy languor on her spirit, and sad eyes gazing on the settled pure peace of the evening light among the flowers. When at last she rose she thought the house was very quiet, and in a sudden terror of her own company went into the chamber at the front where she thought her husband would be writing.

He was not there. She looked at the brass clock and found it later than she thought, then her glance fell to the table and she saw a paper with her name across it. In one second she knew that he had left her—that it was over. She opened the letter and read it by the light of agony.

"I am gone to the camp thus privately, being strong enough for anything but your farewells. Behind the clock you will find papers with the account of my affairs. I will write to you from Flanders. May all your saints bless and protect you, Sweetheart!

"CORNELIUS DE WITT".

She thought, stupidly, that this was the first time he had signed his own name to her; then she dashed his letter to her heart and went to the press in the corner and drew out a box and tore it open in impetuous haste. It contained his long tawny curls cut off in his illness, lovingly tied with silver thread and treasured by her. She went on her knees now and stared at them, and the reluctant sun stole through the lattice and turned them to gold in her hand.

CHAPTER III. THE INLAID BOX

Miss Elizabeth Villiers sat at the window through the long hours of the brilliant afternoon and watched the eventless flight of time in the placid garden at the back of the palace, where formal trees, neat walks, and beds of flowers lay in the steady glamour of the sun. Her work was beside her, but she never touched it nor moved her idle hands, yet her remarkable tranquil face bore no expression of languor, and her eyes were alert and ardent even though they gazed on such a spot of silent peace as the empty garden. She wore a gown of brown ribbed silk of the same colour as her heavy hair, and no ornament save at her waist a crystal watch shaped like a four-leaved tulip set in gold. No one came to disturb her through the passage of the still afternoon, and the shadows were beginning to lengthen from the box hedges when the door was at last opened. Miss Villiers turned indifferently to flush at once into animation. It was Mynheer Bentinck.

"You!" she cried, rising with a stiff rustle of skirts.

"Back from the war as you see," he answered rather grimly.

"We had no notice of this..."

"No, our movements were so uncertain. We have been at Soestdyck." He sat down heavily and frowned.

"The Prince?" asked Miss Villiers.

"He is at the Hague."

"Here?"

"No, he has gone, without dismounting, to Mynheer Fagel."

Miss Villiers, silent and awkward with her own sex, was all sparkle and easy animation with men, who repaid her by treating her as a creature of sense. "Tell me," she asked, "what does this mean, this sudden return from the war?"

Mynheer Bentinck answered passionately: "It means that the States are resolved to clap up a peace with France in face of the Prince."

"After all!" she exclaimed.

"Yes, after all, Madam," he said bitterly. "Mr. Hyde is at Nymegen arranging it. Temple can do nothing, the States will hold out no longer, the Loevestein faction is so strong—the French will get their terms."

Miss Villiers coloured and clasped her right hand on the corded ribbon at her breast. "How can people be so base and weak! I wish I was a man that there might be one sword the more to draw in the Prince's cause!"

"He has come to the Hague for a last attempt to move the States, but after the loss of Ghent and Ypres, they are deaf to reason."

"And there must be a peace," breathed Elizabeth Villiers, "on the terms of France—after all this endeavour. How does the Prince take it?" she added.

"In silence, as always; but it has been an agony for him almost beyond even his bearing."

Miss Villiers paled and bit her full lower lip.

"Where is the Princess?" asked Mynheer Bentinck abruptly.

"At church, I believe."

"And the other ladies?"

"I do not know," she answered impatiently.

Mynheer Bentinck laughed drearily. "How quiet this seems after the camp!"

"Yes, quiet," she said passionately, "but I have hardly noticed it. While I have been sitting here idle as a waterman in a frost my spirit has been in the mêlée, leading the charge with you in the retreat, and I have hardly felt the pain of inaction, so little notice has my soul taken of the doings of my body!"

Mynheer Bentinck's eyes glowed. "If we had more with hearts like yours, Madam, we should not be discomfited now. The great bitterness is that we are thwarted by the timidity, the hesitancy, the littleness of others."

"That," she said hotly, "has hampered the Prince always."

"But he has overcome it so far—yet now I do think he can do no more." Mynheer Bentinck spoke in a tone of despair and pushed back the fair curls from his brow. "I tell you, Madam, that I, who have known him all his life, do marvel at the great spirit in him that supports him through all these reverses. Over-stately and stern he may seem to the English..."

"Never to me," flashed Miss Villiers.

"You understand him," answered Mynheer Bentinck, "but even you do not know him. If you could see him at the war! The thousand crosses, the overwhelming odds, the indifference, the incompetence he has to face—and all borne with serenity, patience, and unflagging resolution. At Bouchain now, he might have beaten King Louis himself, but the Emperor's general Monterez would not risk his troops on the hazard and so the Prince must see the town fall under his eyes! But never a complaint, even when he is sick to death. I have seen him, Madam, so giddy with headaches that he could not stand, get on to his horse and hold himself there in the saddle for hours, the spirit and soul of all!"

His listener flushed and glowed. "And is all this to end in ultimate defeat?"

"I cannot think it!" cried Mynheer Bentinck hotly. "Yet I will admit to you, Madam, that never have the Prince's affairs looked darker than at this moment. He is even losing what was ever his greatest strength outside his own genius—his popularity."

"Why is that?" she asked eagerly.

"They blame him for the ill success of the war, when, but for him, we had all been slaves long since!...and the French have handled the Republican faction so cleverly that this marriage, which was reckoned so sore a hit for them, they have turned to their advantage by making the people jealous of so near a connection to the English throne."

"This marriage," said Miss Villiers slowly, "seems to me every way unfortunate."

"Save that the Prince has got a good woman to his wife."

"An obedient creature, yes," admitted the lady, "but hardly one, I think, who will suit the humour of the Prince. Besides," she added with some feeling, "good women are not so rare?"

Mynheer Bentinck sighed. He looked very dispirited and tired, his buff coat and rough appointments accentuated his haggard air.

"What of England?" asked Miss Villiers. "Have you no hope there?"

"No," he replied fiercely. "The French have betrayed Danby's forced dealing with them under the King's commands, because under no commands would he go further with Louis—and he lies in the Tower..."

"So the marriage was his downfall—and the King?"

"Strains back to France, without whose money he cannot long rest. He is a false friend. Talk not of England, Madam—policies of that island vary with the weather-cock!"

"And the allies, Spain—Sweden—Brandenburg?"

"If the States sign a peace they must follow, and France will be triumphant."

He dropped his open hand upon his knee with a movement of disconsolate vexation. Miss Villiers crossed over to him and placed her hand on his shoulder.

"Keep up your heart," she comforted; "have faith in the Prince, who has never failed you yet."

"Ah, Madam, I do not doubt the Prince—but I think that he has before him what no mortal can perform. To break off the peace now is, I fear, impossible, even to him."

Miss Villiers was about to answer when they were disturbed by the entry of the Princess, flushed, and, it seemed agitated. Mynheer Bentinck rose and saluted her with tender respect.

"What is this?" she asked. "I was never told—the Prince is in the Hague, they say."

"We have just arrived from Soestdyck." He stopped rather awkwardly; he thought the Prince had written to her of his return.

Mary looked at Miss Villiers quickly. "What brings his Highness back from the war?" she asked, and laid her prayer book down.

"An endeavour to prevent the peace, Madam," said Mynheer Bentinck; "but there is no need why I should trouble Your Highness," he smiled, "with these cumbrous matters."

Again the narrowed soft brown eyes glanced from one to another as if she saw she had interrupted confidences from which she was shut out; she gave the slightest sigh and asked; "When is the Prince arriving here?"

"When he has done with Mynheer Fagel, Highness."

Miss Villiers looked at her crystal watch and said, "It is now near five, Highness..."

"I will give orders that they hold the dinner back," said Mary simply, and left them.

As the door closed Elizabeth Villiers broke into bitter laughter. "Is that all she can think of?—at such a time as this!"

Mynheer Bentinck sighed. "Yet I am sorry for the Princess," he answered.

William Bentinck (1649-1709). Engraving by J. Houbraken.

Miss Villiers looked at him; the defect in her eyes was very noticeable and gave her a sinister aspect. Silence largely robbed her of charm, and Mynheer Bentinck found himself thinking that, entrancing as she might be, she was a plain woman and Mary a beautiful one even if she had not a mind above the ordering of her household. An almost unconscious coolness fell between them; their converse became dull; they parted after a little. Elizabeth Villiers went into the garden where some other of the Prince's officers walked, and entertained them with her enthusiasm, her sparkle of interest and animation, her frank admiration of their exploits.

The dinner waited but the Prince did not return. In place of him came a message to say that he was dining with the Grand Pensionary. The sweet summer evening wore on and he did not come. The little palace that had lain so quiet these months among its trees was now noisy and excited with the coming and going of men, talk of war, of battle, of great events. Mary left them all; she could not speak their language nor understand their allusions. Mynheer van Zuylestein was courtesy itself but she felt that it wearied him to talk trivialities to her ignorance and so spared him. Miss Trelawney absorbed the one Englishman, Mr. Mompesson, and the other ladies were in some way amusing themselves. The Princess withdrew into her private sitting-room that had once belonged to Amalia of Solms, and to still the insistent throb of loneliness at her heart sat down at the beautiful lac cabinet which had always stood locked in one corner of the chamber. She had only today recovered the key which Anne Trelawney had carelessly lost months before, and, as a distraction, she put in practice a long since formed design of examining the contents of this rich piece of furniture.

She opened the flap and looked at the multitude of drawers with their handles of costly stones with but a languid interest; the candlelight sparkled in vain on marvels of craftsmanship and gorgeous gems. The Princess was thinking of other things. With an indifferent air she pulled open one of the smaller drawers; a fine gold miniature case fell out. With the romantic curiosity always awakened by discovery of a picture carefully preserved, Mary snapped open the case.

She beheld the enamel portrait of a woman, a young dark face with an old-fashioned falling collar and smooth ringlets. It gave the Princess a little start to see her own name, "Mary Stewart," inscribed beneath on the white enamel among the fine spiral ornament. At the top was a lover's knot also in white enamel, and on turning it over she saw the delicate painting of a violet, above it a crown, and beneath these words: "J'aime un seul."

The Prince's mother! she thought and she gazed at the motto earnestly with a painful sense of wondering sympathy. How had this woman of her blood, her name, exiled in this same country, united to a Prince of the same title, found her life? Mary remembered that she had died young, in the full height of her beauty, of a hideous disease, and the unbidden recollection rose of some careless remark once made to her that the name of Mary Stewart was fatal to its possessor. She held the enamel in her hand and sat back in her chair. She felt sure that by now the Prince must have returned and equally sure that he would not want her welcome. She did not care to see him join the group about Elizabeth Villiers so remained gazing at the proud pale face of this dead kinswoman of hers, whose pictured likeness seemed to evoke a faint friendly presence in this quiet room where she must often have sat, not so many years ago.

The door opened. Mary turned, expecting to see Miss Trelawney and shrinking from the interruption, but it was a gentleman. The candles were sparse and her eyes, never strong, were dimmed of late with tears; it was a second before she saw that it was her husband. Her hand closed instinctively over the enamel as she rose.

"Good evening," he said, as if he had left her yesterday.

Instantly she thought of her own shortcomings. "I should have been there to meet Your Highness," she faltered.

"I am but this moment returned," he answered, "and have been so deafened with talk of late I did shrink from joining those without. I do commend, Madam, your taste for quiet."

Her heart gave a bound that he should have actually sought out her company in preference to those she felt held all his favour.

"I do leave them," she answered humbly, "because I do not understand what they speak of."

"There is no marvel in that," he said, "since so many talking together can scarce make sense." He took the chair against the wall beside the cabinet and she her former seat. She was too shy to say that she was glad to see him back, or to remark upon an absence that he himself ignored; indeed the strangeness of suddenly having beside her this lord of hers of whom she had seen so little kept her altogether silent.

"What have you there?" he asked. He was, for the moment, too fatigued even for despondency, too worn out with fierce passion even for the sympathetic talk of his friends. He looked round the room in a kind of lassitude, noted with pleasure the difference in it, as in the whole palace that used to be so sombre, then glanced at his wife in her white lawn gown with the drawn thread cap over her rich curls and her lovely sensitive face.

"A little painting," she answered in some confusion, "of her Highness the late Princess of Orange..."

"Ah, yes," he said in a kinder tone than he had yet used to her, "there are some old things of mine in there. Is this the first time that you have opened it?"

"I did lose the key," she replied. She laid down the picture reverently.

He looked at her shrewdly; she was careful not to look at him. "You have been dull here?" he asked.

"Oh, no, Highness," she answered hurriedly. "I hope," she added, "that you find the house to your liking."

"It is very well," he answered, "but too small, is it not? I mean, when I can, to build another house at Loo, where it will be pleasant in the summer."

She was utterly at a loss to explain this new tone of kindness; he did not speak to her now as if he considered her his enemy; her spirits rose. "I do love good lodging and neat gardens," she confessed, "and I never saw either so fine as in this country."

"Yet you have excellent gardens in England," said the Prince, "and I do think you could get all this house into the cockpit at Whitehall—yet let me not interrupt your amusement, Madam."

She opened other drawers. Under his unwonted gentleness she expanded happily, even ventured to laugh as she pulled out a little tray of gems.

"Your Highness has wealth here!" she cried.

"Yet not enough to pay my debts," he answered, finding more ease at this moment of his utter weariness in her simplicity than in any brilliancy.

Mary held up a snuff-box of root of amethyst, a milky grey shading into lavender and set with little rubies that blinked in the candlelight. She gave a little exclamation of pleasure at the beauty of it and pulled out another of root of sardonyx, opaque white embellished with clear green jargons and violet spinel stones in the design of a wreath of flowers on the lid.

"You like them?" asked the Prince, looking at them critically.

"Oh, yes," said the Princess, happy in his good humour. She took up a necklet of dull mauve iolite heads and studied the faint variations of colour in them, then a ring of orange and black tourmaline and a small watch of gold filigree over green enamel.

"It is broken," said William with some interest. He ignored the case, which he opened, and looked at the works. "It never kept good time," he added. "My grandmother bought it, for the design I think."

Mary made bold to look at him now that his attention was engaged. He was as plainly dressed as she had ever seen a gentleman, in a suit of black corded tabinet with a lawn cravat with no lace to it, a sword-belt of simple leather and a weapon with a cut-steel handle, high close soft boots still dusty, and black braid buttons to fasten back his sleeves. This fashion of his clothes, his slight stature, air of delicacy, the natural hair falling over his shoulders made him so different from the men she was used to with their splendid clothes height and pomp, their long perukes and jewels, and again she wondered at this difference in him. She noted his face, stately, composed, with that expression she could not understand, sombre yet with a flashing fire behind it, cold yet conveying a quenchless ardour, even now, when his brown complexion was pale with fatigue.

Mary broke the silence. "What is this, Highness?" She held up a piece of unset lumachella or fire marble, lights of green and orange flashed dimly through its dark surface; it was cold and smooth to the touch, yet revealed fire at its heart. It reminded her of the Prince. As she gave it to him he looked up and their eyes met.

"I take it kindly of you, Mary," he said, "that you took my part to your Uncle Hyde."

This coming suddenly from his reserve left her silent, stormed with blushes. She saw now to what she owed his present humour. Laurence Hyde had conveyed to him, directly or indirectly, that she was not of his enemies.

"I have," he continued, "so many troublesome affairs in these unhappy times and am so vexed with opposition and enmity that I am glad that you do not join the array against me." His eyes expressed more; his glance thanked her, and more warmly than his words.

"I could do no less than I did," murmured Mary. "I never meant to be other than dutiful. I pray you impute it to my ignorance—for I am stupid—not to my desire if ever I displeased Your Highness." She ended rather breathlessly and bent her head over the cabinet. The Prince said no more; he returned the watch and the fragment of lumachella in silence. She guessed his thoughts were already far from her and she turned the trinkets over without speaking. The copious candlelight was over her bowed head, glimmered in the silver-gilt thread and spangles of her linen cap and the little escaping curls in her neck, left her face in shadow and ran riot in the rich gems of the lac cabinet. She opened the large receptacle under the rows of drawers, and, with her mind not on what she did, took out an inlaid box. Instinctively she tried to open it, found it locked and desisted.

William, who was watching her without appearing to do so, rose to see what she had discovered. "That is not mine," he said at once.

"It must be, Highness," she answered. "I do not know it..."

The Prince, whose memory was never deceived, even in trifles, knew that he had not seen the box before, and, as it was large and locked, his curiosity made him take it up.

Mary recalled the circumstances now of the box being brought her from her coach and locked in the lac cabinet by Anne Trelawney, who carried off the key and lost it, and had only found it again this very day.

"Found in a coach!" said William.

"Yes," she smiled. She was too pleased with his changed humour to care what was in the box, nor could she feel any interest in its history; her eyes were on the Prince, not on what he held as he studied the silver lock.

"Have you a key?" he asked.

She had none except that of the cabinet, which was manifestly too large. He took his own from his pocket and tried them, but with no results.

"A locksmith could open it tomorrow," she suggested.

But the Prince would not have that. Out of all proportion to his real interest in the thing was his desire not to be baffled by it. He seemed to take the resistance of the lock as a challenge and in a few moments was absorbed in the endeavour to force it open. He took it to the light, looked at it closely, and tried to prise the lid up with the sharp bow of one of his keys. The attempt was a failure. He made the same endeavour with the scissors of the Princess and only succeeded in breaking them. Mary could not forbear a smile that he, with so much on his mind, should so throw himself into this trivial task.

"I'm sure it is empty, after all," she said gaily.

"No—it is too heavy—and I do detect a perfume from it like spices."

She came over to him where he stood under the branch of candles and he looked up with a good-humoured smile.

"You think I have turned bedlamite," he said. "But I cannot endure to be worsted by these things."

She, only too glad to have him in this mood upon any occasion, laughed too with pleasure. "Your sword?" she suggested.

"I have no wish," he said, "to break that." But he drew it, nevertheless, held the box on the table with one hand and forced the fine sword-point under the lid. There was a sharp crack and a portion of the box split away.

"There! You have spoilt it!" cried Mary gaily.

The Prince dropped his sword, seized the box and tore the lid off, a fragment at a time. "There is," he said, "something silver within..."

"A barbarous manner to open a casket!" said the Princess. "What have you found—is it jewels?"

He set the defaced box down; his keen senses noticed the peculiar scent of pungent spices that rose and the unusual shape of the silver case now lying exposed to view. His whole bearing changed; he looked at Mary. "You know nothing of this?" he asked.

"No," she faltered, in instant fear. "What is it?"

"I think," he said, "it is a human heart."

Mary gave a little shriek and stepped back from the table.

"This is some ill-thought-of trick or jest," continued the Prince sternly. "Who has dared to give you such a thing?"

"Oh me!" she cried, very pale. "What can it be?"

"Bring a candle here," he answered, "there is some writing."

She came obediently, shivering, and he lifted the silver case from the shattered box while she held the candle up for him to read the fine lettering by, and averted her own eyes from the ghastly shape of the thing. The careful, delicate inscription stood out clearly in the red light that gleamed in the silver.

The heart of Cornelius de Witt, Admiral and Ruard of Putten, who was barbarously massacred the twentieth day of August 1672, together with his brother, John de Witt, Grand Pensionary of Holland, between the Gevangenpoort and the house in the Kneuterdyck, by the people of the Hague, who did this murder in the name of William Henry of Nassau, Prince of Orange.

The Prince put the casket down and walked away. "Who has done this?" he said. He seemed faint and overcome as one struck by a blow of physical agony; he wiped his brow and his lips and shivered violently.

Mary watched him in a staring horror; she did not dare to speak. He turned round suddenly and confronted her. "You must know something of this. Who brought it to you? Where was it found?"

Trembling, she forced her mind back. "It was the day after I brought home the Spanish gentleman..."

"Ah!" He drew himself up with the flashing look of one who suddenly sees his foe form out of obscurity. "And it was in the coach—now I understand."

Mary clasped her hands. "Tell me—what is this..."

"The heart of Mynheer Cornelius de Witt," he answered "who was my great enemy and murdered in my name."

"How is this possible?" she murmured bewildered, and tears of agitation sprang to her eyes.

"Any one in Holland will tell you the story!" he said passionately. He sat down and took his brow in his hand, wrapped in a black and bitter absorption that she could only be silent before. She was glad of what a moment before she would have regretted—the entry of a servant to say that Mynheer Fagel was at the palace to see his Highness.

"Tell Mynheer Fagel to wait," said the Prince fiercely. He took up the broken box and the silver case and left the room, leaving Mary in a wondering fear as if a nameless ghost had glimpsed across the chamber, chilling the air.

CHAPTER IV. THE UNCONQUERABLE RESOLVE

Mynheer Gaspard Fagel waited for the Prince in agitation and despondency. He felt himself overwhelmed by the crisis he was in the midst of. Though he did not understand the motives of the Prince, he wished to support him, and though he disagreed with the policy of the States he was bound to obey them, since their High Mightinesses, thanks to John de Witt, and not his Highness, were still the masters when it came to a vital issue. The Prince had saved the States, and now they began to think he was not so necessary to their security as they had at first imagined. The Republican party, rising on French intrigues, spread a jealousy of his royal marriage and ambitious designs that was potent to destroy his popularity, and his late steady ill success at the war seemed an argument against listening to his passionate demand for the continuation of a struggle in which, it appeared, he could not be victorious. It was remembered how Prince Maurice had prolonged the war that he might be more powerful in the State, nor were there wanting those to recall the words of John de Witt, uttered in warning in the Senate, that Princes could only satisfy their own ideas of greatness by sacrificing the liberty of their people. The States were also disappointed by the apparent failure of the Prince's diplomacy in England, where his friends were now in disgrace, and his party out of power before they had succeeded in inducing Charles to a firm alliance with the United Provinces or a hearty acceptance of the will of Parliament in wishing to put a check on France.

Against these failures of the arms and statecraft of the Prince, which might be explained, but could not be denied, Mynheer Fagel and his friends had nothing to oppose sufficiently tangible to satisfy biased understandings and inflamed tempers. Therefore he came now, exhausted, to tell the Prince that France had the laugh of him, and that nothing would prevent the States from concluding a peace with Louis, regardless of their allies, of their future safety, of the warnings of the man who had saved them not so long ago from the overwhelming peril courted by indifference, and this same impatience of war. His unpleasant anticipations of this interview were not lessened by the appearance of the Prince, who was in a mood even more silent and stern than he had been at their meeting earlier in the evening. He sat down by the open window with the curtest greeting.

"You have seen the States, as I advised you, Mynheer Fagel?"

"Such as I could, Your Highness."

"Well?"

The Grand Pensionary paused. "They were," asked William, "unmovable?"

"I am sorry to disoblige Your Highness..."

"Disoblige me!" said the Prince shortly. "There is greater matter at stake than that."

"I do fear I must confirm what I earlier said to Your Highness..."

"Which is the worst that can be."

"Which is that the States will make a peace," said Mynheer Fagel.

There was no change in the face of the Prince. "You think this unalterable?" he asked.

"I do," admitted the Grand Pensionary hopelessly.

"They are no way to be threatened or entreated?" demanded the

Stadtholder.

Mynheer Fagel shook his head. "All that has been done."

William looked at him shrewdly. "You, then, are resolved to despair?"

"I am convinced, Your Highness, that there is no altering the mind of the States."

"You speak, Mynheer, as if you would justify their action."

"I must admit their reasons."

"Their reasons for a peace?"

"Yes, Highness."

"So, you, sent to persuade them, have been yourself overcome by their arguments," returned the Prince grimly.

Mynheer Fagel answered firmly: "I have, these months past, done all I can to bring the States to the mind of Your Highness—but events have been unfortunate..." He hesitated.

"You mean in the war," said William calmly. "Well continue, Mynheer."

"The Loevestein faction has a growing hold..."

"And I," put in the Stadtholder with a bitter smile, "am not so popular as I was in '72. I do not doubt there are those who would do for me what they did then for the Mynheeren de Witt."

"You have still," protested Mynheer Fagel, "the heart of the country. If the people seem ungrateful, Your Highness must consider the misery of the war, the great expense, the ruin the inundations caused, the fluctuating policy of England, which forbids us to hope for an ally there; the impossibility of ever checking France by ourselves, the stagnation of trade, the rivalry of the English in the Indies, where they come and go freely while our ships are not safe on the seas, so that the shares in that company dwindle to nothing, the general cessation of all business—all this leads people to consider that no evil can be greater than the present war, and no blessing so much worth a sacrifice as an immediate peace."

The Prince sat pale and silent; the Grand Pensionary was encouraged by his quiet. "Add to this," he went on, "that the proposals France offers leave our liberty untouched, secure us another town, renew a commercial treaty that was to our advantage, and it will seem that there are inducements for the States to disregard the advice of Your Highness."

"You are a ready-tongued advocate in the service of their Mightinesses," answered William coldly.

"Not that," protested Mynheer Fagel. "I have the utmost confidence in the wisdom of Your Highness, which has brought us through our perils, but I can see no way for us now but this of the peace..."

William interrupted, "Which is to be concluded, it seems, in defiance of my wishes. Come, Mynheer, would the States do that?"

Mynheer Fagel was silent

The Prince looked at him with narrowed eyes. "If I was to exert all my authority, would they obey me?"

Mynheer Fagel's answer was not without pride.

"We are, Highness, a Republic, and no one man can force his will upon the rest."

The Prince rose and clenched his hand on the window frame. "I know well that you are a Republic," he said haughtily, "and therefore you dare to take the insolence of the common people for your law. If I were a King over you, you should know it!"

Mynheer Fagel flushed. "Your Highness takes an imperious tone— the States are our masters."

"Your predecessor might have made those words becoming on his lips, Mynheer; they sound ill from you," answered William. "You have served me, and no one but me, and you know very well that I alone have held this country together since John de Witt died, that I, and not your calculating burghers, have made possible this peace they are so eager to conclude."

"I do admit it," said the Grand Pensionary.

The Prince eyed him with the full-roused and brilliant fire of his powerful eyes. "And I have no man to my master," he said. "I swore my oaths to my country, not to this confederacy of traders—and I will do my service as God and my honour shows me, not as plebeian caution commends. If they like it not, let them raise some pure patriot from their counting-houses to their councils, and see how he will protect them against Europe. John de Witt was a great man, but he had them on the rocks from which they came to me to bring them off. Now, if my steering pleases not, let them find another captain to guide them through these deceitful shallows of a peace, for I am so made that I must steer the vessel or be set on shore."

"Your Highness speaks bitterly," answered Mynheer Fagel.

The Prince laid his hand lightly on his breast; his black clothes, his pale face and bright hair, his slender figure and sparkling eyes were set off by the candlelight against the dark background of the open window. "Do you not think," he said with full and intense passion, "that I have some cause to speak bitterly? You can argue very well from the standpoint of the people, can you not see how I stand in this matter?"

"I can see, Highness, that to you we owe our present security."

"You do indeed owe me something better than this constant contempt with which I am served."

"Not contempt, Highness..."

"What else?" demanded the Prince. "All I do is cavilled at—all my wishes opposed, all my designs opposed..."

Gaspard Fagel felt himself caught on the full tide of the bitter anguish and wrath of a strong and passionate nature, against which his ablest arguments were of no more avail than twigs before a flood. He was silent.

"Answer me," said the Prince, "how I have been repaid—answer me how I have been judged! What has been my reward for every hour of day and night given to hard work for constant striving, in incessant labour, against every difficulty? Calumny and disdain have I been repaid with. I might have taken my ease and secured my own advantage and still have been better thanked."

Mynheer Fagel answered in a troubled manner. "This seeming ingratitude..."

William interrupted, "I do not want gratitude, laudation, and submission. Had these things been my aim I had sought for them in another fashion. I want trust, belief, confidence. By God's grace," he added with deep force, "have I not *proved* I have the power to perform what I conceive? I tell you, I am so conscious of the strength Heaven has given me that even now I know I shall overcome it all." He stopped, coughed, and turned his blazing glance on Mynheer Fagel. "What have I done already, hampered and unaided? Something to make Europe listen to me, and had I but a handful who would stand by me, I would change the face of the continent. I know I can do these things; I *know* that the most vast designs any can contemplate I am equal to frustrate or further—and must I be stopped because some shopkeepers cannot get their ships home and the price of shares falls? Is every timid, trembling commoner to be listened to when he shouts out for the loss of his comforts, and I, whose life has been one toil, not heeded when I speak my mind against this piteous policy of Peace? If they have given something of their ease to the general good, have I not given all? If they have spent their fortunes on the war, have I not spent mine?" He took a turn about the room. Mynheer Fagel had never seen him so moved from his usual unfathomable reserve to such an open passion of emotion.

"You and the States," the Prince broke out again, "call the loss of towns and battles failure. You do not see that one may rise stronger from every fall and that there is no failure if one admit it not. You do not see that to have snatched back the country from such dire peril, to have maintained her liberty against such odds, to have brought the enemy to wish for peace, to have half Europe for an ally, is a triumph for you greater than these bloody and useless captures of forts that King Louis is praised for. If so much can be done in these few years, in a few more we could force our own terms, as we could have done now had King Charles stood firm."

"Yet," said Mynheer Fagel desperately, "the States are too set on a peace to see these reasons."

The Prince paused before him. "How long do you think this peace will last?" he asked breathlessly. "Only till Louis is strong enough to break it with impunity—and we, disarmed, slothful, are become an easier prey. What is to turn an arrogant warlike King into a peaceful neighbour? Do you suppose that the French will lay aside their ambitious designs because they have put their name to a treaty with us? I say that they cannot be cajoled—they must be subdued!"

"Who is to do that?" cried the Grand Pensionary in despair.

"I," answered the Prince proudly, "if you do not tie my hands. I who have taken you so far will take you to the end if you will only be true to yourselves."

"God knows, if it rested with me..."

"Do you realize what this peace will mean? Spain disabled, our frontier at the mercy of France, and that country confirmed in robbery, licensed to injustice. This war was the most unprovoked, the most shameful ever waged. Is it to end in sanctioning the oppressor in his spoils?"

"Your councils, Highness, are too true to prevail."

The Prince turned to the open window and stared out into the night. Mynheer Fagel marked his hollowed cheek, his stooping pose, his constant asthmatic cough, the unconscious movements of pain and weariness with which he shifted his head and raised his hand. "The war is killing you, Highness," he said abruptly.

"I shall live long enough," answered the Stadtholder. "I have no wish to grow old in ease and comfort, which it seems is the main desire of some of you..." He put his hand over his eyes as if weary with his expressed passion. "Now, there is enough of this, Mynheer. Get you back to your obdurate Assembly, and tell them that I am gone to Flanders."

"Your Highness is not returning to the war?" exclaimed Mynheer Fagel.

"Peace," answered the Prince, sunk again to his fierce reserve, "is not declared yet, and until it is I am with the army."

"Highness, I think it will be signed at Nymegen in a few days."

"Let them send me news of it at the camp. I shall be near Mons, where Luxembourg is. Good night, Mynheer." He gave the Grand Pensionary a sudden smile, which put him far beyond the comprehension of that statesman, who left disheartened and amazed at this great immovable spirit his Highness showed. The Prince snatched a note-book from his pocket and fluttered over the pages. The States would not listen to him; Charles had failed him; he fell back on what was always his greatest resource, his own valour, his own daring. Luxembourg would be at Mons waiting for the news of the peace to return to France. William noted distances in his pocket-book. He might reach the French camp before the news of the peace reached either of them; a fierce, bloody battle might break off the negotiations. It would at least be his protest to the world against the sheathing of the sword.

He went to call Bentinck and bid him make ready on the moment to return to the camp.

———————

CHAPTER V. TWO WIVES

The Princess Mary sat before a table against the wall of the magnificent Orange Saloon on which stood her spinet. It was a beautiful Venetian instrument that had once belonged to her great-aunt, the fair and sad Queen of Bohemia. Every one of the twenty-seven keys was deep blue enamel and the sharps were blue stones, dark and rich; the raised lid was gorgeously ornamented with antique scenes, framed in hawthorn blossoms, and the exposed wires gleamed golden in the light of the afternoon sun that poured in through the tall window. Beside the spinet lay a book that the Princess had been reading; a fine volume lately published in Amsterdam which re-told in modern French the adventures of Charlemagne and his paladins, among whom was William of Orange, ancestor of her husband's illustrious house. Neither book nor spinet engaged her attention now. She held an open letter in her hand and as she, for the tenth time, re-read it, she was forming the first independent and definite resolution of her life.

The writer was Mynheer Balthasar Bree, of whom she had heard, from Mynheer Bentinck, as the donor of the beautiful lac cabinet that now held a faint horror for her, and it began with a preamble of compliments, but the real gist of it was set forth plainly enough.

"Madam, yesterday a man was arrested for brawling in the streets of Amsterdam, and being inflamed with wine, insulted his judges, for which he was like to be heavily fined, but seeing the case go against him, he cried out that he was cognisant of plots against his Highness, and that he could tell of a wide-spreading intrigue the object of which was to overturn the government and assassinate his Highness the Stadtholder. Upon which they bade him be silent for a half-wit and discharged him, because, Madam, the city of Amsterdam is ruled by those who are in the interest of France, and this man knew too much. I, who was in the court, followed and got into converse with him, and he, not knowing me, and being a boastful fellow, was led to speak of his declaration. It, was he said, the son of the late Mynheer Cornelius de Witt who was to murder his Highness, and he was now following the camp with an English priest, and as soon as the deed was done the Republican party were to rise up and call in the French.

"Madam, I could get no more from him. I was bound to part with him, but marked his lodging and went to the burgomaster with my tale. He could not refuse to credit me and sent, reluctantly, some soldiers to arrest the man this morning. But either he had been warned or prudence had come with the morning, for he was fled, and they gladly abandoned all search for him.

William II of Orange (1626-1650). Painting by Gerard van Hondthorst.

"Madam, I feared a letter to the Prince would have no effect, as he is so heedless of his life, and there may be nothing but idle boasting in what I heard. Yet I am resolved to place it before Your Highness, who is the most fit person to decide what action is to be taken. If anything should happen to his Highness now, it would be a misfortune half the world would never recover from, since in his courage, wisdom and steadfastness we all rest our hopes of justice and   liberty."

Mary put the letter down at last, and her eyes rested on the glowing paintings on the walls, the triumph and splendour of Princes of her husband's line. She sat so, motionless, with her hands folded in the lap of her muslin gown. She recalled the young man whom she had brought home in her coach, what the pastor had said of him, her meeting with him afterwards, his unusual-looking wife who had confessed to being a Romanist, the box found in her coach, containing the heart of Cornelius de Witt, and doubtless dropped by this same young man—the words of the Prince, "I understand now."

The Spanish wrestler *was* the son of the late Ruard, and William knew it. She had now no doubt of that, but was he, was it possible that he could be, an intending murderer? Her soul revolted against that belief, yet she did not dare dismiss it. She had a great responsibility suddenly thrust on her, and she, who had lived in sheltered idle ignorance all her short life, rose instantly and quietly to the need. She remembered the house where Bab Mompesson had called the day of the fair, and the name of the street. It was not two weeks ago since she had seen this young man, still weak from his illness. If he was still at the Hague, the tale was proved wrong at least in detail. The Prince had only left yesterday. Though her knowledge of the country was vague, she knew that he could not yet be at the seat of war; but she had no means of sending to him had she so wished. She thought of Mynheer Fagel, but shrank from informing him of such a vague accusation. She took a courageous resolution, and without telling any of her household she ordered her little chariot and drove alone to the house of the Spanish wrestler. Her intense loneliness was made more manifest to her by the reflection that this had to be decided and undertaken alone, because there was not one person whom she could confide in; comment and reproof alone would follow on what she did, but she never hesitated, though she trembled.

She sent her page to ring and waited, cold at heart, in the chariot. A girl in native dress came to the door and answered that her mistress was within. Mary, feeling the empty sunny street full of curious eyes, stepped on to the paving-stones and through the tall door into the narrow passage. She told the page to wait in the chariot and bit her lip desperately.

The servant asked her something. Mary shook her head; she could not understand Dutch. The girl seemed surprised and motioned her upstairs and showed her into a parlour that overlooked a small garden with a beech-tree and one rose-bush growing among beds of herbs. The maid set a chair and left her. With a heart beating high at her own audacity Mary looked round the room, as if she thought it would give her some clue to the character of its owner. It was very neat, dark and simple; the table and the stools about it shone with a deep wax polish; there were pleasant homely picture tiles on the empty hearth, a glimmering brass clock on the mantleshelf; a most beautiful lute in the window-seat and in one corner a closed clavichord.

The Princess felt it must all be a foolish mistake—surely these were the quiet people they seemed—and yet, and yet, the room reminded her of the air of breeding she had noticed and found so incongruous in a young wrestler. After a few moments the dark mistress of the house entered, wearing a deep blue gown, her face very colourless under the artificial red on her cheeks.

"You!" she cried; and the button of the door slipped out of her hand and the door fell to behind her.

"I could not give my name as I do not speak Dutch," said Mary rising.

Teresa made an effort, but an obvious effort, to control herself. "If Your Highness has sent for me, I would have waited on you. You do me too much honour by this..."

"It was more expedient, Madam," returned the Princess with a dignity that did not betray her inward trepidation "for me to see you here."

Teresa came to the table. Mary thought her whole bearing defiant under her courtesy. "Will Your Highness tell me what you want of me?" The sunlight was over the childish figure of the Princess, her white dress, her grey cloak and hood, her sweet troubled face. The older woman looked at her with intent eyes.

"I do not even know your name, Madam," said Mary gently.

"I am the wife of Don Ramon de la Rosa, Highness."

"I did not know the name of your husband," replied the Princess. "Is he, Madam, in the Hague?"

"No," said Teresa steadily. "He is, Your Highness, in Brussels."

Mary quivered. "I am sorry for that!" she said.

"Why, Madam?"

The Princess spoke more coldly. "What business has your husband in Brussels?"

"He has gone to look after some land he has outside the town—it is, Your Highness, the place he comes from."

Mary sat down; Teresa remained standing, alert and erect by the table.

"You are a Romanist, Madam?"

"Yes, Your Highness."

"Is your husband?"

"No."

Mary paused, she saw that the other woman was baffling her by guarded answers and seeming frankness; she summoned all her dignity and courage, all the royal manner she had learnt. "Are you sure, Madam, that your husband has not gone to the camp?"

"The camp?" repeated Teresa stupidly.

Mary pressed her hands together. "Do you know," she asked, "that his name is Cornelius de Witt?"

Teresa did not blench; she began to laugh.

"Do you know," continued the Princess, "that he is in a plot against his Highness?"

Teresa's laughter died into sobbing breaths. "Forgive me," she said. "What Your Highness says is so strange!"

"It is very strange and very terrible," answered Mary, "but I do fear that it is very true."

An awful shadow passed over the face of Teresa; she looked in one second old and hopeless, but she still spoke from the echoes of the painful laugh. "Who has been giving these tales to Your Highness?"

"I have them," said the Princess, "from a sure source in Amsterdam."

Teresa drew a half-step back. "Amsterdam!" she repeated unsteadily. "What should we have to do with that city?"

"I do hear it is the place for all these plots," replied Mary simply. "A man has been arrested there who mentioned all this."

Teresa shuddered. Her father was in Amsterdam and all the chiefs of the intrigue; she could not doubt that they were discovered. "Why have you come?" she demanded.

"In the hope," answered Mary, "that I should find your husband here and able to disprove what I was so reluctant to believe."

Teresa came slowly round the table. The strong late sunlight caught the folds of her gaudy silk gown and the dusky curls on her shoulders. "There is no truth in any of it," she said harshly.

"I do fear there is," said Mary, coldly but trembling.

"It is a fantastic story. I do marvel that Your Highness should have taken it so seriously!" retorted Teresa.

"It concerns the life of my husband."

"And mine, it seems!"

"And yours, Madam."

Teresa forced the piteous laugh again. "What does Your Highness mean to do?"

Mary flushed. "It is very difficult. I pray God to direct me, Madam."

"*Your* God, yes!" cried Teresa desperately.

"Yours it seems, would sanction murder," answered Mary.

"You do not understand." Teresa spoke roughly. She sat on one of the dark chairs against the wall and held her side. "I am in great trouble. I beg you leave me."

"You are in trouble," said Mary, "because you do know your husband for a villain."

Teresa repeated with dry lips: "You do not understand. I'll not betray him by one word."

"Listen to me." The Princess spoke proudly. "There is in the Stadtholder's possession a box which contains the embalmed heart of your husband's father and which he lost when I did take him wounded to my house."

Teresa shuddered. "He never had such a thing!"

"I pray to God," said Mary with dignity, "that you be not lying, but I know enough, Madam." She rose and turned toward the door, agitated but resolute.

Teresa lifted her head. "What do you mean to do?"

"I must," answered the Princess, "tell what I know to Mynheer Fagel."

Instantly Teresa got to her feet. "You will not!" she cried.

Mary's soft eyes did not flinch. "Do not doubt that I shall," she said. "I would do it were it to save the meanest man, much more when it is...the Prince."

Teresa looked at her strangely. "But supposing you are wrong, that my husband is innocent?"

"He can prove it and I shall be glad," said Mary simply.

"His father could not prove it," flashed Teresa.

"I do not know that story, Madam."

"It would not be one," was the grim answer, "that your husband would be like to tell you."

"Madam!" Mary crimsoned from chin to brow. "Let me pass, I beg you."

"No," Teresa was before the door, protecting it desperately.

The Princess spoke with a flash of the imperious Stewart. "Your manner is a bad advocate for your innocence!"

Teresa answered swiftly: "Think how much mischief you will do if you breathe these hasty suspicions!"

"Madam," said Mary, "it is an insult to me to suppose that I should be silent on such a matter."

The black eyes of Teresa flashed fiercely and despairingly. "You know nothing!"

"Enough."

"Nothing, I say."

"Stand from the door, Madam."

"For you to pass out and kill my husband with your tongue!"

"For me," retorted Mary, "to save your husband from a hideous crime." She held herself very erect, and though she was colourless as her lawn gown, her wonted gentleness had given place to a calm and a poise that seemed marvellous in her youth. "You," she added, "would have stood silent and seen it done. May God forgive you!"

Teresa moved from the door. "Will you be merciful?" she asked.

"I will be just," answered Mary, drawing back from her.

"Your justice would be cruelty to me. Listen, if I tell you all, will you spare him?"

Mary shrank back against the wall. "It is not in my power," she said with a tremble of horror.

"Yes—you could..."

Mary broke into her speech. "I could make no such promise—and it is not needful that you should betray your husband to me, Madam. I know enough."

"You do not know where he is."

"He follows the Prince to murder him," said Mary, and her eyes were so full of pained terror that the other woman blenched before them, "but before his Highness reaches the camp, he will have had the warning from Mynheer Fagel—this is sufficient."

"Oh!" broke from Teresa with such passion that it was Mary who winced now, "and you will not save him?"

"You would have seen my husband slain," said the Princess in a voice as cold as her face. "Let me go, Madam."

Again Teresa flung herself across the door. "I make no pretences— I admit it all, and I am not ashamed—not ashamed. The Prince had his uncle and his father murdered..."

"You must not say that to me, Madam," Mary spoke, turning her face away.

"I will tell you everything if you will promise me his life!"

Mary put her hand on the button of the door. "I have no power to make any promises," she repeated. "You must take that offer to the Prince—but I will tell you this for your present comfort, that his Highness has long known who your husband is, also, I think, that he plotted against him, and he has kept the secret, so you need not fear his generosity."

Teresa cried vehemently: "It is not possible! He never knew!"

Mary did not answer; there was no change in her face, no hesitancy in her intention. To Teresa's anguish the composure of her features was an expression of cruelty.

She asked suddenly: "How old are you?"

Mary raised her still face. "I have fewer years than you would think."

"So young! What can you understand of any of it? I am older than you and I tell you that you do not know..." She broke off incoherently as if the thread of her thought had snapped. The sun was setting and through the open window could be seen like a torch inverted, quenching its ruddy flames in smoky vapour; the leaves of the beech-tree glittered in thin flecks of gold and the late roses were a blur of crimson in the dusky twilight.

An infinite sadness came into Mary's straining eyes. "I am very sorry for you," she said in her childish untouched fashion. "I do not think you need fear for his life. I shall say as little as possible—not mentioning you."

"What do I care about myself?" cried Teresa fiercely.

"I am very unhappy that I have to do this. Tell me that you—never wished—that you are innocent."

"No more so than my husband," replied Teresa. "What he wished, I wished; what he would have done, I would have done."

Mary opened the door. "I do not doubt that you know of some horrid plot in Amsterdam, but I shall not ask you of it," she said faintly, "though I tell you others may discover it through me."

"I have said nothing," cried the other woman eagerly. "I will never say one word—no—not before the rack."

The darkening room obscured them from each other.

The Princess spoke again in an unsteady voice. "I am very sorry for all of it...I hope God will have pity on you and let your husband live to repentance." Her slight white figure passed into the darkness of the stairway. Teresa stood staring at the sun, whose last rays were being licked up by the encroaching vapours.

CHAPTER VI. ENEMIES

The Stadtholder was sitting alone in a room in an inn at St. Ghislain with the window open on the August night. Above the village streets hung the moon, which was very brilliant in a mist of brightness and appeared detached from the heavens and hanging low over the earth; the steady white light revealed the roof-lines of the clustering houses and beyond the silent ruined fields of Hainault. The Prince was writing by the light of a single candle at the gate-table in the centre of the room; he was facing the window and continually looked up and out at the glittering sky and large vivid moon. He wore a buff coat and a blue ribbon across his breast. At the end of the table were his gorget, hat, gloves, pistol, and sword. The candle lit only the table and the figure of the young man bending over it; the rest of the low dark room was in fluttering shadows. He covered several sheets with his large careless hand, sealed the packet, using the common taper-holder of the inn, and laid down his pen.

A clock struck ten out of the obscurity. William Bentinck entered, carrying a rushlight in its iron and well-worn wooden stand; it cast a leaping glow over his damascened cuirass and orange scarf.

The Prince looked over his shoulder.

"You have heard?" asked Mynheer Bentinck in a toneless voice of depression.

"What?" asked William.

Mynheer Bentinck placed his rushlight on the table and crossed to the window. "From Nymegen," he explained. "This post brought me a letter from Sir William Temple there..."

"You mean," said the Prince, "that the objection of the Swede is removed?"

"Yes."

"And that a peace has been signed?"

"Yes."

"Three days ago," said William calmly.

"You will wait here to receive the news from the States?" asked Mynheer Bentinck despondently.

The Prince snuffed the candle and ignored the question. "I am glad," he remarked, "that Sweden did raise an objection to the terms."

"What was the use of it, since it but delayed the negotiations without breaking them off?"

"It gave me," returned the Prince, "a pretext for keeping the army together."

Mynheer Bentinck looked at him curiously. He had an air of elation rather than depression. He was ever in good spirits when at the war, but his friend had expected to see him in the depths at this final triumph of France and the Republican party. The peace was signed at Nymegen. Louis had Franche Comté, the frontier of Holland. He was at the height of his glory. He had disabled Spain, silenced England, gained the smaller Powers, and if the valour and wisdom of the Prince had brought Holland out of the war that aimed at her extinction without the loss of a single town, he had none the less reason to be dissatisfied with the weak perfidy of Charles and the impatient mistrust of the Republic that forsook him at the moment when their support would have enabled them to force the terms of Westphalia again on France. Yet he appeared unmoved, even elated.

"I had a curious letter from Mynheer Fagel today," he said.

"On what matters, Highness?"

"Plots, of course."

"What has been discovered?"

"That," said William, "is nothing. The strange part is that he says the Princess informed him."

"The Princess!"

"Yes. Now how could she know, for one thing; and why should she care, for another?"

"The Princess!" repeated Mynheer Bentinck wondering. "I thought she had no interest in these matters."

"I thought," answered the Prince dryly, "that she did not care whether I was intrigued against or no—but Mynheer Fagel says she was vehement with him that my safety might not be endangered." He smiled. "I believe," he added, "that she must hate me."

"You are wrong there," returned Mynheer Bentinck. "I think her feeling for you has another name. What service has she done you now?"

"Some man," answered the Prince, "has, it seems, taken the trouble to journey here from the Hague with the purpose of making an end of me."

"Has he been discovered?" asked Mynheer Bentinck, startled.

"He was arrested this morning in a neighbouring village," said William calmly. "This candle gives an ill light—get them to bring another and some ale, my friend. You look," and he smiled again, "somewhat downcast."

"You are very strange, Highness!" exclaimed Mynheer Bentinck, "I had thought to see *you*downcast tonight."

"I am pleased," answered William with inscrutable eyes on the moon, "that the Princess has discovered this tender interest in my affairs, and I was thinking that my fond and submissive wife as Queen of England would be a useful ally."

Mynheer Bentinck looked a little puzzled.

"You are dull," said the Prince calmly. "This package is for the grave Fagel. Who is in the inn?"

"None but our men. The people of the place are fled or slain."

"The work of Luxembourg," remarked William;

"He is at St. Denis."

"I know." The Prince laughed outright. "He is waiting the news of the peace, as I am." He tossed the letter he had just completed to Mynheer Bentinck, and when that gentleman had left the room he rose and went to the window and pushed the lattice even wider, leant on his elbow on the sill and gazed down the street. The party he was expecting to see came round the corner of the half-demolished houses; a few soldiers and in their midst a young man weaponless—a prisoner. He was uncovered and looking about him. The torches the soldiers carried showed his serene face and his close tawny hair. As the little cavalcade passed into the inn he glanced up and saw the slight figure of the Stadtholder leaning from the lit window and gazing down on him. For a second the eyes of the two met across the torchlight, then the prisoner disappeared into the inn between his guards and the Prince returned to the table.

His gentleman entered with a gilt sconce of candles and placed them on the low mantle; a page followed with a tray of bottles, tankards, and glasses. William desired him to bid the officer bring up the prisoner he had sent for.

The two left and William Bentinck re-entered. "Who is the fellow below?" he asked.

"The man Mynheer the Grand Pensionary warned me of," answered William. He took up a tankard and the pearl edge gleamed in the moonlight that crept over his shoulder; he sat now with his back to the window. Mynheer Bentinck poured out his ale and helped himself to the wine his Highness disdained.

"Why is he here, Highness?"

"Because, my friend," said the Prince, "I am going to see him."

"Here?"

"Yes, and alone."

"I cannot conceive the object of it."

"Well, I can," returned William, who seemed in an imperturbable good humour.

Mynheer Bentinck drank his wine and sighed. "Of course you are quite obstinate," he said.

"I do think I am," smiled William.

"I am not liable to fears," remarked Mynheer Bentinck, "but I do think you must have marvellous stout nerves to endure this constant risk of murder."

The Prince's expressive eyes dwelt on him a second with a half-wild, sad expression.

"My cough will kill me before any assassin," he said; then added instantly, "this is vile ale, being no better than sour beer."

Mynheer Bentinck turned away. "You want me to leave?" he asked drearily.

William gave him a kindly glance. "For a little, yes. I shall have news for you later on."

Mynheer Bentinck saluted and went slowly; his firm tread was heard descending the wooden stairway. William quenched the candle on the table and moved the rushlight so that it did not shine on his face. He picked up his pistol, a wheel-lock weapon with a walnut muzzle and silver mountings, looked to it and laid it down; then took his note-book from his pocket and glanced at some of the entries. His motto, "I will maintain," showed on the engraved title page. He looked at it thoughtfully, then added with a rapid quill one of the favourite mottoes of William the Taciturn, and one that the Prince had seen on his great tomb in the bare altar-space of the Church of St. Ursula at Delft, *Saevis tranquillus in undis*—"Calm amid the raging billows" the Prince translated it, and it was so often in his mind that he wrote it almost mechanically.

The soldiers entered with their prisoner. The Prince glanced up, then instantly down again.

"Return this gentleman his weapons," he said, "and leave us."

It was done. The Prisoner took his sword, pistol, and a little dagger *a la main gauche*, Spanish, with long quillons, guard and pommel in burnished gold, which he thrust into his belt. The soldiers left the chamber, while the Prince kept his eyes on the quill he held. As the clumsy wooden door closed he said quietly: "Good evening, Mynheer de Witt."

The prisoner stood back against the wall with his pistol in his hand as the officer had returned it to him, and his cloak falling back from his black velvet coat; the lustre of the candles on the mantle-tree was over his tall person and cast a long soft shadow behind him toward the door. As the Prince used his name a quick breath shook his bosom, his lips parted but he was silent.

William raised his eyes. "Be seated," he said.

Cornelius de Witt made no response.

"I think," added the Stadtholder, "you had an intention to murder me."

"I have been traveling day and night," answered the prisoner, "that I might shoot you when I met you."

"Why?" asked the Prince quietly.

"You know," said Cornelius de Witt.

The Prince leant back in his chair and looked curiously at the splendid, youthful, strong face, pale above the black coat and crowned with the close ruddy hair. "You are very like your father," he remarked, biting the end of his quill. "It startled me when I first saw you—you remember—at the East India Company their bazaar."

"You—you knew me?"

"Yes, I knew you."

Cornelius de Witt flushed violently. "You have known of me since then!"

"The Hague," answered William, "is better policed than you imagine, Mynheer. You and a man named Lacruez, whose daughter you have married, an English papist priest, and an Irishman named Dermot Fairfoul have been the chiefs of a plot against my government this year past."

The colour faded from the face of the prisoner; he looked intently at the Prince.

"Last year your Irishman came to me with a full account of this intrigue. I sent him to Loevestein, as it was not my wish that he should talk, but you, Mynheer, seem determined to force my hand."

"I have been fairly fooled!" cried Cornelius de Witt softly. "So you knew!"

"I had no desire to shed the blood of a De Witt," said the Prince. "I would have spared you even the humiliation of a pardon, but, as I say, you forced my hand."

The prisoner drew himself up against the wall; his eyes were narrowed and full of a smouldering fire of passion. "Why were you so tender with me?" he demanded.

"I answer you in your own words," said William. "You know!"

"I know that you hate me even as I hate you."

"No," replied the Prince quietly, "I rather pity you."

"Pity me! This is humiliation indeed. *You* pity me!"

William smiled. "You come of a great family, Mynheer de Witt, and I pity you that you have become what you have."

Cornelius laughed shortly. "Those are fine words from my father's murderer!"

The Prince was unmoved. "You see, Mynheer, that I allow you to insult me because I am pitiful of your misfortunes," he said. "Your uncle was a great man; he took a place that was not his; he made blunders and he atoned. Your father was always my enemy, and not bending had to break. I will say of both of them that they loved their country and fulfilled their fate without shirking, as I will fulfil mine, Mynheer."

Cornelius looked at him in baffled wrath and agony. "What cold cunning moves you I know not," he cried; "but with every word you say you dispel my last lingering doubts that you and you alone inspired that base and bloody deed!"

William gazed at him steadily. "To no man am I accountable," he said, "and to no man will I explain. Think what you will. I am not eager for your good opinion nor moved by your enmity. Let the Mynheeren de Witt rest in their graves, Mynheer."

Cornelius flung down his pistol. "You tempt me to use it," he said hoarsely.

"Well, I thought you did not stop at murder?" smiled William. "A design to end my life was believed to be your father's crime, and you have already proved that a De Witt can lend himself to assassination."

Cornelius answered in a tone of anguish: "Send me out to be shot. I deserve no more for so dallying with my vengeance. I should have killed you while their blood was yet warm on the Plaats..."

"You are free," said the Prince, "to go when you will and where you will. You need not thank me for your life—it is a poor gift—for I do not think that you will ever do much with it."

Cornelius read in his stern contained face some fierce pleasure that the son of the man whom he had always hated should stand before him to take his clemency, some satisfaction that the son of the proud commoner who had been the cause of many a humiliation to him should come to the final humiliation of accepting his mercy. "I'll not go like this," exclaimed Mynheer de Witt hotly. He came a step nearer the table; he put his hand to his sword. "Why do I not kill you as you sit there?"

"Because," answered William with gleaming eyes, "you ask yourself the question instead of doing the deed. It is not in your nature to be decisive, Mynheer."

Cornelius stood silenced, gazing at him, his fingers still round the pommel of his sword. He was more completely astonished, confused, and baffled by the personality and manner of the Prince than he had believed he could be by anything.

"Go back and plot if you will," said the Stadtholder. "Men like you are never dangerous."

"I do not understand you," cried Cornelius on a deep breath, his blue eyes straining onto the face of the other.

"My life is given to one thing alone," replied the Prince quietly. "Nothing much matters to me but that one thing, which I am appointed by God to perform. What bears not on it has little interest for me, and since I know that neither plots nor any scheming can injure me till what I have to do is done, I trouble not about you nor such as you."

"God, according to John Calvin?" exclaimed Cornelius wildly. "This is your cold creed!"

"God according to John Calvin," repeated the Prince. "What do *you* believe?"

"Nothing."

"Therefore you will do nothing, but like a straw on the river be swept with the tide to extinction on the ocean—a useless thing."

Cornelius asked desperately: "In the name of this God of yours, were you guilty of the death of the Mynheeren de Witt?"

"Do you think I would say yes or no to that?"

"Why not? Their murderers went unpunished. You could have prevented it! You do not dare to say that you could not have prevented it!" he cried brokenly and desperately.

A dark flush rose to the Stadtholder's thin cheek. "Mynheer de Witt, lay the death of your father to the account of his own presumption in meddling in what was not his province—not to me."

"You are as secret as hell and as guilty," answered Cornelius, "and I curse myself that I have not had the resolution to put a bullet through your cold heart." With a gesture of misery he brought his hand to his brow and thrust his fingers through his hair. "But you are one of fortune's favourites," he said, "and I one of the slaves to be kicked from her path...You have conquered...I shall not molest you again. You will always be a great man and I a broken one."

The Prince rose and came round the table. "You say you believe in nothing, not even your country?"

"My country is but a name to me."

"You would not fight for Holland as your father did?"

"To be paid as he was!"

"True service considers not the payment, Mynheer de Witt. Tomorrow I am to attack Luxembourg before St. Denis."

"The peace is signed!"

"No matter for that," answered William. "I want more gentlemen—if you will fight under me I will give you a company."

Cornelius was utterly amazed. "You offer me this!" he cried. "You tell me this! I might take this news to Luxembourg."

"But you will not," said the Prince, "because I have told you and because I let you go free. I know you, Mynheer, better than you know yourself." He was breathing an air of ardour, of enthusiasm difficult to resist; his whole face was altered by the glowing commanding expression of his hazel eyes; his thin beautiful hand rested on the edge of the table and a great chrysoberyl ring he wore, a cat's-eye stone, with a rib of pulsing light down it caught the candle flame, and shone vividly.

"You cannot think that I should serve you!"

"Call it your country," said William.

Cornelius stepped back against the wall and put his hand before his eyes. Up from the street came the sound of the light artillery passing over the cobbles—the shout of the men, the crack of the whip, the rumble of the wheels.

"No," said Cornelius, as if answering his own thoughts, "I am pledged to France."

"Pledged to Louis, pledged to that bloody devil Luxembourg, pledged to all your father hated, against all he strove for—freedom, liberty, honour!" William smiled as he finished. "Think before you decide," he added.

Cornelius was silent; he was so under the grip of an overwhelming personality that his very soul seemed invaded; he was baffled beyond expression by the extraordinary attitude of the Prince, his extraordinary proposal; all his own thoughts, hopes, fears, schemes of the last years suddenly became intangible to him in the presence of this young man, who told him, simply, of a tremendous act of daring and asked him to participate in it; he steadied himself by the memory of his long hate, by the memory of that awful day that had shattered his happiness. "The past is not forgotten so easily," he said at length. "And I meant to take your life."

"You would never have done it," returned the Prince. "When was a gentleman an assassin?"

The plain words seemed to show him his own soul; he would never have done it; that was the reason of his long delays, his hesitations, his excuses. He had never meant to do the deed, he had only been playing with the idea; he was no man of action but a dreamer and a lover of music; therefore the Prince had left him his weapons as he would have left them to a child. Cornelius saw this in a helpless pain. "Let me depart," he said thickly.

"One moment," answered the Prince. "I have told you I wish to break off this unjust peace. On which side will you fight tomorrow?"

He looked intently at Cornelius, who could not avoid his searching eyes. He was so much the shorter, slighter, that he looked frail to weakness beside the fine easy strength of the other, yet the purpose, the will, and the passion he expressed made that very strength appear merely cumbrous. "Come, on which side?" he repeated.

Cornelius made an effort against the sensation of domination. "France," he said in a strained voice.

For a second the eyes of the Prince rested on him in silence, then he answered: "It is very well, I will give you a passport through the lines. Take up your pistol, Mynheer."

Almost unconsciously Cornelius stooped for the weapon; when he raised his head the Prince had returned to his place at the top of the table and was lifting his heavy black cloak from the chair. From under the folds he took a silver object which he held out across the candle-lit space. "This is yours," he said, "take it into the fight against your country."

Cornelius came forward stupidly; he knew at once what it was William showed him. "So you—had that," he murmured.

"You lost it the day you were brought to the *Huis ten Bosch*. Take it, Mynheer."

Cornelius took the case containing his father's heart. A great sigh heaved his bosom; the painful rush of memory became almost unendurable. Mynheer Cornelius de Witt had served his country, in every way, in battle, in agony..."I dishonour him!" burst from the white lips of his son.

William was watching him intently. "On which side would *he* have fought?"

Cornelius lifted his eyes hot with tears. In that moment France, England, were hateful to him, the thought of vengeance nothing.

The traditions of his race awoke in him; his father and his country were not enemies, but one. He saw clearly at last, saw how that dear memory might be best honoured.

"A De Witt will again serve Holland tomorrow, Prince," he said abruptly.

CHAPTER VII. THE BATTLE OF ST. DENIS

Monsieur de Luxembourg and his officers were celebrating the peace that they were waiting official confirmation of, in the village of St. Denis, close to the great fortress of Mons, which they blockaded. They amused themselves by picturing the extreme discomfiture of the Prince of Orange at the miserable ending of his strenuous opposition to a conclusion of the war; the uselessness of the marriage that had been considered such a stroke at the time of its accomplishment; his failure to secure the English alliance and the general triumph of the arms and arts of his most Christian Majesty,' who was now great indeed, in the eyes of his subjects of an almost superhuman dazzle.

The rejoicing at the peace was the greater because William of Orange was the one man in Europe whom King Louis feared (lesser opponents, such as my Lord Danby, now in the Tower of London, the power of France soon swept aside), and under the scorn expressed for the servant of a republic who had dared to set himself against the might of the greatest nation in the world was the secret vexation that this young man alone had prevented the United Provinces being added to the conquests of France; and brilliant as the peace might be for them, of the country they had undertaken so light-heartedly to conquer they had not succeeded in retaining a single acre; so though they magnified their triumph after the manner of their nation, the wisest of them admitted to themselves that the greatest glory lay on the side, not of the victorious Louis, but of the defeated Prince of Orange.

Monsieur de Luxembourg had burnt the village of St. Denis and put the inhabitants to the sword some months before; his gorgeous camp was spread among the ruins of orchards and cornfields, farm-houses and humbler dwellings, and strangely in the midst of it rose the dumb stark church with blank windows and broken doors. The moon was now high in the heavens and of a great luminous brightness. The officers who had been at the supper given by Monsieur de Luxembourg had returned to their quarters, save one young captain of cavalry, the Marquis de Croissy, a relation of the general.

The tent of Monsieur de Luxembourg was large and splendid; the canvas hung with velvet and stamped leather, the floor spread with carpets from Persia and the new factories as Aubusson, lamps of silver, crystal, gilt, and bronze were skilfully hung to the polished tent-poles and cast a soft shaded lustre. At the back was a rich, violet satin curtain, before which was a couch covered with a fine tiger-skin and a scarf of Eastern embroidery. On a low carved chest were guns, swords, gauntlets, and all the appointments of war; on a long table covered with a lace cloth, painted glasses, gold plate, agate-handled forks, silver-gilt knives, baskets of fruit, bottles of wine and bowls of white and yellow roses. A great Venetian mirror with a frame of pale-hued glass flowers hung by scarlet silk cords from the roof-pole and reflected dimly the glittering table. A box of books stood by the entrance, where the flap was lifted up to court the hesitating breeze, and Terence in gilt and leather, a volume of French comedies and a bundle of the latest pamphlets from Amsterdam lay scattered on the carpet. By a small table near this entrance sat a man on a folding chair of pierced steel-work with a leather seat; on the table was a glass of iced sherbet, a table watch in rock crystal and a tiny monkey asleep on a white satin cushion. The man wore a flowing dressing-gown of red damask, black silk breeches, scarlet stockings and slippers of white watered silk, laced with silver. He was hunchbacked, but this was largely concealed, as he sat, by the heavy curls of his fair peruke. His face was nearly colourless, his eyes pale and very steady, his hands white, small, and fine; in his long lace cravat was a large brooch of jewels. He held a book in his hand and alternately read a sentence and sipped his sherbet, which he was proud of securing in this barbarous wilderness, as he considered the Low Countries. He was Francois Henri de Montmorency, Duc de Luxembourg, peer and marshal of France.

By the looped-back entrance-flap stood Monsieur de Croissy gazing out at the encampment, the dark steeple of the desecrated church and the wonderful moon. He sang softly a little song by Lambert, fashionable when he had left Paris.

> *"Voici les charmants où mon âme ravie*
> *Passait à son temple Sylvie,*
> *Ces tranquilles moments si doucement perdus,*
> *Que je l'aimais alors! que je la trouvais belle!*
> *Mon coeur, vois soupirez, au nom de l'infidèle,*
> *Avez-vous oublié que vous ne l'aimez plus?"*

Monsieur de Luxembourg looked up. "You are very doleful tonight," he remarked.

"Doleful, Monsieur!" The young man turned quickly as if he was startled. The moonlight was full over his habit of pale lemon-coloured silk and his black hair; it gave him a ghostly look.

"Yes, I thought so."

De Croissy smiled, though faintly. "On the contrary, I should feel very joyful tonight since the war is at an end at last," he answered.

Monsieur de Luxembourg laid down his book. "Are you so glad of that?" he asked.

"Well, you know, Monsieur, that I am, for one thing, tired of being exiled from Paris."

"Yet one soon becomes weary of Paris," remarked the Duke dryly.

"And besides," added De Croissy lightly, "there was the prediction of the wise woman…"

"Your wise woman!" smiled Monsieur de Luxembourg, stroking the monkey.

"I hear she is more the mode than ever," returned the young man.

"No doubt she will continue to be the fashion, even when she is being burnt on the Place de la Grêve. What did she tell you? That you would be slain in this war, was it not?"

"Yes," said De Croissy, "and that would be very unpleasant."

"Well, you cannot be slain in this war," answered the Duke, "because, as you know, the peace was signed three days ago."

"Which is the reason, Monsieur, why I am so lighthearted."

Monsieur de Luxembourg glanced at him curiously. "What is the matter with you, De Croissy?" he asked abruptly.

Again the Marquis gave him that startled look. "What do you mean, Monsieur le Duc?" he asked unsteadily.

The general sipped his sherbet and surveyed him over the glass. "You seem to me," he said quietly, "to look very strange."

Monsieur de Croissy laughed. "I will spare you my company—I am dull tonight." He crossed over to the table, poured out some wine and drank it. The light eyes of Monsieur de Luxembourg watched the noble, slender figure in the rich setting. He stood leaning against the table, the wineglass in his hand, singing under his breath.

"C'est ici que souvent, errant dans les prairies
Ma main des fleurs les plus chéries
Lui faisait des présents si tendrement re us..."

He broke off suddenly, looked slowly round and the glass slipped from his fingers.

"You are not well, De Croissy," said the Duke, leaning forward.

The Marquis made an effort. "It is nothing..." He filled up the glass again.

"Que je l'aimais alors! que je la trouvais belle!
Mon coeur, vous soupirez, auprès de l'infidèle
Avez-vous oubliè que vous ne l'aimez plus?"

As his words ended he came a step forward into the tent and again looked round with an air of startled suspension, as of a sensitive creature alarmed by some distant and ominous sound.

"Get to your quarters, De Croissy," said Monsieur de Luxembourg. "I have a great mind to sleep if you have not—ring for my gentleman."

But the young officer seemed reluctant to depart; he laughed uneasily and sank down on the tiger-skin couch. "I am glad the peace is signed," he said.

The Duke answered grimly. "I am not—for if it had not been I should have taken Mons."

"Ah, Duke, you think of nothing but glory—I think..." He broke off and looked sharply round.

"What is the matter?" cried Monsieur de Luxembourg impatiently.

The Marquis rose, trembling violently. "I do not know," he muttered, "it must be the moon. I never saw the moon so bright—it is shining behind that church like an evil dream."

"You have the fever," said the Duke quietly, "you had really better, my friend, go to bed." He touched the bell beside him and a black page with a bronze collar appeared from behind the violet curtain.

"Fetch my surgeon," said Monsieur de Luxembourg. The boy slipped away noiselessly. Monsieur de Croissy appeared not to hear; he stood in an expectant attitude.

"What is going to happen?" he murmured. "I feel..."

Monsieur de Luxembourg closed his book. "What?" he asked.

"As if some one was coming for me..."

"My faith, De Croissy," said the Duke anxiously, "you are certainly ill with the cursed Dutch fever." He rose slowly from his chair and at that moment the surgeon and the page entered from behind the curtain. They saw a curious scene: the soft shaded light of the rich lamps falling on the glittering table; the fluttering wine-coloured shadows concealing the roof and corners of the tent, the looped-up entrance showing the vivid moonlight and the stark outline of the ruined church without; the dwarfish, hunched figure of Monsieur de Luxembourg in his flowing dressing-gown, and the tall young man gleaming in pale satin, powdered with gold, holding his hand to his heart and gazing before him as if he saw some disembodied terror, the black hair about his brow and shoulders intensifying the unnatural whiteness of his face.

Monsieur de Luxembourg laid his hand on the arm of the Marquis. He turned slowly at the touch. "My dear De Croissy," he said, "let my surgeon cup you..."

On the soft and utter silence broke a fierce sound that caused the Duke to stop his speech and swing round with a violent ejaculation. It was repeated, threatening, louder; the crystal lamps shook and the glasses on the table danced.

"Cannon!" cried Monsieur de Croissy on a deep breath. "I knew it." He pulled a crucifix out of his breast and kissed it violently.

"Cannon!" exclaimed Monsieur de Luxembourg. He seized the frightened page by the ear and cast him against the curtain. "Get my clothes—armour..."

A breathless officer of the Black Musketeers burst in with a drawn sword. "Monsieur le Duc," he gasped, "the Prince of Orange is attacking us—his artillery is on the heights—by the woods."

Monsieur de Luxembourg flew into a violent passion. "Fools! Dolts!" he cried as he snatched off his dressing-gown and kicked his slippers across the tent. "Is this the first you knew of it? Where were the outposts? I'll have some of you broken for this. Are you all blind and deaf?" He stamped passionately. "To arms, I say—get all these sluggards to arms—get to your troop, De Croissy..."

That young man, now perfectly calm, stooped and kissed the Duke's hand. "Good-bye, Monsieur," he said.

Monsieur de Luxembourg did not notice the words. "No delays!" he shouted. His gentlemen were busy about him and as he spoke he struggled into his coat and was buckled into his cuirass. "This is a trick! He would fall on us while we rest under faith of a treaty, this little Prince—which is a move I was not prepared for!" His tent was filling up with the officers of his staff and he nodded to them curtly as he sat down to draw on his boots.

The cannon sounded again and again. The Duke, booted, sprang up and shook his fist in the direction of the sound. "You think you have me this time," he said, "but that remains to be seen." Strapping on his sword he turned to his officers, who were loud in anger against the Prince of Orange, who must know, they said, that the peace was signed.

"Gentlemen!" cried the Duke, "I admire him for it—and if this move of his breaks off this same paltry peace I shall not be sorry." His horse was at the door of his tent and he mounted and was riding along his hastily summoned ranks a few moments after the first alarm.

It was said afterwards that no man but the Prince of Orange would have dared the attack and no man but the Duc de Luxembourg would have rallied so soon to meet it. The French battalions had to form in face of the Dutch shots, cannon-balls and bombs that dropped into their midst from the shelter of the slightly rising woods where the Prince had his artillery, and many a man dropped as he rode up to take his place. But the ranks of France were not easily discomposed, and before the moon had paled before the hot August dawn, Monsieur de Luxembourg had recovered from the surprise and disposed his infantry in order of battle about the hastily constructed earthwork round the encampment; the cavalry rode up the incline, and succeeded, in spite of many losses, in spiking several of the Dutch guns; upon which the Prince sent out a regiment of Spanish horsemen which, skirting St. Denis, fell on the right flank of the French.

The infantry were ready to receive them; the first rank knelt, the second leant over their shoulders, and the third stood erect. All being armed with pikes, fusees, and bayonets they represented a front impossible to break, as the fire of the fusees maddened the horses and sent them charging backwards into the ranks behind them and so broke the advance into confusion.

The Prince, coming up to the scene with the Dutch regiments, perceived the disorder occasioned by the firm array of the French foot and dismounted his cavalry, who, advancing to the attack with pike and musket, succeeded in breaking the French line.

Monsieur de Luxembourg, having his attention drawn to this, rode up from the centre of the battle, where a confused fight was raging round the French entrenchments, and made a fierce effort to rally his men, who were being rapidly driven off the battle-field under the onslaught of the Spanish and Dutch. Thus it happened that in the very first hours of the battle these two commanders came near enough to distinguish each other through the smoke of canon and musket, the pale glare of fire, the flare of the rising sun reflected from cuirass, sword, and bayonet.

Monsieur de Luxembourg had withdrawn his men a little within the shelter of their entrenchments and was riding along the front of them with his sword unsheathed, when, in a slow clearing of the smoke, he perceived an officer galloping before the Dutch lines and pausing to give commands to his troops. They were but divided by a few trenches and palisades and it needed not his perspective glass to tell Monsieur de Luxembourg that he beheld the Prince of Orange. He knew him by his blue ribbon and more certainly by that instinct the great have for one another.

At the same moment the Prince saw him and instantly lifted his hat, smiling. Monsieur de Luxembourg uncovered and bowed with an answering laugh. The two bodies of troops rallied and fell upon each other in a fierce disordered combat. The French, who had not sufficient time to form in order of battle fell back before the impetuous charge of the Dutch, which threw them into confusion; they gave way and were pursued into their own entrenchments.

Meanwhile, in the centre and right of the battle they had not broken their ranks and it was the allied army that was being repulsed. On news being brought of this, the Prince flew to encourage his troops, but though he again and again led them to the charge the Frenchmen held their ground. By now Monsieur de Luxembourg had brought up his artillery, disposed it to advantage and turned it on the enemy. The sun was high and swooningly hot; the metal belfry of the church shone like molten gold above the dun smoke. There was no breeze to stir the leaves of the beeches in the little wood where the Dutch gunners worked. Here and there a trail of fire licked along the parched grass or caught the roof of some dismantled cottage on the outskirts of the fighting. With undaunted persistency and energy each side maintained their own without obtaining any advantage. It was the most bloody, obstinate and furious battle of the war.

Time after time the cuirassiers and musketeers of France charged the ranks of the allies; time after time the shock was met without flinching and a steady fire of shot emptied saddles and thinned ranks. The Prince led now this regiment and now that, dismounted to encourage the infantry and exposed himself with a reckless ardour that called forth the protests of his officers. He gave his usual answer that he did not risk his life needlessly out of mere foolhardiness, but on due consideration to encourage his comparatively unpractised troops against the veteran arms of France.

By midday he had had two horses killed under him, and mounted on a third steed led a detachment of the Spanish cavalry right against the now slightly wavering centre of the enemy. The violent shock of their onslaught brought them into the midst of the French ranks, which fell to right and left before them; and the Prince brought his men into the centre of Monsieur de Luxembourg's body-guard. He rose in his stirrups to shout to those behind when a French officer clapped a pistol to the forehead of his horse, and at the same instant another knocked him out of the saddle with the butt-end of his musket. The Prince sank to the ground, the horse reared and fell; the Spanish troops broke unto disorder. A hand-to hand fight followed round the Prince, who was actually under the hoofs of the maddened horses and in danger of being bruised to death. Two of his men dismounted and dragged him with difficulty out of the press. He was borne backwards, hatless, with a broken sword, the fire of the French so hot upon him that the balls struck down those about him and carried away the end of the pistol at his waist, even passing through the skirts of his coat. It was believed by all near that he was doomed; but he stopped the first riderless horse that passed him, flung himself into the saddle, grasped one of the swords offered him, waved it aloft, his arm streaming with blood, and again led his men against the French, who this time began to reel back and stagger under the vigorous onslaught; routed squadrons pressed back on those behind them and the invincible Luxembourg cursed heartily, after his fashion when enraged. He began to be in want of powder; he was losing men heavily and he had just been told that a reserve of a thousand that were coming up from the outskirts of the fight had been met and put to confusion by the Dutch.

Engagement followed engagement throughout the stifling August day; neither would give way and neither could gain a definite advantage. Monsieur de Luxembourg was the better general as the Prince was the finer man, and he put the whole force of his genius into resisting the attack, as the Prince put the whole strength of his courage and resolve into leading it. There was a generation between them in years and experience. The French general had served under Conde and Turenne; the Dutch commander had been his own master, but the ardour of youth and high aims supplied the deficiency. Luxembourg made no headway against the dauntless young Stadtholder, whose troops had never been heartened by a victory and had none of the glory of prestige which was such a power to the French.

In clouds of dust and smoke the contest raged on the plains of Hainault. As the sun reached the meridian, declined, sank, France and her enemies still swayed to and fro amid the discharge of cannon, the rattle of musketry, the shouts of command, the last words of the fallen and wounded. As the purple evening, fiery and easeless as the day, drew on, a little company of Dutch, being broken from the main ranks, were pursued by some of the French cavalry out of the general melee of the dreadful and doubtful combat. They crossed a little stream and gained a mill grown about with meadowsweet, alders, willows, and wild roses yet pure from the evil smoke, and there turned at bay. The French forded the water and attacked the mill. The fight continued till darkness, when the French became discouraged and drew off to the centre of the fighting, and the Dutch breaking from their cover dashed after them, in their turn the pursuers. They left behind them many dead and one living—a young man wounded, sick and shuddering, who sat by the wooden door and stared vacantly before him. The distant roar of the cannon was incessant, but there was no nearer sound. About the ruined mill was a ghastly peace. The young man could see the dark shape of the water-wheel, the fluttering tendrils of the eglantine, the masses of blue forget-me-nots crushed near the stream on which still floated great calm water-lilies. The dark shapes of dead men broke the sward and weapons showed scattered on the powder-charred grass. Even through the smell of blood and smoke was a perfume of summer sweetness from the meadowsweet, which grew waist-high beyond the mill to the edge of a young coppice of beech.

The Hollander rose stiffly. He felt lifeless with fatigue and loss of blood, as if he was under water, floating, a mere weed among the wreckage of the ocean, but he heard the confused sound of battle and fumbled in the twilight for his sword that he might return to the fight. As he came to the edge of the stream a man raised himself on his elbow from beneath a willow-stump and held out his hand silently. He wore a light and gold glimmering dress which rendered his figure noticeable in the dusk. By reason of this habit the Dutchman knew him for the leader of the French cavalry and stood hesitating, with his hand instinctively closing round his sword.

"Monsieur," said the French officer mournfully, "will you help me to my feet?" In the twilight and with dimmed eyes he possibly thought that he spoke to one of his own nation. The other, who was no soldier, but a gentleman volunteer, threw down his weapon and raised him in his arms.

The cannonade was becoming more intermittent and the stars brighter overhead.

"Shall I take you into the house?"

The Frenchman pressed his hand. "It is no matter," he said faintly and courteously.

"Where are my troops?"

"Returned to the battle."

"And you?"

"I am Dutch."

"My enemy, then..."

"You are wounded...I think the battle is nearly over." He helped the officer into the lofty bare room of the mill, long since emptied, and arranged for him a bed of straw and sacks still white with flour, near the open window.

"I am dying," smiled the Frenchman. "Will you bring me a little water? My name is Louis Anne de Croissy—yours?"

The other answered with bent head: "Cornelius de Witt."

"Ah," the Marquis strove to rise. "Monsieur de Witt, I am indeed honoured..." He gasped and swooned.

Cornelius fetched the water though he had nothing better to bring it in than an empty powder-flask he washed in the stream. With unaccustomed fingers he sought for the hurts of the wounded man, and was bending over him, when the bright and painful light of a lantern streamed across the obscurity and he looked up to see the figure of Father Constant, in jack-boots, buff, and cloak, standing on the threshold with the lantern held up. He beheld him without surprise or emotion.

"Cornelius!" exclaimed the priest.

"Yes—I—here is a dying man. Can you do anything?"

The Englishman stepped into the room and flashed the light of the slim unconscious figure. "Monsieur de Croissy," he said. "Monsieur de Luxembourg will be sorry—but you," he turned his piercing eyes on Cornelius, "what of you?"

Cornelius smiled. "Does it matter?

"You were arrested—yesterday?"

"Yes."

"And taken before the Prince of Orange at St. Ghislain?"

"Yes."

Father Constant coloured darkly. "What does it mean—why are you here?" he asked haughtily.

Cornelius lifted his haggard face and eyed the priest steadily across the lantern beams. "It means that I fought today for Holland."

"You—a renegade and a traitor!"

"Neither the one nor the other."

"You fought for William of Orange!"

"For my country. Look to this dying man."

The priest knelt at the other side of De Croissy and opened his blood-stained coat and shirt. Cornelius had already removed the rich gorget.

"Why are you here?" asked Cornelius.

"My duty—I look to the souls of men."

Cornelius fixed his bloodshot blue eyes on the white face of the Frenchman. "You blame me. I said I believe in nothing, it was not so—I believed in my country and the God of my country," he said in a low voice. "Yesterday I knew...I could not take my father's heart into French ranks...my country and liberty...I am Dutch and *his* son, there was nothing else to do—you should understand."

"I understand," answered the priest stubbornly, "that you have forsworn and failed us." He was busy with Monsieur de Croissy and did not look up as he spoke.

"No," said Cornelius earnestly, "for that was all false. When I put it to the touchstone I found it so. Did *he* die that I might serve France?"

"A man of nothing, turning with the weathercock. I should have known better than to trust you."

Cornelius rose from his knee. He looked beyond the prone figure and the stooping one to the loveliness of evening wood and field, dark beneath the last saffron glow of the cold sky.

"If it had been England, would you have stood to France?"

"To God," answered the priest.

"God!" repeated Cornelius sadly. "If a man finds his God is not in his country where shall he find Him?"

Father Constant took the dark head of Monsieur de Croissy on to his knee. "Maybe I should prove it so," he said. "But France and England are one. I am not like to be put to the test."

A swallow darted past the gaunt window; the scent of the wild rose and meadowsweet was of an aching pungency, like the memory of ancient pleasures.

"Are *you* wounded?" asked the Englishman.

"No—but wearied. I am no soldier."

The priest looked at him over his shoulder. "Yet you fought today for the man you vowed to kill."

"For my country," said Cornelius, "and my father's God."

Monsieur de Croissy stirred and half sat up; he put his fingers to his lips and seemed to be listening to the random distant shots of the cannon.

"Monsieur le Marquis," said Father Constant, "it is I..."

The black eyes turned on him and lit with a flash of returning light. "A priest!" he gasped. "Absolve me, my father—the Cross!"

Father Constant held the crucifix he took from his bosom to the mouth of the dying man, who clutched it convulsively and passionately.

"Christ!" he cried, "and France! France!" His last breath was spent on the word, he fell back smiling and his face was as calm as that of a child in the long beams of the lantern.

The priest whispered a prayer and Cornelius fell to his knees again and looked wistfully into the fair fearless countenance of the dead. "What was there for him," he murmured, "but his God and his country—which are one?"

The Romanist looked at him. "Go," he said commandingly, "and unblamed by me. No man can accomplish save if he believe in what he sets his hand to. We have made the mistake. Return to your heritage and farewell."

Cornelius picked up his sword. "Farewell," he answered, and went slowly, without looking back, into the wonder of the night and made his way through the dead men about the stream and so back to the Dutch lines. His mood was sad but calm; he had touched the truth of his own soul. Each man where he is set, let him stand for his own things and so he shall serve the highest he knows, which is God.

CHAPTER VIII. A HEART INDOMITABLE

The house of the Stadtholder at Soestdyck was so surrounded with trees back and front that the sun rarely entered the cool dark rooms. It was so silent that the humming of bees, the scattered notes of birds, the rippling sound of the foliage in the breeze made a delicate harmony in its chambers no ruder noise disturbed. It was scantily, even ill furnished, and the garden was a mere tangle of wild green, but the trees were lordly and the house itself old and finely built. On the red brick frontage small red roses climbed, and the curved drive was green with moss. Here the long, long drowsy summer afternoons were invested with an exquisite sense of sad peace, and the sunshine falling on the upper branches of chestnut, elm, and beech seemed eternal and full of tender memory. This was a harbour from all trouble, a refuge from all conflict, a place for rest, for thought and yearning, so remote it was, so still and melancholy.

Here, in late August, the Stadtholder returned from the war. The Peace of Nymegen was signed, and his daring and undaunted efforts to break it culminating in the battle of St. Denis had availed nothing. King Louis saw his advantage too clearly in the peace to notice the Prince's endeavour to force him into a continuation of the war; so the exploit outside Mons served for nothing save to make the world wonder and to warn the French that they had an implacable enemy in William of Orange, who had, by this last act, directly in the face of the wish of the States, risked and almost lost his popularity and his position in the country he had saved. The admiration of Europe was barren return for what he had staked and what he forfeited, and this hero, respected and famous at Versailles and Whitehall as one of the most powerful men in Europe, came home as quietly as any private gentleman and with a heart as heavy as ever returned from a campaign.

A few hours after his arrival at Soestdyck, Cornelius de Witt was admitted to his presence and stood before him in the still, bare, dark room with the panelled walls and simple furniture. The whole chamber was in shadow. The Prince sat listlessly and languidly in the window-seat, behind him the boughs of elm, chestnut, and lime quivering in the sun. He was dressed in black, with a plain leather swordbelt, and soft high boots dusty as he had ridden from Utrecht along the dry summer high roads. On a chair beside him was his hat with a black feather, his worn gauntlets, some letters torn hastily open, and a small Bible.

Cornelius de Witt was speaking. "I wish to take my leave of Your Highness. I am making my residence in Brussels."

The large eyes of the Prince surveyed him calmly. "You have my good wishes, Mynheer de Witt."

Cornelius bowed his head. He held himself with an air of fatigue; his face was slightly hollowed, tanned, and changed in contour, but the old expression of serenity was intensified. "Highness, I have been to the Hague," he said, "and laid my father's heart at rest in the Nieuwe Kerk."

The Prince slowly brought his handkerchief to his lips and was silent. He was thinking of the past, its passions, its pains, all as still now as the brave heart of Cornelius de Witt.

"I am more content than I have been since his death. I have to thank Your Highness."

Still William did not speak; his pose was one of utter weariness and his eyes were half veiled.

"I am wholly for the United Provinces," continued Cornelius. "And if Your Highness should ever wish to call on me..."

"You would serve me again?" asked William.

Cornelius answered simply: "Holland—always."

The Prince gave a sad smile. "I am glad your father's son should say that to me..."

Cornelius coloured faintly. "Your Highness has to forgive me that I have conspired against your life."

William's eyes brightened. "What of your vengeance now?" he asked.

"Now I know you," said Cornelius, "I think it is impossible; or if you did that, then all good is false. You are a Prince to serve, a man who stands for God."

William moved a little. "Mynheer de Witt," he said gravely and sternly, "I will tell you that I am innocent of this deed, which I cannot think of without horror...they should have lived for me."

Cornelius paled, lifted his hand and let it fall. "I do believe Your Highness—no more of them."

"They were not unhappy," said the Prince, "in that they did their duty to the last. I do hope I may die as steadfast."

The blue eyes of Cornelius lifted with a bright sharp light in them. "God," he said, "preserve Your Highness. Though I will not live under you, being a De Witt, I will, at need, serve Holland as loyally as any Royalist."

"What will you do with your life?" asked the Prince.

"I have a wife," answered Cornelius, "and she is my great comfort now."

"Tell her father to be careful," said William. "She, being a good wife, will meddle no more with plots."

"She is a devoted servant of Your Highness, because you have spared my life."

The Prince sighed. "Farewell, Mynheer. If we never meet again have me sometimes nevertheless in your prayers. It is not forbidden us," he smiled, "to pray for our enemies."

"I shall, from my soul, for my country and—Your Highness."

They parted, and the door closing on the tall young man left the Prince in the perfect summer silence of the drowsy afternoon, cool shadow within and bright beams of sunshine in the rich trees without. He loved warmth and light, and unlatched the window now, that the sun-heated breeze might enter the chamber. For awhile he sat with his elbow on the sill, his chin on his hand, looking over the garden and passing a review of his life since that terrible bloody hour that put his task before him.

Toil, difficulty, discouragement, opposition, defeat, failure, sickness, and utter weariness of mind and body, that was the sum of it. At first he had pleased the people and been absolute in the States; now only the three provinces he had wrested from Louis were unflinchingly loyal; the others had forced this peace upon him in spite of his passionate protests, his far-seeing judgment, his utter conviction of the folly of it. Charles had played with and deceived him when he might by so little have turned the scale in his favour. The English marriage, entered into with the one idea of gaining the English alliance of his country, had made him unpopular at home, and brought him no added power abroad. The army he had with such incredible labour brought together would be dispersed by order of the States, while Louis would keep his men under arms and in training ready for the next attack on the defenceless liberties of Europe. The frontier of Holland was in the hands of France, and he had no means to protect it; Spain was despoiled and supine, England more estranged than ever from the United Provinces since the fall of Danby. At the end of five years of labour the Prince saw all his task still to do if he was to accomplish his object, the preservation of the liberty and religion of his country.

Hampered by lack of money, of men, of power, forsaken by England, opposed by his own nation, worn out by increasing ill-health and continual fatigue, misunderstood even by his friends, William of Orange saw the way so dark before him that cruel doubts assailed him of his ability to go on. He knew not one person who could completely comprehend his desires, his motives, nor could he see any help ahead. It seemed that God had forsaken him, humiliated him, and taken from him his work; no ardour, energy, courage, nor steadfastness could continue strongly in face of such overwhelming odds, such continual disappointment. He was too young to despair, but that apathy which is its forerunner laid a cold chill on his hitherto unconquerable spirit. He struggled to submit to inscrutable decrees, but in submitting his faith in that Divine protection he had always felt about him in his darkest moments was unconsciously obscured. Europe was at peace, her courage broken, France confirmed in her spoliation, sanctioned in her conquest, and, bitterer than this by far, no one cared; no one could be roused, each was intent about his own little business, his own small hopes and fears. Why should I fret about them? thought the Prince bitterly. Let it all go. I have done my utmost.

He rose from the window seat, called the steward of his household and told him of his intention to move at once to Dieren; there he might at least enjoy the one distraction he cared for, his long arduous hunts in the forests about Arnhem. He then asked where the Princess was, whom he had but seen for a quick moment or so since his return. He was answered that she was abroad in the garden with her ladies and Mynheer Bentinck. The Prince said no more of that, but demanded his dog, the white boarhound of the Russians that he had desired to be brought to Soestdyck to meet him.

The steward replied with some trepidation that the dog was dead since the last departure of his Highness to the war.

"How should he be dead?" asked the Prince.

"I do think the creature very sorely missed Your Highness, so much so all our care was of no avail to comfort him."

The Prince said nothing. The steward left, wondering that his master did not display some emotion at the death of his favourite, and again that summer stillness of silence fell on the lofty shadowy chamber, while the birds in the sunny branches without gave faraway calls. The Prince sat at the table in a dull attitude thinking of his dog and holding his hand before his eyes. Behind him was an open door into another room, dark, cool, and barely furnished, and at the end of this stood the Princess, having just entered from the garden, looking at the back of his bowed figure.

She stood motionless, breathing lightly, in her hand a bunch of long-stalked, striped carnations, like in colour to her gown, clear pink and white. As she paused, alone in the shadow of the peaceful room, her thoughts presented to her, as a pack of cards huddled together, painted and plain, all that had gone to make her life: the first days at Twickenham, the river and the sunlight on the old red wall of the garden, St. James and the hayfields, Whitehall and her talk with Baptist Mompesson, the game of blindman's buff when the Prince had entered upon them, her first sight of him at the ball, her wedding on a sad November day, her long hours of tears, her dreary departure from England and dreary arrival amid snow and storm, doubts, passions, jealousies, regrets, loneliness, a short severe schooling for her ignorance, pitiless test for her youth, then of a sudden a lift into upper regions where none of these things mattered.

It was as if she had come down a long avenue full of shadow, crossed here and there with fitful radiance, full of confusion and distraction, and then stepped quietly into eternal and steady light. Softly she smiled to herself and was moving forward when an instinct held her arrested.

The Prince was now bent over the table, his head resting on his arms, the dark locks falling over his shoulders. She knew with a swift shock of intuition that he was weeping. She paled and waited. She saw him raise his head, struggle to contain himself and heard him sob painfully as he rose and moved to the window.

Pale but unhesitating she came forward. At her first movement he must, she knew, hear her. When she entered the chamber he was gazing out of the window.

She laid her flowers on the table. "Sir," she said steadily.

He glanced round at her. "Well, Madam," he answered kindly, "this was an ill house to bring you to."

Mary came a step toward him. "Mynheer Bentinck has been telling me of this last battle."

"To what purpose?" he asked.

She laid her hand on the breast of her tight striped bodice. "I would to Heaven it had succeeded," she said, gravely and earnestly. "Your desire to break off the peace, I mean."

The force with which she spoke brought him to look at her searchingly. "My child, what can you know of it?" he asked slowly.

She was silent a moment, then said simply: "I understand—indeed, Sir, you may believe it."

The words came as a rebuke to him who had been despairing because he stood alone. Yet was it possible a foreigner, a woman, almost a child, brought up to dislike him, could—comprehend?

"What do you understand?" he asked incredulously.

She answered instantly in a sweet, still fashion. "What you are doing—what God has appointed you to be."

The dark pale face of the Prince flushed. "Do *you* believe in me?" he asked, looking away from her. He thought of what Cornelius de Witt had said of his wife, "She is my chief comfort," and his heart gave a curious stir to think that perhaps from this neglected despised lady might come the sympathy which would strengthen when all earthly supports failed and Heaven itself was dark.

"I do believe," she said, "that you will accomplish your task."

He could not answer steadily and would not betray himself, so was silent.

"Oh, if you would trust me with your thoughts and designs," she murmured, "even as I trust Your Highness to accomplish them."

He answered now in a low tone: "Do you not find, Madam, that these designs are discomfited and utterly undone?"

"I do not think such words possible to you. If God has appointed you His captain, how could you be discomfited?"

It was the first time he had heard his own calm enthusiasm on the lips of another—the first time any one had spoken to him of his life-work without misgivings, discouragement, or doubts. A glow came into his tired eyes; he straightened his shoulders.

"Surely," said the Princess ardently, "you have great things before you."

Like a failing flame blown up again by an eager breath, his indomitable resolution re-arose at the touch of her understanding and belief. He let the moment take him out of the long reserve of loneliness, the containment of years. "With your dear company," he answered, "I might yet accomplish much."

She turned her face from him then and the happy tears sprang to her eyes as she bent over the rich blooms on the dark table. Mynheer Bentinck entered from the outer room with a half-sighing laugh on his lips.

"What will Your Highness do now peace is signed?" he asked, between despondency and tender mockery.

The Prince looked at his wife with an expression of strength and resolve, and answered as if he spoke to her alone: "I shall go back to my task."

Mary lifted her deep serious glance. "I would give you one of our English titles—'Defender of the Faith'—for such you are to God's Church." She turned to Mynheer Bentinck. "Sir, do you not hope to see it after the name of his Highness yet?"

"Why, what is this?" asked William Bentinck lightly. "Are you plotting, Madam? What are you going to do Prince," he repeated, "now peace is signed?"

"Plan another war," said the Stadtholder, still looking at his wife.

————————

APPENDIX
GENEALOGY OF
WILLIAM III OF ORANGE NASSAU
AND MARY STEWART II

Genealogy of William III of Orange Nassau

William of Nassau [William the Rich] (1484-1559) & Juliana of Stolberg (1506-1580)

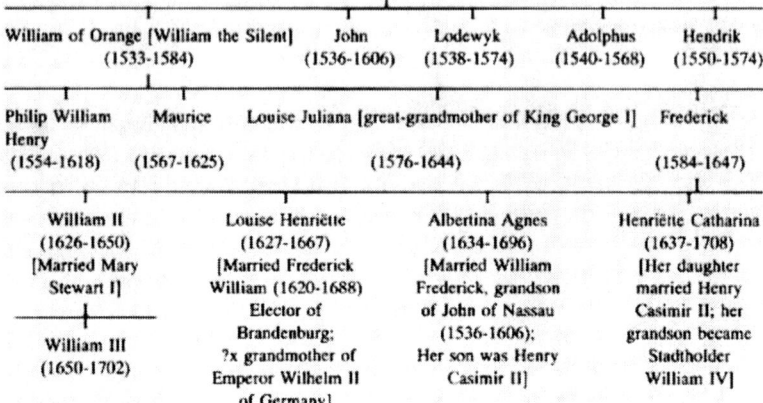

William of Orange [William the Silent] (1533-1584)	John (1536-1606)	Lodewyk (1538-1574)	Adolphus (1540-1568)	Hendrik (1550-1574)

Philip William Henry (1554-1618)	Maurice (1567-1625)	Louise Juliana [great-grandmother of King George I] (1576-1644)	Frederick (1584-1647)

William II (1626-1650) [Married Mary Stewart I]	Louise Henriëtte (1627-1667) [Married Frederick William (1620-1688) Elector of Brandenburg; ?x grandmother of Emperor Wilhelm II of Germany]	Albertina Agnes (1634-1696) [Married William Frederick, grandson of John of Nassau (1536-1606); Her son was Henry Casimir II]	Henriëtte Catharina (1637-1708) [Her daughter married Henry Casimir II; her grandson became Stadtholder William IV]
William III (1650-1702)			

Genealogy of Mary Stewart II

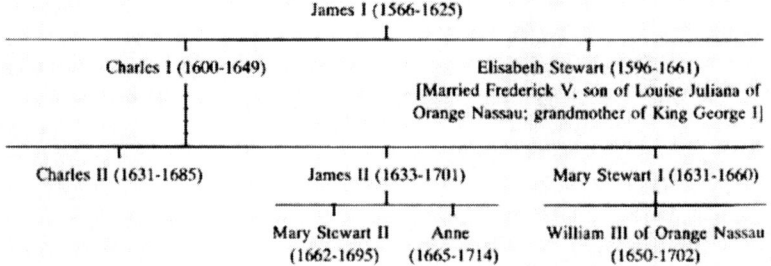

James I (1566-1625)

Charles I (1600-1649)	Elisabeth Stewart (1596-1661) [Married Frederick V, son of Louise Juliana of Orange Nassau; grandmother of King George I]

Charles II (1631-1685)	James II (1633-1701)	Mary Stewart I (1631-1660)
	Mary Stewart II (1662-1695) Anne (1665-1714)	William III of Orange Nassau (1650-1702)

CPSIA information can be obtained
at www.ICGtesting.com
Printed in the USA
LVOW10s1337060917

547750LV00023B/564/P